WEIRD TALES VOL. 1 NO. 2, APRIL 1923

PULP FICTION CLASSICS

CARL RASMUS   HAROLD WARD
OTIS ADELBERT KLINE   J. PAUL SUTER
VARIOUS

Edited by
EDWIN BAIRD

MYTHBANK.COM

This edition is Copyright © 2020 by Jason Hamilton

All rights reserved.

No original part of this book may be reproduced in any form or by any electronic or mechanical means, including information storage and retrieval systems, without written permission from the author. All short stories found therein are in the public domain.

MythBank

www.mythbank.com

Cover design by Jason Hamilton.

CONTENTS

About MythBank and the Pulp Fiction Classics	v
Disclaimer	vii
The Scar, by Carl Ramus, M.D.	1
Beyond the Door, by Paul Suter	29
The Tortoise Shell Comb, by Roylston Markham	46
A Photographic Phantasm, by Paul Crumpler, M.D.	52
The Living Nightmare, by Anton M. Oliver	54
The Incubus, by Hamilton Craigie	60
The Bodymaster, by Harold Ward	71
Jungle Death, by Artemus Calloway	107
The Snake Fiend, by Farnsworth Wright	116
A Square of Canvas, by Anthony M. Rud	126
The Affair of the Man in Scarlet, by Julian Kilman	143
The Hideous Face, by Victor Johns	157
The Forty Jars, by Ray McGillivray	167
The Wish, by Myrtle Levy Gaylord	184
The Whispering Thing (Part 1), by Laurie McClintock and Culpeper Chunn	187
The Thing of a Thousand Shapes (Part 2), by Otis Adelbert Kline	227
The Conquering Will, by Ted Olson	249
Six Feet of Willow, by Carroll F. Michener	259
The Hall of the Dead, by Francis D. Grierson	271
The Parlor Cemetery, by C. E. Howard	282
Golden Glow, by Harry Irving Shumway	289
The Eyrie	300
More Pulp Fiction	309

ABOUT MYTHBANK AND THE PULP FICTION CLASSICS

MythBank is a website devoted to the documentation and study of storytelling. As part of that initiative, this collection was created with the purpose of ensuring all public domain pulp magazines had attractive, uniform, and readily-available print copies and ebooks.

Through print on demand, many classics that are lesser known or have limited runs can still be available for anyone who wants it, keeping the price steady and reducing the need to search the dregs of used books for a copy that might cost ten times what it's worth.

We hope you enjoy this collection of classics, and recommend you visit our website to learn more. Additionally, you will find other classics in this collection that are designed to match the same branding and tone of this volume, so they look amazing on your shelf or your device. Check them out!

About the Pulp Fiction Classics

Our modern popular culture would not exist in its current form without the enormous influence of pulp fiction. So named due to the cheap wood-pulp paper used in the printing process, pulp magazines brought affordable fiction options to the masses.

Popular magazines at the time, such as *Weird Tales* and *Amazing Stories*, became the start of what we now call the fantasy, horror, and science fiction genres. Before these magazines, such categories did not really exist. Hugely influential authors such as H.P. Lovecraft, H.G. Wells, Robert E. Howard, and Edgar Rice Burroughs all contributed to some of these pulp magazines.

This collection attempts to create a modernized version of these magazines, taking the short stories from each public domain issue and assembling them in a more modern collection format. For a scanned facsimile of the original issue, complete with original ads and formatting, visit MythBank.com.

Disclaimer

These magazines were produced decades ago when there were different standards regarding women and minorities. As such, some of these stories may contain content that ranges from passive to blatant depictions of racism, sexism, and homophobia. We have kept all stories for archival purposes, however, we caution those who may be sensitive to such occurrences that some stories may contain elements of that are distasteful or even hurtful. We ask all to remember that this was a different era of our history with different standards, and while that does not excuse such behavior, it can allow us to learn about the history of storytelling and even enjoy these pulp age stories, while being critical of their more problematic or pernicious aspects. Such instances of bigotry do not represent the views and opinions of MythBank.com and its associates.

DISCLAIMER

These magazines were produced decades ago when there were different standards regarding women and minorities. As such, some of these stories may contain content that ranges from passive to blatant depictions of racism, sexism, and homophobia.

We have kept all stories for archival purposes, however, we caution those who may be sensitive to such occurrences, that some stories may contain elements that are distasteful or even hurtful.

We ask all to remember that this was a different era of our history with different standards, and while that does not excuse such behavior, it can allow us to learn about the history of storytelling and even enjoy these pulp age stories, while being critical of their more problematic or pernicious aspects. Such instances of bigotry do not represent the views and opinions of MythBank.com and its associates.

THE SCAR, BY CARL RAMUS, M.D.
A THRILLING NOVELETTE

"Thanks for the lift, Edwards. Come in for a minute, won't you?"

"No. I was up nearly all last night, and must get some sleep."

"To be sure! But you've time for a nip before you go."

"Well—since you put it that way, and in these arid times—"

"Good! Come along."

Dr. Herbert Carlson opened the door of his office on the first floor with his latch key, snapped on the lights, and entered with his colleague, Dr. Clark Edwards. Carlson hung up his overcoat and hat, and Edwards threw his own over a chair, and then Carlson produced from an inner room a bottle, two glasses, and a siphon of carbonic.

"Like the good old days," smiled Edwards, sipping his glass. "*How* did you get it?"

"A voluntary donation from a grateful patient, a second steward on the board the—but that would be telling."

Edwards took another sip. "I wish I had one or two patients like that!"

"You're not likely to get them as long as you stick to *your* specialty."

"I suppose not—Hello! What's all that shouting for?"

Both men listened. Newsboys were yelling an "Extra." Carlson opened a window, leaned far out, and drew up a paper.

"Just another bank robbery. They're so common now as to be hardly worth mentioning."

"Exactly. Anything new in the Holden case?"

"Let's see…O yes! Here it is: 'Father of Ina Holden gets another threatening letter."

Edwards' jaw set. "If I had my way," he said, "every kidnapper would go to the chair!"

"I'll go you one better. If I had *my* way, they'd get the Georgia treatment!"

"What's that?"

"Lynching!"

Edwards was silent.

"The trouble is," Carlson went on, "that we have too much legal red tape, too much politics, too many lawyers and too little real law."

"I suppose so," said Edwards. "When we haven't children of our own, it takes some special circumstance to bring home to us the meaning of a damnable crime like kidnapping. This Holden case brings it home to me."

"Indeed?"

"Very much so. It has to do with an unusual surgical case, which I believe was reported in the International Journal of Surgery or *The London Lancet* by Professor Meyerovitch."

"I don't remember reading it. Please tell me about it."

"I will. It was when I was house surgeon at the Presbyterian Hospital in Chicago. One night a child of seven was brought in with all the signs of fulminating appendicitis. That child was Ina Holden."

"Ah!"

"It was a private case of old Meyerovitch's, and he decided on immediate operation. Now Meyerovitch was one of the few really good surgeons who wouldn't use either the McBurney or Kamerer incision for appendicitis. He just cut down over the trouble and through everything in one line."

"Fool!"

"Most of us thought so then, but somehow Meyerovitch always got good results—*always*."

"Pure accident."

"Perhaps so. But, anyhow, when little Ina was under the anesthetic, and Meyerovitch had his knife in one hand—his left, by the way—and was testing the tension of the abdomen with the other hand, he said, 'I will need plenty of room here.' And then he surprised us all by making a reversed Senn incision."

"I don't seem to remember that incision," said Carlson, after a slight pause, "What is it?"

"An S-shaped incision devised by Nicholas Senn when he was Professor of Surgery at Rush Medical College. You young fellows in New York don't as a rule know about that incision."

"But, Edwards, as I remember, Senn recommended the McBurney method in his book."

"Yes, for appendicitis. He only used the S in neck operations. And so when Meyerovitch used it on Ina Holden, it was the first time on record for appendicitis, and probably the last."

"Most likely. And how did the case get along?"

"Better than any of us expected. It was a drainage case, of course, and took some time to dry up. But the wound finally healed perfectly, with no suggestion of weakness and left a large scar like a reversed S."

"Meyerovitch's bull luck."

"Yes. I saw the child every day for more than a month and got much attached to her. She wouldn't let anyone else dress the wound, and after she went home, the family often invited me to the house."

"They're very rich, aren't they?"

"They are, now, but they weren't then. Mr. Holden owned some manganese land in California, and when the Western Pacific laid its tracks over a corner of his property, he was a rich man."

The colleagues silently finished their illegal glasses. Then Edwards looked at his watch and rose from his chair.

"Good night, Herbert, and many thanks for the drink."

Carlson, alone, looked at a memorandum that his sister had left on his desk.

"Nothing more for tonight, thank God," he thought with relief.

He closed and fastened the window, bolted the door, and was passing into his bedroom, when the telephone rang.

"Damn! Why didn't I muffle it?"

He put the receiver to his ear.

"Well?" he said abruptly.

"Doctor Carlson speaking?"

"Yes."

"Can you come at once to a very sick case?"

"I'm sorry, but I can't. My car is out of order, and I'm not very well myself tonight."

"But this case is extremely urgent, sir, and we don't want anyone else but you."

"Thank you, but---"

"Please listen, Doctor. I'll have a car for you in five minutes, and take you home afterwards, if you'll only come."

"Try another doctor first."

"We *have* tried, but can't find one of the only other two we have confidence in. Money is no object. Please do reconsider, Doctor."

"Who recommended me to you? Do I know you?"

"I do not know you personally. But you are highly recommended by the Brooklyn Hospital. Once more let me say that your fee can be as large as you like."

Carlson did not answer for a while.

"All right, I'll go," he said at last. "What is it—a medical or surgical case?"

After a short silence, the voice replied: "Medical, I think. But you had better come prepared to do whatever is necessary."

"Very well. I'll be ready when you call for me."

Carlson placed his medical and surgical bags on the table, put on his overcoat and hat, and sat down to wait.

In less than five minutes he heard the *honk-honk* of an automobile under the window, and he picked up his two bags, snapped off the lights, and went down to the waiting car, a large limousine.

As Carlson emerged from the house, the chauffeur got out of his seat and opened the car door. He wore a wide slouch hat, the brim of which hung down and so shaded his face from the corner electric light that Carlson could not make out his features. All he was sure of was a long heavy moustache. The lower part of the man's face was concealed in a muffler. He opened the door and stood as if at attention.

When Carlson was inside with his bags the man closed the door silently, got into the driver's seat, and the car was soon rushing up the street. It turned at the second corner, and after that made so many sharp turns among small and narrow and dark streets that Carlson began to feel uncomfortable.

At last they came to a long stretch of vacant lots, and went faster for half a minute or so, and then slowed down again. The chauffeur sounded three *honks*—one long and two short. Carlson bent forward and peered ahead, but could see nothing.

He did not like it at all, and he regretted that he had not brought his revolver. He was wondering what he had got into when, suddenly, the car slowed down with a loud grinding of the brakes, and stopped with a jerk that threw Carlson violently forward

A moment later both doors opened together, and he realized that masked men stood on either side of the car, covering him with revolvers or magazine pistols.

Then came a few moments of the most eloquent silence that Carlson had ever experienced. He said nothing and waited.

"Don't be afraid, Doc," said a thick voice, obviously disguised. "Just do as you are told and you'll be O.K. But if you try any stunts—T.N.T. for you. Do you get me?"

"Yes. What do you want me to do?"

"You'll be told later. My partner'll sit by you now, and I'll sit facing you. So---"

They got inside and shut the doors, and the car started forward at high speed.

"Sorry, Doc, but we'll have to blindfold you," said the masked man.

And then a heavy muffler was wound about his face.

II.

As the car rushed on, Carlson sat still with his captors in a kind of stupefied silence. Only that morning he had been wishing that his life was more eventful, less common place. Well, here was adventure with a vengeance.

He was only twenty-seven and he had been two years in the city. The first year and a half had been slow and discouraging, as often happens with young doctors. But in the last six months patients had begun to come, in steadily increasing numbers, until now he had about all he could handle. He was five-feet-eleven, well-built and athletic. He had clear hazel eyes with a very direct look, and thick and wavy brown hair, which was much admired by his women patients. All this with good and strong features and a pleasant expression, made an ensemble which expressed health, confidence and efficiency.

And now what was he in for? It was hardly reassuring, especially when blindfolded, to know that at least one gun was probably pointed at him all the time, and that any involuntary move of his might bring a bullet into his brain.

Yet, for all that, he did not feel exactly fear; it was more like strained interest, a burning curiosity to know where the adventure was to lead.

For a long time—or so it seemed—the car sped on what might have been an isolated suburban road. Occasionally another car passed, going in the opposite direction, but otherwise there were no other sounds than the rolling of the limousine.

At last they slowed down and turned off to the right, and from then on, for perhaps five minutes, the car went slowly over rough ground, turning so frequently that Carlson lost all idea of direction.

Presently they were on a good road again, and once more traveled very fast. More and more automobiles passed them, and they went slower and slower, until Carlson knew they were in a town again. Once they had to stop for a minute or two, as it seemed, at a crossing, and he distinctly heard a policeman's voice allowing them to make a turn to the left on a side street. After that interruption they moved for the most part rapidly for another five minutes or so, making several turns and passing many machines, until they slowed own and came to a full stop.

Carlson could hear people passing to and fro on the sidewalk, talking and laughing. He sat still, careful not to make any movement that might alarm his captors, feeling that their weapons were leveled at him.

When at last the voices and footsteps had become almost inaudible, the voice spoke again.

"Now, Doc—no fooling."

He put his own slouch hat on Carlson's head and drew the brim far down over his face. Then he opened the door toward the curb stone and got out.

"Come along, Doc, give me your hand."

Carlson took the hand and got out of the car. The man put his hand within his arm and drew him across the sidewalk. Carlson heard the other man open an iron gate, and close it again after they had passed through. A few steps more, and another stop.

He heard a key turning in a lock, and a door open, and he was led into a warm room. The door *clicked* after them. A woman's harsh voice impatiently exclaimed:

"I thought you'd *never* come."

"Shut up!" said Carlson's guide. "Here's the Doctor. Take him upstairs. Step lively, will you! Keep right hold of my arm, Doc."

Carlson counted three flights of stairs, then he heard a key turned just beyond the head of the stairway, and he was led into a room.

"Shut the door!"

It was done.

"Now take off the blinder!"

Carlson's eyes blinked as the muffler was removed. But as soon as his eyes got accustomed to the light, he realized that the room was only dimly lighted.

Two men and one woman, al masked, stood nearby. One of the men had come with him in the car. The other was a huge man, a giant. The woman was short and rather scrawny-looking, to judge from her hands and neck.

"Now, Doc, a word with you alone," said one of the men. "Come here!"

He stepped into a small dressing room and Carlson followed.

"Shut the door!"

Carlson obeyed.

"Now, here's the proposition. We've got a sick woman on our hands—damned sick! But she's got in trouble with the law and the police are after her. Get me?"

"Yes. Go on."

"Well, that's why she doesn't go to a hospital, and that's why we had to get you. Get me?"

"Go on."

"Very good! Now your job is just this: Look at her and find out what in Hell is the matter with her, and write out a prescription—No! That won't do, either. Somebody might get on to it. You've got your medicines with you, have you?"

"I have some medicines in my bag."

"Good! You'll give me the dope she needs, and then get out and away from here as fast as you can and keep your mouth shut. You'll be taken home safe, and you'll get your money all right. Do you get me?"

"I understand."

"Good! Just one other thing. You can't see her face, and there can't be any talking, not one word. You understand?"

Carlson felt that the time had come for him to say something, and he said it:

"You damned fool! What kind of an examination do you think a doctor can make if he can't see his patient or hear her talk? Have you never been to a doctor yourself?"

The man hesitated, fingering his automatic.

"Open that door!" he commanded, after a pause. Carlson did as he was told.

"Teresa!"

She appeared so quickly that Carlson was sure that she had been listening behind the door.

"The doctor will have to ask her a few questions, and she will have to answer. God and tell her. And tell her from me-that if she says anything she doesn't have to say—T.N.T. for her! Do you get me?"

"All right, Boss, I'll tell her."

She spoke with a cruel chuckle that all but made Carlson shudder. While he waited for further orders from his captor, he tried to get a line on the mystery he was involved in. but nothing came to him. Was the sick woman he was about to visit a fugitive or a captive? Probably the latter; and if so, why?

He furtively inspected the dressing-room and its contents. It was richly and beautifully furnished—like the large bedroom it adjoined, as far as his very brief glance had discovered. It was on a corner and had two windows, with curtains tightly drawn. At the end, farthest from the door of entrance, was another door, standing half open and showing a glimpse of a lavatory and bathtub. Nothing hopeful thus far.

Then he noticed a small black box on the wall nearest the corner, with a green cord leading from it and disappearing behind a screen. Not until his anxious glance had shifted elsewhere did Carlson realize the possible significance of that green cord. Surely, what else could it mean but a telephone behind that screen! A *telephone*.

The masked woman suddenly appeared at the door.

"She's ready for the doctor," she snapped out viciously.

Carlson looked at his masked companion for orders.

"Go with her," he said. "And don't ask her no questions that are none of your damned business! If you do, you'll go out of this house in two or three suit cases! Get me?"

Carlson did not answer, and followed the woman to a darkened bedside. The man also followed, and stood at the food of the bed.

III.

In the dim light of a shaded table-lamp Carlson saw a large double bed of massive and antique construction. At the head was a high and projecting portion of carved woodwork which overhung like a canopy. On the bed he saw the outline of a human body through the coverings.

The head showed a mass of thick dark-brown hair, unbound and falling about the shoulders. The upper part of the face was hidden by a wade bandage wound several times around the head. The arms were bare and lay outside the coverlet. They were well rounded, and the hands were small and beautiful.

Carlson stood silently beside the bed at first, watching the patient's deep and rapid breathing, and assembling his professional manner. The hand nearest him was trembling slightly. As he took it up, to feel the pulse, the arm jerked and the whole body shook, as if under profound nervous tension. A thrill of compassion and pity ran through him as he held the trembling little hand.

"Don't be afraid, Madam," he said rather huskily. "I'm the doctor. I want to feel your pulse."

Instantly the trembling stopped and her fingers tightened around his. He noted the pulse rate with his other hand, and found it rapid, about 120. The hand and wrist were burning hot.

He let go of the hand and took a thermometer from his vest pocket. After shaking it down several times he placed it in her mouth and closed her lips with his fingers, saying:

"Hold it that way for five minutes, please."

Again he took her hand, pretending to count the pulse beats by his wrist watch, but in reality thinking as hard as he could. The thermometer was actually a one-minute thermometer, but he wished to gain as much time as possible. When at least he took it from her mouth and held it to the light it registered 105. Involuntarily he whistled. Here was a very sick woman, indeed!

"How long have you been sick?"

"Three days." The voice was soft, but deep and sweet.

"Is your throat sore?"

"No."

"Do you cough?"

"No."

"Have you pain anywhere?"

"I hardly know. I feel sick all over."

Carlson thought for a minute. Three days sick, and now a temperature of 105! About time for a skin eruption to begin to show, if it was one of those diseases. He turned to the masked virago who stood beside him.

"I must have more light," he said abruptly.

The woman hesitated and looked toward the man.

"What about it?" she jerked out.

"What's the matter with this light?" the man snapped angrily.

"Just that it isn't enough for me, that's all! She may have typhus or smallpox—"

"Hell!" The man jumped backward so quickly that he upset a small table and chair.

"Damn her!" screamed the woman, retreating to the wall.

Carlson, being a doctor and often in contact with contagious and loathsome diseases, had not counted on the terrifying effect of the word "smallpox" on the criminals he was for the moment associated with. But he instantly realized the advantage it gave him, and decided to capitalize it to the limit in the mysterious woman's interests.

After a short but tense silence he said impressively:

"Yes, it may be smallpox. But I cannot say for certain in this light."

The masked man waited a few uneasy seconds, then went to the chandelier and raised a hand to the light key.

"Teresa. See that the bandage is tight over her face before I turn on more light." His voice was surly.

"I won't touch her again if she has smallpox!" Teresa's strident voice shook.

"Yes, you will, or I'll brain you." He took a step toward her.

The woman muttered, but obeyed, though her hands shook as

she fumbled with the bandage. Crossing herself, she said with shaking voice:

"All safe," and stepped back again to the wall. The light was turned on, and Carlson bent down to look more closely at his mysterious patient.

A deep, feverish flush was over the arms, neck and the strip of forehead above the bandage. But Carlson's trained fingers could not feel even a suggestion of the "shotty" feeling which goes with the first rash of smallpox.

"What do you make of it, Doc?" asked the man impatiently.

"Highly suspicious, but I cannot tell certainly until I have finished my examination. Madam, may I listen to your lungs and heart with y stethoscope"

'Yes," she faintly murmured.

Carlson looked around at the man.

"I am not in the habit of examining women in the presence of strange men," he said sharply.

The man mumbled a curse and turned his back. Carlson then looked at the masked woman.

"Turn down the bedclothes and open her nightgown!"

"Do it yourself! I won't touch her again!"

Carlson took his stethoscope from his pocked at bared the patient's chest. The nightgown was coarse and cheap, but the form within it was rounded and beautiful. The sleeves of the garment had apparently been roughly hacked off with scissors.

Carlson's examination of lungs and heart found absolutely nothing to account for the very high fever. Then he thought of appendicitis or peritonitis.

"Now, please let me examine the abdomen for a moment."

She lay still while he delicately arranged the clothing. The light from the chandelier showed obliquely, so that the lower part of the abdomen was in the shadow cast by the rolled-down bedclothes. Carlson felt and carefully sounded, but she gave no sign of pain or involuntary resistance.

As his sensitive fingers passed over the place under which the appendix is located, he felt something that broke the smoothness of the perfect skin. It was a surgical scar. That fact along should almost certainly ruled out a present attack of appendicitis!

"So you have had appendicitis?"

"Yes."

"It must have been a bad case—to judge from the size of the scar."

She did not answer, and he drew the covering a little lower and brought the scar out of the shadow into full view. Then he started, and, involuntarily, a gasp escaped him.

The large surgical scar was in the form of *a perfect reversed letter S.*

IV.

So much had happened to Carlson that night that his mental receiving instrument was somewhat dulled, and did not immediately register the momentous significance of what his eyes now saw. That curious scar-that reversed S—symbol of the great Senn. Great God! *Now* he remembered. The only case on record in which that Senn S-incision had been made for appendicitis was the case of Ina Holden.

He heard the masked man muttering in angry impatience, and then his brain began to work again. The Holden *child*. Edwards had spoken of her as "little Ina."

Though the papers had been full of accounts of the Holden kidnapping case for the last five days, he, Carlson, had read nothing but the headings, and his impression from them and from Edwards' talk was that Ina was a small girl, quite a child. And yet this was a woman, or a well-grown girl of 16 or 17 at the least. He looked up at her bandaged face.

"How long ago did you have this operation?"

"I—when I was a child."

"How long ago was that?"

"About eight or nine years ago."

"Ah—"

"You're takin' a hell of a long time, doc. Has she got smallpox?"

The man still stood with his back to the food of the bed, but Carlson realized that he could not temporize much longer.

"Just about a minute more and I can tell you," he said, as nonchalantly as he could say the words.

How could he get rid of the kidnappers and telephone for the police? Then came an idea—a wild, forlorn hope; but he would try it.

"I will have to examiner her throat," he said, with professional voice.

He walked to the table where his medical bags were and took out a circular mirror with an aperture in the center, a small electric bulb, and a black elastic band with a buckle in it. Next, he detached a connecting-plug from a cell battery in the bottom of the bag, being careful to conceal the battery from the gimletlike eyes of the two men and the woman. With the plug hidden in his hand he crushed the two contactors together.

Then he adjusted the elastic band and mirror to his forehead, connected the two wires with the small bulb on the head mirror and deliberately unscrewed the bulb from the table lamp. He drew a deep breath; then quickly inserted the crushed battery plug into the lamp socket.

Flash! The room was in complete darkness. Carlson had short-circuited the current and fulminated the fuse, probably for the whole house.

"Damn it!" he exclaimed, ostentatiously. "What am I going to do now?"

Almost instantly the beam of a pocket flashlight came from the hand of the "boss."

"Take this, doc," he said, holding it toward Carlson.

He took it, asked the girl to open her mouth, and looked within.

"No good at all. I *must* have the electric light. Where is the fuse box?"

The "boss" looked at Teresa.

"It's in the cellar with the meter," she said.

"Go down and put in a new fuse."

"I don't know how. You'll have to come with me."

The man hesitated. He glared at Carlson through his mask, and at the sick girl on the bed, and then at the giant near the door.

"Tony!"

"Huh?"

"Come here!"

The giant slouched nearer.

"Where's your flash-light?"

He produced it.

"Good! Now stay right here till we come back. If the doctor tries to leave this room, or if he talks to the girl—you know what to do."

Tony grunted, and showed a magazine pistol in his other hand. The other man and Teresa left the room. The man slammed the door and locked it on the outside.

Carlson felt almost overcome by a feeling of powerlessness and despair. He and the girl were alone with the giant Tony, who sat stolidly by a table in the center of the room, flashlight in one hand, the automatic pistol in the other. His narrow, piglike eyes gleamed through the mask and seemed never to relax their sinister gaze.

Carlson's plan was completely frustrated by the baleful presence of this Frankenstein Monster.

Suddenly he heard the blindfolded girl give a sob, and he saw her shoulders trembling. As the sound of that despairing sob a new impulse to action surged through him. Her only hope lay in him. He would not fail her. He would save her or die in the trying.

He took her nearest and burning hand in both of his.

"There, there. Everything will be all right."

As her fingers gripped his convulsively, a horrible snarling sound, as from an angry hippopotamus, came from Tony. Carlson disengaged the girl's hand and faced the giant.

"Tony!" he said commandingly.

"Huh?"

"Help me to fix up this head light of mine. Bend those points out straight—so!"

Carlson had seen some remarkable demonstrations in hypnotism in Zurich, and he had been told by Professor Jung that he had exceptional personal power in that line, if he chose to develop it. He remembered that advice now, and he was trying it on Tony.

The giant hesitated, but at last obeyed the imperative and hypnotic voice of the young doctor. He laid the pistol and flash-light on the table, but just within reach of his hand, and then hold out one hand for the electric plug.

"There—twist them out again, right there," said Carlson in a slow, monotonous voice. As he spoke, his other hand closed over a heavy glass paper weight that lay at the farther end of the table. Tony put the plug on the table and bent his face over it.

Carlson felt that he could soon have Tony completely under his own hypnotic power. But time was too precious to wait for that. The "boss" might return any minute. There was only one thing to do, and Carlson did it.

He raised the paper weight slowly, and just beyond Tony's field of vision and then—he brought it down on the giant's head with all the force he could put into the blow.

Tony dropped the electric plug and swayed to one side, only slightly stunned by a blow that would have fractured the skull of another man. But before he could recover, Carlson dealt him a second, and then a third bow, the last on the angle of the jaw.

Tony crumpled up and fell face downward across the table. But Carlson, to make sure, gave him a final and terrible blow which seemed to give back a crushing sound.

V.

He rushed to the door and bolted it; then back to the bedside.

"Are you Ina Holden?"

"Yes!"

"Then get out of bed instantly. I'm going to save you."

As she started up, he seized her in his arms, lifted her out bodily, and plumped her into the nearest upholstered chair.

"Take off that bandage as quickly as you can!"

He flew back to the huge bed and began dragging it toward the door. It was heavy as a safe, and incredibly hard to move. Suddenly it became easier, and to his amazement he saw that the girl was helping him. When they had placed it so that the head completely blocked the door, Carlson ran to Tony.

"Help me drag this carcass against the foot of the bed. Take the feet—so! That will brace the bed better. Now take this pistol. You know how to use it?"

"O, yes!"

"Fine! Watch that beast while I telephone the police. If he moves, shoot him."

Carlson rushed into the smaller room, kicking two small chairs out of his way and looked behind the screen. Praise be to God! It *was* a telephone. He jerked the receiver to his ear and began jiggling the instrument frantically. After a few interminable seconds came the blessed words:

"Number, please?"

"Listen, operator—this is a case of life and death. First take down this number—Cartwright 872....Yes....No! No!!—for God's sake don't call it. *This* is it. Now listen. Have you got this number written down?"

"Yes, sir, but—"

"Listen, I tell you!"

"I am listening!"

"Ina Holden is a prisoner in this house, with telephone Cartwright 872. Do you know who Ina Holden is?"

"You mean the kidnapped girl?"

"Yes. Now get me police headquarters at once. Then, while I am talking with them, you look up Cartwright 872 and phone the police station nearest this place. *Quick*, for God's sake!"

Another agonizing wait; then—

"Police headquarters speaking."

"Ina Holden is in a house with phone number Cartwright 872. Mark it down."

He heard the voice of the officer dictating "Cartwright 872. Ina Holden." Then. "What else, sir?"

"There are at least four armed men in the house, and one woman."

"Where is the house?"

"I don't know. I'm a prisoner with her myself. Send enough men at once to surround the house. Look it up in the numerical index."

Carlson could hear the officer giving rapid orders, and, more faintly, their repetition being shouted out through the station.

"All right, sir. We've located the house, and it will take us about twenty minutes to get to you. I'm sending out a general alarm, and maybe some of our men out there can arrive sooner. How are you fixed?"

"I knocked out one of the men. I and the girl are barricaded in a third floor back room, and we'll try to hold out until your men come."

"Good! Stay at the 'phone as long as you can and keep me informed to the last possible moment. Good luck to you!"

"I'll put the girl at the 'phone, and stand guard myself. Ina!"

"Yes, doctor." She came in quickly, the pistol in her hand.

"Please sit down here and hold the 'phone. The police are on the wire. I'll call out to you how things go, and you repot to them. Has Tony moved?"

"No. he doesn't seem to breathe."

Carlson left Ina at the 'phone and went to Tony. He lay absolutely still, just as they had placed him at the food of the bed. Carlson tore off the mask and turned the face around and listened with his ear to the mouth. Not a sound! Then he used his stethoscope over the heard. Silence! Tony was dead!

Carlson picked up Tony's automatic, turned off the light plug in the large bed room, and went back to Ina. She was at her post, her elbows on the little table, the receiver at her ear. She looked up at him with a grave smile.

"The police have been asking me a lot of questions. How about the man in the next room?"

"Dead. I'm sorry I killed him, but there was nothing else to do. Anyway," said Carlson, "it makes our work easier. We won't have to watch him, and his body will help hold the door a little longer."

He looked quickly around the room.

"And now for our plan of defense until the police come. The barricade in the bedroom may hold till then. But, if it doesn't then we will have to barricade ourselves again in here. We ought to be able to hold out easily."

And then Carlson began dragging furniture from the bedroom into the dressing room until the latter was nearly full.

"I guess that'll be enough," he said. "They're taking a long time fixing that fuse, but they can't be too long for us." He stood beside Ina once more, having done all that could be done for the present.

"Yes," she said slowly, "and their bungling delay probably means our salvation. Anyhow, there's nothing for it but to wait—for what is to come."

Carlson had been looking at Ina Holden while they were talking, and he thought he had never seen a more charming girl. Her thick dark hair was unloosed and uncombed and fell over her shoulders. She was clad only in the coarse, sleeveless, night garment, which showed beautifully rounded arms to the shoulders. Her feet were bare. Her eyes were a pure and brilliant blue, shining under heavy but well arched brows. Her features were almost faultless, but the strong jaw and firm though adorable lips expressed unusual force and will power for a woman. A woman worth going through hell for —Carlson thought grimly.

Her face, neck and arms were deeply suffused as with the flush of high fever. But her manner and movements were not those of a very sick person. Carlson was puzzled.

"I confess I don't know what to make of your fever," he said frankly.

She half smiled as she replied:

"Of course. I should have thought of that before. It isn't a *real* fever, but what the Italians call an *impressione*."

"What's that?"

"An effect of a shock."

"But no mere shock can cause actual fever!"

"That's what many doctors have said. But the fact is that it *does* with me. I was always that way. There's something abnormal in my constitution. I can even bring on a fever by willing it. I'm ashamed to say that when I was a child I would sometimes play sick in that way in order to get what I wanted. But I hadn't done it for so long that I'd almost forgotten about it—until this horrible thing happened, and then I remembered and tried it. But they wouldn't call a doctor for three days, not until they got badly scared and thought I might die on their hands. And that is why they brought *you* here."

"I never heard of such a case before," said Carlson. "Never! To be sure, there are a few cases on record where the heart and pulse rate were under the control of the will to some extent; but certainly *not* the temperature."

He then asked: "How does it happen that the kidnappers have a house like this?"

"This house belongs to a wealthy family named Carriello. They are traveling in Europe, and have left the house in charge of an Italian and his wife."

"The woman Teresa?"

"Yes. The two are black-handlers, and their gang figured that the police would never suspect that I might be hidden in such a place."

Suddenly the lights flashed out. The fuse was repaired at last. The kidnappers would be at the door n a few moments!

Carlson gripped Tony's automatic a little harder, and his left hand fell almost involuntarily on the girl's shoulder. They waited thus, tensely, hardly breathing, and with quickened heart-beats, until they heard footsteps hurrying up the stairs. Then Carlson drew a deep breath, and whispered:

"They are coming now—but don't be afraid."

She said nothing, but raised both her hands and clasped them over his for a moment.

He stepped softly into the darkened bedroom, just as a key turned in the lock. The knob was turned, the door tried—then shaken. There was a short silence. Then, from the "boss:"

"Open the door, you fool!"

Carlson was silent.

"Tony!"

Silence.

"Tony! What the hell's the matter with you?"

Silence.

A whispered consultation outside the door. Then:

"Tony! Doctor! Open that door or, by God! I'll---"

More whispering, then a short silence.

"Doctor!"

Silence.

Whispering again; then footsteps running down the stairs; then another and longer silence. Carlson put his ear as near as he could to the door. Soon he heard the footsteps returning, but they stopped at the second floor. A voice called faintly from below:

"I can't find anything but a hatchet."

Smothered cursing told that the "boss" was still on the other side of the door. Then he also seemed to run down stairs. Presently Carlson heard hammering or pounding, far below, and at last a crushing and crumbling sound, as if something heavy had given way. *What* were the scoundrels doing?

Then footsteps again, coming up the stairs, but more slowly this time. And as they came, there was an occasional bumping sound, as if they were carrying some bulky object which now and then struck the walls or stairs.

When they were opposite the door, something heavy hit the floor, then, once more, the sullen voice of the "boss."

"Listen, Doc! I don't know what you've done to Tony, and what's more I don't give a damn, if you open the door now."

Silence. Carlson thought he could hear their heavy breathing. As a psychologist he know that his own silence, and that of Tony, had a horror about it that was telling severely, even on their hardened nerves.

"This is your last chance, Doc! If you open the door now, you can go, and take your fee, and be damned. But if you won't open, I'm going to break down the door, and then—you'll leave here in a couple suit cases. Do you get me?"

Silence! After about a quarter of a minute, the "boss" said:

"Now then! All together!"

Carlson braced himself. But suddenly the woman screamed, "Stop!"

"Shut up! You—"

"I won't. Listen!" and though she spoke lower, Carlson could hear her say something about the doctor and Tony's pistol!

"I know that," muttered the man, "but we've got to risk it!"

Another voice, Carlson thought that of the man who sat beside him in the auto, half whispered:

"Wait, Boss! I don't like this! What did the doc do to big Tony? I wouldn't go into that room again if you killed me! I've lost my nerve, let's chuck this job and make a getaway!"

"No, I won't! and none of you won't by God! We've gone too far to go back. We'll win together, or go to the Chair together! I'll shoot the first—"

"But—"

"Take that, will you, and shut up!" a blow, a fall, and a groan, as if from the level of the floor.

A few seconds of dead silence, then the voice of the "boss":

"Now, get together and smash that door!"

More shuffling of feet and the dragging of something heavy, then the muffled voice of the woman:

"Maybe he found the phone—"

"Quick! Bust in that door!"

Carlson held his breath.

CRASH!

A terrible blow, as of from a battering ram, shook ad shivered the strong oak door. But door and bolt still held. Carlson knew from the impact of the blow that some ponderous solid object had been driven against the door. And he know also that a few more such blows would shatter it, leaving only the bed and an overturned chiffonier and Tony's body as a barricade.

So he quickly began dragging more chairs, tables and what not into the small dressing-room.

CRASH! The door fell inward against the head of the massive bed.

Carlson dragged a davenport into the little room, and then closed its door, locking and bolting it.

CRASH!

The devastating sound that followed told that the heavy overhanging canopy of the bed had fallen inward. Carlson kept steadily working away barricading the second door. "Thank God *this* door opens outward!" he said to Ina. She was still at her post at the telephone.

"Hello?" she said calmly. "They have just smashed in the outer door and are climbing in over the ruins of the bed and furniture. We have retreated into a smaller room, and the doctor is piling furniture against it—" She looked at Carlson.

"The police want to know how long we can hold out!"

"Perhaps another five minutes."

"Five minutes more—what?...O, I hope so!"

CRASH! This time on the inner door. It held perfectly!

"They are attacking our inner door, Inspector—you heard it?"

CRASH! A panel cracked, all the way down.

CRASH! The panel flew in splinters. One splinter struck the girl in the face, making a small wound on the forehead, and blood trickled down into her eyes, but she did nothing more than to wipe it off with the back of her right hand.

Carlson readjusted the shifting barricade, and glanced at Ina.

"You are hurt!"

"It's nothing."

"Into the bathroom, quickly!"

CRASH! Another panel cracked!

She got up calmly, and wiped the blood out of her eyes again with the handkerchief Carlson pressed against her face; then, his arm around her, she walked into the bathroom.

Carlson forced Ina into a chair and knelt beside her, indifferent to everything now but the bleeding cut on her face.

"Let me look at it!"

"It's nothing at all, I tell you! Go back and attend to the door. We must barricade ourselves in here in another minute."

CRASH! The center of the door fell inward against the barricade. As Carlson ran to pick up a heavy chair for the bathroom defense, a hand and pistol came through the breach in the door and a shot rang out. He felt a stinging pain in his side, but kept on with his work. Before he realized it, Ina was in the roo again, dragging another chair into the bathroom. The barricade crumbled still more, and another shot was aimed at Carlson, but did not hit him. Ina deliberately crossed the little room to the telephone and turned off the light.

"They won't shoot *me*—not yet, anyway," she said.

The barricade fell to pieces. There was not a moment to lose. Carlson and Ina rushed into the bathroom and locked and bolted the door and began staking the chairs and tables and one small chiffonier against the door.

Carlson felt blood soaking his clothing. He and Ina crouched together in one corner. He held Tony's pistol in his right hand, and both of Ina's hands in his left.

"Listen, Ina! When they force this door, I will try to pick them off one by one. If I fall, be ready to snatch the pistol and shoot carefully. Don't waste a shot! The police should be here any moment."

CRASH! The lock and bolts snapped, and the door itself was pressed inward several inches, but rebounded by the pressure of the barricade.

CRASH! This time the door yielded more than a foot, and in the opening Carlson could see a man's form. He fired, and a shriek followed. Four or five shots were aimed at Carlson, but did not reach him in his protected corner angle. Suddenly a voice yelled from the outer room:

"The Cops! They're around the house!"

"Damnation! Get the Girl, at all costs!"

When the next rush brought a man into view Carlson fired, and he knew by the scream that he had hit once more. The pistol dropped from his hand, and his body swayed. But the girl realized everything in an instant. Quick as thought she snatched up the pistol with her right hand as she knelt beside him, and her other arm went around him.

At that instant a perfect fusillade of shooting sounded from the outer room, followed by screams, yelling and groaning. Then a masked man with a pistol in his hand bounded wildly into the half-opened door of the bathroom. But Ina fired from their darkened corner before he saw them, and he fell backward among the debris.

Carlson felt everything growing dark.

"Ina?"

"Yes, dear; we've won the fight!"

His head sank against her breast, just as two policemen appeared in the doorway.

She dropped the pistol and put both arms about him.

VI.

"Miss Holden," asked one of the officers, turning his bull's eye lantern on them.

She did not answer, but looked long and tensely at Carlson's white unconscious face. Then she pressed a kiss on his forehead.

"He saved me!" she said, looking up at the officers. "I owe everything to him. Please send for a surgeon and have him taken to my home immediately."

"The police surgeon will be here in a moment, Miss Holden. Let us take him into another room."

As they took him from her arms they saw that her garment was soaked with his blood.

"Who is he?" asked the lieutenant.

"I don't know. He was brought here by the kidnappers when I seemed to be very sick. We had no time for anything but defense."

The lieutenant took off his overcoat and placed it over Ina's shoulders, and then they both followed the two officers who carried the unconscious Carlson out through the wreck of the dressing-room and larger bedroom.

And what a scene of ruin and blood! They had to pick their way through masses of broken furniture. One masked dead man lay just outside the bedroom—the man Ina had shot. Another man, his mask torn off, sat propped up against an overturned chiffonier on the floor of the large bedroom. He was groaning and trying to wring his manacled hands, as two officers knelt beside him and searched his pockets.

The mammoth carcass of Tony lay where Carlson and Ina had first dragged it, but it was now half covered by the mattress and debris of the bed. At least a dozen policemen in the rooms. The woman Teresa stood sniveling in a corner, unmasked and handcuffed.

But there was a sudden silence as Ina Holden appeared, her face bloody, her feet bare, and her form covered by the officer's overcoat. All eyes were fixed on the girl, whose name and picture had been in every newspaper from Maine to California for the last five days.

They carried Carlson through the devastated rooms, into another room and laid him on a bed. The police surgeon arrived at almost the same moment. After a glance at the unconscious man on the bed, the surgeon said:

"But where is the *girl*?"

"I am Ina Holden," she said quickly, "but never mind *me*. Look at *him!*"

"Who is he?"

"The man who saved me. They shot him just before the police came."

The surgeon quickly tore open the blood-soaked shirt and found the bullet wound in the right side. He listened a moment to his hear; then looked up gravely.

"Very serious! There seems to be severe hemorrhage into the pleura. He must be rushed to the nearest hospital for immediate operation."

"Doctor" asked Ina, with shaking voice. "Is he—will he recover?"

"I am sorry to say, Miss Holden, the chances are against him. Quick, boys! The stretcher. One of you telephone Mercy Hospital to have the operating-room ready."

And then another man burst like a whirlwind into the room—a

large, bearded man of about fifty—a man of commanding presence, before whom everyone made way.

"Ina!—my Girl!—"

Slowly Ina turned her eyes from Carlson and looked at her father. Then she stood up and held out her arms, and was gathered into his embrace.

"Father, dear!" she panted, as soon as his joyful greetings would allow; "Listen! I am all right. But that man lying there saved my life. If he had not come—"

"Yes, my girl! Go on!"

"He was shot defending me before the police could get here. And now—he may be—*dying!*—" Her voice broke.

Two men entered with a stretcher, just as the surgeon gave Carlson a hypodermic of some powerful heart stimulant. Deftly they moved him from bed to stretcher. Mr. Holden drew the surgeon aside and they exchanged a few earnest words.

"We'll do our best, sir, that's all I can say. Good night, sir! Good night, Miss Holden!" He hurried down stairs after the stretcher.

"Where's the telephone?" said Holden.

Ina took him to it, and then he called the hospital and several famous surgeons, telling them that the man who had saved his daughter *must* be saved! *Must be saved!*

"What is it, Lieutenant?"

"I have found his name, sir. It's on his surgical bag. He is Dr. Herbert Carlson of New York."

"Thank you very much! Please fid his 'phone number and I will call his wife and tell her what we are doing for him."

As her father was calling Carlson's telephone number, Ina listened with strained attention. His *wife!* Somehow, it had never occurred to her that he might be married!

"Hello! Is this Dr. Carlson's residence?...Yes, yes, I know he's not there now. May I speak with his wife?...What's that?...*Not* married?...O, I beg your pardon! His sister?—yourself? Thank you! Now listen to me, please!..."

Ina did not try to analyze her feelings when her father's words at the telephone seemed to prove that Carlson was unmarried. But then she suddenly remembered, as with a stab at her heart, what the police surgeon had said! Yes: As her father had ordered, He *must* be saved! Nothing else mattered!

At 2:53 A.M. the telephone at the Holden residence rang for at least the hundredth time that fateful night. The butler had instructions not to call Mr. Holden except for communications from the police or the hospital. Ina and her mother, in Ina's bedroom heard the muffled buzzer in the study below, and looked at each other anxiously. Ina snatched up the extension receiver at her bedside and listened.

"Hospital speaking. I have a message for Mr. Holden."

It was the second message from the hospital. The first had told the hopeful news that Dr. Carlson had been successfully operated on, that hemorrhage had been checked, and that his heart had responded to stimulants. Mr. Holden at his desk, lifted the receiver.

"Mr. Holden speaking. Quick! What's your message?"

"Dr. Carlson slept until five minutes ago. Then he woke up suddenly and asked: 'Is Ina all right?' we told him that Miss Holden was safe at home, and he said: 'Thank God!' and went to sleep again."

BEYOND THE DOOR, BY PAUL SUTER

CREEPING HORROR LURKED BEYOND THE DOOR. AN UNUSUAL STORY.

"You haven't told me yet how it happened," I said to Mrs. Malkin.

She set her lips and eyed me, sharply.

"Didn't you talk with the coroner, sir?"

"Yes, of course," I admitted; "but as I understand you found my uncle, I thought—"

"Well, I wouldn't care to say anything about it," she interrupted, with decision.

This housekeeper of my uncle's was somewhat taller than I, and much heavier—two physical preponderances which afford any woman possessing them an advantage over the inferior male. She appeared a subject for diplomacy rather than argument.

Noting her ample jaw, her breadth of cheek, the unsentimental glint of her eye, I decided on conciliation. I placed a chair for her, there in my Uncle Godfrey's study, and dropped into another, myself.

"At least, before we go over the other parts of the house, suppose we rest a little," I suggested, in my most unctuous manner. "The place rather gets on one's nerves—don't you think so?"

It was sheer luck—I claim no credit for it. My chance reflection found the weak spot in her fortifications. She replied to it with an undoubted smack of satisfaction:

"It's more than seven years that I've been doing for Mr. Sarston, sir: Bringing him his meals regular as clockwork, keeping the house clean—as clean as he'd let me—and sleeping at my own home, o' nights; and in all that time I've said, over and over, there ain't a house in New York the equal of this for queerness."

"Nor anywhere else," I encouraged her, with a laugh; and her confidences opened another notch:

"You're likely right in that, too, sir. As I've said to poor Mr. Sarston, many a time, 'It's all well enough,' says I, 'to have bugs for a hobby. You can afford it; and being a bachelor and by yourself, you don't have to consider other people's likes and dislikes. And it's all well enough if you want to,' says I, 'to keep thousands and thousands o' them in cabinets, all over the place, the way you do. But when it comes to pinnin' them on the walls in regular armies,' I says, 'and on the ceiling of your own study; and even on different parts of the furniture, so that a body don't know what awful thing she's agoin' to find under her hand of a sudden when she does the dusting; why, then,' I says to him, 'it's drivin' a decent woman too far.'"

"And did he never try to reform his ways when you told him that?" I asked, smiling.

"To be frank with you, Mr. Robinson, when I talked like that to him, he generally raised my pay. And what was a body to do then?"

"I can't see how Lucy Lawton stood the place as long as she did," I observed, watching Mrs. Malkin's red face very closely.

She swallowed the bait, and leaned forward, hands on knees.

"Poor girl, it got on her nerves. But she was the quiet kind. You never saw her, sir?"

I shook my head.

"One of them slim, faded girls, with light hair, and hardly a word to say for herself. I don't believe she got to know the next-door neighbor in the whole year she lived with your uncle. She was an orphan, wasn't she, sir?"

"Yes," I said. "Godfrey Sarston and I were her only living relatives.

That was why she came from Australia to stay with him, after her father's death."

Mrs. Malkin nodded. I was hoping that, by putting a check on my eagerness, I could lead her on to a number of things I greatly desired to know. Up to the time I had induced the housekeeper to show me through this strange house of my Uncle Godfrey's, the whole affair had been a mystery of lips which closed and faces which were averted at my approach. Even the coroner seemed unwilling to tell me just how my uncle had died.

"Did you understand she was going to live with him, sir?" asked Mrs. Malkin, looking hard at me.

I confined myself to a nod.

"Well, so did I. Yet, after a year, back she went."

"She went suddenly?" I suggested.

"So suddenly that I never knew a thing about it till after she was gone. I came to do my chores on day, and she was here. I came the next, and she had started back to Australia. That's how sudden she went."

"They must have had a falling-out," I conjectured. "I suppose it was because of the house."

"Maybe it was and maybe it wasn't."

"You know of other reasons?"

"I have eyes in my head," she said. "But I'm not going to talk about it. Shall we be getting on now, sir?"

I tried another lead:

"I hadn't seen my uncle in five years, you know. He seemed terribly changed. He was not an old man, by any means, yet when I saw him at the funeral—" I paused, expectantly.

To my relief, she responded readily:

"He looked that way for the last few months, especially the last week. I spoke to him about it, two days before—before it happened, sir—and told him he'd do well to see the doctor again. But he cut me off short. My sister took sick the same day, and I was called out of town. The next time I saw him, he was—"

She paused, and then went on, sobbing:

"To think of him lyin' there in that awful place, and callin' and callin' for me, as I know he must, and me not around to hear him!"

As she stopped again, suddenly, and threw a suspicious glance at me, I hastened to insert a matter-of-fact question:

"Did he appear ill on that last day?"

"Not so much ill, as---"

"Yes?" I prompted.

She was silent a long time, while I waited, afraid that some word of mine had brought back her former attitude of hostility. Then she seemed to make up her mind.

"I oughtn't to say another word. I've said too much, already. But you've been liberal with me, sir, and I know somethin' you've a right to be told, which I'm thinkin' no one else is agoin' to tell you. Look at the bottom of his study door a minute, sir."

I followed her direction. What I saw led me to drop to my hands and knees, the better to examine it.

"Why should he put a rubber strip on the bottom of his door" I asked, getting up.

She replied with another enigmatical suggestion:

"Look at these, if you will, sir. You'll remember that he slept in this study. That was he bed, over there in the alcove."

"Bolts!" I exclaimed. And I reinforced sight with touch by shooting one of them back and forth a few times. "Double bolts on the inside of his bedroom door! An upstairs room, at that. What was the idea?"

Mrs. Malkin portentously shook her head and sighed as one unburdening her mind.

"Only this can I say, sir: He was afraid of something—*terribly* afraid, sir. Something that came in the night."

"What was it?" I demanded.

"I don't know, sir."

"It was in the night that—it happened?" I asked.

She nodded; then, as if the prologue were over, as if she had prepared my mind sufficiently, she produced something from under her apron. She must have been holding it there all the time.

"It's his diary, sir. It was lying here on the floor. I saved it for you, before the police could get their hands on it."

I opened the little book. One of the sheets near the back was crumpled, and I glanced at it, idly. What I read there impelled me to slap the covers shut again.

"Did you read this?" I demanded.

She met my gaze, frankly.

"I looked into it, sir, just as you did—only just *looked* into it. Not for worlds would I do even that again!"

"I noticed some reference here to a slab in the cellar. What slab is that?"

"It covers an old, dried-up well, sir."

"Will you show it to me?"

"You can find it for yourself, sir, if you wish. I'm not goin' down there," she said, decidedly.

"Ah, well I've seen enough for today," I told her. "I'll take the diary back to my hotel and read it."

∼

I DID NOT RETURN to my hotel, however. In my one brief glance into the little book, I had seen something which had bitten into my soul; only a few words, but they had brought me very near to that queer, solitary man who had been my uncle.

I dismissed Mrs. Malkin, and remained in the study. There was the fitting place to read the diary he had left behind him.

His personality lingered like a vapor in that study. I settled into his deep morris chair, and turned it to catch the light from the single, narrow window—the light, doubtless, by which he had written much of his work on entomology.

That same struggling illumination played shadowy tricks with hosts of wall-crucified insects, which seemed engaged in a united effort to crawl upward in sinuous lines. Some of their number, impaled to the ceiling itself, peered quaveringly down on the aspiring multitude. The whole house, with its crisp dead, rustling in any vagrant breeze, brought back to my mind the hand that had pinned them, one by one, on wall and ceiling and furniture. A kindly hand, I reflected, though eccentric; one not to be turned aside from its single hobby.

When quiet, peering Uncle Godfrey went, there passed out another of those scientific enthusiasts, whose passion for exact truth in some one direction has extended the bounds of human knowledge. Could not his unquestioned merits have been balanced against his sin? Was it necessary to even-handed justice that he die face-to-face with Horror, struggling with the thing he most feared? I ponder the question still, though his body—strangely bruised—has been long at rest.

The entries in the little book began with the fifteenth of June. Everything before that date had been torn out. There, in the room where it had been written, I read my Uncle Godfrey's diary.

> "It is done. I am trembling so that the words will hardly form under my pen, but my mind is collected. My course was for the best. Suppose I had married her? She would have been unwilling to live in this house.at the outset, her wishes would have come between me and my work, and that would have been only the beginning.
>
> "As a married man, I could not have concentrated properly, I could not have surrounded myself with the atmosphere indispensable to the writing of my book. My scientific message would never have been delivered. As it is, though my heart is sore, I shall stifle these memories in work.
>
> "I wish I had been more gentle with her, especially when she sank to her knees before me, tonight. She kissed my hand. I should not have repulsed her so roughly. In particular, my words could have been better chosen. I said to her, bitterly: 'Get up, and don't nuzzle my hand like a dog.' She rose, without a word, and left me. How was I to know that, within an hour—
>
> "I am largely to blame. Yet, had I taken any other course afterward than the one I did, the authorities would have misunderstood."

Again, there followed a space from which the sheets had been torn; but from the sixteenth of July, all the pages were intake. Something had come over the writing, too. It was still precise and clear—my Uncle Godfrey's characteristic hand—but the letters were less firm. As the entries approached the end, this difference became still more marked.

Here follows, then, the whole of his story; or as much of it as will ever be known. I shall let his words speak for him, without further interruption:

"My nerves are becoming more seriously affected. If certain annoyances do not shortly cease, I shall be obliged to procure medical advice. To be more specific, I find myself, at ties, obsessed by an almost uncontrollable desire to descent to the cellar and lift the slab over the old well.

"I never have yielded to the impulse, but it has persisted for minutes together with such intensity that I have had to put work aside, and literally hold myself down in my chair. This insane desire comes only in the dead of night, when its disquieting effect is heightened by the various noises peculiar to the house.

"For instance, there often is a draft of air along the hallways, which causes a rustling among the specimens impaled on the walls. Lately, too, there have been other nocturnal sounds, strongly suggestive of the busy clamor of rats and ice. This calls for investigation. I have been at considerable expense to make the house proof against rodents, which might destroy some of my best specimens. If some structural defect has opened a way for them, the situation must be corrected at once."

"July 17th. The foundations and cellar were examined today by a workman. He states positively that there is no place of ingress for rodents. He contented himself with looking at the slab over the old well, without lifting it."

"July 19th. While I was sitting in this chair, late last night, writing, the impulse to descend to the cellar suddenly came upon me with tremendous insistence. I yielded—which, perhaps, was as well. For at least I satisfied myself that the disquiet which possesses me has no external cause.

"The long journey through the hallways was difficult. Several times, I was keenly aware of the same sounds (perhaps I should say, the same

IMPRESSIONS of sounds) that I had erroneously aid to rats. I am convinced now that they are mere symptoms of my nervous condition. Further indications of this came in the fact that, as I opened the cellar door, the small noises abruptly ceased. There was no final scamper of tiny footfalls to suggest rats disturbed at their occupations.

"Indeed, I was conscious of a certain impression of expectant silence—as if the thing behind the noises, whatever it was, had paused to watch me enter its domain. Throughout my time in the cellar, I seemed surrounded by this same atmosphere. Sheer 'nerves,' of course.

"In the main, I held myself well under control. As I was about to leave the cellar, however, I unguardedly glanced back over my shoulder at the stone slab covering the old well. At that, a violent tremor came over me, and, losing all command, I rushed back up the cellar stairs, thence to this study. My nerves are playing me sorry tricks."

"July 30th. For more than a week, all has been well. The tone of my nerves seems distinctly better. Mrs. Malkin, who has remarked several times lately upon my paleness, expressed the conviction this afternoon that I am nearly my old self again. This is encouraging. I was beginning to fear that the severe strain of the past few months had left an indelible mark upon me. With continued health, I shall be able to finish my book by spring."

"July 31st. Mrs. Malkin remained rather late tonight in connection with some housework, and it was quite dark when I returned to my study from bolting the street door after her. The blackness of the upper hall, which the former owner of the house inexplicably failed to wire for electricity, was profound. As I came to the top of the second flight of stairs, something clutched at my foot, and, for an instant, almost pulled me back. I freed myself and ran to the study."

"August 3rd. Again the awful insistence. I sit here, with this diary upon my knee, and it seems that fingers of iron are tearing at me. I WILL NOT go! My nerves may be utterly unstrung again (I fear they are), but I am still their master."

"August 4th. I did not yield, last night. After a bitter struggle, which must have lasted nearly an hour, the desire to go to the cellar suddenly departed. I must not give in at any time."

"August 5th. Tonight, the rat noises (I shall call them that for want of a more appropriate term) are very noticeable. I went to the length of unbolting my door and stepping into the hallway to listen. After a few minutes, I seemed to be aware of something large and gray watching me from the darkness at the end of the passage. This is a bizarre statement, of course, but it exactly describes my impression. I withdrew hastily into the study, and bolted the door.

"Now that my nervous condition is so palpable affecting the optic nerve, I must not much longer delay seeing a specialist. But—how much shall I tell him?"

"August 8th. Several times, tonight, while sitting here at my work, I have seemed to hear soft footsteps in the passage. 'Nerves' again, of course, or else some new trick of the wind among the specimens on the walls."

"August 9th. By my watch it is four o'clock in the morning. My mind is made up to record the experience I have passed through. Calmness may come that way.

"Feeling rather fatigued last night from the strain of a weary day of research, I returned early. My sleep was more refreshing than usual, as it is likely to be when one is genuinely tired. I awakened, however (it must have been about an hour ago), with the start of tremendous violence.

"There was moonlight in the room. My nerves were 'on edge', but, for a moment, I saw nothing unusual. Then, glancing toward the door, I perceived what appeared to be thin, white fingers, thrust under it—exactly as if some one outside the door were trying to attract my attention in that manner. I rose and turned on the light, but the fingers were gone.

"Needless to say, I did not open the door. I write the occurrence down, just as it took place, or as it seemed; but I can not trust myself to comment upon it."

"August 10th. Have fastened heavy rubber strips on the bottom of my bedroom door."

"August 15th. All quiet, for several nights. I am hoping that the rubber strips, being something definite and tangible, have had a salutary effect upon my nerves. Perhaps I shall not need to see a doctor."

"August 17th. Once more, I have been aroused from sleep. The interruptions seem to come always at the same hour—about three o'clock in the morning. I had been dreaming of the well in the cellar—the same dream, over and over—everything black except the slab, and a figure with bowed head and averted face sitting there. Also I had vague dreams about a dog. Can it be that my last words to her have impressed that on my mind? I must pull myself together. In particular, I must not, under any pressure, yield, and visit the cellar after nightfall."

"August 18th. Am feeling much more hopeful. Mrs. Malkin remarked on it, while serving dinner. This improvement is due largely to a consultation I have had with Dr. Sartwell, the distinguished specialist in nervous diseases. I went into full details with him, excepting certain reservations. He scouted the idea that my experiences could be other than purely mental.

"When he recommended a change of scene (which I had been expecting), I told him positively that it was out of the question. He said then that, with the aid of a tonic and an occasional sleeping draft, I am likely to progress well enough at home. This is distinctly encouraging. I erred in not going to him at the start. Without doubt, most, if not all, of my hallucinations could have been averted.

"I have been suffering a needless penalty from my nerves for an action I took solely in the interests of science. I have no disposition to tolerate it further. From today, I shall report regularly to Dr. Sartwell."

"August 19th. Used the sleeping draft last night, with gratifying results. The doctor says I must repeat the dose for several nights, until my nerves are well under control again."

"August 21st. all well. It seems that I have found the way out—a very simple and prosaic way. I might have avoided much needless annoyance by seeking expert advice at the beginning. Before retiring, last night, I unbolted my study door and took a turn up and down the passage. I felt no trepidation. The place was as it used to be, before these fancies assailed me. A visit to the cellar after nightfall will be the test for my complete recovery but I am not yet quite ready for that. Patience!"

"August 22nd. I have just read yesterday's entry thinking to steady myself. It is cheerful—almost gay; and there are other entries like it in preceding pages. I am a mouse, in the grip of a cat. Let me have freedom for ever so short a tie, and I begin to rejoice at my escape. Then the paw descends again.

"It is four in the morning—the usual hour. I returned rather late, last night, after administering the draft. Instead of the dreamless sleep, which heretofore has followed the use of the drug, the slumber into which I fell was punctuated by recurrent visions of the slab, with the bowed figure upon it. Also, I had one poignant dream in which the dog was involved.

"At length, I awakened, and reached mechanically for the light switch beside my bed. When my hand encountered nothing, I suddenly realized the truth. I was standing in my study with my other hand upon the doorknob. It required only a moment, of course, to find the light and switch it on. I saw then that the bolt had been drawn back.

"The door was quite unlocked. My awakening must have interrupted me in the very act of opening it. I could hear something moving restlessly in the passage outside the door."

"August 23rd. I must beware of sleeping at night. Without confiding the fact to Dr. Sartwell, I have begun to take the drug in the daytime. At first, Mrs. Malkin's views on the subject were pronounced, but my explanation of 'doctor's orders' has silenced her. I am awake for breakfast and supper, and sleep in the hours between. She is leaving me, each evening, a cold lunch to be eaten at midnight."

"August 26th. Several times, I have caught myself nodding in my chair. The last time, I am sure that, on arousing, I perceived the rubber strip under the door bending inward, as if something were pushing it from the other side. I must not, under any circumstances, permit myself to fall asleep."

"September 2nd. Mrs. Malkin is to be away, because of her sister's illness. I can not help dreading her absence. Though she is here only in the daytime, even that companionship is very welcome."

"September 3rd. Let me put this into writing. The mere labor of composition has a soothing influence upon me. God knows, I need such an influence now, as never before!

"In spite of all my watchfulness, I fell asleep, tonight—across my bed. I must have been utterly exhausted. The dream I had was the one about the dog. I was patting the creature's head, over and over.

"I awoke, at last, to find myself in darkness, and in a standing position. There was a suggestion of chill and earthiness in the air. While I was drowsily trying to get my bearings, I became aware that something was nuzzling my hand, as a dog might do.

"Still saturated with my dream, I was not greatly astonished. I extended my hand, to pat the dog's head. That brought me to my senses. I was standing in the cellar.

"THE THING BEFORE ME WAS NOT A DOG!

"I cannot tell how I fled back up the cellar stairs. I know, however, that, as I turned, the slab was visible, in spite of the darkness, with something sitting upon it. All the way up the stairs, hands snatched at my feet."

This entry seemed to finish the diary, for blank pages followed it; but I remembered the crumpled sheet, near the back of the book. It was partly torn out, as if a hand had clutched it, convulsively. The writing on it, too, was markedly in contrast to the precise, albeit nervous penmanship of even the last entry I had perused. I was forced to hold the scrawl up to the light to decipher it. This is what I read:

"My hand keeps on writing, in spite of myself. What is this? I do not wish to write, but it compels me. Yes, yes, I will tell the trust, I will tell the truth."

A heavy blot followed, partly covering the writing. With difficulty, I made it out:

"The guilt is mine—mine, only. I loved her too well, yet I was unwilling to marry, though she entreated me on her knees—though she kissed my hand. I told her my scientific work came first. She did it, herself. I was not expecting that—I swear I was not expecting it. But I was afraid the authorities would misunderstand. So I took what seemed the best course. She had no friends here who would inquire

"It is waiting outside my door. I FEEL it. It compels me, through my

thoughts. *My hand keeps on writing. I must not fall asleep. I must think only of what I am writing. I must---"*

Then came the words I had seen when Mrs. Malkin had handed me the book. They were written very large. In places, the pen had dug through the paper. Though they were scrawled, I read them at a glance:

"Not the slab in the cellar! Not that! Oh, my God, anything but that! Anything—"

By what strange compulsion was the hand forced to write down what was in the brain; even to the ultimate thoughts; even to those final words?

~

THE GRAY LIGHT FROM OUTSIDE, slanting down through two dull little windows sank into the sodden hole near the inner wall. The coroner and I stood in the cellar, but not too near the hole.

A small, demonstrative, dark man—the chief of detectives—stood a little apart from us, his eyes intent, his natural animation suppressed. We were watching the stooped shoulders of a police constable, who was angling in the well.

"See anything, Walters?" inquired the detective, raspingly.

The policeman shook his head.

The little man turned his questioning to me.

"You're quite sure?" he demanded.

"Ask the coroner. He saw the diary," I told him.

"I'm afraid there can be no doubt," the coroner confirmed, in his heavy, tired voice.

He was an old man, with lackluster eyes. It had seemed best to me, on the whole, that he should read my uncle's diary. His position entitled him to all the available facts. What we were seeking in the well might especially concern him.

He looked at me opaquely now, while the policeman bent double again. Then he spoke—like one who reluctantly and at last does his duty. He nodded toward the slab of gray stone, which lay in the shadow to the left of the well.

"It doesn't seem very heavy, does it?" he suggested, in an undertone

I shook my head. "Still, it's stone," I demurred. "A man would have to be rather strong to lift it."

"To lift it—yes." He glanced about the cellar. "Ah, I forgot," he said, abruptly. "It is in my office, as part of the evidence." He went on, half to himself: "A man—even though not very strong—could take a stick—for instance, the stick that is now in my office—and prop up the slab. If he wished to look into the well," he whispered.

The policeman interrupted, straightening again with a groan, and laying his electric torch beside the well.

"It's breaking my back," he complained. "There's dirt down there. It seems loose, but I can't get through it. Somebody'll have to go down."

The detective cut in:

"I'm lighter than you, Walters."

"I'm not afraid, sir."

"I didn't say you were," the little man snapped. "There's nothing down there, anyway—though we'll have to prove that, I suppose." He glanced truculently at me, but went on talking to the constable: "Rig the rope around me, and don't bungle the knot. I've no intention of falling into the place."

"There *is* something there," whispered the coroner, slowly, to me. His eyes left the little detective and the policeman, carefully tying and testing knots, and turned again to the square slab of stone.

"Suppose—while a man was looking into that hole—with the stone propped up—he should accidentally knock the prop away?" He was still whispering.

"A stone so light that he could prop it up wouldn't be heavy enough to kill him," I objected.

"No." He laid a hand on my shoulder. "Not to *kill* him—to *paralyze* him—if it struck the spine in a certain way. To render him helpless, but not unconscious. The *post mortem* would disclose that, through the bruises on the body."

The policeman and the detective had adjusted the knots to their satisfaction. They were bickering now as to the details of the descent.

"Would that cause death?" I whispered.

"You must remember that the housekeeper was absent for two days. In two days, even that pressure—" He stared at me hard, to make sure that I understood—"with the head down—"

Again the policeman interrupted:

"I'll stand at the well, if you gentlemen will grab the rope behind me. It won't be much of a pull. I'll take the brunt of it."

We let the little man down, with the electric torch strapped to his waist, and some sort of implement—a trowel or small spade—in his hand. It seemed a long time before his voice, curiously hollow, directed us to stop. The hole must have been deep.

We braced ourselves. I was second, the coroner, last. The policeman relieved his strain somewhat by snagging the rope against the edge of the well, but I marveled, nevertheless, at the ease with which he held the weight. Very little of it came to me.

A noise like muffled scratching reached us from below. Occasionally, the rope shook and shifted slightly at the edge of the hole. At last, the detective's hollow voice spoke.

"What does he say?" the coroner demanded.

The policeman turned his square, dogged face toward us.

"I think he's found something," he explained.

The rope jerked and shifted again. Some sort of struggle seemed to be going on below. The weight suddenly increased, and as suddenly lessened, as if something had been grasped, then had managed to elude the grasp and slip away. I could catch the detective's rapid breathing now; also the sound of inarticulate speech in his hollow voice.

The next words I caught came more clearly. They were a command to pull up. At the same moment, the weight on the rope grew heavier, and remained so.

The policeman's big shoulders began straining, rhythmically.

"All together," he directed. "Take it easy. Pull when I do."

Slowly, the rope passed through our hands. With each fresh grip that we took, a small section of it dropped to the floor behind us. I began to feel the strain. I could tell from the coroner's labored breathing that he felt it more, being an old man. The policeman, however, seemed untiring.

The rope tightened, suddenly, and there was an ejaculation from below—just below. Still holding fast, the policeman contrived to stoop over and look. He translated the ejaculation for us.

"Let down a little. He's stuck with it against the side."

We slackened the rope, until the detective's voice gave us the word again.

The rhythmic tugging continued. Something dark appeared, quite abruptly, at the top of the hole. My nerves leapt in spite of me, but it was merely the top of the detective's head—his dark hair. Something white came next—his pale face, with staring eyes. Then his shoulders, bowed forward, the better to support what was in his arms. Then—

I looked away; but, as he laid his burden down at the side of the well, the detective whispered to us:

"He had her covered up with dirt—covered up..."

He began to laugh—a little, high cackle, like a child's—until the coroner took him by the shoulders and deliberately shook him. Then the policeman led him out of the cellar.

∽

IT WAS NOT THEN, but afterward, that I put my question to the coroner.

"Tell me," I demanded. "People pass there at all hours. Why didn't my uncle call for help?"

"I have thought of that," he replied. "I believe he did call. I think, probably, he screamed. But his head was down, and he couldn't raise it. His screams must have been swallowed up in the well."

"You are sure he didn't murder her?" He had given me that assurance before, but I wished it again.

"Almost sure" he declared. "Though it was on his account, undoubtedly, that she killed herself. Few of us are punished as accurately for our sins as he was."

～

ONE SHOULD BE THANKFUL, even for crumbs of comfort. I am thankful.

But there are times when my uncle's face rises before me. After all, we were the same blood; our sympathies had much in common; under any given circumstances, our thoughts and feelings must have been largely the same. I seem to see him in that final death march along the unlighted passageway—obeying an imperative summons—going on, step by step—down the stairway to the first floor, down the cellar stairs—at last, lifting the slab.

I try not to think of the final explanation. Yet *was* it final? I wonder. Did the last Door of all, when it opened, find him wiling to pass through? Or was Something waiting beyond *that* Door?

THE TORTOISE SHELL COMB, BY ROYLSTON MARKHAM
THE FANTASY OF A MAD BRAIN

"Well, the ghosts of the men hung at Is-Sur-Tille have company. For myself, I wouldn't even want a photograph of the place. No, sir, not me. I can remember it without that. That's why they've put me in this hospital with all these crazy people. Yet a tortoise shell comb is as good an alibi as any...

"What? Ghosts? No sir, of course not; I don't believe in 'em, not on *this* side of the Atlantic...who ever told you *I* believed in ghosts.

"The hospital interne?...If they'd kept me 'round that chateau in the woods at Is-Sur-Tille, it might 'a' been different. It had a queer story about it, that chateau. That's what set *me* off; that and the fact that I never did like Captain Bott.

"He was hardboiled, that guy was. No, sir; he didn't own that French chateau, although at one time he acted as though he thought he did....I'm coming to that.

"Over there the frogs said the original owner of the place, in his youth, had fallen madly in love with a young girl and married her. He must 'a' been crazy about her all right because, according to their story, he often was seen combing her hair—yes, sir, the French folks are like that; that's romance—combing her long red hair as it hung over the back of her chair, touching the floor.

"I particularly remember that they said her hair was long, very long, and red, like copper is red in candle light. After a year, she died, suddenly, of heart disease—'killed by love itself,' one of the frogs said; that's romance, and he, her husband, the owner of that chateau there in the woods at Is-Sur-Tille, left that part of the country on the very day of her funeral. The place, probably, is there yet, like it was when I saw it, late in the summer of 1918.

"The house was set back from the road among the trees. It looked, then, as though it had been deserted for a long time. Most of the furniture had been removed from it, except in one room—I'm coming to that—and the gate leading into the yard had fallen open on one rusty hinge. Grass filled the paths; and you couldn't tell the flowerbeds from the lawns except by the weeds.

"Nobody had used the place, even in wartime, until our outfit was billeted at Is-Sur-Tille. That ghost story of a dead bride begging some one to comb her hair had kept the Frenchies off the place. But Captain Bott was a hard-boiled guy.

"We went into the house late one afternoon, Captain Bott and me. He led the way into the kitchen and through the first floor into a large hall, where the stairs went up to the floor above. Dust was over everything. The only room in the house that looked at all as though it had been occupied in years was that bedroom upstairs where, they had told us, the bride had slept and died. We recognized it because it was the only room in the house where the door was shut.

"We opened it—that is, Captain Bott did—and went in. I stood in the doorway until he swore at me and ordered me to follow him in. the room smelled moldy. It smelled dead. It was a fine room for a ghost. It was dark in there, but gradually my eyes got accustomed to the gloom enough to make out that there was a bed in it. On the captain's orders, I went to the window to open it for light, but I had to break the rusty hinges of the outside shutters before I could loosen them.

"At the court martial inquiry they wouldn't believe me when I said that was the only reason I went into the room, and on the captain's orders

"The room was on the north side of the house and the sun was setting, so opening the window didn't help much. There was pillows and a mattress and sheets—yellow sheets, yellow with age—on the bed. The chairs seemed all in confusion. There was another door in the room, probably leading to a closet. It was closed.

"Captain Bott went over and felt of the mattress and patted the pillows—the pillows on which they had said the bride's head, nestled in its mass of copper-colored hair, had rested when she died. Captain Bott was hard-boiled, like I just said. He didn't believe in ghosts.

"He said it was the best shakedown he'd seen in weeks.

"'I'll damned soon get a good night's rest,' he said.

"And he ordered me to go for some candles and his stuff; and, when I got back, I was to clear the place up. I went. I was glad to go. But I hated like hell to return."

∽

"When I did get back into the house, it was twilight and, inside, as dark as a black cat's belly. Downstairs, in the kitchen, I lighted one of the candles and held it before me in one hand, the other being occupied with the captain's luggage. Then I went through the first floor into the large hall where the stairs went up to the floor above.

"In the light of my candle at the landing I saw that the door into the bedroom was closed again, as it had been the only room in the house where the door was shut when we first went up there together —the captain who didn't believe in ghosts and I, who did, over there...No sir, of course not; I *don't* believe in 'em, not on *this* side of the Atlantic. But, in the woods, at Is-Sur-Tille at night, that's different.

"And it must be worse, since they hung those men there...and with Captain Bott who thought the bed of a dead bride was a handsome billet. He was sure hard-boiled, that guy. I hated him for it.

"When I left him to go for the candles, that door had been open. When I returned it was closed. I didn't like to open it again. But he was alone there in the dark in that bedroom. I knew that if I waited for him to come to open the door, stumbling across chairs and things, he sure would cuss me out—that's the hell of being a private and a servant to an officer; no white man likes it—so, finally, I opened the door, with the hand which held the candle.

"Everything seemed as before, but so quiet. My ears were straining for sound like they used to do at the sudden cessation of barrage-firing. But I heard nothing, nothing at all. And the place smelled moldy. It smelled dead. It was a fine room for a ghost. I thought of it then.

"And, as I stepped across the threshold, I noticed that that other door in the room, probably that of a closet, was open. It had been closed. I thought perhaps that the captain had opened it while I was gone. It wasn't so dark when I left him as when I returned, and maybe he would 'a' been snooping around a bit, out of curiosity, perhaps. *I'm not curious like that.* But Captain Bott was hard-boiled. And he didn't believe in ghosts...

"All these things I'm telling you about what I saw and thought and felt, they wouldn't hardly listen to at the court martial inquiry...

"I don't know how long it was from the time I lighted the candle in the kitchen downstairs until I stood with it in the doorway of the bedroom of the dead bride. Not very long, probably, because the melting candle grease was just beginning to run hot onto my fingers when I turned to glance toward the bed, wondering why the captain had kept so damned quiet. It wasn't like him.

"And there he was, lying across the bed on his back, the tips of his shoes just touching the floor. Asleep? No. I don't know how I knew he wasn't asleep...the court martial inquiry kept asking me that...

"But I saw he had something wound round his neck, something that glinted in the candle light like the braid of a woman's copper-red hair. And his hands were above his head. One of them clutched a tortoise-shell comb. I knew he wasn't asleep. I knew he was *dead!*....

"How I knew, I couldn't tell you nor any damned court martial inquiry on earth. God knows they drove me crazy enough asking me that and what else I saw....

"Didn't I see nothing else? No, but I thought I *heard* or *felt* something move near that black hole where that other door opened yawning into a closet. My candle went out—maybe it was only the night wind from the window—and I dropped it. I dropped the bundle of things belonging to Captain Bott. I crossed the threshold. I went down the stairs in the dark, running.

"I fell at the bottom. I remember that...And I told the court martial inquiry so; 'twas about the only thing those smug guys believed that I told them...But I was on my feet and out of that house before I knew I had fallen..."

∽

"HA! I can see it! You, too, think I'm soft-boiled....So did the court martial inquiry. That's why they sent me here, among these crazy people. But say, Buddy, don't believe what the hospital interne tells you. He's crazy, like the rest of 'em. He's as hard-boiled, too, as Captain Bott was. And *that* guy was so hard-boiled he didn't believe in French ghost stories."

∽

"THAT NUT you just talked with tells his story to anyone who will listen," the interne remarked casually, as we returned to the office of the commandant of the Army and Navy Insane Asylum. "Probably you think you've heard a crackin' good ghost story, but what you really heard was the confession of a crazy murderer who ought to have been the third on the gallows at Is-Sur-Tille."

"Isn't there a haunted chateau at Is-Sur-Tille, and dint' the officer he tells about die in the bedroom there?"

"*Oui, mais certainement!* As the frogs have it. If that chateau isn't haunted, it ought to be. There's a story in the village of the bride's death there. And Captain Bott died there all right enough. But that thing they found twined around his neck 'like the braid of a woman's copper-red hair' was, in fact, real copper—copper wire stolen from a lineman's kit. It might *look* like hair to a crazy man."

"But that comb?" I persisted. "What about that tortoise-shell comb?"

"That? Oh, the nut stole that, too. It belonged to one of the girls of the town whom the private knew before the captain beat his time with her."

A PHOTOGRAPHIC PHANTASM, BY PAUL CRUMPLER, M.D.

I have always believed that there is a simple and natural explanation for all seemingly supernatural happenings; but I recently had occasion to question this belief.

I cannot doubt my own personal knowledge, nor can I deny what my own eyes have seen, therefore, I cannot dismiss it as a figment of imagination. The facts are as follows:

There is a rural section near me into which I frequently make visits in the practice of my profession as physician. The people are a quaint, simple and kindly sort, honest, unsophisticated.

I was called, not long ago, to see a little girl in this neighborhood and found her very ill and with a poor chance for recovery. She was the younger of two children of a very intelligent farmer and his wife, the latter, however, having a rather nervous temperament. I had treated the woman before the little girl was born, and, although she, too, was above the average in intelligence in her neighborhood, she was a person who would be classed medically as a neurasthenic.

Realizing the seriousness of her child's sickness, she was becoming very nervous, so much so that I found it necessary to leave her some sedatives. She was worrying a great deal because she did not have a picture of the little girl. It seemed that the family had planned on several occasions to have a group picture made in the village, but each time something had prevented their doing so. This, she informed me, was preying on her mind and accentuating her grief.

The child died and I heard nothing more from the family until about two months later. This time my call was to the mother. I found her in a state of hysteria bordering almost on insanity. She was holding a number of photographs to her breast, and alternately laughing and crying; it was impossible to get any coherency into her actions.

Her husband, however, told me that just before he sent for me, the Rural Mail Carrier had delivered the photographs which had been taken of himself, his wife and the remaining little girl about six weeks after the death of their child.

After much persuasion we were able to get the photographs from her and after glancing at them we saw the cause of her hysteria. THE DEAD CHILD WAS PHOTOGRAPHED IN THE GROUP ALMOST AS PLAINLY AS THE OTHERS.

She was sitting on her mother's lap, and on her feet were the little white shoes which had been bought after her death to satisfy the mother, who did not want to bury the child in the old and ragged pair which were all she had. She was dressed exactly as when she was buried, wearing the dress that the mother had made for her to wear when the family group was to be photographed.

Did this phenomenon happen by mental telepathy from the mother to the camera? The mother had grieved unusually and her mind was entirely filled with thoughts of her child. If the explanation is not to be had from this line of reasoning, I am unable to solve it.

The picture is there, and also the photographer to verify the truth of this. The pictures shows the two children and the mother and father. The photographer is ready to swear that only one child was visible to his eye when he made the negative.

THE LIVING NIGHTMARE, BY ANTON M. OLIVER

ONE "CREEPY" NIGHT IN A HOUSE OF DEATH

"You mean to tell me," demanded Jim Brown, "that those people left town and expect you to stay in that house alone tonight?"

"Why, yes," said MacMillen, preparing to leave. "They've gone to Virginia and will be back Thursday, when the funeral will take place."

"And they left the body lying in the living-room?"

"Of course. Where did you expect them to leave it—on the porch?"

"And you are going to sleep in that house alone—with the corpse?"

"Yes. What of it? There's nothing to be afraid of."

Taking his hat and coat, MacMillen departed.

"Pleasant dreams!" called Brown, as the door slammed behind him.

The night was cold and the atmosphere was clear and "hard." The snow crackled under his feet as he walked.

"Silly idea." He muttered; but he couldn't help wondering why the Mitchells, with whom he made his home, had left the house on the same day that Mrs. Mitchell's grandmother had passed away.

In his mind he went over Mrs. Mitchell's explanation. She had told him that they were going to Wheeling, the deceased lady's old home, where a sister lived, and would remain there until the funeral. And she had asked, "You are not afraid to stay here alone, are you?"

No, of course, he was not afraid; but it was strange that they should leave the corpse in his charge and depart.

Then it came to him. Funny he hadn't thought of it before. The Mitchells must be superstitious. They probably had some silly notion about a house being haunted while a corpse was in it, or something of that sort. That must be it. But how ridiculous!

Still, the Mitchells were a little queer anyway, reflected Mac, as he turned up the ice-covered path of the Mitchell residence.

It stood, surrounded by high buildings and stores, in a section of town which in days gone by had been the very heart of the city's social life. It was one of the largest and oldest homes in the city. And now it was an outcast, so to say, among the monuments to industry and progress. Built years ago by the husband of the woman who now lay dead within its walls, it was in a style of architecture long since abandoned. Everything about it was high and narrow—the building itself, the windows and doors, the porch columns, and the roof high up among the tree branches.

Mac walked unhesitatingly toward the big dark house. But, somehow, the formidable brick walls that always looked so inviting seemed cold and inhospitable tonight. Strange shadows were playing in the windows.

He looked up at his own window. He didn't exactly fancy the idea of going past the room where lay the dead woman, he admitted to himself, but her certainly was not afraid. Not he!

With a grim resolution, he thrust the key, which he had taken from his pocket while coming up the walk, into the lock of the front door. The huge, glass-paneled door squeaked as he did so, and he was almost startled by his own reflection in the shining glass. He turned the key in its lock and threw the door wide open with unnecessary vigor.

A hot wave of air greeted him. The house was warm, surprisingly so, considering that it had been unoccupied all day. His heart, for some unexplainable reason, was beating rather fast as he entered the dark hall.

He turned sharply to the left and reached for the electric light switch. His hand had often turned that switch, had often found it instantly in the dark; but tonight he had to feel for it. He turned it once, twice—three times—*but the hall remained dark.*

The dark suddenly seemed to give him almost physical pain. Listening acutely, he tried to account for this. Why were the lights out? The street lights were on, and there was light in several of the homes he had passed. He stood motionless. There was no sound. The dark house was buried in deathlike silence.

Then, with nerve-shattering suddenness, came a sound as real as that of his heart, which was beating so that the blood was throbbing in his ears. He whirled to face it, but, as suddenly as it had started, it stopped. With clenched teeth and damp forehead, Mac stood motionless. Then it came again—a sound like the distant scream of a siren.

Gradually he collected his senses, and reason took the place of bewilderment. He reached for his matches, and, striking one, he stepped over to the gas chandelier, turned the valve, and presently a blue flame leaped high from the lamp, which had not been adjusted for months.

With somewhat trembling hands, he turned the air adjustment, then the gas, until finally the familiar yellow light illuminated the hallway. Then he again heard the noise—this time a little louder and *nearer.*

His decision to investigate suddenly left him. He stood motionless, unable to move, for he not only *heard*—he also *felt!* Then, with a sudden resolve, he stepped swiftly to his room, which was on the same floor and adjoined the library.

The light from the hall cast a long, distorted shadow on the floor before him. It was so still now that the silence surged in his ears. Lighting his own gas lamp, he locked and bolted his door. His pipe lay on the dresser, and he lit it nervously. Then he looked at himself in the mirror.

"How ridiculous!" he said, half aloud, with a forced laugh. Then he began slowly to undress.

All was quiet and peaceful here in his own room. How foolish to let himself get so excited. The lights had probably gone out all over the city since he had entered the house, and, as for that noise, it was probably outdoors somewhere and in his mind he had associated it with the perfectly harmless corpse lying in the net room.

"Darn Brown!" he murmured. "He got me all wrought up over nothing with his kidding."

And, having finished undressing he retired, leaving his light on full, however. In spite of the fact that his own explanation of the origin of the strange sounds had, in a measure, satisfied him, he lay awake for a considerable length of time.

He was drifting off on the first soft currents of sleep when he suddenly sat up with a jerk. He had heard a noise!

His lamp was flickering weirdly and he could hear its faint singing—barely audible—yet it seemed to his ears like the mighty rush of steam from a boiler, for his ears were strained to hear a different sound, a sound he *must* hear again, the source of which he *must* locate.

His body began to ache from sitting rigidly in one position. Still all was silent.

Suddenly, with a sense of being jerked to consciousness, he again heard the noise, like the shriek of a siren. It seemed distant, yet close. His heard labored so hard that he could feel its beat all through his body. The shriek continued for several moments, and then all was silent again.

He wanted to rise, but he could not.

He was not afraid, he told himself,--and yet...

Suddenly he heard the sound of footsteps—steps that seemed to come from the interior of the wall, pass through his room and die away gradually. Holding his breath, he listened.

The big clock in the front room struck the hour of midnight. He counted each beat as it rang through the house. He was wide awake now. The white curtains seemed to glimmer like sunlit snow, and the clock chimes, in the deathly silence, sounded like those of a mighty tower clock.

As the last note died away, Mac suddenly remembered that *the clock had been stopped by Mrs. Mitchell* as a mark of respect to her, who, in the adjoining room, was awaiting burial.

∽

A SUDDEN FEELING of relief came over Mac. It was clear now; somebody had come back, Mr. Mitchell perhaps. That explained everything.

Confidently, Mac got out of bed and, unlocking his door, stepped into the hall. How different everything looked, how natural and homelike! The light that had had such a ghost-like appearance, a short time ago, seemed friendly and quite natural now. At the foot of the stair Mac stopped and called. He called louder and louder, but all remained silent. Suddenly, for some inexplicable reason, he approached the door of the room next to his, seized the doorknob resolutely and, with a sudden push, swung the door open. The rays of the gas light in the hall fell directly into the room, and what they revealed sent a cold shudder of horror through him. Before him stood two *empty pedestals*. The body had disappeared!

Turning violently, he almost ran to the front door and pulled it open. An icy gust of wind hit his thinly clad body. For several moments he stood breathing the cold night air, then, with a sudden determination, he slammed the big oak door shut.

As the door slammed, there came a sharp report, like the snapping of a wire, followed by a thunder and crashing and wailing. The electric light came on, and the same footsteps that had sounded through the house before came closer and closer. He felt a sharp pain, like the thrust of a knife, between his shoulder blades...And then he fell in a swoon.

Weeks passed before Mac was well again. Excessive exposure had brought on pneumonia. As soon as he recovered he summoned me to the hospital and begged me to find a new lodging for him and remove his belongings from the Mitchell home.

I tried in vain to explain that he had misunderstood Mrs. Mitchell regarding the disposal of the corpse, for they had taken the body with them for burial in Wheeling, and it was not in the house at any time after their departure. But Mac was resolute. He listened indulgently, patiently, then, laying his white, hot hand upon my shoulder, he looked earnestly into my eyes, and with a voice that carried conviction he said:

"I know what I felt in that room that night. It had a *hold* on me, and it is waiting for me, and I am not going back!"

Mac is well again now, and one can see him at the club most any night. But whenever anybody starts to speak of the Hereafter he rises and hurriedly leaves the room.

THE INCUBUS, BY HAMILTON CRAIGIE
A MAN'S FRIGHTFUL ADVENTURE IN AN ANCIENT TOMB

F ear beset Gerald Marston at the very moment of his entry into the chamber—an intense, gripping horror which laid an icy hand upon his forehead and fingers of a damp coldness about his heart.

It was as if one invisible from within had reached forth to make him prisoner to its atmosphere, which, heightened physically by the slimy walls, the velvet darkness, and the ceaseless, slow dripping of liquid upon stone, chilled his soul with a nameless foreboding, a daunting menace of unutterable dread.

And yet that Something, as he told himself, was behind him—his victim, the man whom he had killed.

Even now It walked, rather, upon the surface of the oily night, felt, but unseen, driving him forward inexorably, pitilessly—so that now he stood in the entrance to this lesser blackness, his huge bulk shaking in an anguish of uncertainty but one degree removed from the panic which had ridden him until, at length, distraught and near to madness, he had stumbled into this subterranean oubliette in his frantic flight.

It seemed a week since he, together with Professor Pillsbury, had descended into this whispering labyrinth of tombs—long galleries of Aztec construction vying in completeness with the catacombs of early Rome—sinuous corridors crossing and re-crossing in a maze of underground warrens of apparently interminable extent.

It had been the Professor himself, an archaeologist whose devotion to his calling amounted almost to an obsession, who had suggested the exploration—nay, insisted on it—nor had he in his singleness of purpose, remembered that it had been Marston, his friend, who had, as it were, with a very triumph of casualness, implanted in his mind the first tiny seed of suggestion.

Scarcely a month before Marston had felicitated his friend upon the latter's engagement to Lucille Westley, beautiful and imperious, but there had been death in his heart. Perhaps, however, he had fancied, with the perverted hope which had grown in his heart like a green and pallid flame of lust, that, given his chance, he might has possessed this incomparable creature for his own.

And so, like a destroying fire, his obsession had mounted until, with the cunning of his twisted brain, he had evolved a plan, or, rather, deep within his consciousness, had spawned a thought: foul, slimy, furtive—even to himself half-born—an abortion, in truth and yet...

∼

As they had passed from the clean sunlight into the Stygian darkness of the cavern, somehow, unbidden, there had arisen in Marston's mind an echo of the classroom—a fugitive whisper which, he could have sworn, took on suddenly the form and substance of mocking speech: "*Facilis decensus Averni,*" it whispered in his ear, as in a dim current of the whispering wind.

Marston had brought with him a ball of stout twine as a necessary precaution in threading the uncharted deeps of the underground corridors. This he had knotted firmly in a clove hitch (for Marston had been a sailor). There could have been no fear of its working loose, and less danger of its fraying out against the rough walls of the passageways, since at all times it would be loosely held. Like a thin snake, it spread itself behind them, and like a snake...

The accident had been impossible to foresee. He had *known* that it could not happen; and yet....

The Professor, leading the way with lantern held well aloft, had exclaimed aloud at the vivid beauty of a stalactite in his path, adjacent to a broad, deep ledge some three feet in height.

"Ah, Gerald!" he had cried. "It is *alive*—it writhes with motion—observe how it has grown, layer upon layer of smooth perfection! And the ledge—a perfect replica of an ancient sarcophagus! Look—"

But he was destined never to complete the speech.

For with the words he stumbled—a bight of the line snaked out to coil around his ankle—tottered, even as from behind him something moved, flashed, descended upon his head—something cold and hard. He fell, with a sodden crash, face downward in the mold. And with his fall the lantern crashed to the floor of the cavern, sputtered a moment feebly in a brief spark of life, and then died abruptly. And at the feet of Marston that which had been sentient, alive, now lay still and motionless in the dust.

Marston stood for a moment, with groping fingers extended into the void about him; his head song, his eyes blurred. The velvet black became suddenly, as it were, endowed with life and movement, mysterious, whispering. Near at hand there sounded abruptly a horrible, fetid panting—a gross intake of whistling breath which, in a sudden, overmastering panic, he did not recognize as his own labored breathing.

"God!" he cried, insanely, and then, in panic-struck terror at the sound of his voice, fell silent and stood shivering like a frightened horse.

With fumbling fingers he felt in his pockets and produced a box of matches, finally, after many attempts, lighting one which he held tremblingly above his head. He did not glance at the figure at his feet, but over and beyond it, where his shadow, monstrous and grotesque, seemed flung headforemost into a shallow niche, within which there rested a flat slab of rock perhaps three feet in height.

To his distorted imagination the sudden suggestion seemed filled with a vague menace—as if the brooding shadow of death had reached forth to touch, to summon, to beckon with an imperious, chill finger there in that stifling abode of changeless dark.

Abruptly, as the quick flame ate downward to his finger-tips, he made a short, backward step—stumbled—and the box fell from his nerveless hand, the match winked out, and at one stride the dominion of the dark enveloped him.

He bent swiftly, with frantic fingers searching in the mold, scratching, clawing in a fever of anxiety.

He found—nothing. Then, as if impelled from behind by an inexorable Force, he began to run, stumbling, falling, bruising himself against the sharp, unseen angles of the passageway along which he fled....

Time had merged into an eternity of physical pain and mental torture, of corroding fear which left him in a sweat of agony as he fared onward in his blundering flight. The sense of direction which in the pitch blackness renders the familiar outlines of one's very bedchamber strangely distorted—this had become confused in his first headlong rush away from the scene of that which was branded upon his heart in letters of fire.

Now, in his warped and twisted brain the germ of a though grew, expanded, flowered abruptly in an insane cacophony of sound.

A laugh, reedy, discordant, cackling echoed in his ears, beginning in a low chuckle, then rising all about him in a furious stridor of sound. It was as if the demons of the place were welcoming him to their midst as one worthy of their company.

Again he fell prone, groveling in the mold in an ecstasy of terror at the unrecognizable mouthings which issued from this throat. But even as his insanity peopled the void about him with shapes of terror, in especial the hideous Shape which he knew even now followed him, he got somehow to his feet, arose, and lurched headlong into a recess in the rocky corridor, which would have been familiar could he have but beheld it even in the brief flaring of a match.

It was then that he heard the ceaseless, slow dripping that smote him afresh with an indescribable, crawling fear, beside which his previous insane panic had been as nothing. For a moment he heard also a gibbering—a squeaking, a rustle which with his coming ceased abruptly in a faint shadow of sound. For the moment, he could have sworn that a slinking, furtive, Something, unbelievably swift, had brushed past his leg, touched him lightly as with the faint, furtive contact of a dead, windblown leaf.

That slow, continuous dripping—too well he knew its meaning, or thought that he did. And in the same breath he became aware of the place in which he stood—*recognized* it for what it was even in the enveloping blackness.

At any other time he would have known that measured dripping for what it was: the curiously suggestive rhythm of the stalactite's slow *drip-drip*, like the sluggish dripping of blood.

In his headlong flight, cleaving an unimagined depth of Cimmerian darkness, through which it seemed he was breathing the oily tide of a dim nightmare of viscid flood, all sense of direction had been completely lost.

Now, as he stood, within this fearsome catacomb, of a sudden he stumbled, knelt, put forward a groping hand, and then recoiled with a windy shriek—as his shaking fingers encountered *the clammy surface of a human face!*

∼

HE HAD RETURNED, willy nilly, as it seemed, to the body of his victim. It was the face of Pillsbury, cold, clammy, silent, unresponsive.

Domed! He was doomed, then, to kneel there, in that groping blackness of this frightful charnel—alone, yet prisoner to that silent figure—forever to hear that ceaseless dripping, regular as the beating of a heart, of a heart that was stilled forever, yet strangely pulsing in its slow *drip-drip*—inexorable, insistent, ever louder, as it seemed— rising in a veritable thunder against the low-hung curtain of the dark.

Trembling, urging his will by the severest effort he had ever known, in a sudden lucid interval he passed an exploring hand over the rigid outlines of the body, which lay, as upon a bier, on a sort of rocky shelf, perhaps three feet in height, just level with his shoulders as he bent before it. But it had not been there before! When he had left it in his overmastering panic *it had been lying, face downward in the mold!*

But it did not occur to him to question its position: the strange significance of the fact affected him not at all, for, curiously enough, with the contact there came a measure of reassurance: the Thing which had been Pillsbury, his friend—the Thing which he had left behind—had not been following him; it had existed merely in his coward imagination. Or, if it had hunted him through the maze of corridors, it was now returned to its chosen resting-place. There it was, under his hand!

It was absurd to think that he had been followed, for dead men did not walk, save in dreams, and he had returned to prove that it lay where he had left it, silent, cold, incapable of movement without volition.

On his hands and knees, his questing fingers, tracing the rigid outline of the limbs, came suddenly upon a length of line, knotted about the ankle. *Ah!*

Feverishly he felt about him in the blackness, clawing forward on hands and knees. Yes, the line ran clear, unbroken, away from the niche. He was saved!

In his sudden revulsion, he gave way to primitive emotion—he chuckled, moaned, cried, wept, laughed in a horrible travesty of mirth.

Like a drowning man, he seized upon it with clutching fingers as if by some sudden magic he might be drawn, on the instant, out of this labyrinth of black terror which was eating into his soul with the corroding bite of an acid. For at the other end of that thin thread lay sunlight and life and liberty. He held that within his shaking grasp which was in truth a life-line, a tenuous yet certain means of safety, of escape from a death, the grisly face of which had but a moment before leered at him out of the tomblike depths.

In his eagerness to be gone, he straightened from his kneeling posture with a convulsive movement, his fingers holding the line, jerked it violently, and, before he could rise, there came a rustle, a thud, and a suffocating weight descended upon his back. As he fell, face downward in the mold, he squeaked like a rat as, out of the dark, two hands went round his neck and clawlike talons encircled his throat.

Curiously alive they seemed, and yet—with his own hand he had accounted for that life. It was not possible—no, it could not be!—it was unthinkable...

For a space he lay, inert, passive, but, notwithstanding his terror, his fingers still clutching the line, spread out before him in the blackness. Presently, when his panic had somewhat abated, when he found that he was still alive, unharmed, by slow stages of tremendous effort he rose to his knees, tottering under the Incubus upon his back.

Now that he knew what it was, after an interval he attempted to disengage the fingers around his neck, but he could not. He found that grip rigid, unyielding. Like a bar of iron, it resisted his utmost efforts.

It was as if a Will, implacable, inexorable, had informed those stiffened talons with purpose; it was as if the last sentient effort of an Intelligence had, by some supernatural quality, *bequeathed* to those fingers a message, a command to be performed. *Rigor mortis*—that was it—the unbreakable hold of those implacable fingers: Pillsbury's vengeful fingers, reaching out, even after death, in a dreadful cincture of doom!

But Marston rose slowly to his feet, staggering, swaying beneath that frightful burden whose fingers wrenched by a superhuman effort from his neck, bit into his shoulders like hooks of steel.

"God!" he mumbled, again, in an unconscious travesty—a hideous burlesque of supplication.

It *was* the end, then. Weakened as he was, his nerves a jangle of discordant wires, his mind a chaos of bemused and frantic thought, he stood, helpless, swaying, foredone, beaten, trapped by the insensate clay of his own making.

No longer a man but a beast, his brain wiped free of every

thought but the blind, unreasoning impulse to live, like an animal he drew, from some unsuspected physical reservoir within him, the strength to proceed.

Tottering, swaying, he reverted to the brut, and, with the dumb, inhuman impulsion of the brute, roweling even his apelike strength to superhuman effort, he continued to advance, falling at times, and rising as with the last spent effort of a runner at the tape, yet somehow going on and on, feeling his way along that thin thread whose other end, miles distant, centuries away, stretched into the ether of Heaven!

In a nightmare of suffocating blackness, shot through at times with the red fires of the Pit, he fared onward, and now he saw, with a sudden, agonized return to the perception of the human, that those fires were all about him. They were Eyes, venomous, hateful, red with the lust of unholy anticipation...

He heard about him the lither of gaunt bodies, the patter of innumerable feet—rats they were, but of an unconscionable size, huge and voracious, such as infested this underground kingdom of the dead.

While he moved he knew that they would not attack him. While he lived, even without movement, he believed that he was safe.

But why had they refrained from that which he had given them to feast upon, the thing which even now flapped about him, the inanimate yet strangely animate shell which he had transformed at a stroke from life to death, its legs striking against his as he moved, as if to urge him onward, rowel him forward as in a race with death?

The sounds that he had heard, the squeaks, the gibbers—as of ghouls disturbed at a ghastly rendezvous—could there have been any significance in these? Somewhere he had heard of drunken miners, asleep in the deep levels of coal, brought to a sudden, horrid awakening by cold lips nuzzling cheek or neck, but his brain considered this dully, if at all.

An odd hallucination began to possess him; dimly he dreamed that his dreadful burden was alive, but unconscious, insentient. But he knew that it was an hallucination.

He would make no immediate effort to rid himself of the Thing he carried—not now, at any rate. When he became stronger he would bury it, hid it. Years might pass—perhaps a chance party might discover in one of the innumerable corridors a moldering skeleton—but the body of his guilt would be a *corpus delicti*—there could be no conviction without evidence, and no murder without a victim produced as of due process of law.

But in a moment it seemed this thought gave place to the overmastering panic terror of escape. Instinct alone held him to his course. If there had been light one might have seen the foam which gathered on his lips, the glassy stare of his eyes.

Again he fell, and this time he fancied that the narrowing circle had drawn nearer. Even to his dulled brain he was aware of an intelligent rapacity in those burning eyes, an anticipation which sprang from knowledge.

Somehow, once more, he rose upright, after a multiplied agony of straining effort, but he felt, deep within his consciousness, that he was but a puppet in the hands of a ruthless fate, doomed to wander forever under his detestable load.

Of a sudden, also, an illumination, like a fiery sword, cut through the dulled functioning of his intelligence: the beast that was Marston reeled with the suggestion that penetrated the surface of his physical coma.

What if the line he followed led, not into the clean brightness of the outer air, but, by some frightful mischance, still further into the womb of the hills, deeper and deeper into oblivion, down and down into the uttermost hell of one's imagining?

In the flux and reflux of images which had taken the place of coherent thought he saw all this, he felt it to be a possibility, and with the terror of the brute he strove once more to rid himself of this insensate tyrant, this incubus which rode him, roweling his sides with grotesquely dangling feet, spurring him on in a made welter of fear and pain from which he could not escape.

But it was useless. Try as he would, he could not disengage that grip of steel, and thewed mightily as he was, he found that every last ounce of his great strength was needed to go on. He was just weak enough to render futile any effort to dislodge those clinging fingers, and just strong enough to continue his progress, like a mole in the dark—and that was all.

He must go on and on until flesh and blood could endure no more, the victim of his own contriving, the veritable bond-slave of his passionate soul. And when at length he should fall, no more to rise, then would come, not swift oblivion, but death, indeed, lingering, horrible, unthinkable, even for a beast...

∽

TIME HAD CEASED, feeling had ceased; thought remained only in the faint spark which glowed somewhere within him, flickering now, glowing at the core of his being even as about him there narrowed the fell circle of the blazing eyes.

*Slap—slap—shuffle—slap...*With the infinite slowness of exhaustion, his feet moved, dragged, went forward, while ever at his back those other lifeless feet rose and fell in a grotesque travesty of life, of movement, spurring forward his all but fainting soul.

Dimly he perceived that the floor upon which he moved had taken an upward trend; he felt the line go suddenly taut; then, abruptly, before him, for a single instant, a pale glimmer flickered and died as from dim leagues of distance.

Summoning the last remnant of his strength, he began to run, or thought that he did, but in reality he moved by inches, and by inches the faint glimmer grew, expanded, broadened to a luminous grayness.

Stumbling, slipping, swaying from side to side, the sight of hat pale shadow of the day intoxicated him with a feverish exultation, despite the weakness which seemed to dissolve his being to water. He was saved.

By a last, titanic effort, a tremendous wrenching of the will, he fell rather than staggered into the outer air—beheld, with lack-luster eyes, the ring of faces about him, all staring eyes and white lips and working faces.

Then he sank abruptly to his knees as eager hands relieved him of his burden. He heard voices, meaningless, yet filled with meaning...

He fell instantaneously down a long stairway to the deep, enveloping mercy of unconsciousness.

PRESENTLY, after a timeless interval, he opened his eyes, and then closed them again, blinking owlishly at the strong sunlight. He heard a voice, incoherent, babbling, which, after a moment, he recognized as his own:

"The stalactite—it was the stalactite that killed him, I tell you...it was an accident—an *accident*..."

He rolled his eyes wildly from right to left; and at what he saw a strangled, mad cry of sudden comprehension—of understanding—issued from his throat ere the thick veil of a retributive insanity descended upon him forever:

"*The rats...knew...*"

Before him, his face death-white, his hands scarred from the rough stone up which he had clawed to the rocky shelf, a clean bandage about his forehead, was the face of Pillsbury. In that brief instant, like a lightning flash, illumination seared into the brain of Marston, and, by its very white-hot intensity, shriveled it to the dust of a gibbering madness:

The drunken sleep of the miners...The nibbling of the rats...Pillsbury's awakening to consciousness....His instinctive, *upward* effort to escape the ledge from which, with the half-conscious, and then wholly conscious grip that would not be denied, he had fallen upon Marston...

Potential murderer that he was, Marston himself, by a poetic irony of justice, had been the unwitting savior of his intended victim!

THE BODYMASTER, BY HAROLD WARD
AN AMAZING NOVELETTE FILLED WITH WEIRD HAPPENINGS

Foreword

*P*erhaps I have been suffering from an hallucination. Possibly during the weary months that I was lost to family and friends I was wandering about the country, my brain in the ferment which afterward developed into the attack of brain fever from which I have just recovered.

Yet the maggots of madness inside my skull could not have created all that I have seen. The proof of my sincerity lies in the fact that within these pages I have confessed complicity in crimes for which the law can hang me if it so desires. I am willing to admit that to the man of science my tale bristles with errors—errors of interpretation, but not of fact—for I am a detective, not a scientist.

Did such a man as The Bodymaster really exist? Or was it only the writhing of my tortured imagination which transformed Doctor Darius Lessman, theologist and philanthropist, into a fiend incarnate? His lair is gone. A pile of charred ruins now occupies the place where it stood. Its inmates died with it. The Bodymaster is no more. But is he really dead?

Time alone will tell. The records of the police department of the City of New York will bear out my story up to a certain point. From there on the *affair is a puzzle to me. It is from this that the reader must draw his own deductions. I can give only the facts.*

Chapter I.

Through the thick tangle of underbrush and trees, which surrounded Doctor Darius Lessman's private sanitarium just outside the city of New York, dashed a young man, coatless, hatless, his shirt and trousers torn to shreds by the thorns and brambles.

With blood streaming from a hundred scratches on his face and hands, he presented a savage, almost inhuman, aspect as he leaped before the automobile rapidly coming down the smooth asphalt pavement.

His face was drawn, haggard, contorted; and the snow-white hair, which crowned his youthful face, was matted and unkempt. His eyes bulged from their sockets like those of a maniac as he glared at the oncoming machine.

The afternoon, which was just drawing to a close, had been unusually hot; the storm, hovering over the countryside, filled the air with a strange foreboding—an unusual degree of sultriness. The sky was dull save when an occasional flash of lightning tore through the lowering heavens. Not a breath of wind. Not the rustle of a leaf. Yet the teeth of the man in the roadway rattled like castanets, and upon his clammy brow the cold sweat of terror stood out in beads.

The driver of the big machine brought it to a stop with a sharp grinding of brakes. As he caught a glimpse of the ghastly face of the man before him he involuntarily hunched his body back further into his seat.

"What the hell!" he exclaimed.

The other leaped to the side of the machine and fumbled clumsily—his fingers shaking like those of a man with the palsy—at the catch of the door.

"Quick!" he exclaimed hoarsely. "He—the Bodymaster—is after me! Get me to the police station. I must—Oh, my God! I *must* tell my story before he seizes me again!"

He managed to open the door and stumble into the machine. The driver turned to him.

"All right, old man," he said in the soothing tone that one uses in addressing a lunatic. "We'll get you there in a jiffy. Are you from the big house up yonder?" he jerked his thumb in the direction of the sanitarium.

An involuntary shudder ran through the young man. His eyes dilated. He shrank away from the motorist.

"My God! Not there! Not there again!" he implored. "Please don't take me back to that den! You think that I'm a madman. I can see that you do. I'm sane—as sane as you. But heavens knows why—after the hell I've been through."

He turned to the driver and grasped him by the arm.

"Give her the gas!" he exclaimed. "Can't you see that I'm doomed? But no. You know nothing of the Bodymaster and the strange hold he has over his subjects. He is after me—he, the Bodymaster! It is to save others from the same fate that I must tell what I know!"

With a sudden bound he leaped forward, his eyes wild, his hair in a tousled mass, his hands stretched out, the fingers clawing wildly, his whole body quivering. Then he dropped to the floor of the machine as if hurled by unseen hands.

"He is *here! The Bodymaster is here!*" he shrieked. "Drive—for the love of God, dr—"

The words ended in a dull, throaty gurgle as he writhed upon the floor of the machine at the other's feet. The driver, bewildered by the strange scene, threw in the clutch, and the machine dashed madly down the pavement.

They young man was on his back now, his knees drawn up, his face ghastly and twisted, his eyes bulging, his fingers clawing as if unseen hands were gripping at his throat. His mouth was open— gaping as he fought for breath.

With a wile yell of terror, the driver leaped from the machine. The automobile swerved, skidded—then hurled its weight against a nearby tree.

Summoning his courage, he rose to his feet from the side of the road, where his fall had thrown him among the brush and brambles, and approached the wreck.

In the bottom of the car the stranger lay dead!

And upon his white throat were the black marks of fingers!

Chapter II.

John Duncan was arrested, charged with the murder of the unknown young man.

He had no defense. The evidence was all against him. The body of the stranger had been found in his damaged car. Death was the result of strangulation. The marks of fingers were upon the dead man's throat.

The defendant admitted that the deceased had been alive when he entered the machine. And the story he told was so strange, so unbelievable, that even his own attorney scoffed at it. How, then, could a judge believe his tale?

Doctor Darius Lessman was called upon to testify at the preliminary hearing. Tall, gaunt, saturnine, his raven hair, slightly tinged with gray, brushed back from his high forehead, he looked the student, the man of research, and as such he impressed the jury.

Carefully, painstakingly, he made an examination of the body. To the best of his knowledge and belief, he testified, he had never seen the man in life. How he chanced to be wandering about the grounds of the Lessman sanitarium he did not know. He added to the already favorable opinion formed of him by the judge and jury by asking that he be allowed to pay the funeral expenses of the ragged stranger.

One man alone believed the tale told by John Duncan. He was Patrick Casey, captain in command of the homicide squad of the Metropolitan Police Department.

The alleged murder had happened outside of Casey's jurisdiction; but the captain chanced to be present at the hearing. Immediately afterward he sought an interview with the defendant.

For a second time he heard the story, questioned Duncan closely and, at the close of his visit, advised the accused to retain the private inquiry agency of which I am the head. He even interested himself to the extent of calling me up, telling me of what he had done and asking that I take the case as a personal favor to him.

John Duncan, being a wealthy man, accepted the policeman's advice. And thus I became a figure in what I am forced to believe as the strangest series of happenings that ever fell to moral man.

I admit that I am ashamed of the part fate forced me to play. The reader will probably term me either a fool or a lunatic. I am certain that I am not a fool. As for being a lunatic—as I have stated in my foreword, I do not know. But I digress.

Three days later, armed with letters of introduction from some of the most celebrated alienists in the city, all vouching for my character and ability, I applied to Doctor Darius Lessman for a position as attendant.

I secured the position.

AN UNCANNY EERIE, ghost-like place, this sanitarium of Doctor Lessman's.

My first glimpse of it recalled to mind a description I had read somewhere of a ruined castle "from whose tall black windows came no ray of light and whose broken battlements showed a jagged line against the moonlit sky." It had been built—some half century before—for a madhouse. Its owner, a better physician than a business man, had lost his all before its completion, and it had fallen badly into decay when Lessman purchased it.

It stood in the midst of an arid thicket of oaks, cedars and stunted pines. Lessman, evidently, had done little to improve the place or its surroundings save to finish that part that had been left uncompleted by the former owner, and year after year it had grown more gloomy and less habitable. The state highway ran a scant half mile away, crowded on both sides by the stunted forest, a macadamized driveway which wound about through the trees, leading to the house. The nearest habitation was several miles away.

How such a place could be approved by the state as a hospital for the cure of nervous disorders has always been a question to me. Yet investigation proved that Lessman had a state license, although to the best of my knowledge his institution had no patients, nor did it seek them. It was a sanitarium in name only.

In my character of a man seeking employment, I thought it best to walk the last lap of the journey. Dismissing my chauffeur at the edge of the forest, lest some one from the house discover my means of transportation, I sent him home and trudged down the pathway toward the ancient pile.

I must digress long enough to state that this was the last time I was seen until I made my reappearance months afterward, to all appearances a raving maniac. Naturally, after several weeks had passed and nothing was heard from me, my family and friends commenced an investigation. Doctor Lessman was able to prove to them that I had never reached his place, in spite of the statement made by Hopkins, the chauffeur. The latter was arrested and would probably have been held for my murder had it not been for my timely reappearance. But more of this later.

I approached the great door, studded with iron nails and set in a doorway of massive brick and stone. There was no sign of a bell, and I was finally forced to resort to my knuckles to hammer a tattoo on the weather-beaten panel.

I had almost decided to try the door in the rear, when I heard the approach of a heavy step. There came a sound of rattling chains and the clanking of massive bolts. Then a key was turned with a grating noise, and the big door swung back.

Something told me to flee; but I shook off the feeling as unworthy a man of my profession and stood my ground. Had I but obeyed that impulse I would have been a happier man today!

Doctor Lessman, clad in a faded bathrobe, his forefinger between the pages of the volume he had been reading, greeted me. For an instant his gaze traveled over me from head to foot, then went past me as if seeking my means of approach. Apparently satisfied with his inspection, he took my letters of introduction and read them carefully, questioning me on several points.

With a gesture of his slender hand he invited me to enter—*the lair of the Bodymaster!*

Chapter III.

What better proof that I was not insane during those horrible months than that during my rational periods I kept a diary? Fragmentary though it is, showing as it does the awful strain under which I was placed, the detective instinct must have been uppermost at all times.

I remember nothing of writing it. Yet here it is in my own handwriting. Evidently so deeply impressed upon my subconscious mind must have been my mission—the fact that I was there to save an innocent man from the gallows—that, like a man in his sleep, I wrote, not knowing that I did, obsessed with the one idea—to preserve the evidence which I was accumulating against Darius Lessman. Why he did not destroy the diary I do not know. Possibly I had it too well hidden. Or he may not have thought it worthwhile, believing that I would never escape.

THE DIARY.

"The ragged stranger was right. Less *is* a Bodymaster. Already he holds me in his power. My body is his to do with as he wills. Those into whose hands this writing may fall will probably think me demented, for the human mind declines to believe that which it can not understand. And while I am under his uncanny power I may do some act—commit some deed—which, under happier circumstances, would fill me with loathing. Do not judge me too harshly. Remember that Lessman's is the will which forces me."

ANOTHER ENTRY IN THE DIARY.

"Last night I killed a man. Of this I am almost certain. I, a man sworn to avenge crime and to track down criminals, have the brand of Cain upon my brow. My hands are dripping with blood. I should be in a cell in murderers' row, waiting for an avenging law to hang me, instead of breathing the air of freedom. But am I free? No! A thousand times no! I am as much a prisoner as I would be behind the bars of a felon's cage.

"As one watches a motion picture thrown upon the silver screen, I see myself with Meta by my side...We cross a darkened thoroughfare...The details are fragmentary—occasional. I know that we are near a house. A window is open. We enter. At her command, I approach a safe placed in the wall. It seems to open to my touch... Meta is holding a flashlight—And yet it is not Meta! It is another—a girl, fair-haired, sweet of face—yet her will is the will of Meta. Meta's is the driving force behind her actions, just as my body is driven onward by the iron will of the Bodymaster...

"Some one is approaching. We step behind the curtain. He enters and snaps on the light. At sight of the open safe, he turns. He is about to give the alarm...There is a knife in my hand...I strike! God in Heaven! *I have killed him!* ...We seize the jewels from the safe and escape...

"There was the stain of blood on my hand when I awoke this morning. I am a murderer! Oh God! I pray that it was all a dream. Yet it was so realistic that I am forced to believe that it is true.

"I have discovered the evidence which I set out to find. But what a terrific price I have paid for what I have learned. Under his will, my brain is a vacuum, rattling around within its pan like a pebble in a tin bucket, functioning only when he so commands. But wait! This can not be entirely so. I must still have some reasoning power left, else I would not be writing these lines. Thank God for that!

"Yet even as I write I know that The Bodymaster is planning my death. He has it within his power to drive my soul from out my body —to usurp this tenement of clay with his own polluted brain. How he works his wonders I will describe later if I am able. It is hard for me to think consecutively.

"Lessman's is the greatest brain, his the most wonderful intellect, the world has ever known. His is the accumulated wisdom of the centuries—since Jesus of Nazareth trod this earth there has been none who could accomplish the wonders he has performed. Think what a power for good he might have been!

"I must publish his devilishness to the world. John Duncan lies festering in a felon's cell, perhaps to stretch a hempen rope for a crime that Lessman committed. I must save him if I can. Yet who will believe me? Wise judges and learned counsel scoffed and jeered at what Duncan had to tell. What, then, will they say when they read these lines? I see them smile derisively and tap their bulging brows in token of my madness.

"Meta is the lure he used to hold me in his power. My instinct told me to flee the minute I crossed the threshold. Would to heaven I had! Lessman must have read my thoughts, for he pressed the bell which summoned her to his side.

"One glimpse of Meta Vinetta and I was lost.

"Lessman introduced me to her as his sister. I know now that she is more to him than that—that she is his soul mate, his affinity. She is his accomplice in all the devilish schemes which incubate within his wondrous brain.

"Together they can rule the world. Lessman holds that the body is a shell, a house built only to hold the soul, deriving its power from the spirit, the will. To him there is no crime in murder, for his theology holds that the snapping of the thread of life is merely the release of the soul which soars away to realms on high. His is the belief that might is right. He needs the bodies of his victims in order to practice his devilish arts. He has the power to take them, and he uses it to the utmost. He holds that the body is not a prison house, but a slave to will. In his philosophy, it is simply a useful tool over which the spirit possesses absolute control. He is neither a spiritualist nor a theosophist. His is a theory all by itself and of itself.

"*Lessman has elected to live forever!* Of that I am certain. He and Meta—the woman he loves."

ANOTHER ENTRY.

"There are other poor dupes here—at least a dozen of them. Some of them are maniacs; and Lessman is holding them, I think, with the hope that he can cure their awful malady. For, as I understand it, he has no power over a diseased brain. It is only those that are normal that bow to his bidding.

"We have compared notes. Collins, of Chicago, has rational streaks during which he is able to talk freely. He, like myself, was a detective. I remember reading of his strange disappearance over a year ago. He was on a robbery case, and certain clues led him to New York. Instead of reporting to the police, he thought to take all the credit and capture the criminals himself. He trailed them to Doctor Lessman's place. He, like myself, fell a victim to the wiles of Meta. Now he is at intervals a jibbering idiot.

"Several of the poor devils, Collins tells me, were placed here by distant relatives. Lessman, wearing the garb of sanctity, talks of his desire to cure them of their nervous disorder, and their relatives, poor fools, glad to rid themselves of the millstones around their necks, turn the wretched creatures over to him. He charges a low rate for their board and medical treatment.

"To one and all he is known as 'The Bodymaster.' He teaches them to call him that. They fear him like the very devil. They talk occasionally of a revolt. But when he is near they tremble at his frown. His hold over them is absolute—complete."

Chapter IV.

Evidently several weeks elapsed between the last entry in the diary and what follows. This is to be inferred from the fact that several things are mentioned as having happened of which there is no record. In all probability, I was in a semi-somnambulic state during the interval, as a result of Lessman's strange power over me. During my entire incarceration there were times when everything was a blank; at other times, I remember there were dim, hazy vistas of things into which I peered. They seem like dreams.

Yet, if they were dreams, of what was their substance? A dream must have some foundation.

FROM THE DIARY.

"The unforeseen has come to pass. That which I have just witnessed God never intended that mortal eyes should see. At the very thought of it my body trembles and every nerve tingles as if from electric shock.

"Where is Lessman? Did the Bodymaster and his female accomplice perish in the ruins of their own diabolical art? I hope so. It is better that I—that all of us—die of starvation, locked as we are in this horrible den, than that others should share the fate which has been meted out to us.

"Last night I am almost certain that we exchanged bodies—the Bodymaster and I!

"At least, my waking consciousness tells me that we did. Yet it is all so hazy that I can remember only fragments of what happened. Perhaps I only dreamed. I tell only what I can remember.

"At his command, I slunk from my narrow cell like a mangy, half-starved, dope-filled circus lion from its cage. And, like the king of beasts, beaten into servitude in the arena, I fawned at my master's feet, ready to do his bidding. Such is the state that I have reached. For my body is not my own. It is his—his to do with as he wills. Fight as I may, an unseen force compels me to do his bidding.

"They were together, he and Meta. From another door entered a girl—young, beautiful, fair-haired. She is, I am certain, the woman who accompanied me on that other occasion of which I have a recollection—the night I found the blood upon my hand and knew that I had killed a man. I dream of her nightly. She is Meta's dupe. Like me, her mind is not yet a blank. She entered slowly, reluctantly, as if every fiber in her body rebelled against the awful crime in which she was to take a part, her great blue eyes staring straight ahead.

"Like a woman who walks in her sleep, she approached Meta's

side. For an instant they stood there—the fair-haired girl and the beautiful, raven-tressed woman. Lessman's hands hovered over them.

"She screamed! God in heaven, how she shrieked! Then the body of Meta staggered to a nearby chair and dropped into its recesses.

"*And from the throat of the fair-haired girl with the angel's face came the voice of Meta!*

"'*It is done!*'

"He, the Bodymaster, turned to me. My whole being fought within me against the sacrilege which was being committed. As well attempt to stem the oncoming tide. I felt my body in a convulsion. Something seemed to be tearing at my very vitals: My mind reeled. My brain was filled with fire. The face—the devilish, diabolical, mocking face of the Bodymaster appeared before me. I could see nothing else. His baleful, gleaming eyes seemed to burn into my very core. My body seemed to be hurled through space....Then came oblivion.

"I must have been unconscious but an instant. I stood leaning against the table, my fingers pressed against my aching brow. Dazed, I passed my hand across my face. I was bearded. *It was the face of Lessman, the Bodymaster!*

"The clothes were his. *I was inhabiting his body!*

"My startled gaze turned across the room. To all intents and purposes it was I who stood there, my arm about the waist of the golden-haired girl.

"I knew that it was not I—that it was Lessman, the Bodymaster, who offered his foul caresses to the beautiful face upraised to his. I knew that the rich red lips were not those of the girl whose slender body he had defiled. It was Meta—Meta and Lessman, not the girl and I...

"A burst of rage swelled up within me. Something snapped. For an instant a flood of red appeared before my eyes. I leaped forward, the lust for killing within my brain.

"Lessman's body is fat with nourishment, his muscles fed by good living, while mine is half famished, ill-nourished, weak as a result of worry and nerve strain.

"It was my own body I was punishing. Yet Lessman's was the soul that inhabited it. As a man sees his face in a mirror, so did I see my face before me. I hurled my stolen body to the floor. Screaming with rage, I showered blow after blow upon it. It writhed with pain.

"And all the time, within me, there was being waged a terrible struggle for mastery. I felt the will of Lessman commanding me to desist. Yet the love of a woman was stronger than his power. I gouged at the gleaming eyes which stared up into mine, while I choked at the throat—*my throat*—which lay beneath my fingers.

"The woman was screaming. I knew that it was Meta who was cursing me, who sought to pull me from my victim. Yet it was the body of the unnamed girl I loved, her face contorted into a frenzy of malignancy, who showered blow after blow upon my bared head....

"I awoke to find myself here in my cell again. My head aches. My face is covered with bruises. My hair is matted with blood. Lessman must have conquered. I wonder how fared the girl with the mass of shimmering, golden hair. Surely, with all these bruises, it could not have been a dream."

Chapter V.

"She loves me! We med today for the first time, unfettered by the insidious chains the Bodymaster has woven about us. Her name is Avis—Avis Rohmer. She has told me all.

"Perhaps it is a part of his diabolical plan to allow us to see each other. He knows that I will never seek to escape until I can take her with me. Since my rebellion of the other night—I know not how long ago it was, for time is as nothing in a brain that is partly dead—he has been more careful.

"She, Avis and I, alone of all those who have fallen under his supernatural power, still retain our minds. The others are mental wrecks, their skulls mere empty shells in which their addled brains sizzle and froth like half-worked wine in kegs. She has begged me to protect her. And I have sworn to take her from this den of iniquity, although God alone knows how I can ever keep my promise. For I am as completely under his power as she.

"Victory makes him careless while failure makes him redouble his efforts. That is why this narrative appears piecemeal. I am like a man sleeping the sleep of the exhausted, waking up occasionally for food, then dropping off again. What is he doing during the intervals when I am not myself I can only imagine."

ANOTHER ENTRY.

"I must work fast if I am to save Avis. I care not for myself now—since I have felt love. She is an orphan. She came here from a western state, determined to make her fortune on the stage. Like thousands of others, she found that her talent was mediocre. She sought to make a living in other ways when she found that all that was open to her was the downward path. Meta—again it was Meta who served as the lure—read her advertisement. Meta appeared before her as the Good Samaritan—a woman, wealthy, refined, seeking a companion. She brought her here.

"Lessman allows me to see her every day now. What devilish plan has he in view that he should torture me with her sufferings?"

Chapter VI.

Occasionally through the clouds of obscurity there appears some incident which I remember distinctly. Strange as it may appear, there is no record of these occasions in m diary. I can explain this only by the supposition that at such times Lessman withdrew his power over me, while on all other occasions I was, as I have said before, in a semi-somnambulic state.

THE DIARY CONTINUES.

"I awoke as one awakens from a horrible nightmare. My brain was as clear as a crystal. For an instant I imagined that I was in my own apartment—that the suffering I had gone through were but the conjurings of my own mind.

"A single glance at the barred window brought me back to a sudden realization of my condition. But my mind was my own. I was freed from the horrible thing that had obsessed me.

"On the table in one corner of the room was food. I ate ravenously. I do not remember how long it had been since I had eaten. My meal completed, I looked about me for some means of escape. Once I could find a way out of the accursed place—some weapon with which to defend myself—I would return, free Avis and flee.

"It must have been midnight. Outside, the rain was falling in torrents. It beat a regular tattoo upon the window. Cautiously, lest I be heard, I tiptoed to the door and tried the knob.

"The door was unlocked!

"In an exultation of excitement, I peered out. There was no one in sight. My mood was detached, strange, vague—marked by an indescribably something I could not explain. Save for the single kerosene lamp, which burned low in its bracket at the end of the long hallway, the place was in darkness.

"Removing my shoes, I tiptoed my way across the floor. Avis' room was the fourth door from mine. That much she had told me. Reaching it, I tried the knob. It was locked. I tapped softly against the panel. Receiving no answer, I rapped more loudly. I dared not raise my voice. Failing to arouse her, I was forced to leave her for a moment to continue my exploration.

"In one corner of the hallway stood a huge stick—evidently a cane that had been carried by one of the keepers in the days when the place was used as an asylum for maniacs. With this in my hand, I felt more secure.

"Where was Lessman? Had he made his escape while I slept, leaving my door open? Had he forced Avis and the other poor creatures who were under his command to accompany him? The thought startled me. Grasping the cudgel more firmly, I took the lamp from its bracket and started on a tour of investigation. Al of the doors opening into the hallway, with the exception of my own, were locked. The silence was tomblike, uncanny.

"At the end of the long corridor a pair of stairs wound upward. Mounting them, I found myself in a long passage similar to that which I had just quitted. One or two of the rooms near the end were open. There was nothing in them except old furniture, moth-eaten and dusty with age. The entire floor seemed deserted.

"Continuing onward, I came to a door which, though it seemed to be locked, seemed to give a little under the pressure of my knee. Setting my lamp upon the floor, I put my shoulder against it and gave a long, steady shove. Under this force it opened quite readily.

"My stockinged feet made no noise, while the ease with which I was able to force the door showed that the hinges had been recently oiled. Inside, a lamp was burning.

"I hesitated in the doorway. Then my startled gaze made out a second room, partitioned from the first by curtains, pushed partly back.

"Across my field of vision moved the gaunt figure of The Bodymaster. He was clad in the faded bathrobe in which I had first seen him, and he held a lamp in his hand. The light shone upon his thin, cruel face. He approached the side of the bed and stood gazing down upon its occupant.

"Something seemed to draw me closer. Upon the bed lay a corpse —a blond-haired giant—stripped to the waist. As Lessman, his evil gaze still upon the mammoth figure, held the lamp a trifle aloft, *the dead man writhed and twisted as if in moral agony!*

"The Bodymaster stretched forth one thin hand. The man upon the bed stiffened—then sat bolt upright, his bloodshot eyes glaring!

"Involuntarily I took a step backward.

"*As God is my judge, the eyes were those of a corpse—glassy, unseeing!* And while I still looked, the body slipped backward, the curious writhing movements ceased, and that which lay upon the bed was only insensate clay.

"Now or never was the time to strike. Grasping my cudgel more firmly, I raised it over my head. The back of the Bodymaster was turned toward me. I had him off his guard. I was about to bring the club down across his head when, without turning his gaze, he spoke:

"'Sit down, my friend, and throw your cane aside. You can not strike. Your arm is palsied.'

"The cane dropped from my fingers. I attempted to lower my arm to recover it. Impossible. I was unable to move. My arm was held aloft as by an unseen hand.

"The Bodymaster turned toward me with a smile.

"'Sit down!' he commanded.

"My arm dropped to my side. Like a drunken man I staggered to a chair."

Chapter VII.

'Seating himself opposite me, Lessman pushed a box of cigars across the table.

"'Help yourself,' he smiled, selecting one for himself. 'You are some sixty seconds ahead of time. I hardly expected you to be so prompt.'

"'Expected me!' I ejaculated.

"He nodded. 'Naturally' he responded. 'How else do you suppose you got here? You certainly did not expect that I would make so great an oversight as to leave your door unlocked! I wanted you—wanted to have a talk with you. My mind willed that you should come, and you are here.'

"He waved his hand with a slight gesture as if dismissing the entire subject. For a second there was silence. Then he resumed:

"'Our little fracas of the other night taught me that you are a man of more than ordinary mental ability; in fact, you are the first who has ever disobeyed my unspoken commands. And, more than that, you showed me that you are the man I have been seeking all these years.'

"His eyes burned with enthusiasm as he continued.

"'Man,' he went on, 'my experiments have been a success. True, lives have been destroyed. But what is life? Your man-made theology teaches you that life is but a span of a few years in eternity; you snap the cord which binds you to this earth, and immediately you enter the paradise which your God has prepared for you. Why, then, prolong matters? I, rather than being the monster you think me to be, am a benefactor to the human race. Every man who dies in my hands before his allotted time has that much longer to spend in heaven.'

"He leaned back in his chair and laughed mirthlessly for an instant.

"'I am not here to argue the right or wrong of the thing, however,' he continued. 'I am a man born to rule; I would rather be a big devil in hell than a little angel in heaven—if there be such places as heaven and hell, which I greatly doubt.

"'I need help in my work—my experiments. True, I have Meta— but she is only a weak woman. I need others—men whom I can teach —men whom I can trust—men with the will to conquer. You have proved to me that you are such a man. The world is yours—the world and all that it contains—if you accept.'

"He stopped suddenly and gazed into my eyes as if trying to read my very soul. In fact, I believe that he did read my mind, for he answered my unspoken thoughts before I had voiced them:

"'Yes, the devil took Christ upon the mountain and offered him everything,' he exclaimed, his eyes blazing. ' Call me the devil if you like—I care not a rap what you term me—I offer you the same. I said before, and I say again, the world is yours—money, power, pleasure and---'

"As he spoke, as if in obedience to some rehearsed cue, the door opened. A vague perfume assailed my nostrils—a faint, elusive scent —a zephyr from the East. Through the opening Meta stepped. She wore a kimono—a soft, silken, figured affair reminiscent of the Orient. I can only remember that beneath its folds protruded a glimpse of tiny, bare feet clad in the smallest of sandals.

"There are silences more eloquent than words. For an instant my eyes sought hers—deep, dark, lustrous, glowing like great pools of liquid fire.

"She smiled. Then, suddenly, she sprang forward, her arms from which the folds of the kimono had slipped, bared—outstretched toward me, her rich red lips upraised to mine.

"I leaped to my feet. My mind was filled with wild, insane thoughts. I took a half step toward her. Like a frightened bird, she darted backward. Then, as if filled with a wild abandon, she tore open the neck of her kimono, revealing to my startled gaze a glimpse of transparent white skin.

"Stretching forth one rounded arm, she displaced the curtain, discovering to my view a room opposite that in which lay the body of the man from the grave.

"My God! Crouched in a corner like a frightened animal was Avis! Her dress was torn, her golden hair matted and unkempt. She shrunk away from the light as one who fears its rays. Her big blue eyes gazed into mine. They were wide with fear. Yet her lips moved. It seemed to me that they were trying to form some message—to convey something to me.

"She held up her hands appealingly. They were fastened together with chains.

"From behind me came the voice of Lessman:

"'Choose!' he commanded. 'On one hand wealth, luxury, power, beautiful women; on the other—*this!*

"'*Choose!*'"

ANOTHER EXTRACT FROM THE DIARY.

"I awoke in my own bed. I have the word of Avis for what happened. She says that when Lessman made his terrible offer to me that I stood for an instant like a man too astounded for utterance. Suddenly I turned and struck him squarely in the face. Meta screamed. Lessman, however, merely dropped back a step and stretched forth his hand. I had my arm drawn back to strike him again. I wavered, staggered for a second like a drunken man, then my knees gave way under me and I fell forward on my face.

"That is all she knows. She was hurried back to her own room by Meta, where she fell in a swoon."

Chapter VIII.

A man suffering from amnesia has, upon his return to normal, no recollection of what happened while he was in that condition. While I do not say that I was amnestic in every sense of the word, yet my condition must have resembled that peculiar malady to a certain degree. I can positively state that I have absolutely no remembrance of the events which are described below. Yet they are in my own handwriting in my diary. My own idea of the subject is that I was in a sort of twilight sleep, as it were—not completely under Lessman's influence, yet partly so. I give the contents of my diary just as they were written, venturing the assertion, however, that they must have been put down several days after the events of the previous chapter:

"A strange thing has come to pass. The Bodymaster evidently bears me no ill will, for last night Avis and I dined with him. Ordinarily, we are fed like animals, the food served out to us by a deaf and dumb mulatto who shoves the edibles through the bars to those who are too dangerous to be allowed outside their cells, while such of us as Lessman evidently considers harmless are occasionally permitted to dine at a long, bare table in the hallway. Here we sit and wolf our food like swine, our only thought being to fill our bellies quickly, lest the others get more than their share of the meal.

"Imagine, then, my surprise last night when, an hour before tie for eating the mulatto brought to my room—for I am not yet confined to a cell, probably because I am not yet stark mad—a dress suit. Everything was there—even down to the studs. With it was a shaving outfit. Laying the things carefully upon my cot, he handed me a note. It read:

"'*Let us forget our troubles for tonight. Dine with me. I have a surprise in store for you.*

"'*Lessman*.'

"I was shaved and cleaned and feeling like a new man by the time the dumb servant called for me. Following him down the stairs, I was ushered into the large parlor. Lessman, in full dress, seized me by the hand and greeted me warmly, while and instant later Meta, looking truly regal in an elaborate decollete, stood before me. But the real surprise came a minute later.

"Avis was ushered in!

"Attired in some fancy gown—what man can describe a woman's dress?—she looked like an angel from heaven. I pinched myself to see whether I was awake or dreaming. What object had the Bodymaster in this masquerade?

"How can I describe the dinner which followed? For weeks we had been on a diet of little more than bread and soup. And now we sat down to a feast. Lessman was the perfect host; Meta the perfect hostess. Under their deft manipulations we forgot ourselves—forgot that they were monsters—remembered only that we were honored guests. Never have I met as charming a conversationalist as he. The man is a veritable storehouse of knowledge, with the added ability of imparting it to others. He has been everywhere, seen everything.

"He is far too subtle for me, for I have fallen a victim to his insidious wiles. Yet it is for another that I have sold myself, body and soul, to this monster.

"He knows that I love Avis. My every look shows it. And he is wise enough to seize the golden opportunity. That is the reason for all these courtesies, the dinner, the clothes, the brilliant conversation.

"Meta and Avis left the room, leaving Lessman and myself to our cigars. For weeks I have been without the solace of nicotine. Under the soothing influence of the weed and the charm of his conversation, I settled back in my chair, at peace with all the world. Lessman sensed my mood. He turned to me, his black eyes dancing with energy.

"'You are the first who has ever been able to combat my power.' He said slowly. 'And instead of being angered, I think the more of you for it. I need you—need your badly. Without a man of your caliber my work—my experiments—must temporarily halt.

"'You love the golden-haired girl in yonder—and if I am not greatly mistaken, she loves you. She is yours—yours if you agree to my demands. Otherwise---.'

"At a gesture the door opened. Into the room came the mulatto dragging a woman—a mere slip of a girl. In her eyes shone the light of insanity. Her hair was matted, her clothes in tatters and covered with vermin. Her talonlike fingers worked spasmodically as she babbled meaninglessly. I shrank back from her in horror.

"The Bodymaster stepped across the room and with a sweeping movement of his hand, drew back the curtain. In the further corner of the adjoining room sat Avis—a veritable queen among women, in conversation with Meta. He withdrew his hand and the curtain fell again. He stepped back to his chair and reseated himself. The mute withdrew, dragging the poor insane creature with him.

"For a moment there was silence. Then Lessman turned to me again.

"'Within a fortnight,' he said, 'she—the girl in yonder—the girl you love—will be like *that!* I know the symptoms. Her mind is on the verge. It is for you to say whether she goes over the abyss.

"'Obey my commands, give me the assistance I demand, and the girl you love stays as she is now—the companion of Meta. Luxury, clothes, good food—everything that a woman cares for—will be hers. Refuse, and she goes back to her cell—to the squalor and dirt and vermin from which came the poor wretch you have just seen.

"'You and you alone can save her!'

"He stopped dramatically. There was but one answer. May God in Heaven have mercy on my soul! I have become Lessman's partner in crime—an accomplice of that foul thing, the Bodymaster—I who have sworn to bring him to justice!

"But I have saved Avis."

Chapter IX.

I judge that several weeks must have elapsed between the time the foregoing was written and what follows:

"What does mankind know about psychic phenomena? I remember reading the attempts of various novelists to exploit the subject. Combining a smattering of psychology with a vivid imagination, they succeed in knocking together a readable, though unreliable, story, trusting to the general lack of knowledge to cover their untruthfulness. And who can blame them? Secure behind the ramparts of the grave's grim silence, they can defy the world to prove them wrong. Their weird hypotheses bring them gold, power and position in the world of letters. And I—I, the only man who ever sent his soul hurtling through the realms of space to explore the mysteries of the great unknown—I must keep silent.

"The human mind refuses to believe what it does not understand. Were I to make public what I *know*—even if it were possible—I would be derided, held up to ridicule by press and public. For, despite our vaunted civilization, we are still slaves to superstition and ignorance, ever ready like those of old, to strike down one who dares utter the truth.

"Who among the millions on this globe would believe that I have spent days—weeks—months—in the dim past? As a man looks upon a motion picture of himself thrown upon the screen, so I have seen myself in the ages gone by. In shining armor, a plumed lance in my hand. I have ridden with the crusaders, or fought with the devil-may-care gallantry of the times for the favor or a damsel's smile. I have been the head of as bloody a gang of cutthroats as ever slit a weasand or scuttled a craft.

"I smile with I think of the things that I have been—I who am now the head of a modern detective agency, hired to run down the man whose gigantic brain has made these things all possible. I have been among the best and the worst of them in days gone by. Yet who would believe such a story? Lessman is too far in advance of his time. Yet there is a possibility that a few centuries hence some eye may read these lines and wonder how the men of today could be so dense.

"I am no longer afraid of death. I know now that such fear is only a superstitious idea. There is no such thing as death. That which we term death is but a step from one life to another. Lessman has taught me that life is a cycle and that when we leave it we enter into another existence, better or worse than the one we are quitting in accordance with our own actions.

"Lessman! Ah, there is the intellect! It is he who has made it possible for me to view wonders which no man ever looked upon before. I wonder how I could have doubted him.

"Lessman is a scientist—a thinker ahead of his time. Now that he has shown me that there is no death I feel no compunction about taking life, for by taking life we merely assist nature by a few years, leaving the body for us to experiment on. He has promised me that some day he will publish the results of his conclusions in order that the world may know and study. When he does, I will occupy a star part on the pages. For it is I who, at the command of Lessman, have explored the realms unknown, bringing back to him the fruits of my knowledge.

"And I have met Avis again and again. I have found that she has been with me through the ages—my loved one, my affinity. In every period of the past she has accompanied me-just as she will in the future, until the time comes where Divine Intelligence brings all things to an end.

"Let me start at the beginning. No more do I live in a cell-lie room, eating like an anima with the cattle whose brain power is not as great as mine. With Avis by my side, I dine in state with Lessman and Meta.

'The next evening, immediately after dinner. The Bodymaster summoned me to his library. He was anxious to commence his experiments. At the beginning I was nervous, keyed up to the highest pitch, regretting the bargain I had made with him. But within five minutes he had wrought a change in my mind, and under the mastery of his words I soon reached a point where I was as enthusiastic as he.

"Remember, I have dabbled in philosophy to a certain extent myself. I took a degree at Princeton before I took up the business of crime detection. But my knowledge is elementary compared with that of Lessman. But I am getting away from my subject.

"Under the spell of his eloquence, I forgot that I was the servant, and he the master—that I was merely a prisoner, subservient to my jailor's will. For an hour we discussed the subject; I was as interested as he. There is, he claims, no heights to which man can not climb, providing he so wills. To him man is—or should be—absolutely the master of his own body and soul.

"His is a mind that has reached on where others stopped. Hypnotism, to him, is child's play. Soul transference, the exchange of bodies—these are the things that this man dabbles with. But he has his limit. He can go so far and no farther.

"However, with my will submissive to his—with my mind attuned to his—he believed that he could send me hurling through space. In other words, he was to be the power station which would furnish me the energy to make the voyages of exploration.

"I was like wet clay in his hands. With the enthusiasm of a youngster, I gave myself over to him. Leaning back in my chair, at his command I made my mind nearly as possible an absolute vacuum. It was probably but for an instant—but enough. There was none of the pain that I felt before on that never-to-be-forgotten occasion when my soul was divorced from my body. Instead, I felt my soul—my mental being—leave my body. I stood beside myself sitting there in the chair. There was no fear—nothing except a feeling of buoyancy..."

Chapter X.

I must digress from my diary again.

As I have stated elsewhere, I have a recollection of certain things which transpired while I was in Lessman's power, although the greater part of the time that I passed with him is but a blank.

There is nothing in my diary which touches upon my trips into the unknown under his strange influence, aside from an occasional vague mention. I am certain that the greater part of the time I was in a sort of daze, imagining myself in a perfectly normal condition, yet held by The Bodymaster in a state where I would respond immediately to his will.

Yet even now I can recall, vaguely, incidents which happened to me on these trips. I remember meeting Avis on numerous occasions and under many names. Had my adventures happened consecutively, and could I remember them, they would be interesting food for thought for the men of science. But, unfortunately, they jump here and there, the story, ofttimes, remaining unfinished.

There are so many, many adventures, the details of which I can not recall, that I will make no attempt to set them down. Suffice to say that all the time my brain was steadily growing weaker while I, poor dupe that I was, imagined that I was again normal.

During my lucid intervals I was constantly troubled by a gnawing conscience. Here was I, an officer of the law, lending myself to the worst form of outlawry. I attempted to reconcile myself with the thought that I was a prisoner, yet I was ever obsessed with the idea that I had proved a traitor to myself and to my oath. My only recompense was the feeling that by becoming a traitor I was saving the life and reason of the woman I loved.

I wonder now why I did not kill Avis and then commit suicide. So great was Lessman's influence over me that I sincerely believed that death was a myth. My own adventures beyond the pale had proved to me the correctness of his theory. Why, then, I did not end it all is something that can not be explained, especially when one recollects that from my warped viewpoint death would have been the easiest solution of the dilemma. My only explanation is that my mind was not functioning properly. As I have remarked again and again the reader must form his own conclusions, draw his own deductions, for I am dealing in facts, not surmises.

Lessman allowed me the freedom, to a certain extent, of the house. With Avis by my side, I wandered up and down the long, dusty corridors, exploring, searching. I told myself that I was looking for evidence—that sooner or later I would make my escape and bring The Bodymaster to justice. And I found none—nothing but the poor wretches locked in their cells, made—all of them. And who would believe a maniac? No, there was absolutely nothing that could be used against the monster. It would be my word and that of Avis against that of Lessman and Meta. Such a case as that would be laughed out of court.

Why did I not make my escape? I could not. I only know that with the door wide open an invisible hand seemed to keep me from crossing the threshold.

Chapter XI.

Again I must resort to my diary:

"I know now how the stranger was killed—the man for whose death John Duncan is being held. Who the medium was through whom Lessman worked I do not know. I imagine that it was Collins, the Chicago detective. I have questioned him, and he does not remember anything about the affair, so far gone is his mind. Yet he has a hazy recollection of having at one tie done Lessman's bidding. Nor have I learned the name of the poor fellow who met death in the heroic attempt to unmask The Bodymaster.

"The dean of Dagget College is dead—murdered! Another professor has been arrested as the murderer. Lessman showed me the paper this morning, chuckling over the gruesome details. There is absolutely no hope for the poor wretch who has been seized by the police, for the evidence is all against him. They will hang him, and the law will consider itself satisfied. I laughed with Lessman at the newspaper account. Is he not right when he states that both of them are merely being ushered into paradise ahead of their time?

"I am certain that I killed Professor Ormsby!

"Years before he and Professor Jacobs had been teachers in the same college where Lessman held a chair. To them Lessman, then a young man, presented some of his astonishing theories. They turned upon him with ridicule, rebuked him, and then reported him as a heretic to the head of the university. It was their testimony which caused Lessman's dismissal in disgrace. He swore to get revenge.

"Two nights ago Lessman hurled my ego—my spirit—through space. I am certain of it, although my memory is indistinct and is growing weaker every hour. At his command I went to Ormsby's apartments. Jacobs was seated with his old friend engaged in a heated discussion, for both were argumentative men.

"Before the eyes of Professor Jacobs, Dean Ormsby shrieked as an invisible hand struck him down—then fell writhing to the floor, the purple marks of fingers upon his throat.

"They arrested Jacobs for the murder. Others had heard them arguing. Vainly he tried to tell them the truth—that the argument had been a friendly one and that his friend had been killed by some unseen force.

"They scoffed at his story—for the mars of fingers showed too plainly upon the dead man's neck."

ANOTHER ENTRY IN THE DIARY.

"I wonder if my mind is weakening? I seem to do Lessman's bidding too easily. I fall in with his every suggestion. I know that he is using me in his crimes—that he is getting rich as a result of my efforts—and I do not seem to recollect what transpires, as I used to. Everything is hazy, with here and there some specially vivid remembrance standing out amidst the chaos.

"Occasionally he reads me the papers, or hands them to me after calling my attention to some mysterious crime of which there is an account. Often he tells me, with a sneer, that he is the author and I the perpetrator of these horrible affairs. Innocent men are being made to suffer for things that I have done.

"The police are on the lookout for a mysterious woman who has been seen often where strange crimes have been committed. Can it be that they—Lessman and Meta—are using Avis as they are using me? They both deny it. And Avis tells me that she has no recollection of such things...I wonder...

Chapter XII.

MORE REMARKABLE THINGS FROM THE DIARY.

"They hanged John Duncan today for the murder of the unknown young man. And I, the man who swore to save him from the gallows, could do nothing.

"I am an accomplice—an accessory after the fact. Lessman is a fiend; and if Meta is any better it is only because she lacks his scientific ability. I am beginning to hate them both.

"I have been tricked. I am but a dupe. My brain is steadily growing weaker. When they have sucked me dry they will cast me aside, as they have Collins and the others. I realize this when I am alone, but when I am with Lessman I do his bidding gladly, happily.

"The papers are often filled with accounts of his work among the poorer classes. They say that he gives thousands of dollars away yearly. Little do they suspect that it is money that he has secured through crime—that he interests himself among the poor only because he occasionally is able to secure some new type of human brain upon whom he can work his nefarious experiments."

ANOTHER EXTRACT.

"Damn the Bodymaster! I hate him! His hold over me is absolute—supreme.

"Vile as I have become, degraded as he has made me, my very being revolts at the thought of what he has forced me to do. It were better that I were dead—a thousand times better. But I can not even die. For he, curse him, will not let me. He owns my body and my soul.

"Yesterday I am certain that I killed another man. It was Johnston, the broker—a man I knew well in my other days—as kind-hearted an old fellow as ever lived. Many is the favor that he has done for me. Yet, at the dictation of Lessman, I took the poor old fellow's life.

"God in Heaven! What a mixup it was! Lessman planned it all. He might have made it different—easier for those left behind to bear. But no—that is not his way. He loves the dramatic, the theatrical. But let me tell it just as it happened:

"Together, we went to Johnston's house—Lessman and I. the poor old fellow has been under the weather for several days, but he has not allowed his illness to interfere with his philanthropic work. Lessman, in his guise of a worker among the poor and afflicted, had no trouble in gaining entrance. He introduced me as another laborer in the vineyard. I have changed so much as a result of what I have been through that Johnston failed to recognize me.

"Alone in the room with the old man, Lessman commanded me to do his bidding. I swear that I tried to withhold my hand, but I was powerless. It was not I, but another, who seized the scrawny neck in my muscular fingers and pressed-pressed—pressed against the windpipe until the haggard white face turned black and the gray eyes bulged forth under their shaggy white brows like glass beads.

"He tried to fight back—to defend himself—but what was his puny strength compared to mine? His efforts only incensed me the more. I shook him as a terrier roughs a rat. And the agonized expression on his face! It was awful. He tried to shriek for help, but so firm was my hold upon him that he could only splutter and gurgle.

"Lessman watched it all. He chuckled with glee at the feeble old man's weak gasps and urged me to further efforts. Then, when I had laid the old fellow down upon the couch, it was The Bodymaster who, with a tremendous show of hypocrisy, shouted for help and jerked frantically at the bell which summoned family and servants.

"Never shall I forget the look of pathetic grief upon the face of the dead man's aged helpmate. Liar that he is, Lessman told her a story of the old fellow's sudden choking and of his death before we could summon help. The servants carried her swooning from the room."

A FURTHER ENTRY.

"Mrs. Johnston is dying, they say, from grief. Lessman chuckles over it, thinking it a huge joke. When I am with him, I laugh, too. Away from him, I can see the horror—the devilish horror of it all.

"Lessman is richer by thousands of dollars. Mrs. Johnston, if she lives, will be almost a pauper. The sum of which she was filched represented practically their all—the savings of a lifetime. For Lessman presented a forged will in which almost everything, except a small amount for the widow, was left to charity *with Lessman as the administrator.*"

Chapter XIII.

Following the above, my diary is filled for several pages with meaningless, childlike scrawls. I seem to have tried to write, but evidently my brain and hand failed to co-ordinate. Here and there I can make out a curse against The Bodymaster, but nothing else can be read. From this I take it that several weeks passed between the time the last entry was written and that which now follows. During that time I was probably in one of my trance-like states, so deeply under Lessman's influence that I had no control over my actions. At the same time the fact that I even attempted to write shows that, deep within my subconscious brain, there was ever that desire to give the horrible truth to the world.

FROM THE DIARY.

"I have denied the truth. I have betrayed those in whose pay I am, and now I know the remorse of Judas.

"Can it be that The Bodymaster seeks my Avis? Are those glances which he darts at her from beneath his half-closed lids intended to be messages of love?

"Of late she has appeared distracted and filled with a vague melancholy when I am around. Does she wish to tell me something, yet fears to open her lips?

"She knows my cataclysmic temper. She has seen me throw off the baleful influence of The Bodymaster when a wild fit of passion seized me. She probably fears that I will again rise against him and that he will blast me where I stand.

"My hands are tied. In turning myself over to The Bodymaster I have betrayed the woman I love. May Heaven have mercy on my soul!"

ANOTHER ENTRY.

"In prowling about the ruins of the old building today I found the remains of an ancient chapel. In one end was an altar, tumbling to ruin. In a little niche, dust covered, was a bottle of Holy Water. I have seized upon it and have hidden it in my room. Perhaps it will save us both.

"I wonder if The Bodymaster has sold himself to the devil? I have heard of such things. No one would believe that such a thing is possible. Yet who would believe that the happenings which I have recorded in my diary could have taken place? They sound like witchcraft, so strange, so diabolical are they. I never believed in such things, but now I am ready to believe anything."

A SUBSEQUENT EXTRACT.

"My mind is made up. I talked with Avis again today. She practically admitted that Lessman has been annoying her with his attentions. Who knows to what steps he will go while she is under his devilish influence?

"Meta, too, is showing her teeth at poor Avis. Heretofore she has shielded the innocent girl to a certain extent. Of that I am certain, and Avis also believes it. But of late she has acted strangely, even showing her temper on several occasions. Lessman treats her at such times with amused contempt. He knows the absolute hold that he has over her.

"But she may injure my loved one. How, I do not know. She is a woman capable of anything. And the 'green-eyed monster' has neither brains nor conscience.

"I am going to be a man at last. I am summoning all of my will power for the battle which is sure to come within a few days. I must—I will—break the bonds which he has placed about me. Just as I arose in rebellion against him on those other occasions, so will I rise against him again for the sake of the woman I love. But this time there will be no surrender. I will conquer him and save her, or die in the attempt.

"To die for Avis may mitigate my sin in the eyes of God.

"I feel The Bodymaster summoning me...My every nerve tingles... These may be the last lines I will ever write...I wonder if these pages will ever be read by other eyes than mind?...I go now to answer his call...*God help me...*"

Chapter XIV

The remainder of my tale is from memory, for the preceding lines are the final entry in my diary. As I have stated elsewhere, I can recall certain things which occasionally happened during my trance-like periods. Remember your dreams—vague, indistinct, hazy—leaping here and there? So are my recollections of that last hour with The Bodymaster. Probably many things happened of which I have no memory. In my desire to stick to facts, I give only that which I remember, leaving the blank places to the reader's imagination.

It must have been immediately after making the final entry in my diary that Lessman summoned me, for the book was in my pocked when I eventually found myself.

Of this, however, I have no memory. My first recollection is of floating through space on one of those strange exploring expeditions in the Great Beyond on which The Bodymaster so often sent me, several of which are described in my diary. Whether I was just returning, or was on my way, I do not know. I only recall that something seemed to be dragging me back—that my whole thought—if thought I could be said to have had—was to get back to my own body as soon as possible.

My next recollection is of being in the room with Lessman. My body lay back in an easy chair, cold, stark and deathlike. I attempted to enter it. But the will of Lessman held me back.

I could see, I could hear, yet I had no visibility. I was but a wraith —an ego as it were—a thought-a spirit—a vapor!

And I was controlled wholly by the brain of Lessman. Just as the invisible current sent out by a central station causes the tiny submarine miles away to hurl itself here and there, so was his magnetic brain master of my actions.

I knew then—or *felt* rather than knew, for I do not believe that a wraith is able to think—I felt that it was Lessman's will that I should never return to my body shell. Something—it was his thought—seemed to hurl me back into space. And at the same time another—an even stronger thought—seemed to hold me transfixed.

It was the will power that I had concentrated for weeks past, aided by the desire for help from Avis. Her whole being was calling out for me.

∼

SHE WAS in the beast's arms. For once in his career his terrible will had no effect upon his victim. Her golden hair was torn from its coils and lay in a shimmering cloud about her shoulders. Her tiny fists beat a tattoo upon his face; his black, lustful eyes gazed, snakelike, into hers, seeing to charm her with their power.

It was awful! I knew that she was calling me—calling me with every bit of her being. And I was helpless, chained to the floor, unable to regain the cold form which was myself.

Suddenly, she tore herself from his grasp. Her clothing was hanging in shreds; across her cheek was an ugly scratch; upon one white, rounded arm stood a livid red welt where his cruel fingers had seized her. She was screaming madly. The furniture was overturned.

Now he had her cornered. But she fought herself away from him, striking him across the head with the leg of a chair that had been broken in the fray.

He pursued her across the room....Once more she was in his grasp. I could hear her breath come gaspingly as she put every ounce of her strength into a final effort to free herself...

The door opened. Meta entered. Her black eyes were blazing. Her mouth worked convulsively. She was a raging demon—a woman scorned—cast aside for another. Like a devil from hell, she threw herself into the fray. Lessman swept her aside with a single motion of his muscular arm.

For an instant she lay there stunned....She dragged herself to her knees, her lips mouthing curses....She half rose to her feet and staggered toward them as Lessman dragged his shrieking victim toward the door which led to the other room. He turned toward her, his fiery eyes snapping with uncontrolled anger.

For the moment I was forgotten....Something snapped. I found myself again within my own body, the lust for battle raging within me....Lessman surrounded by his enemies, turned like a stag at bay....I felt the currents of his powerful mind surge around me again like great waves beating against a rockbound coast.

Every bit of energy I possessed was necessary to hold myself together. He caught me within the power of his will! I felt myself slipping—slipping—*slipping!* Everything grew black before me. I could see nothing save his eyes—burning—*burning* into my very soul.

Like a man who is fighting an overdose of chloral, I strove to free myself from the web which his mind was weaving about me. It was of no avail. Again I felt a wave of fire shoot through my veins.

I lurched against the table. Seizing the lamp, with a final effort. I hurled it straight at the face of the mocking demon before me.

I KNEW NO MORE until I awoke in the hospital.

They say that the place Lessman called his sanitarium was burned to the ground the night before they found me wandering, almost a maniac, several miles away.

As I stated in the beginning, I am unable to distinguish between the truth and the wanderings of my diseased brain. The reader must draw his own conclusions.

What happened? Did I kill Lessman? Did he and Meta and Avis perish in the fire with the other poor unfortunates? Nobody knows.

I HAVE JUST LEARNED that a woman—a golden-haired woman—was found a week ago in a demented condition in a far distant town. The reports say that she mumbles something about "The Bodymaster!" Can it be Avis? I leave tonight for the hospital where she is confined. If it be she, perhaps my presence will recall her to herself.

The End.

JUNGLE DEATH, BY ARTEMUS CALLOWAY
CROCODILES AND VOODOOISM PLAY IMPORTANT PARTS

The very atmosphere seemed surcharged with mystery—danger—death.

Even the clear blue sky above seemed to shrink away from The Tropical Gem Plantations as from a thing accursed. Out in the muddy waters of the Ulua, apparently as lifeless as a water-soaked log, a sleepy-eyed crocodile waited—waited as if he, too, sensed impending calamity for the creatures on shore and intended being at hand to assert his rights should the threatened catastrophe bring food for his kind.

All this impressed Bart Condon, standing in the protecting shade of the softly rustling banana jungle, eyes focused on the busy scene across the river, brain busy with the disquieting events of the past few weeks.

Bart Condon was troubled. Here was something he knew not how to fight, because it was something he could not see. Until recently, he had thought himself fairly familiar with Honduras and the trials of a plantation manager there, but this was something new—something which hid in the shadows and struck when one was not looking.

First there had been the matter of the cistern water in the laborers' quarters. Some one had poisoned it—not in a manner to cause death, but illness. Condon had been mystified by the epidemic which descended upon the place until the plantation physician made an examination of the water. Then he was the more at sea. Who could have done this—and why?

Close upon this trouble came whispers—rumors that the place was bewitched. More than a dozen of the more superstitious blacks and half blacks slipped away. And their places had been hard to fill.

Then had come the fires, starting no one knew when or how. Once a manacca shack, in which a sick man lived, burned; and he was brought out half-stifled, scorched and raving about the devils that infested the place.

Other things occurred. And there was more whispering, more dissatisfaction.

And then had come death. A partly devoured body had been found lodged against a mud bar in the river. The work of crocodiles, Condon had thought, until examination disclosed the fact that there was a bullet in the man's brain. And then he knew that the crocodiles had profited from the work of a murderer.

And now all the plantation laborers threatened to leave. Somehow Condon felt that he could not blame them, though he knew that their desertion meant his ruin.

The activity along the river bank increased. The crocodile moved slowly downstream. Simultaneously with the arrival of a noisy fruit train on Condon's side of the river, another chugged into view on the opposite shore.

As soon as the trains came to a stop natives commenced transferring bananas from the cars to the fruit racks at the water's edge; here they would later be picked up by the river boat of the big fruit company which purchased the output of many Ulua River plantations, afterward shipping the bananas to the States on its own steamers.

Condon saw George Armstrong standing to the right of the train across the river, and, for some unknown reason he disliked the man more than ever. There was no real reason why he should dislike and distrust Armstrong. Yet he did dislike him, and never, from the first moment his eyes rested upon the man, had he trusted him. For two years now Condon had known he manager of the Royal Palm Plantation Company, and for that length of time some instinct had whispered that the other would be a dangerous foe.

True, Armstrong had always evinced the greatest friendliness, frequently coming across the river, which separated the plantations, to visit Condon. And occasionally—when common courtesy demanded—Condon had returned the visits.

Bard Condon had been in Honduras one year longer than Armstrong, and this year's experience as manager of the plantation of which he was majority stockholder had taught him many things of value, which he had passed on to the newcomer. But Armstrong's company was stronger financially than Condon's, and was desirous of expanding. So, for three months now, Armstrong had been trying to buy the Tropical Gem. And for nearly that length of time the Tropical Gem had been having trouble.

~

But it was only this morning that Condon had first commenced wondering what connection, if any, there might be between Armstrong's desire for the Tropical Gem and the trouble which had come to that plantation. Of course such thoughts were silly. Unworthy. He should be ashamed of himself....And yet...

Standing where he was, in the shelter of the tall banana plants which at a distance resembled a forest of green trees, Condon knew Armstrong had not seen him. And for some reason, which he himself did not understand, he did not want the other man to see him this morning.

Bart Condon turned and slowly made his way from the river to a trail about two hundred yards away. There he paused to watch some men cutting fruit which would be carried by mule cart to the river, the railroad being employed only for longer hauls.

Finally he turned to his pony, fastened to a young avocado tree, mounted and rode away. Twenty minutes later he was at plantation headquarters.

An hour after reaching headquarters Condon was sitting at his office desk, a slender young native opposite him. This man—Juan Hernandez—one of Condon's foremen, possessed intelligence above the average. He was one of the very few natives of that section of Honduras who boasted pure Spanish blood, but at the same time he understood thoroughly the mixed breeds in whose veins there flowed the blood of African, Indian, Chinese and others, to say nothing of the full-blood negroes from Jamaica, Barbadoes, and elsewhere.

Once facing Hernandez, Condon lost no time in getting to the subject:

"The men—they are very much upset?"

Hernandez nodded.

"They are, Mr. Condon," he replied in perfect English, thanks to a States education. "They are whispering that there is a curse upon the plantation; that you are the cause of it; that the spirits are displeased with you, and I don't know what else. They—"

Hernandez hesitated. Then:

'Why, they are even beginning to blame you for the death of that man found in the river, although they don't know, as we do, that someone shot him."

Condon frowned. "Somehow I suspect as much. But you are sure your information—what you tell me is correct?"

Hernandez nodded. "I am positive of it. Further than that I feel that I have discovered what is behind it all. You know you told me a week ago to look into it—"

"Yes?"

"It is voodooism. A witch doctor who lives in the jungle is behind the trouble here. And a white man is behind the witch doctor!"

Conon started. "You mean--?"

For a moment Hernandez said nothing, staring at the desk before him. Then:

"Armstrong!"

Condon's hands twitched nervously. "How do you know—or suspect—this, Hernandez?"

"I am positive, Mr. Condon. I have a man working under me whom I trust implicitly. He is an Indian—one of those commonly known as a Mosquito Indian—they live down on the Mosquito Coast, you know—"

"Yes. Go on. What about him?"

"Well, he is a very intelligent fellow. Not a drop of black blood in his veins. Of course, many of the Indians in this country have their own superstitious beliefs, but not so this man. For years he has worked around foreigners—those ideas, if he ever had them, have been supplanted by those of civilization.

"This man told me that the witch doctor—an old dried-up black fellow, no telling how old he is—has been coming to the plantation. He was here the night before the water was poisoned. He has been here since. And lately the laborers have been going to see him—holding ceremonies and that sort of thing.

"And tonight—" Hernandez lowered his voice—"they go again! They are to be there at ten o'clock. The witch doctor is going to tell them that their lives are not safe on this plantation as long as you have anything to do with it. Tomorrow they will leave. And no other laborers will come here. Then—Armstrong thinks he can buy you out. You see, with Armstrong in charge, the curse will be removed."

Condon secured a box of cigars from his desk, handed it to Hernandez, found a box of matches, lighted a cigar himself.

'*Hmm!* Pretty clever scheme. But—Oh! Hang it, Hernandez, do you suppose this *can* be correct?"

Hernandez regarded his cigar thoughtfully. "I *know* it is!"

"Well---"

"Just a moment, please, Mr. Condon. There is one chance for us—only one. That is to discredit the witch doctor. Once the superstitious mixed breeds and blacks find that he is not infallible, that there is something more powerful than he, they will lose confidence in him. They will believe nothing he has told them. But until that is done the case is hopeless. You see, many of the men working here were raised on superstition—on voodooism. The blacks brought it from Africa, and their descendants in this and the other nearby countries cling to it. And, as I have said, we have them here from many places."

"How are we to discredit the witch doctor?"

Hernandez smiled. "Armstrong visits him at eight o'clock this evening, to pay half the price for running the laborers away from here. He is to pay the other half when they are gone. Of course, he has paid something all along for the various little jobs, but this is the big one—the big money job."

"What on earth would that old fellow want with money?"

Hernandez laughed. "Square-faced gin. He stays soaked all the time. But I have a plan—"

"But how," interrupted Condon, "did your man learn all this?"

"By pretending to believe in voodooism—and by watching. He has attended the ceremonies with the others. And he has followed Armstrong there when the witch doctor was alone. That is how he learned of the poisoned water. He has heard nothing there about the murder of the native, but I am sure there is a connection there somewhere if we can find it."

Hernandez made a significant gesture.

"You don't know the confidence those people have in that old fellow. He has a pond there in front of his cave. A natural sort of pond. Been there for centuries, I suppose, and it is full of crocodiles. Sacrifices to these crocodiles have been hinted at—but of course I couldn't swear to that. I do know, however, that the laborers here are blind enough in their belief of him to do anything he might tell them."

Condon's face was wrinkled in thought. "But your plan?"

Hernandez leaned nearer. "Listen…"

∽

SEVEN-THIRTY O'CLOCK that evening found Bart Condon, Juan Hernandez and the Indian of whom Condon had been told concealed on the side of the little jungle hill above the witch doctor's cave. Almost at his doorway was the pond of which Hernandez had spoken. An occasional *swish* of the water told of life in it. Just in front of the cave, squatted on the ground beside a faint brush fire, was the witch doctor, an old, shriveled, dried-up, gray-headed black.

"We can hear from this place?" Condon whispered.

"Yes," replied Hernandez, "but be quiet. He might hear you."

Back in the jungle, monkeys chattered. Baboons howled nearby. A macaw set up a shrill shrieking. Once Condon heard the helpless, hopeless cry of some small animal as it met the death of the jungle. Some beast of the tropics slipped past them. Bart Condon griped his revolver.

And then they heard somebody approaching. Down a little trail —the same trail which Conon had traveled part of the way—a man was coming. A few moments later Armstrong was standing before the witch doctor's fire.

With every nerve on edge, Condon watched. Armstrong and the witch doctor, both now seated before the blaze, wasted no time on inconsequential talk.

Armstrong was speaking in Spanish: "You understand exactly what you are to tell those people when they come here tonight."

"I do."

"Very well. Here is half of the money. You will receive as much more—provided you get Condon's laborers away tomorrow—and keep them and all others away."

The witch doctor nodded. "They will be away before tomorrow. When they leave here they will be afraid to return to the man Condon's plantation."

"They won't even return for their things?"

The old man laughed shrilly. "They will believe everything on that plantation accursed when I have finished with them and will never desire to see their things again. I intended telling them that they must leave tomorrow. Now I have decided to have them leave tonight. It is better so."

Again the witch doctor laughed.

"But—" and now there was something in his voice Condon had

not detected there before—"there is more money to come to me, Senor."

Armstrong's tone was impatient. "You get that when the laborers have quit the plantation."

The old man chuckled. "But I mean other money."

"What other money?"

"The money for keeping your secret about the man you shot!"

George Armstrong jumped to his feet. "You're crazy! I shot no man."

The witch doctor also was on his feet. "But you did, Senor, I *saw* you! I don't blame you for what you did. The fellow saw you coming from here and he might have been suspicious. I, also, would have killed him, but you did the job for me. And now you will pay me for keeping the secret."

The witch doctor's words seemed to madden the manager of the Royal Palm Plantation. Straight at the old man's throat he sprang. The fought like wild animals. The witch doctor, for all his frailness, possessed enormous strength.

Suddenly Hernandez caught Condon's arm: "Look! Down the trail!" he whispered.

Condon looked. Then he gasped in amazement. The trail was filled, as far as he could see, with men.

∼

Suddenly Condon's attention was brought back to the struggle by a scream of terror, which burst from Armstrong's lips. And then, locked in embrace, the plantation manager and the witch doctor disappeared in the crocodile pool.

There was a sudden rush—horrid grunts—the crushing of bones —and Condon imagined he could see the water redden. Armstrong and the witch doctor were no more.

Then, from Condon's laborers in the trail came cries of denunciation. "He is no witch doctor! He fought with the white man and was eaten by crocodiles—he who told us that he could destroy white men by pointing his finger at them. He told us that the crocodiles could not harm him."

Unafraid of that which was now no mystery, some of the bolder ones advanced to the fire. One picked up some gold pieces, which the witch doctor had dropped. Another found Armstrong's purse.

They turned and rejoined their companions. Five minutes later the entire party had passed out of hearing.

Hernandez touched Condon on the shoulder. "We can go now. And our troubles are over. The men will remain on the plantation perfectly satisfied."

"But I don't understand," said Condon slowly, rising to his feet and rubbing his cramped legs, "why they came so early. I thought they were to get here at ten o'clock."

"So Armstrong and the witch doctor thought," laughed Hernandez." But the message was carried by our friend here—and he asked my advice before delivering it. And he made the hour earlier so they would find Armstrong here. That alone would have destroyed their confidence in the witch doctor, for he is supposed to have nothing to do with white men."

Hernandez smiled.

"They were told, although this man professed not to believe it, that there was a report to the effect that Armstrong had bought the witch doctor—had paid him to betray them. That is why they understood everything so readily when they saw the end of the fight."

"Voodooism," said Condon thoughtfully, "loses its strength when it mixes up with white men."

THE SNAKE FIEND, BY FARNSWORTH WRIGHT

ANOTHER TALE OF DIABOLIC TERROR

Even as a child. Jack Crimi delighted in collecting reptiles, and he seemed to absorb much of their venomous nature. His best- loved pet was a large blacksnake; but when it caused him a whipping by crawling into his father's bedroom, he roasted it over a slow fire in a large pot, listening with glee to its agonized hissing and pushing it back with a stick when it strove to crawl out of the searing container. It is no cause for wonder, then, that his burning love for the girl of his dreams turned to fierce hate when she became the bride of another.

Crimi's sentiment for Marjorie Bressi was aroused by her fine Italian beauty, which reminded him of his mother. He could have fallen in love with any other girl as easily, if he had set his mind to it in the same way. By dint of comparing her with his mother's picture, he conceived a groat admiration for her: then he wished to possess her, to be her lord and master, to marry her. Gazing on her every day with this thought in his mind, his admiration grew to a burning passion. Of all this he said nothing to Marjorie, and then it was too late.

Marjorie loved, and was loved by Allen Jimerson, a young civil engineer. Crimi neither threatened nor cajoled. He simply accepted the fact, and meditated revenge. He was all smiles at their wedding, and he gave them a wedding present beyond what he could reasonably afford, while he planned to tumble their happiness in rains about their ears.

After a short honeymoon, Jimerson departed with his wife to take up his duties as resident engineer of some construction work on a western railroad. Crimi, his face glowing with friendship and good will, was the last to clasp Marjorie's hand in farewell, as the train pulled out of the station.

"Write to me often, Marjorie." was his parting injunction. "Send me a letter as soon as you get settled, and let me know how you are getting along. I don't want to lose touch with either of you."

And he meant it.

MARJORIE WAS fond of the handsome, manly-looking Italian youth, and liked him immensely as a friend, although she had never been in love with him. No sooner was she settled in her new home than she wrote him a long letter, telling of her husband's work, the bleakness of the desert country, and the strange newness of her life. She and her husband occupied a cabin together, apart from the bunk-houses of the construction camp, in the sagebrush region of northern California, not far from the Nevada border.

A fierce joy and exultation leapt in Crimi's heart as he read Marjorie's letter.

> "You would like the country better than I do", she wrote, for it is infested with rattle-snakes. The bare desert rocks on the ridge four miles from our cabin are swarming with them. Ugh! They sun themselves in tangled masses, Allen says, but truly I can't bring myself to go near the place. I get quite too much of snakes without that, for we are constantly killing them in the sagebrush. This country has never been settled, and except for an occasional prospector, there was nobody to kill them before the surveyors

came. The Indians never bother the snakes, but pass by on the other side of a sagebrush and leave them in peace."

Crimi scored these lines in red ink, word by word, as if to blazon them on his memory, and he drew little pictures of snakes on the margin. He burned out Marjorie's signature with acid, spitefully watching with minute care as the letters faded, and cleaning a savage satisfaction from seeing the paper rot away under the venomous bite of the poison. Then he fed the letter to the flames, as he had roasted his blacksnake, years before, and watched the missive burn into black ashes and crumble slowly away, page by page, into gray dust.

Followed Crimi's pursuit of the pair. His arrival was not expected by either Jimerson or Marjorie, but it was none the less welcome, for both of them liked the genial, companionable Italian. Life on the edge of the desert had few distractions at best. Crimi's eyes lit with genuine pleasure at sight of his prospective victims. The joy on both sides was sincere.

"No, this isn't a pleasure trip," he explained to them, "although I expect to have pleasure enough out of it before I get through. I have turned from collecting reptiles to studying their lives and habits. I intend to write a monograph on rattlesnakes. When I got your letter. Marjorie, I knew that I could do no better than to come here. I expect to become very well acquainted with that ridge you wrote about, where the snakes sun themselves in tangled masses."

Marjorie shuddered, and Crimi laughed.

"Well, don't bring any of your snakes around here,'" she said. "I turn cold and something grips at my insides every time I hear one rattle."

Crimi built himself a small cabin about a mile from the Jimersons, in the direction of the rattlesnake ridge. He adorned the shack tastefully, and Marjorie's deft hand gave a distinctly feminine neatness and charm to its appearance.

He became a frequent visitor at the Jimerson cabin, and evening after evening he read to them in his melodious, well modulated voice.

Sometimes the draughtsman or transitman would come in, and Crimi would join in playing cards until late at night.

He seemed to take keen pleasure in the company of Marjorie and her husband, and his face always lit up at sight of them, especially when they were together. But it was the joy of a boy who sees the apples ripening for him on his neighbor's tree, and knows that they will soon be ready for him to pluck. He was most happy when he was meditating his frightful revenge. As his preparations drew near their end, he often spent whole hours gloating over the fate in store for the couple. For Marjorie, in loving Jimerson, had aroused him to insane jealousy, and Jimerson, having robbed him of his heart's desire, was included in Crimi's fierce hate for the girl who had crossed him.

When, one evening, Marjorie and her husband happened in at Crimi's cabin, Marjorie expressed her horror at the though of Crimi wandering among the snake-infested rocks of the rattlesnake ridge. The snake-hunter seated her on a box that contained a twisting knot of the venomous reptiles.

Marjorie, serenely unaware, talked cm blithely, and Crimi's merry laugh pealed out at regular intervals. He was in right jovial mood that evening, for he was ready to spring the death- trap prepared for his two friends. He only awaited a favorable opportunity to strike.

~

THE OPPORTUNITY CAME WHEN THE SURVEYORS' cook, crazed by bad whisky, smashed up the kitchen. Jimerson discharged him, and the cook muttered threats of a horrible vengeance.

"Shut up." Jimerson ordered. "This is the third time you've been seeing snakes, and now you've wrecked the cook shack. You ought to be sent to jail—or a lunatic asylum."

"It's you that will be seeing snakes," the cook spluttered. "You an' that Italian wife of yours 'll see plenty of 'em—red. an green, an'—"

Jimerson struck him across the mouth and sent him on his way. This was in the evening. The draughtsman and rodman went to town the next day to hire a new cook, while Jimerson and Marjorie went on an outing up the headwaters of Feather Creek. It was Sunday, and they intended to spend the day there.

Crimi declined their invitation to accompany them. It was the moulting season, he explained, when the snakes were casting their skins. He could ill afford to lose a day of observation at this time, for he had several perplexing points to clear up before writing his monograph.

Crimi walked fearlessly from rock to rock of the rattlesnake ridge, chuckling to himself. The tangled masses of snakes, of which he had been told, existed only in rumor, although there were snakes in plenty if one but looked for them. Tangled masses would serve his purpose later, but he had gathered them here and there, one or two at a time.

By noon the little cluster of cabins occupied by the engineers was deserted. Marjorie and her husband had been gone since sun- up, and the surveyors were all in town. Not a soul was stirring in the neighborhood of the shacks, and the men at the construction camp were mostly lying around in their bunks, or playing cards.

Crimi nailed fast the windows of Jimerson's cabin. Then he entered and secured the bed to the floor so that it could not be moved. He laboriously carried his boxes of snakes a mile or more, from his room to the little gully behind the surveyors' cabins, and hid them in the sagebrush.

Marjorie and her husband came back from their tramp after dark that evening, dog-tired. Marjorie cooked a little supper, and by 10 o'clock the two were asleep. Crimi entered their cabin about midnight. They were fast in the chains of dumber, and he did not even find it necessary to muffle his tread. He removed the chairs, shoes, clothes, and even the hand mirror and toilet articles. Everything that might serve as a weapon, no matter how slight, he took away.

Then he brought his snakes from the gully, and collected them in front of the cabin. When he had assembled them all, he knocked the top from the largest box, carried it into the room, and, in the audacity of his certain triumph, he dumped the twisting mass of rattlesnakes on the bed where Marjorie and her husband lay asleep.

The other boxes he emptied quickly just inside of the door, and withdrew, for he had no wish to set foot among the venomous serpents. Revenge is never satisfied if retribution overtakes the avenger, and Crimi had no wish to share the fate of his victims. He locked the door from the outside, and battened it. Then he removed the boxes that had contained the snakes, and returned to his cabin and peacefully went to sleep.

~

MARJORIE AWOKE with the first rays of the sun, and lazily opened her eyes.

Her heart leapt suddenly into her throat, and she was wide awake in an instant. The flat, squat head of a rattlesnake was creeping along her breast. Its beady eyes were fixed on her face, and its red tongue flickered before her like a forked flame. For a moment she thought she was still dreaming, but the familiar outlines of the room limned themselves in her consciousness, and she knew that what she saw was real.

Her shriek rent the air, as she threw back the bed clothes and sprang to the floor. She stepped on a coiled serpent, which sounded an ominous warning as it struck out blindly.

She quickly climbed back on the bed, and stood on the pillow, screaming. Her husband was beside her at once, hazily trying to understand the import of the hysterical torrent of words she was sobbing into his ears. For an instant he thought she must be in the clutch of some horrible nightmare. Then a quick, startled glance around the room turned his blood to ice.

There was now a continuous rattling, as of dry leaves blowing against a stone wall, for Marjorie's screams had galvanized the snakes into activity. The room was filled with their angry din. It sounded in Jimerson's ears like the crack of doom. The floor seemed covered with the creeping reptiles. Some were coiled, the whirring tips of their tails making an indistinct blur as they rattled, and their heads swaying slowly back and forth. Others writhed along the floor, their venomous squat heads thrusting forward and withdrawing, and their tongues darting out like red flames.

On the bed itself there was motion underneath the thrown-back coverlet, and the ugly, gray head of a thick, four-foot snake protruded from under it, its evil eyes shining dully, as if through a film of dust. It extricated itself, and coiled as if to strike, while Marjorie shrank fearfully against the wall, wide- eyed with horror.

Jimerson attacked the reptile with a pillow, sweeping it from the bed onto the floor. He quickly looked about him for a weapon, and saw at once that he was trapped. There was not even a shoe or a pincushion with which to fight the crawling, rattling creatures.

He tried to rock the bed toward the window, as boys move sawhorses forward while sitting on them. But the bed was firmly fastened to the floor, and in his efforts to release it he was bitten on the wrist by the strike of a large snake coiled near the foot of the bed.

Jimerson flung the reptile across the room, and sprang to the floor with an oath, crushing a large rattler with his heel as he jumped. He raced to the door, and wrestled with it for a full minute before he discovered that he and Marjorie were locked in that serpent-hole.

He sprang to the window, and felt a sharp stab of pain in the flesh of his calf as the open jaws of another reptile found their mark, and the poison fangs were imbedded deep in the flesh. The window, like the door, was nailed fast, but he broke out the glass with his bare fists.

Unmindful of the blood on his lacerated hands, he was back at the bedside, treading over reptiles with his bare feet. Marjorie lay on the bed, unconscious.

He lifted her in his bleeding arms and hurled her through the window to safety. He struggled out after her, tearing open his bitten leg on the jagged pieces of glass still left in the window frame. The spurting blood drenched him, and he leaned, faint and dizzy, against the cabin as three of his surveyors came running up, having been attracted by Marjorie's screams.

In almost incoherent words he told them what had happened. He asked them to make immediate search for the discharged cook, for there was no doubt in Jimerson's mind that it was the cook who had placed the snakes in the room.

Then the sky went suddenly black before his eyes, and he lost consciousness.

∼

At that minute Crimi was waking from peaceful dreams. He recalled what he had done the night before, and blissfully mused on what must be taking place in the Jimerson cabin.

A phantasmagoric succession of pictures weltered in his mind—Marjorie and her husband fighting with bare hands against the serpents—bitten a score of times by the angry fangs of the rattlesnakes—clinging to each other in terror—sinking to the floor in agony as the poison swelled their tortured limbs and overcame them—lying green and blue in death, with rattlesnakes crawling and hissing over their dead bodies.

It is remarkable how few people die from rattlesnake bites even when as badly bitten as Jimerson was. Probably not one adult victim in a hundred succumbs to the venom, although mistaken popular belief considers rattlesnake poison as fatal as the death-potion of the Borgias.

Jimerson had known too many cases of snake bite to believe his ease hopeless. He did not give up and die, nor did he try to poison his system with whisky. He knew that his condition was serious but he let rest and permanganate of potash, rubbed into his wounds, effect a cure. The Weeding from the lacerated leg had almost entirely washed out the poison, and there was little swelling. The pain of his swollen wrist, however, distended almost to bursting, kept him from sleeping, and the sickly green hue of the bite distressed him. But it did not kill him.

Crimi, careful observer of reptiles though he was, had never known an actual case of snake bite, and he shared the popular illusion that the bite of the rattlesnake dooms its victim to death. Hence he was certain of the complete success of his revenge, and his gloating glee was unclouded by even the shadow of a doubt that Marjorie and her husband had been killed in his death-trap. He awaited only the supreme joy of drinking in the details of his success, to feel the exultant thrill of complete victory.

As Crimi sat alone, two days after that horrible morning, Jimerson was limping slowly toward his cabin. His swollen hand still pained him badly, and there was a dull ache in his ankle when he put too much weight on it, but he thought the fresh air would benefit him.

Supporting himself with a cane, and leaning heavily on Marjorie at times, he went painfully toward the young Italian's desert home. Not once had his suspicion pointed toward Crimi as author of the crime, for the guilt of the lunatic cook seemed all too clear. Besides, he liked Crimi for his genial camaraderie, his joviality and good humor, and his frank interest in everything that concerned either him or Marjorie.

So intent was the snake fiend on passing the torments of his victims before his fancy, that he did not hear the knock on his cabin door. His brain was too busy to heed the message sent by his ears, for he was feasting on the mental and physical tortures that Jimerson and Marjorie must have endured before they lay cold in death on the floor of the cabin, hideously discolored by the venom of the rattlesnakes.

By degrees he became conscious that he was not alone. Two persons stood before him, and he raised his eyes in eager anticipation, to feed his revengeful spirit on the story he had waited two days to hear.

Even when he gazed on those whom he had consigned to a horrible death, the thought that they were alive did not penetrate his consciousness. The idea of failure had never entered his mind for even an instant. They were dead, beyond the peradventure of a doubt, and now—*their avenging ghosts stood before him!*

CRIMI DROPPED to his knees in white terror and crawled behind his chair. He clasped and unclasped his hands in agony of fear. Sweat poured from his face and bathed his body. He implored mercy. He screamed for forgiveness. He gibbered like a frightened ape. Half forgotten words of Italian, learned at his mother's knee, fell from his lips.

He pleaded and begged for his life, crawling on his face toward the amazed couple in an endeavor to clasp their knees.

As the meaning of his broken ejaculations was borne in on them, a tremendous loathing and disgust overcame them. Marjorie clung to her husband, unnerved at the repulsive sight of the malicious coward groveling on the floor and trying to kiss their feet.

Crimi shrieked and gnawed his hands as he saw the avenging angels of his victims leave the cabin.

∼

IT WAS impossible for the stern hand of the law to inflict a greater punishment on Jack Crimi than his own malice had wrought for him. Today he occupies a padded cell in a hospital for the incurably insane.

A SQUARE OF CANVAS, BY ANTHONY M. RUD

A REMARKABLE STORY OF AN INSANE ARTIST

"No, Madame, I am *not* insane! I see you hide a smile. Never mind attempting to mask the expression. You are a newcomer here and have learned nothing of my story. I do not blame any visitor—the burden of proof rests upon us, *n'est-ce-pas*?

"In this same ward you have met several peculiar characters, have you not? We have a motley assemblage of conquerors, diplomats, courtesans and divinities—if you'll take their words for it. There is Alexander the Great, Richelieu, Julius Caesar, Spartacus, Cleopatra— but no matter. *I* have no delusion. I am Hal Pemberton.

"You start? You believe *this* my delusion? Look closely at me! I have aged, it is true, yet if you have glimpsed the Metropolitan gallery portrait that Paul Gauguin did of me when I visited Tahiti...?"

I gasped, and fell back a pace. This silver-haired, kindly old soul the mad genius, Pemberton? The temptation was strong to flee when I realized that he told the truth! I knew the portrait, indeed, and for an art student like myself there could be no mistaking the resemblance. I stopped, half-turned. After all, they allowed him freedom of the grounds. He could be no worse surely, than the malignant Cleopatra whom I just had left playing with her "asp"—a five-inch garter snake she had found crossing the gravel path.

"I—I believe you," came my stammered reply.

What I meant, of course, was that no doubt could exist that he was, certainly, Hal Pemberton. His seamed face lighted up; it was plain *he* believed that establishment of identity made the matter of his detention absurd.

"They have me registered as Chase—John Chase," he confided. "Come! Would a true story of an artist's persecution interest you? It is a recital of misunderstanding, bigotry...."

He left the sentence incomplete, and beckoned with a curl of his tapered, spatulate index finger toward a bench set fair in the sunshine just beyond range of blowing mists from the fountain.

I was tempted. A guard was stationed less than two hundred feet distant. Notwithstanding the horrid and distorted legends which shrouded our memories of this man—supposed to have died in far-off Polynesia—he could not harm me easily before assistance was available. Beside, I am an active, bony woman of the grenadier type. I waited until he sat down, then placed myself gingerly upon the opposite end of the bench.

"You are the first person who has not laughed in my face when learning my true identity," he continued then, making no attempt to close the six-foot gap between us—much to my comfort. "*Ignorance* placed me here. Ignorance keeps me. I shall give you every detail, Madame. Then you may inform others and procure my release. The *cognoscenti* will demand it, once they know of the cruel, intolerance which has stolen nine years from my career and from my life. You know—" and here Pemberton glanced guardedly about before he added in a whisper, "*they won't let me paint!*

"My youth and training are known in part. Alden Sefferich's brochure dealt with the externals, at least. You have read it? Ah, yes! Dear Alden knew nothing, really. When I look at his etchings of buildings—at his word sketch of myself—I see behind the lines and letters to a great void.

"At best, he was an admirable camera equipped with focal-plane shutter and finest anastigmatic lenses depicting three dimensions faithfully in two, yet ignoring the most important fourth dimension of temperament and soul as though it were as mythical as that fourth dimension played with by mathematicians.

"It is not. Artistic inspiration—what the underworld calls *yen*—has been my whole life. Beyond the technique and inspiration furnished by Guarneresi, one might scrap the whole of tutelage and still have left—myself, and the divine spark!

"I was one of the Long Island Pembertons. Two sisters still are living. They are staid, respectable ladies who married well. To hell with them! They *really* believed that Hal Pemberton disgraced them, the nauseating prigs!

"Our mother was Sheila Varro, the singer. Father was an unimaginative sort, president of the Everest Life and Casualty Company for many years. I mention these facts merely to show you there was no hereditary taint, no connate reason for warped mentality such as they attribute to me. That I inherited the whole of my poor mother's artistic predilection there is possibility for doubt, for she was brilliant always. I was a dullard in my youth. It was only with education and inspiration that even a spark of her divine creative fury came to me—but the story of that I shall reach later."

∽

"As a boy, I hated school. Before the age of ten I had been expelled from three academies, always on account of the way I treated my associates. I was cruel to other boys, because lessons did not capture my attention. Nothing quiet, static, like the pursuit of facts, *ever* has done so.

"When I tired of sticking pins into younger lads, or pulling their hair, I sought out one or another of my own size and fought with him. Often—usually—I was trounced, but this never bothered. Hurt, blood and heat of combat always were curiosities to me—impersonal, somehow. As long as I could stand on my feet I would punch for the nose or eyes of my antagonist, for nothing delighted me like seeing the involuntary pain flood his countenance, and red blood stream from his mashed nostrils.

"Father sent me to the New York public schools, but there I lasted only six or seven weeks. I was not popular either was my playmates or with the teachers, who complained of what they took to be abnormality. I had done nothing except arrange a pin taken from the hat of one of the women teachers where I thought it would do the most good. This was in the sleeve of the principal's greatcoat.

"When he slid in his right hand the long pin pierced his palm, causing him to cry out loudly with pain. I did not see him at the moment, but I was waiting outside his office at the time, and I gloated in my mind at the picture of his stabbed hand, ebbing drops of blood where the blue steel entered.

"I longed to rush in a view my work, but did not dare. Later, when by some shrewd deduction they fastened the blame on me, Mr. Mortenson had his right hand bandaged.

"Father gave up the idea of public school after this, and procured me a tutor. He thought me a trifle deficient, and I suppose my attitude lent color to such a theory. I tormented the three men who took me in hand, one after the other, until each one resigned. I malingered. I shirked. I prepared 'accidents' in which all were injured.

"It was not that I could not learn—I realized all along that simple tasks assigned me by these men could be accomplished without great effort—but that I had no desire to study algebra, geography and language, or other dull things of the kind. Only zoology tempted in the least, and none of the men I had before Jackson came was competent to do much of anything with this absorbing subject.

"Jackson was the fourth, and last. He proved himself an earnest soul, and something of a scientist. He tried patiently for a fortnight to teach me all that Dad desired, but found his pupil responsive only when he gave me animals to study. These, while alive, interested me.

"One day, after a discouraging session with my other studies, he left me with some small beetles which he intended to classify on his return. It was a hot day, and the little sheath-winged insects were stimulated out of dormance to lively movement. I had them under a glass cover to prevent their escape.

"Just to see how they acted, I took them out, one by one, and performed slight operations upon parts of their anatomy with the point of my pen-knife. One I deprived of wings, another lost two legs of many, a third was deprived of antennae, and so on. Then I squatted close with a hand-lens and eyed their desperate struggles.

"Here was *life, pain, struggle*—death close by, leering at the tiny creatures. It fascinated me. I watched eagerly, and then, when one of the beetles grew slower in moving, I stimulated it with the heated point of a pin.

"At the time—I was then only sixteen years of age—I had no analytical explanation of interest, but now I know that the artist in me was swept through a haze of adolescence by sight of that most sincere of all the struggles of life, the struggle against *death!*

"A fever raced in my blood. I knew the beetles could not last. An instinct made me wish to preserve some form of record of their supreme movement. I seized my pencil. I wrote a paragraph, telling how I would feel in case some huge, omnipotent force should put me under glass, remove my legs, stab me with the point of a great knife, a red-hot dagger, and watch my writhings.

"The description was pale, colorless, of course. It did not satisfy, even while I scribbled. As you may readily understand, I possessed no power of literary expression; crude sentences selected at random only emphasized the need of expression of a better sort. Without reasoning—indeed, many a person would have considered me quite mad at the time—I tore a clean sheet of paper from a thick tablet and fell to *sketching* rapidly, furiously!

"As with writing, I knew nothing of technique—I never had drawn a line before—but the impelling force was great. Before my eyes I saw the picture I wished to portray—the play of protest against death. I drew the death struggle...."

"By the time Jackson returned the fire had died out of me.

"The horrid sketch was finished, and all but one of the beetles lay, legs upturned, under the glass. That one had managed to escape somehow, and was dragging itself hopelessly across the table, leaving a wet streak of colorless blood to mark its passing. Exhausted in body and mind. I had collapsed in the neared chair, not caring whether I, myself, lived or died.

"Poor Jackson was horrified when he saw what I had done to the *Coleptera*, and he began reproaching me for my needless cruelty. Just as he was waxing eloquent, however, his eye caught sight of my crude sketch. He stopped speaking.

"I saw him tremble, adjust his pince-nez and stare long at the poor picture I had made, and then at the dead beetles. Finally, seeming in a torment of anger, he read the paragraph of description, turning to examine me with horror and amazement in his glance.

"Then, suddenly, he sprang to his feet, gripping the two sheets of paper in his hands, swung about, and made off before I could rouse from my lassitude sufficiently to question him. I never saw Jackson again. The poor fool.

"An hour later father sent for me. I knew that the tutor had been to see him, and I expected another of the terrible lectures I had been in habit of receiving each time a new lack or iniquity made itself apparent to others. On several occasions in the past father had flogged me, and driven himself close to the verge of apoplexy because of his extreme anger at what he deemed deliberate obstinacy. I feared whippings: they sickened me. My knees were quaking as I went to his study.

"This time, however, it was plain that father had given up. He was pale, weighed down with what must have been the great disappointment of his life; but he neither stormed nor offered to chastise me. Instead he told me quietly that Jackson had resigned, finding me impossible to instruct.

"In a few sentences father reviewed the efforts he had made for my education, then stated that all the tutors had been convinced that my lack of progress had been due more to a chronic disinclination for work rather than to any innate defect of body or mind.

"'So far,' he told me, 'you have refused steadfastly to accept opportunity. New we come to the end. Mr. Jackson has showed me a sketch made by you in which he professes to see real talent. He advises that you be sent abroad to study drawing or painting. Would you care for this last chance? Otherwise I must place you in an institution of some kind, where you no longer can bring disgrace and pain upon me—a reform school, in short. I tell you frankly, Hal, that I am ready to wash my hands of you.'

"What could I do? I chose, of course, to go to Paris. Father made the necessary arrangements for me to enter Guarneresi's big studios as a beginner, paying for a year in advance, and making me a liberal allowance in addition.

"'I shall not attempt to conceal from you, Hal,' he told me at parting, 'that I do not wish you to return. Your allowance will continue just as long as you remain abroad. If, in time, a moderate success in some line of endeavor comes to you I shall be glad to see you again, but not before. The Pembertons never were failures or parasites.'

"Thus I left him. He died while I was in my third year at the studio, and by his express wish I was not notified until after the funeral was over. I wept over the letter that came, but only because of the knowledge that now I never could make up in any way for the great sorrow I had caused my father. Had he lived only ten years longer—and this would not have been extraordinary, as he died at the age of fifty-two—I could have restored some of that lost pride to him."

∽

"Is it necessary to tell of my years with Guarneresi? No; you confessed some slight knowledge of me. Very well, I shall pass over them lightly. Suffice it to say that here at last I found my forte. I could paint. The *maestro* never valued my efforts very highly, but he taught with conscientious diligence nevertheless. In the use of sweeping line and chiaroscuro I excelled the majority of his pupils, but in color I exhibited no talent—in *his* estimation, at least.

"It was strange, too, for through my mind at odd intervals swept riots of crimson, orange and purple, which never could be mixed satisfactorily upon my palette for any given picture. I told myself that the fault lay as much in the subjects of my pictures as in myself—the excuse of a liar, of course.

"There *was* some excuse there, however. For instance, when we painted nudes Guarneresi would assemble a half-dozen old hags with yellowed skin, bony torsos and shriveled breasts, asking us to portray youth and beauty. Instead of attempting to pin a fabric of imagination upon such skeletons, I used to search out the more beautiful of the cocottes of the night cafes, and bring with me to the studio the next day memories and hurried sketches of poses in which I had seen them. This was more interesting, but unsatisfactory withal.

"I had been five years in the studio, and had traveled three winters to Sicily, Sardinia and Italy, before the first hint of a resolution of my problem came to me. It was in the month of July, when north-loving students take their vacations.

"I was alone in the vast studio one afternoon. Guarneresi himself was absent, which accounted for the holiday taken by the faithful who remained during the hot days. On one side of the room were the cages, where the *maestro* kept small live animals, used for models with beginners. There were a few rabbits, a dozen white mice and a red fox.

"Wandering about, near to my wits' end for inspiration to further work, I chanced to see one of the rabbits looking in my direction. Rays of sunlight, falling through the open skylight, caught the beast's eyes in such a manner that they showed to me as round discs of *glowing scarlet.*

"Never had I witnessed this phenomenon before, which I since had learned is common. It had an extraordinary effect upon me. In that second I thought of my delinquent boyhood, of dozens of cruel impulses since practically forgotten—of the mutilated, dying beetles which had been instrumental in embarking me upon an art career.

"Blood rose in torrents to my own temples. A fever consumed me. There was life and *there could be death.* I could renew the inspiration of those tortured beetles."

∼

"WITH AGITATED STEALTH, I glanced out into the empty hallway, locked the door of the studio, drew four shades over windows through which I might be seen, and crept to the rabbit cage.

"Opening it, I seized by the long ears the white-furred animal which had stared at me. The warm softness of it palpitating body raised my artistic desire to a frenzy. I pulled a table from the wall, and holding down the animal upon it I drew my knife. Overcoming the mad, futile struggles of the rabbit, I slit long incisions in the white back and belly. The blood welled out...

"Perfect fury of delight sent me to my canvas. My fingers trembled as I mixed the colors, but there was no indecision now, and no hint of muddiness in the result. I painted....

"You perhaps have seen a reproduction of that picture? It was called "THE LUSTS OF THE MAGI," and now hangs in one of the Paris galleries. Some day it will grace the Louvre. And all because our white rabbit had sacrificed it heart's blood.

"At eleven next morning Guarneresi himself, coming to the studio, found me exhausted and asleep upon the floor. When he demanded explanations, I pointed in silence to the finished picture upon my easel.

"I thought the man would go frantic. He regarded it for an instant, with intolerance fading from his bearded face. Then his mouth gaped open, and a succession of low exclamations in his native tongue came forth. His raised hands opened and shut in the gesture I knew to mean unrestrained delight.

"Suddenly he dashed to the easel, and, before I could offer resistance, he snatched down my picture and ran with it out of the studio and down the stairs into the narrow street. I followed, but I was not swift enough. He had disappeared.

"In half an hour he returned with four brother artists who had studios nearby. The others were more than lavish in their praise, terming my picture the greatest masterpiece turned out in the Quarter for years. Guarneresi himself was less demonstrative now, but I detected tears in his eyes when he turned to me.

"'The pupil has become the master,' he said simply. 'Go! I did not teach you this, and I cannot teach you more. Always I shall boast, however, that Signor Pemberton painted his first great picture in my studio.'

"The next day I rented a studio of my own and moved out my effects immediately. I started to paint in earnest. There is little to relate of the next few months. A wraith of the inspiration which had given birth to my great picture still lingered, but I was no better than mediocre in my work. True the experience and accomplishment had improved me somewhat in use of color, but I learned the galling truth soon enough that never could I attain that same fervor of artistry again—unless...

"After four months of ineffectual striving—during which time I completed two unsatisfactory canvases—I yielded, and bought myself a second white rabbit. What was my horror now to discover, when I treated the beast as I had treated its predecessor, that no wild thrill of inspiration assaulted me.

"I could mix and apply colors a trifle more gaudily, yet the suffering and blood of this animal had lost its potent effect upon me. After a day or two the solution occurred. *Lusts of The Magi* had exhausted the stimulus which rabbits could furnish.

"Disconsolate now, I allowed my work to flag. Though I knew in my heart that the one picture I had done was splendid in its way, I hated to believe that in it I had reached the peak of artistic production. Yet I could arouse in myself no more than the puerile enthusiasm for methodical slapping on of oils I so ridiculed in other mediocre painters. Finally I stopped altogether, and gave myself over to a fit of depression, absinthe and cigarettes.

"Guarneresi visited me one day, and finding me so badly in the dumps prescribed fresh air and sunshine. As I refused flatly to travel, knowing my ailment to be of the subjective sort, not cured by glimpses of pastures new, he lent me his saddle mare, a fine black animal with white fetlocks and a star upon her forehead. I agreed listlessly to ride her each day.

"Three weeks slipped by. I had kept my promise—actually enjoying the exercise—but without any of the beneficent results appearing. I was in fair physical health—only a trifle listless—it is true, yet whenever I set myself to paint a greater inhibition of spiritual and mental weariness seemed to hold me back. Little by little, the ghastly conviction forced itself upon me that as an artist I had shot my bolt.

"One day, when I was riding a league or two beyond Passy, I had occasion to dismount and slake my thirst at a spring on which it was necessary to break a thin crust of ice. Drinking my fill I led the mare to the spot, and she drank also. I raising her head, however, a sharp edge of ice cut her tender skin the distance of a quarter inch. There, as I watched, *I saw red drops of blood gather on her cheek.*

"I cannot describe adequately the sensations that gripped me! In that second I remembered the beetles and the rabbit; and I *knew* that this splendid animal had been given to me for no purpose other than to renew the wasted inspiration within me. It was the hand of Providence."

∽

"Preparations soon were made. I obtained the use of a spacious well-lighted barn in the vicinity, and put the mare therein while I returned to Paris for canvases and materials. Then, when I was all ready for work, I hobbled the mare with strong ropes, and tied her so she could not budge. Then I treated her as I had treated the rabbit.

"Deep down I hated to inflict this pain, for I had grown to care for that mare almost as one cares for a dear friend; but the fury of artistic desire would not be denied.

"Next day, when all was over, I took the canvas in to Paris and showed it to Guarneresi. He went into ecstasies, proclaiming that I had reawakened, indeed. Yet when I told him of the mare and offered to pay his own price, he became very white of countenance and drew himself up, shuddering.

"'Any but as great a man as yourself, Signor,' he shrilled, his cracked old voice breaking with emotion, 'I should *kill* for that. Yourself are without the law which would damn another, but *not* outside the sphere of undying hatred. You are great, but awful. *Go!*'

"I found, then, that no one wished to look at my picture. Guarneresi had told the story to sympathetic friends, and it had spread like a fire in spruce throughout the Quarter. I was ostracized, deserted by all who had called me their friend.

"A month later, nearly broken in spirit, I came to New York. I was done with Paris. Here in America none knew the story of my last painting, and when it was put on exhibition the critics heralded it as greater far than the finest production of any previous or contemporary American artist. I sold it for twenty thousand dollars, which was a good price in those days.

"I was swept up on a tide of popularity. As you know, in this country even the poorest works of a popular man are snatched up avidly. Criticism seems to die when once a reputation is attained. I got rid of all the canvases I had painted in Paris, and was besieged for portrait sittings by society women of the city.

"Because I had no particular idea in mind for my next painting I did allow myself to drift into this work. It was easy and paid immensely well. Also I was called upon to exercise no ingenuity or imagination. All I did was paint them as they came, two a week, and get rich, wasting five years in the process.

"Then I fell in love. Beatrice was much younger than myself, just turned nineteen at the time. I was first attracted to her because my eye always seeks out the beautiful in face and form as if I were choosing models among all the women I meet.

"She was slim of waist and of ankle, though with the soft curve of neck and shoulder which intrigues an artist instantly. She was more mature in some ways than one might have expected of her years—but the more delightful for that reason.

"Her eyes were dark pools rippled by the breeze of each passing fancy. The moment I looked into them I knew that wrench of the heart which bespeaks the advent of the one great emotion. Many times before I had thought myself in love, yet in company of Beatrice I wondered at my self-deception. In the evening, as she sat beside me in a nook of Sebastian's Spice Gardens—you know, the great indoor reproduction of the famous gardens of Kandy, Ceylon—I gloried in her beauty, and in the way soft silk clung to her person. The desire for possession was intolerable within me. Before parting I asked her, and for answer she lifted her soft, white arms to my neck and met my lips with a caress in which I felt the whole fervor of love. That was the sweetest and happiest moment of my life.

"We married, and built ourselves a home upon Long Island. After three months of honeymoon we settled there, more than ever in love with each other if that were possible.

"A year sped by. Ten months of this I spent without lifting a brush to canvas. It was idyllic, yet toward the last a sense of shame began to pervade my mind. Was I of such weak fibre that the love of one woman must stamp out all ambition, all desire for accomplishment?

"At the end of the year I was painting again, making portraits. The long rest and happiness had made me impatient with such piffle, however. I had all the money that either of us could need in our lifetime, so I could not take the portraiture seriously. I dabbled with it another full year, without once endeavoring to start a serious piece of work.

"Then, after Beatrice bore me a daughter, I began to lay plans for continuing serious endeavor. It is useless to repeat the story of those struggles. It was the same experience I had had after that first successful picture.

"My technique now was as near perfection as I could hope to attain, and the mere matter of color mixing I had learned from those two wild flights of frenzy. I found myself, however, psychologically unable to attack a subject smacking in the least of the gruesome—and that, of course, always had been my talent and interest."

∼

"I REBELLED against the instinct which urged me to try the experiment of the mare again. In cold blood I hated the thought of it, and also I feared, with a great sinking of the heart, that I should find no more inspiration there even if I did repeat.

"I turned to landscape painting, choosing sordid, dirty or powerful scenes. I painted the fish-and-milk carts on Hester Street, showing the hordes of dirty urchins in the background playing on the pavement. Somehow, the picture fell short of being really good, although I had no difficulty in selling it.

"I portrayed, then, a street in the Ghetto on a rainy night, with greasy mud shining on the cobblestones and the shapeless figure of a man slouched in a doorway. This was called powerful—the 'awakening of an American Franz Hals' one critic termed it—but I knew better. Beside the work I *could* do under powerful stimulus and inspiration, this was slush, slime. I *hated* it!

"Even waterscapes did not satisfy. I painted half of one picture depicting two sooty, straining tugs bringing a great leviathan of a steamer into harbor, but this I never finished. I felt as if I drooled at the mouth while I was working.

"Thus two more years went by, happy enough when I was with Beatrice, but sad and savage when I was by myself in the studio. My wife had blossomed early into the full beauty of womanhood, and yet she retained enough of modesty and reticence of self that I never wearied of her. Because up to this time, when I turned thirty-three years of age, the powers of both of us, physical and mental, had been on the increase, we still were exploring the delights of love and true affection.

"There was an impelling force within me, however, which would not be denied. I had been born to accomplish great things. Weak compromise, or weaker yielding to delights of the mind and body, could but heap fresh fuel on the flame which consumed me when I got off by myself. I fought against it months longer, but in the end I had to yield. With fear and trepidation struggling with ambition and lust within me. I took a trip to a distant town of New York State, procured a fine, blooded mare, and repeated the experiment which had lost me the friendship of Guarneresi and my Parisian contemporaries.

"All in vain. Out of the hideous slaughter of the animal I obtained only a simple grim picture—a canvas which I painted weeks later, when the shudder of revulsion in my frame had died down somewhat. I called the picture 'CANNIBALISM,' for it showed African savages gorging themselves on human flesh. It never sold, for the instant I placed it on exhibition the art censors of New York threw it under ban—and, I believe, no one really wanted the thing in his house.

"I did not like it myself, and finally, after much urging by my wife, I burned it. This sacrifice, however, merely accentuated the fury in my heart. I *must* do better than that!

"Since I have told you of my other periods of frenzy and self-hatred, I may pass over the ensuing month. One day the inspiration for my last great picture came, and as with the second, through pure accident. Beatrice was cutting weeds in the garden with a sickle, while I sat cross-legged beside her, watching. I always could find surcease from discontent in being near her, and watching the fine play of animal forces in her supple body.

"The sickle slipped. Beatrice cried out, and I jumped to place a handkerchief over the wound that lay open on her wrist, but not before my eyes had caught the sight of the red blood bubbling out upon her satiny skin.

"A madness leaped into my soul. My fingers trembled and a throbbing made itself felt in my temples as I laved on antiseptic and bound a bandage over the wound. This was the logical, the inevitable conclusion! She was my mate; she was in duty bound to furnish inspiration for the picture I must paint, my *masterpiece*."

∽

"I OF COURSE, told Beatrice nothing of what was passing in my mind, but went immediately about my preparations.

"I placed a cot in the studio, fastening strong straps to it. Then I made ready a gag, and sharpened a keen Weiss knife I possessed until its edge would cut a hair at a touch. Last I made ready my canvas.

"She came at my call. At first, when I seized her and tore off her clothing she thought me joking, and protested, laughing. When I came to placing the gag, and bound her arms and legs with strong straps, however, the terror of death began to steal into her dark eyes.

"To show her that I loved her still, no matter what duty impelled me to do, I kissed her hair, her eyes, her breast. Then I set to work...

"In a few minutes I was away and painting as I never had painted before. A red stream dripped from the steel cot, down to the floor, and ran slowly toward where I stood. It elated me. I felt the fire of a fervor of inspiration greater than ever had beset me. I painted. *I painted!* This was my masterpiece.

"Drunk with the fury of creation, I threw myself on the floor in the midst of the red puddle time and time again. I even dipped my brushes in it. Made with the delight of unstinted accomplishment, I kept on and on, until late in the evening I heard my little daughter crying in her room for the dinner she had not received. Then I went downstairs, laughing at the horror I saw in the faces of the servants.

"They found Beatrice, of course. The servants 'phoned immediately for the police. I fooled them all, however. I knew that they might do something to me, such is the lack of understanding against which true artists always must labor, so I took the canvas of my masterpiece and hid it in a secret cupboard in the wall known only to myself. I did not care what they did to me, but this picture, for which Beatrice had offered up her love and life, was sacred.

"They came and took me away. Then ensued a terrible scandal, and some foolish examinations of me in which I took not the slightest interest. And then they put me here.

"I have not been in duress all the tie, though. Oh, no! Three years later some of my old friends contrived at escape, and secreted me away to the South Seas. There they gave me a studio, meaning to allow me to paint. I was guarded, though. They would not allow me full freedom.

"I painted, but I have not the slightest idea what was done with those canvases. I had no interest in them personally. All I could think of now was the one great masterpiece hidden in the cupboard of my old studio. I wanted to see it, to glory in the flame of color and in the tremendous conception itself."

∼

"At last I gave my guards the slip, and after long wandering about in native proas, made my way to this country again, to New York. I found the canvas, and, rolling it, secreted it upon my person. Then I went out and gave myself up to them. I was brought here again.

"Imprisonment was not important to me any more. I was getting old. Though I would like to be released now it is a matter of less urgency than before, because I have with me always my masterpiece. *See!*"

The old man tugged at something inside his blouse, and brought forth a dirtied roll which he unsnapped with fingers that trembled in eagerness.

"See, Madame!" he repeated triumphantly.

And, before my horrified eyes, he unrolled *a blank square of white canvas!*

THE AFFAIR OF THE MAN IN SCARLET, BY JULIAN KILMAN

DO YOU WANT A SLICE OF LIFE FROM THE THIRTEENTH CENTURY? IF SO, DON'T FAIL TO READ

Two French peasants, the one young, the other old and hale and toothless, both carrying baskets and garbed in ragged breeches and tunics, gaped at the pair of horses struggling to haul the closed coach up the steep incline in Angouleme Wood.

At the instant it seemed as if the animals were about to fail. The driver, a sober youth in drab livery with undecipherable shoulder insignia, used his whip mercilessly. The lash cracked, the horses plunged frantically, while a stream of invective sped from the driver's lips.

"You pair of oafs!" he cried, finally. "Lend a hand."

The peasants willingly put shoulder to wheel. The coach gained way and topped the rise. As it do so, the two peasants set out at a run, their baskets bobbing, but a shout came from behind.

"'Ware the road, ye clodhoppers!"

The clatter of horse hoofs was upon them, they were just able to fling themselves to the side as three horsemen, presumable outriders of the equipage ahead, swept by.

The peasants gazed in admiration after the flashing figures.

"That'll be good Kind Philippe's riders," announced André, the younger. "Mark ye the emblems on their jackets?"

"I do that," returned Jacques, the light of understanding in his ancient eyes. "Methinks I know what brings them to the village of Peptonneau."

"And, pray, what is it that brings them to the village of Peptonneau?"

"They come to the Man in Scarlet."

At mention of the official headsman, who years before had come from near Fontainebleau to reside in Peptonneau. Jacques companion fell silent.

The old man chuckled.

"Ah! They were gay days when your old Jacques was a gardener at the royal palace. And be it known to you, lout of Peptonneau," Jaques' voice rose, "that my best friend then was old Capeluche, the very father of our neighbor headsman, who to be sure is a man of ugly temper, and hence giving easy understanding as to why he lost favor at Fontainebleau.

"Ah me!" sighed Jacques. "You, André, should have heard the rare stories told by old Capeluche, the son of the son of the son of the son of a headsman, unto four generations. A proper man with the sword, forsooth! There was the Duc de la Trémouille whom old Capeluche led to the block and permitted to begin the Lord's prayer, but when the noble duke got as far as '*et nos inducas intentationem*' he had drawled it so slowly that the good Capeluche, losing patience, swung his blade and made such a clean stroke of it that the head, though severed, remained in exact place while from the lips the prayer continued—'*Sed libera nos a malo*'—until the faithful Capeluche nudged the body and the head toppled off.

"A wonderful man, one may say," continued Jacques, "but a wonderful weapon, too, and the same one now resting with the Capeluche in Peptonneau. Old Capeluche told me that on one occasion, when Madam Bonacieux, a famous lady-in-waiting—now dead, may the Saints preserve her!—brought her baby to his house, the sword rattled furiously in its closet, which was an omen that the child would some day die by the self-same sword wielded by the right arm of a Capeluche unless then and there Madam Bonacieux allowed her baby's neck to be pricked by the point of the sword until blood showed."

"And did Madam Bonacieux permit it?" asked André curiously.

"That she did not," replied Jacques. "She laughed in old Capeluche's face and ran out of his house, and thereat the old man was furious, vowing that the child would some day have its neck severed by the famous sword."

∽

WHILE THUS ENGAGED IN CONVERSATION, old Jacques had steadily led the way by a short cut through the wood, which presently brought them out of breath to the village, ahead of the coach and horses.

The village of Peptonneau was small, having less than a thousand inhabitants, its houses being of stone, and built close together in the manner of the gregarious Latin. Most striking of these structures in their uniformity was one near the center square painted a brilliant red.

In the clear sunshine of that Thirteenth Century July day, the dwelling stood out like a veritable lighthouse, and thither, giving no heed to the leper who passed in the opposite direction, fingerless, noseless, the bell at his neck ringing dolefully, the two peasants complacently padded their barefoot way.

A tall, lean, but well-thewed individual in leather jerkin and girdle, lounged in front of the house of red. With cynical eyes he viewed the approach of the peasants.

"In five minutes M. Capeluche," announced Jacques, a trifle breathlessly, "a coach and riders will arrive."

"And you, old cock, trot hither from your berry-picking to tell me that bit of famous gossip?"

"Ay! I'm an old cock, and many years have passed o'er my head, Monsieur, but it is a head not destined to be removed by a Capeluche, nor yet by the son of a Capeluche."

"Sirrah! Daily I give thanks to the Holy Virgin," retorted the headsman, "that the delicate skill of a Capeluche is not for the hairy necks of such *canaille* as you."

"Who knows," sturdily replied Jacques, "as to the quality or quantity of hair on the neck of one who draws near in yonder coach?"

The grunt that left the headsman betrayed his interest. He peered down the road.

"What do you mean by that?"

Old Jacques permitted himself a toothless grin. It was not often that a Peptonneau villager could stir the equanimity of the great one, whose prerogatives of office entitled him to tithes exacted from towns and monasteries as ruthlessly as those of prince or baron.

"The coach, Monsieur," the loquacious Jacques continued with satisfaction, "is accompanied by three outriders; they are men of the Divine Philippe's, Monsieur, recently returned from 'The Foolish Wars', and wearing on the shoulders of their tunics the sign of the cross, together with—"

"A falcon in full flight?" quickly broke in the headsman.

"Even so, M. Capeluche. A falcon in full—Now, *regardez vous*, the great man is himself in full flight!"

If the headsman had in truth rather precipitately taken himself into his dwelling, his absence was of short duration, for he returned in a moment, clad in a scarlet cloak that reached to his knees.

At the instant there sounded the call of a bugle, and into sight swung three horsemen, followed by the coach driven at breakneck speed.

M. Capeluche took a position midway of the road and presently caught the heads of the horses drawing the coach. His black eyes snapped fire as he noted the quivering flanks of the hard-driven animals.

"High honor you do me, M. le Headsman," cried the driver, leaping to the ground and clapping the palms of his hands against his breeches to relieve them of perspiration.

"No honor to you, you puling son of an ass," retorted Capeluche, crossly.

"Hear the Man in Scarlet!"

The tallest of the horsemen, a devil-may-care appearing young man whose finely-chiseled features and delicate raiment proclaimed him of noble blood, now steppe to the side of the coach and unlocked the door and opened it.

A surpassingly beautiful woman of perhaps twenty-two years, sat within. She had the totally unexpected air of pretty surprise. As she descended, accepting with dainty grace the proffer of the gallant's arm, her wide-set blue eyes were dazzled by the brilliance of the midday light.

"Thank you, Comte de Mousqueton," she murmured.

With is charge, the Comte then approached the headsman, who stood with arms akimbo, his sharp eyes on the newcomers.

"M. Capeluche," said the Comte, graciously. "The Royal Master sends this day the body of Mlle. Bonacieux. These papers, sir, are your warrant. Please to scan them at once."

"The portent! The Portent!" cried a voice from the crowd of rustics.

"Who shouts?" demanded Capeluche, looking about him fiercely, while a silence fell.

With a nod that gave scant heed to the etiquette of the occasion, the headsman accepted the beribboned parchment and ripped open the cover. The writ was of interminable length and inscribed in Latin. A glance, however, at the familiar "Now, therefore," clause at the end quickly apprised Capeluche of his commission, and without a word he turned to enter his house.

"One moment," said the Comte.

The headsman paused, scowling.

"Where, M. Capeluche, are we to lodge the prisoner in the interim?"

A sardonic smile suddenly played on the features of Capeluche.

"In Peptonneau, Comte de Mousqueton," he said, "you will please to understand that since the days of the plague there has been no inn."

The glance of the Man in Scarlet now shifted to the dilapidated, unoccupied structures on either side of his own dwelling.

"These are the only vacant houses in Peptonneau, their emptiness, of a truth, due to the fact that they stand next to the dwelling of red. Of these two you may choose freely, sir."

The crowd dispersed.

"Ho! Ho!" broke in a familiar voice. "There'll be no hair on the neck of Mlle. Bonacieux to dull the edge of M. Capeluche's good sword."

~

It was near dark before the youthful Comte, after his discourteous reception by the headsman, was able to arrange suitable quarters in one of the deserted houses for his charge. As he was leaving her for the night, he seemed to reach a decision and was about to speak when she anticipated him.

"You are kind, indeed, M. le Comte," she exclaimed, "to one in such misfortune."

"Kindness, Mlle. Bonacieux, come easily when one views beauty in distress."

Mlle. Bonacieux shook her head reprovingly.

"Ah, Comte, to one whose tenure of existence is limited by a bit of parchment to ten hours the occasion does not seem fitting for mere compliment."

"The occasion, Mademoiselle, is not entirely unpropitious if one considers all the possibilities."

The woman gave him a quick look.

"To just what, pray, does the Comte de Mousqueton refer?"

The young Frenchman paced the room, giving signs of a state of tension. Then he began to speak rapidly:

"The Mlle. Bonacieux, some of us feel at the court, has been ill treated both by the King and the Dauphin. The King, by his gratuitous harshness, and the Dauphin, by his, his—"

The Comte hesitated. The keenly intelligent gaze of the woman interrogated him.

"Proceed, M. le Comte," she encouraged.

"Will it be permitted a mere Comte to speak frankly of the prince?"

"By all means."

"Then I shall dare to say, by the lack of knowledge and perspicacity of the Dauphin."

In spite of herself, a flush stole into the face of the woman.

"Ah! You are naïve!!" she exclaimed, in pain. "Cruelly so."

"Nay, Mademoiselle. It is not naïveté in the circumstances, for I have a definite plan to defeat the machinations of the Cardinal."

In amazement the woman stared at her companion.

"But how—" she began.

"Listen, Mademoiselle. Everyone, it seems, including both the King and the Dauphin, have forgotten the ancient Merovingian statute, which provides that a woman sentenced to death may, if the headman is 'able and willing' to marry her, be saved. Now, M. le headsman, if a boor, has at least the temporarily strategic advantage of being a celibate. It remains merely for you to captivate the gentleman's fancy, and—who knows?"

The Comte now glanced with interest at his beautiful prisoner. She was smiling.

"Very prettily thought M. le Comte," she said, "and your interest in my cause is flattering. But is not death itself preferable to life with yon crimson-handed churl as a wife whose only contact with her neighbors would be in the night-tie, when they came stealing to buy from her horrid amulets with which to curse their enemies?"

"Ah, but who said that Mlle. Bonacieux would be compelled to endure life with a headsman?"

"Surely it is not to be expected," remarked the woman, "that the headsman would be gallant enough to release me immediately after the ceremony?"

A short laugh broke from the Comte.

"No fear of that. My purpose is to relieve him of his bridegroom embarrassment within ten minutes after he has a wife."

"Ah! A rescue! You, a King's Messenger, would dare that for me?"

"And why not?"

"But why should you?"

The Comte's face flushed slightly.

"One who loves would not regard such an enterprise as a peril."

The eyes of the woman kindled. She approached the Comte. He caught her hand and kissed it.

"Trust in the Comte de Mousqueton," he breathed.

∾

IT WAS LATE when the Comte came from the prison house. The village seemed asleep, but another than himself was abroad. The figure of a man in a cloak was issuing from the neighboring house.

"You walk late, M. Capeluche," said the Comte. "But it is well, for Mlle. Bonacieux wishes to speak with you."

The headsman stopped abruptly to peer into the eyes of the young nobleman. The act was insolent.

"Is M. le Comte," he inquired, coldly, "sufficiently in the confidence of his fair prisoner to advise me what it is she desires?"

"The man is steel," thought the Comte, hotly. "I'll kill him yet." Aloud, he said: "I have some idea, M. Capeluche. But I may not allude to it."

The headsman fell silent.

"Closer examination of the writ," he went on, finally, "shows that it is curiously indefinite in its recital as to the offense of which Mlle. Bonacieux has been guilty."

The Comte laughed easily.

"M. de Briseout will be pleased to hear that the discriminating Capeluche has so found it."

"And who is de Briseout?"

"The ingenious special pleader employed by the Cardinal to prepare the document. It is a work of art."

"Then I can not be mistaken in assuming that one as clever as the Comte de Mousqueton and so recently come from Fontainebleau will be able to tell me the real nature of the case."

The young nobleman was able to smile in the dark at the discernment of this strange man of blood.

"'Tis a proper question, M. Capeluche," he returned. "Be it known to you, therefore, that no less a person that the Dauphin himself entertains the liveliest of sentiments toward Mlle. Bonacieux. The Cardinal, however, through his spies, early learned of the infatuation of the prince and privately remonstrated with him on the score that the mésalliance would definitely imperil the consummation of his proposed nuptials with Katharine of Austria, which, in turn, might embroil the two nations in war.

"But the Dauphin resented ecclesiastical interference. This aroused the ire of His Eminence, who straightway went to King Philippe. The net result is that the Dauphin has been dispatched on a tedious expedition to Sicilia, and I am ordered to convey the pretty person of Mlle. Bonacieux to you for decapitation."

The two men resumed their walking.

"And this, then, you think," came from the headsman, "accounts both for the ambiguity of the writ's phraseology as well as the fact that Mlle. Bonacieux is spirited hither instead of being left to the hand of the headman at Fontainebleau?"

"Undoubtedly, M. Capeluche."

The headsman started away abruptly, in the manner of a man whose mind is suddenly made up. A light still burned in Mlle. Bonacieux's quarters and he tapped at the door.

"Who is it?" called the woman.

"One whom you wished to see."

"Please come in, M. Capeluche."

Mlle. Bonacieux was in truth chilled by the grim expression of the man who now stood composedly studying her; but she gave no sign. Instead, her eyes were sparkling and she was a vision of loveliness as she reclined on the couch that had been provided for her by the Comte.

"An unpleasant business—for both of us, M. le Headsman," she commented.

"There are many persons in *your* position who would so regard it," bluntly agreed the headsman.

"I shall not dissemble, M. le Headsman. I do not desire to die tomorrow."

"Is it for this that you have sent for me?"

The woman laughed.

"Yes, and no, Monsieur," she returned. "It has but recently been mentioned to me that an ancient law is still in effect and has a certain bearing—"

She paused, glancing with studied carelessness at the headsman.

"The Comte de Mousqueton is a very clever fellow," remarked Capeluche, dryly. "What is it he has to say of this old law?"

"That it seems a pity to miss a perfectly legitimate opportunity both to accomplish a humanitarian act and so defeat the machinations of an interfering Italian Cardinal."

Capeluche's features for the first time relaxed into a smile.

"And Mlle. Bonacieux, therefore, of the two evils—death or a headsman—is willing to choose the latter?"

"You put it so bluntly, M. le Headsman," she sighed. "There can be compensations on either hand. If, for instance, the headsman surrenders his celibacy to a pretty woman, it is not inconceivable that she may reciprocate by surrendering her jewels to him."

"On condition?"

In sincere surprise, Mlle. Bonacieux glanced up.

"Your perspicacity is gratifying, Monsieur," she exclaimed. "The condition, suggested by you, is that immediately after the ceremony Madam Capeluche be released and permitted to journey back to Fontainebleau with the Comte de Mousqueton."

The gleaming eyes of the man told much—or little. He approached the reclining beauty.

"Mlle. Bonacieux," he said. "The Merovingian statute is still law, being, in fact, the very write that directs my hand in your case."

For an instant he stood over her.

"The Abbé Kérouec," he added harshly, "will wed us two tomorrow, five minutes before seven in the evening, the hour fixed by the writ for your death."

∼

Shortly after six o'clock next evening old Jacques stole from the Angouléme wood and fell in step immediately behind a man garbed in a long close-fitting black coat with skirts that fell to his feet. This individual was making his way with painful slowness along the road to Peptonneau.

For the space of a minute Jacques followed in silence, his old nutcracker face full of preliminary guile. Then he pushed forward.

"It is a fine day, good father," he shouted.

In surprise the old man surveyed him.

"Ay, a fine day, Jacques, you godless one," he replied in the toneless voice of the deaf.

"But the clemency of the weather is not for the delectation of the young beauty from Fontainebleau now lodged in Peptonneau."

The Abbé Kérouec inclined his head. He was exceedingly deaf and had not heard.

Jacques swore heartily. At the top of his lungs he shouted:

"Bad weather for her who dies at seven this evening by the hand of M. Capeluche."

The light of comprehension came into the features of the ancient Abbé.

"Ah, my good fellow, you mistake. I come to M. Capeluche's dwelling on a more gracious mission than to shrive the soul of one condemned by the King's Writ."

It was Jacques' turn to be surprised.

"Ha! Say you that Mlle. Bonacieux is not to die this eve?"

The Abbe's eyes showed that he understood.

"That I say, indeed, Jacques. You and I be old men and we have seen much, but never before has anyone in our generation in all France and her possessions witnessed that which is about to occur in modest little Peptonneau."

"And what is that?" sharply demanded Jacques.

"The wedding of M. Capeluche, the headsman, to Mlle. Bonacieux, the condemned."

Jacques threw back his head and laughed till the tears rolled down his cheeks.

"That indeed is droll!" he shouted. "M. le Headsman weds a woman and then immediately cuts off her head."

The owl-like eyes of the Abbé regarded Jacques solemnly.

"You do not know the full import of what I have told you, Jacques."

The old peasant sobered instantly.

"What's that?"

"Then you have never heard of the Merovingian statute which provides that the headsman may marry a condemned woman, if he is able and willing, and thereby save her life?"

"Ah! Ah! Ah!" came from Jacques, his small eyes opening and shutting with lightning rapidity. "Thus it proceeds, eh? M. le Headsman surrenders to the charms of the beautiful Mlle. Bonacieux. He plans to take her to wife. Is not the situation amusing?"

Suddenly he shook the arm of the old Abbé.

"But it can not be, Abbé Kérouec," he exclaimed vociferously. "I knew the worthy M. Capeluche at Fontainebleau. He was a friend of mine, and the father of the headsman in Peptonneau, and he confided in me that on a certain occasion a lady-in-waiting one day brought her child to the dwelling in red, whereupon the Capeluche sword rattled furiously in its closet, which meant, of an absolute surety, that the child, unless its neck was pricked by the point of the sword, would some day die by that sword. That woman bore the name of Bonacieux, and now, after eighteen years, old Jacques lives to see Mlle. Bonacieux, the child grown to womanhood, awaiting her death under the famous sword in the hands of a Capeluche."

Jacques paused for breath. The old Abbé had endeavored to follow the harangue of the peasant.

"Understand? A portent!" shouted Jacques, in desperation. "Mlle. Bonacieux is to die tonight by the sword of the headsman, Capeluche."

"Nay! Nay! Jacques," in turn exclaimed the Abbé. "I know not of what you prate, save that it be Godless. But there will be a wedding in Peptonneau this eve, and no woman will die by the hand of Capeluche."

~

A THRONG HAD GATHERED before the house in red by the time the Abbé and his companion Jacques made their way along the village street. The Comte met them. He was in doublet and hose of violet color with aiguillettes of same, having the customary slashes through which the shirt appeared. The dress was handsome, albeit it gave evidence of having been but recently taken from a traveler's box, which had left it in creases.

"We have little time," he said.

He left them, but returned presently with Mlle. Bonacieux, and at sight of her unusual beauty, accompanied by so graceful a figure as the Comte, a murmur of appreciation stirred the rustic spectators.

With the Abbé preceding them, the little party passed into the red dwelling. M. Capeluche, in the cloak of his office, stood awaiting them. The Abbé he treated with marked deference, a manner that sat oddly on him. As a man beyond the pale of both church and society, because of his calling, Capeluche had experienced some doubt as to whether the worthy churchman would perform the ceremony.

As affairs went forward, his face retained its customary grim composure; but his eyes, resting on the entrancing creature who stood demurely at his side, held a light that fully signified his reaction to the potentialities of the occasion.

An hour passed, and old Jacques lay on his bed. He was fully dressed and wakeful and alert, despite the fact that his retiring-time had long since gone by. Presently there came to him the sound of approaching hoof beats.

With the restless activity of a jack-in-the-box, he ran from his house and was in time to see the horseman dash up to the dwelling of Capeluche. The riders, of whom there were seven, wore masks. They pounded for admittance.

A light showed within, and old Jacques could see, through an open window, the headsman. He was making all secure against the attack. However, a window to the right—one that had just been closed—was reopened unexpectedly, and a woman's hand extended. From it there fluttered a handkerchief. Two of the horsemen started toward the open window. But the hand was withdrawn swiftly, and a terrible shriek followed.

A moment later the door gave way. The attacking party hurtled into the dwelling stumbling over one another.

An appalling sight was before them. In the center of the room stood Capeluche, a scarlet Mephisto. His hands held the cleanly severed head of Mlle. Bonacieux, her beautiful tresses of hair depending almost to the floor. At his feel lay the long weapon of his office.

He extended the head before him.

"Perhaps," he said grimly, "the Comte de Mousqueton would relish a kiss from the lips of Madame Capeluche, the wife of a headsman. She was very choice of those same lips—a Dauphin has felt them. And see! See how deliciously cupid they are!"

Suddenly Jacques' voice broke in.

"Before God!" exclaimed the old peasant, with tremendous satisfaction. "*The portent!*"

THE HIDEOUS FACE, BY VICTOR JOHNS
A GRIM TALE OF FRIGHTFUL REVENGE

Marseilles, one hears while traveling through Europe, is the most vicious town in France. Whether or not this ancient seaport, whose history reaches deep into the shadows of antiquity, is deserving of a criticism so sweeping and so condemnatory, I do not know. Such, at any rate, is the reputation it suffers among travelers.

All roads in Marseilles lead to La Cannebiere, a street of splendid cafés. Being a sort of hyphen that connects the waterfront with the fashionable hotels and shops of the Rue Noailles, it swarms with a curious blend of dregs and pickings. Up from the Quai de la Fraternité come sailors hungry for the pleasures a few hours' shore leave will offer; Algerian troops, on their way to Africa, jostle English soldiers back from India; adventurers and *le monde élégant*, pausing in flight to or from the Riviera, and the inevitable Magdalena, spatter its length with color and charge it with restlessness.

Late one afternoon last winter I drifted through this famous thoroughfare, looking for a place among the tables that edge its pavements. It had become my habit to sit for half an hour before dinner somewhere along the street, drink an appetizer, and expect the crowd to entertain me. The rows of iron chairs were filled with earlier comers, who sat contentedly behind their *aperitifs* or cups of chocolate, but at last, in front of the Café de l'Univers, I found a vacant back row table, which I quickly possessed. With a glass of *vermouth cassis* on the table beside me, I yielded to the lure of seaport excitement.

My thoughts were soon interrupted, however, by an American voice asking in French if the other chair at my table was taken. I turned to assure the gentleman it was not, that he was in no way intruding—and I looked into the face of Lawrence Bainridge.

"Hello, Bayard," was his casual greeting. A bit too casual, I thought, considering the fact that we had not seen each other for nearly two years.

I, contrariwise, must fairly have gasped, "Good Lord! What are you doing here?" for, as he swung the unoccupied chair about and sat down, he said,

"Well, what's so strange about meeting me on La Cannebiére?"

There was nothing strange about it; and I wondered at the amazement which so energetically had voiced itself. A rich, itinerant artist, Lawrence had zig-zagged several times around the world to paint unknown by-ways and hidden corners. Astonishment at meeting him in Marseilles was therefore absurd. Also, I felt he might construe my lack of *savoir faire* as a blunt refusal to play up to his well-known and fondly-cherished reputation as a globe trotter. He was childish in certain respects—artists are.

The waiter quickly fetched a champagne cocktail and a package of English cigarettes. The cocktail Lawrence downed in a gulp and called for more. The second he drank with more restraint.

Though I had not seen him since two summers before—at Land's End, an isolated village in Massachusetts—our conversation was rambling and disjointed, like that of incompatible strangers who find no ease in silence. This annoyed me, for our similarity of tastes, I felt, should more than outweigh the separation.

As the late afternoon merged into early evening, the mistral blew its cold and sinister breath out to the Mediterranean. We drank steadily, Lawrence all the while jibing at me for clinging to so impotent a mixture as vermouth, currant juice and seltzer. He had reached his fifth cocktail, but through the exercise of will, apparently, was still sober. Nevertheless, he worried me.

Furtively, almost defensively, Lawrence sat in his chair. I reacted to his attitude by bracing myself against an intangible, though imminent, danger which thickened the atmosphere. He breathed jerkily, emitting from time to time a sharp clicking sound, as though part of his breathing mechanism had suddenly refused to function. Quivers ran through his body and ended in a twitch.

But he spoke with a crisp enunciation, and so precisely that each word seemed to have been scoured and weighed before utterance. On not a syllable was the checkrein loosened. I sensed a splendid effort at self-control.

I suddenly recalled the wild absurdity of Lawrence's recent work. In Paris, three months before, I had gone to his exhibition at the Vendome Galleries and left the place convinced that Lawrence Bainridge had gone stark raving mad.

"*Flowers, Messieurs!*" A flower girl, her wicker tray heaped with heavy-scented blossoms, paused before us. "No? Ah, *Messieurs*, but one little rose apiece—for luck!" she said.

Then she picked up a red rose bud and pinned it to the lapel of Lawrence's coat.

"*Ugh!* Take it away!" he screamed. "I can't stand it!" He tore the flower from his coat and hurled it into the gutter.

"Lawrence!" I reproved, "You're drunk."

"No, I'm not drunk," he protested. Contrition had subdued his voice. "But—I can't stand—the smell—of roses."

Thinking to avoid a scene, I suggested we take a walk. He said it might be a good idea, first, though, he would fill his cigarette case. A subterfuge, I told myself, to regain composure, and an obvious one. Lawrence had never been obvious.

At that moment there passed before us on the sidewalk such a ghastly thing that my scalp tingled and the flesh on my legs seemed to shrivel and fall away.

It was a man whose face was like a hideous mask; the left side—young and unblemished; but the right half—so mutilated that description would nauseate. Fair was divided from foul by a line running down the exact center of the forehead, nose and chin.

~

My exclamation of horror drew Lawrence's attention to the repellent sight. At that moment the gruesome thing turned full upon us.

Lawrence fumbled with his cigarettes: the case fell from his trembling hands and clattered to the pavement. Quickly he reached down, but did not straighten up again until after the man—a sailor, to judge from his rolling gait, though he wore no uniform—had gone.

"Poor soul," I said. "How his fingers must ache to choke the life from the *Bocke* responsible for that."

Lawrence made no reply. He was drained of blood. He sat rigid, petrified.

"In Paris and London," I continued, "one sees hundreds of *mutilés* —the war's driftwood—and I have trained myself to look unflinchingly into their eyes. But" –I glanced in the direction the sailor had disappeared—"my histrionic ability would fail me there."

Still Lawrence made no move or sound. That he was profoundly touched I knew, for a sensitiveness, abnormal in its refinement, had been his lifelong curse. It had prevented his marriage to a young woman in whom were combined, he thought at one time, all the qualities that appeal to a man of esthetic temperament.

In his studio, one afternoon, they were planning for the wedding. Lawrence recalled a newly-acquired *object d'art* and took it from a cabinet. The treasure was an exquisite bit of ancient Egyptian glass, a spherulate bowl, so delicate of line an so ethereally opalescent of color that it always made me think of a bubble poised to float away.

I can imagine how he carried it across the room—with that caressing touch of velvet-tipped fingers peculiar to artists. The young woman, in order to examine it closely, grabbed the bowl and proceeded to paw it as a prospector might a bit of rock. Lawrence said afterward that had she struck him he could not have been more shocked. He broke the engagement that afternoon.

"Come, drink up, man!" I urged. "Stop looking as though you'd seen a ghost."

"Things other than ghosts can haunt one," he answered in a pinched tone.

We ordered drinks again, with misgivings on my part, for I felt the trembling man opposite me already had had too much. He sat slumped in his chair, shoulders hunched forward, and stared straight before him. Reminiscent or speculative, I could not tell.

Then he began to tell me a story that explained many things. His words were no longer crisp; he now spoke in a heave, monotonous way, with many pauses, pressing his hands together in a gesture of anguish.

"The odor of that rose," he said, "and the sight—I can't stand the smell of roses! Not since two summers ago. I met a Portuguese sailor on the Wharf one day—you know—in that damn place—Land's End. Had planned a canvas, and all summer had been looking for a model—a type.

"A Portuguese Apollo he was—but a Portuguese devil, too. Didn't find that out till later. I stopped him and asked would he pose. Conceited swine! From his smile I knew it was vanity, not industry, that made him accept."

A venomous hate wove its way through Lawrence's phrases. He continued:

"Well—he called at my studio—the next afternoon—and I started the picture. He was a find. Dramatic. An inspiration.

"During the rest periods Pedro—that was his name—would lie on the floor and talk about himself while I made tea. God! How vain he was! Boasted of his success with women—his affairs. They were many. Quite plausible. He spurned the Bay and its fishing, and shipped on merchantmen. The ports of the world were his hunting ground, he said. Swashbuckling bully!"

To hear Lawrence speak so bitterly of Land's End and one of its people was puzzling, for the extraordinary note sounded in that small New England town by its so-called foreign settlement, descendants of Portuguese fishermen who came over some seventy years ago and settled along the New England coast, had appealed strongly to his artistic appreciation two years before. He had looked upon these natives as gentle, lovable fold, but to me their black eyes, heavy-lidded and drowsy, had always suggested smoldering fires, not dreams; their excessive tranquility I thought crafty, hinting of vendettas.

Lawrence picked up the thread of his story:

"One afternoon Pedro began talking about a Portuguese funeral in town that day. A friend of his had died. I dislike funerals—corpses and such—even the mention of them. Always have. Told him to shut up. Instead, he began to tell of an interrupted funeral in Singapore he once had seen. Spared no details. Losing patience and temper, I flung a tube of paint which struck him on the head. He was furious. I told him I was sorry.

"'Pedro,' I explained, 'ever since I can remember, things connected with death have been the only things I've feared. I have never in my life been in a cemetery—and I have never seen a dead body. Just to hear of them brings out a cold sweat.' Pedro laughed and said cemeteries—or dead bodies—couldn't hurt one."

This phase of Lawrence's susceptibility I had not known. And then his pictures in Paris danced before me. What had Pedro to do with them? What had Pedro to do with the change in my friend? But I asked no questions lest I rouse Lawrence to a stubborn silence.

I found myself fidgeting about, peering suddenly into the crowd as if to catch the gaze of hypnotic eyes. Once I saw the *mutilé* standing across the street beside a kiosk, watching Lawrence, or so I imagined, with ferocious intensity. My *vis-à-vis* and his emotional recoils had by that time become agitating companions.

Yet, in truth, there was much in his surroundings to breed thoughts of adventure, even crime. Wharf loungers and apaches were slinking among the well-dressed shoppers who drifted down from the region above. Fringing the port, only a hundred meters distant, were the dark, twisting streets of a district noted for its nefarious habits and avoided by the wary; rumors of tourists who had wandered alone at night into that abyss of lawlessness, reappearing days later on the tide, skulls crushed and pockets empty, were far too numerous to pass unheeded. Out beyond the harbor the Château d'If clung to its rocks, guarding well grim secrets of a tragic past.

～

BUT TO RETURN TO LAWRENCE.

"To blot out the Singapore funeral," he said, "I painted quickly. Makes me concentrate. Got too interested I stopped only on account of bad light. Put on my hat and left the studio—with Pedro—for a walk. Fresh air clears the brain. Must have been exhausted, for I walked along without seeing. Just followed Pedro, I suppose. A bend in the road—and I woke up—galvanized with terror.

"Before me stood the entrance to a graveyard. The stones bristled ghostly in the twilight. I halted—alert."

The stem of the glass, which Lawrence nervously had been twirling, broke, and his unfinished cocktail spilled upon the table.

"I couldn't go on—on through that forest of spectral marble. Pedro continued to walk. Was some distance ahead before he noticed I had stopped. He turned and told me to come along. I refused. He laughed—a derisive laugh—then spit out a single word—'*Coward!*'

"I've been through jungles in India. Gone deep into China where no white man had ever been. Know Calcutta—Port Said—explored the worst slums of the world—and I had never been called a coward before.

"'You don't understand, Pedro—I *can't*, I *can't* go on!' He laughed again—like a hyena.

"'Yes,' Pedro said, 'a coward. How they will laugh—when I tell!'

"Had never been called that before—you know. I began walking forward—slowly. My legs trembled, but I walked. Passed through the gate.

"'That's right,' Pedro said. 'There's nothing to be afraid of.'

"'No—nothing.' I answered, my jaws chattering.

"Then Pedro said, 'I'm going to the grave of my friend who was buried to-day and say a prayer, take a rose from his grave and dry it—

to carry in a little bag—always—for good luck. No harm comes then. *You'll* take a rose, too.'

"I saw a large mound of flowers. The air was strong with perfume. Roses....We reached the grave. Pedro stopped, knelt down and said a prayer. Shadows under the trees were black and the leaves rattled like bones. I wanted to run—but I stood beside Pedro—and shivered. Pedro took a rose from the grave and put it in his pocket. Then he took another, got up and offered it to me.

"'No!' I cried, drawing away. 'I won't touch it.'

"Pedro said, 'You've got to be cured.' He pointed to a large flat stone lying flat on the ground beside him, and explained:

"'Over a hundred years ago—you can see the date when it's light—a funny man had this grave made. Built it like a cistern. Brick walls. Look!' and he slid the stone to one side. Pedro was strong.

"I refused to look. Kept my eyes on the path. A gust of wind blew my hat against Pedro, and it fell to the ground.

"As I stooped to pick it up, he pushed me—*into the grave!*"

∾

THE HORROR of this piece of perversity got me.

"Lawrence!" I exclaimed. "You don't mean it!"

"Yes," he answered, in that new tone, so flat and spiritless. "I sank into something—soft....Pedro's laugh sounded far away, and he closed up the grave—with the stone.

"My throat was in a vice. Couldn't make a sound. Tried to gather strength for one big scream—then something somewhere in my snapped. '*Taing!*' it went, soft and little.

"Don't know how long I was there. It seemed an eternity. I loved on—with the dead man—and crawling things. I don't know. There may have been nothing at all. At last I saw a rift above—the night sky —and Pedro reached down to pull me out.

"When he came the next afternoon I told him I must rest for several days. My nerves were bad. All night I lay awake and thought

—and planned. At daybreak I fell asleep. In the afternoon I went to Boston.

"Three days later, back in Land's End, I settled my accounts. All but one. Told the neighbors I was leaving for New York next day. Gave instructions to have my things packed and shipped to me there.

"Pedro came as usual in the afternoon. I worked as though nothing had happened. He got tired and lay on the floor. I boiled some water for tea. Very, very carefully I made that tea.

"'What kind of tea is this?' Pedro asked. 'It tastes so queer.'

"'A new kind.' I told him.

"He drank, then lay back—asleep.

"From a shelf of etching materials I took a bottle. The liquid inside was clear. So harmless it looked! Poured some into a cup. Filled the cup with water, then knelt down beside the sleeping Pedro —dipped a feather into the liquid—and painted half of his handsome face. Nitric acid—bites deep...

"Pedro's groans were silenced with a gag. More tea for rest and sleep.

"The streets that night were empty as I half carried, half dragged Pedro to the shanty where he lived alone. I threw him on the bed and looked without pity on his face.

"No—there was nothing—to be afraid of, I told him. But Pedro didn't hear.

"Don Juan's career was finished. Apollo had become repulsive. My last debt was paid.

"I packed two bags and caught the early train. That afternoon I said 'Good-bye' to the islands of Boston Harbor as I steamed out for England."

Several minutes dragged past before either of us moved.

"Come, let's go," was all I could find to say.

～

I TOOK Lawrence to his hotel and left him at the entrance with a promise to call the following morning. Unable to keep the appointment, I went around during the afternoon. He was not in his room and could not be located.

Decided to take one last look about the Old Port before leaving for Paris that night, I strolled down the Rue Noailles, through La Cannebiére and the Quai de Rive Nueve, where a group of excited men were gathered at the water's edge. As I reached the crowd two sailors with grappling hooks were laying a dripping corpse on the pavement. It was the body of Lawrence Bainridge.

The right side of his face was slashed and crushed into a shapeless mass —but the left half was untouched and fair.

THE FORTY JARS, BY RAY MCGILLIVRAY
A STRANGE STORY OF THE ORIENT

The sands of Bo-hai never quite are dark.

It matters not that a blood-red, maniacal sun deserts this waste; that sullen cloud banks close in with freezing chill of midnight. A misty, spectral light yet emanates from the sand—quite as if stored-up heat and light were retained by the layers of baked, anhydrous surface. At any time sharp eyes may discern the ghostly shadow of a man who walks, even fifty yards distant.

Mad creatures people Bo-hai, creatures that burrow deep beneath the wall, from Ninghia to Langchau, coming out only for orgies of the night. Any Mongol knows that venturing alone to the salt shores of Gileshtai means joining forever the flitting horde of Nameless Ones—for lepers, and the shades of lepers centuries dead, owe no allegiance either to living law or to the kindly teachings of Tao, the All-Wise.

They gibber in tongues ranging from the twanging patois of Jesaktu to the dry gutturals of Yunnan, and take to themselves either for screaming torture or for the slower, more horrid death of the White Dissolution, all whom their distorted, clawing fingers may clutch.

Driving on and on before food robbers the roving, famished mountain bands of Nan-Shan—Selwyn Roberts had come to Bo-hai. He had not wished to come, for the excavations made by his expedition, which had proved most absorbing, lay in the neighborhood of Kulang, forty miles to the southwest.

Persistent attacks by the brigands of Nan-Shan—starving men who coveted the long train of food supplies with such frenzy of desire that even automatic rifles could not dismay them utterly—had necessitated retreat. Roberts, heading the expedition, saw that rich (in the Chinese conception), well-fed white men, bringing with them provisions for eight months' travel, could be naught save the most juicy, irresistible bait. He decided to return to headquarters in Taiyuen, thence shipping back what remained of his provisions as the greatest contribution to charity his purse could afford.

On the edge of the desert this altruistic plan met defeat. The flitting, fantastic shadows of Bo-hai accomplished by stealth and thievery what had balked the bolder spirits of Nan-Shan. Christensen and Porterfield, acting as sentinels, disappeared soundlessly—and with them all save a small remnant of provisions.

There were many tracks of bare feet in the desert—bare feet that rarely left marks of toes....No clues pointed to the direction the captives had been taken, unless scurrying footprints, criss-crossing the sands in every direction, might be considered clues.

These always ended in bare stretches of shifting sand. Their story was for the reading of a moment; next night wind and sand wiped the record clean. Though Roberts, alone now with his diggers and coolie bearers, attempted to trail the party which had come to his camp, the end of a day found him withdrawing to a position in the foothills which might be defended. The coolies, terrified into spineless, crawling things, clung to him because he represented their only protection. His diggers, strong, black-browed mountaineers of Shensi, gave no sign of fear. He could depend upon their loyalty, but not upon their shooting.

For them the half-light of midnight desert was peopled with

strange, sacred shapes—*suan yi,* the giant horse, eighth of the nine offspring of the Dragon; *kuei she t'u,* the mammoth serpent which struggles continuously with a tortoise; these and countless others from Chinese legend. The diggers might defend camp valiantly in daylight combat; at night they were inclined to commend themselves to Maitreya (Buddha), and await his dispensation with fatalistic calm.

Roberts watched, his own rifle and revolvers loaded and ready, and a second rifle reposing before him in the midst of a dozen loaded clips of cartridges. Sunk in a grim, terrible fit of depression at knowledge of his comrades' fate and his own impotence, Roberts repeated over and over a defiance that was near a prayer.

"Let them come! Let them come! Only let them *see* them...!" fell soundlessly from his stiffened lips.

Without cessation, his eyes swept the semi-circle of open desert. At his back, a curious, overhanging basalt cliff denied attack. In front of him, and to the sides, black figures of the Chinese lay or squatted.

Christensen and Roberts, experienced delvers in Oriental antiquity, had planned the journey. At the time they came to Kulang the crisis of Chinese famine had not arrived. They had taken with them Porterfield, an enthusiastic youth from the consulate at Shanghai. It was his first trip to the interior, Roberts, secure in his own reputation, had thought the trip—an investigation of certain definite clues regarding the old palaces of the Yüan dynasty, and particularly dealing with the possible identification of Kublai Khan, first emperor of the Yüans, with the semi-mythical Prester John of mediaeval history—an excellent chance to give a youngster whom he liked a toe-hold on fame.

To be balked by famine, and then to lose his comrade and protégé in the leper caves of Bo-hai! Strong teeth bit into his lower lip until the blood flowed unnoticed. Silently, Selwyn Roberts swore to himself with immovable earnestness that he would remain. Either the three white men would return together, or all would perish. Robert, not in the least sleepy, though his body was fatigued, waited with restless grimness for the dawn of another day.

Bo-hai, the capricious and terrible, is not a silent waste after sundown.

With the descent of cold air from the heavens come buckling squalls of wind, plucking pillars of sand and dust from the surface and flinging them broadcast with a singing be-e-e-e of flying particles. Far out behind, carried on a wind from nowhere, reverberates at times the faint, unrhythmic banging of *boutangs*, the wailing of *juns* and *nakra*.

At there are voices. At times a rising squeal of Chinese chant makes itself distinct for a second but most often a low, formless murmur, as of howling monkeys heard from a distance of miles, is the constant undertone.

Roberts heard all these, but it was sight, not sound which absorbed him. Flitting scarecrows from the caves might approach soundlessly over the sand, but he did not believe they could reach him unseen.

He had not calculated upon the sand and dust. A squall came up, beating upon the watchers with a fusillade of fine, choking particles, and raising a screen before Roberts' eyes. In the midst of this he heard dry coughs. Someone was out there, approaching with the shielding sand!

Still the watcher, alternately brushing grains of sand from his nostrils and eyes and peering along the barrel of his rifle, found no target. A sudden notion came to him that the marauders now were inside his camp, about to leap upon him.

He dropped the rifle, and seized two revolvers, shaking the sand and dust out of their muzzles.

As suddenly as it had risen, the veil lifted. Roberts, peering out eagerly, saw only a single bent, stumbling figure—a man who fell to his knees, head almost in the sand, and tried to arise....a snap shot from the ready revolver stretched him flat, his breath leaving in a sharp exhalation like air drawn from a pneumatic tire.

In that instant Robert stiffened. From out there ten paces had come a gasping sound. It was the wounded man, the desert rat.

"G'bye!" he wheezed. "G'bye...never come...back...now..."

The words were English!

∽

SELWYN ROBERTS, waiting only to draw on heavy gloves of Llama hide, ran, crouching, to his fallen adversary.

Catching the shrunken, bowed figure beneath the arms—arms which at biceps gave only a pinch of flesh and bone into his grasp—he scurried back. Then, stationing the Chinese in a semi-circle further out, so that no marauders might enter without encountering opposition, he turned to the fainting figure of his victim.

Screening electric torch by flaps of jacket, he looked down at the man. He saw a yellowed, meager face, with eyes that had become long and narrow from much squinting in the desert. The man, unconscious now, had his head shaved except for the circle and queue usual among natives of Inner Mongolia. Except that no sign of leprosy showed, he looked the part of a desert exile. Tearing away his black cotton shirt, however, Roberts saw, with a sinking heart, that the intruder's skin was white as his own.

Desperately, casting aside all caution in use of the flash-lamp, Roberts worked. He found the wound, a gaping hole from soft-nosed bullet, which lay just beneath the stretched ridge of the left clavicle. Probably the bullet had punctured the top of the man's lung. This was rendered plausible by flecks of reddish foam gathering in his mouth corners.

Roberts stanched the external bleeding, and fetched whisky from his personal pack. Forcing three tablespoonfuls of the potent fluid between the man's lips, he held forward the lolling tongue which would have shut off respiration. Ten seconds later the patient squirmed, trying to sit up. Roberts, a solicitous tyrant, held him fast.

"Not dead yet?" queried the man, ending his sentence in a ghastly cough. "What the hell....?" He choked, spitting sidewise to the sand.

"No, you're not dead, and you're not going to die!" replied Roberts with forced calmness. "Take it easy. You're among friends."

"Oh yes, I'll die," stated the man with conviction. "Where am I? Who are you? I *Ch'ueh shih hsiang...*" His speech trailed off into a Buddhist prayer unintelligible to Roberts.

"Never mind that now. The first thing is to make you comfortable. You are safe. Don't forget that. Later we can talk. I have many questions to ask you, but the night is long."

The slight frame shook.

"Something over six—maybe ten years. What year is this?..." His voice seemed to fail. He lay back, occasionally coughing, but for the most part silent.

A half hour dragged by. Roberts did nothing save inspect the wound he had made, and occasionally give a spoonful of stimulant to the prostrate man. The latter's heart action was faint, but constant. Roberts knew he would live till morning, at least.

"I have talked to myself, to the lepers' priests, to the sands—in English," he said suddenly. "That's why I remember. My name's Bowen—Wade Hilton Bowen. Calligraphist for the Central Historical Society. My home was on Perry Street, Montgomery, Alabama. A nice house, with barn for six horses. Box stalls...I have said this many times..."

"Montgomery has changed since you were there," put in Roberts, quietly. "I'll tell you more about it tomorrow."

"Tomorrow....tomorrow in hell!" he coughed, and then was silent again.

Roberts, bringing all his mental cohorts to bear upon the possible relation between this queer derelict of the desert and his two companions, made no attempt to strong on the conversation.

One hour before dawn then man tried to sit up, strangled in a fit of terrible coughing, and then fell sidewise.

"Can't—can't lie on my back," he gasped. "Spine bowed. Hurts. How—how long have I got?"

"You'll get well," Roberts assured him. "I'll take care of you. Here, try a little more whisky. I want to ask you a lot of questions when you're able to stand in the strain."

"*Um-m.* Good whisky. Used to like it. Forgot there was such a thing. You've no notion how a man forgets...." His voice was low, rambling, jerky. "Won't get well, though. Hope not. They fixed me. Found out I was immune....you know, leprosy. They all have it. Want everybody in the world to get it. But there are worse things...."

Coughing cut short his speech for a moment.

"Not many," said Roberts with a shudder. "I thought you were one of them, and so I put on gloves. They've captured my two comrades. What I want to know as quickly as possible is whether you can help me rescue them. Can you?"

"Captured two men?" repeated the other vaguely. "Shouldn't allow it. Better die with a nice, clean bullet. That's the way I'm going to finish it. You've got a gun. You'll let me just one bullet? I'm not dying fast enough."

His skinny hand made a weak grab for Roberts' revolver, but the latter shifted his holsters out of reach.

"No! I've got to have your help."

"Help!" sniveled the prostrate man in bitter impotence. "Don't you see what I am? I'm sorry about those men. They'll wish for quick death, but it won't come. Like as not they'll be put in the leper chambers. I was there for two years. There were six of us. All of them got it but me. They were Chinkies and played me dirt, or I'd have made *them* immune, too.

"But maybe it would have been better if I'd caught it. Then they'd have let me alone. They got jealous. Just seeing a healthy man makes 'em crazy. Most people wouldn't understand how mad they get. They want to kill, but not all at once. Oh, no! Death like that is quick and sweet. I used to be a coward about it, but not now. Just give me that gun a minute, and I'll show you....*Why* don' you let me?" His quaver sank in sobs and coughing.

"Mainly because I can't stand by and see a white man kill himself. Then, as I said, you must help me. If you haven't got leprosy, though. I can't imagine why you stay here—or why you want to die. Why is it?"

A light of wild derision gleamed in Bowen's eyes, upturned to the flash. Seizing Roberts' hand he drew the fingers along his bowed ridge of backbone.

"Algae," he gritted. "Algae from Gileshtai the Accursed. Puncture, you know. Scum grows in the spinal fluid. Every month I stoop more and more. The pain, you know. Now when I run I am bent like a question mark. Oh. I tried to escape a dozen times. Always they caught me. Couldn't travel far or fast, you see. And no food to take. They—they did this. They are clever. *Damned* clever!"

Roberts had no answer for this. He was chilled with horror. Such practices had come to his ears as whispered rumors, yet he had not believed. That his big, silent comrade Christensen, and the youth Porterfield, were this minute in the hands of the devils of the caves, perhaps suffering as Bowen had suffered, and certainly absorbing the awful, infectious dampness of the subterranean passages, undermined his nerve as no certainty of instant destruction could have done. He shuddered.

"See here, Bowen!" he cried. "We *must* get them out! You know the way. It will be terrible suffering for you, but you are a man—a *white* man! Even if it costs the life you do not value you must give these men their chance. I will have two of the diggers support you...."

~

SOME OF HIS intense earnestness caught hold in Bowen's dulled brain.

"You're right," he mumbled. "White men...like you and me. Yes, we can get them out, I think, but not yet. Wait till the sun rises. Then all the *Yengi* are below ground. They have no firearms. By quick attack through the Wall corridor...yes, we should succeed. But then? Do you know your peril in venturing, even for a moment, below ground?"

"My peril matter not!"

Bowen nodded slowly.

"You are brave," he mumbled. "But perhaps you have not seen them...the Yengi?"

"I can imagine," cut in Roberts shortly. "How many of them are there?"

"Hundreds. One never knows exactly. They are sent each week. Some die, of course, but most live on and on...."

"Can you shoot?"

Bowen grimaced.

"I used to," he answered. "I'll *have* to, now. Each of us will take as many guns as he can stow away. And plenty of ammunition. Enough so we can give arms to your friends. Merely reaching them will be simple enough. That will not finish it, though. We must go on."

"Fight our way out, you mean?"

"Oh yes, that of course. But first fight our way further *in!* It would not do simply to escape."

"Why not?"

Bowen grinned wryly. He fumbled in a hidden pocket, coming out with a fat bit of green stone oddly carved with interlaced dragons—a jade pendant.

"Know anything about this?" he asked.

The light of dawn was not yet sufficient. Roberts turned on the flash again. Then he nodded shortly.

"Interesting," he said. "A jade, probably of the fourteenth century, the Yüan dynasty. A week ago I was searching for things like that, but now...."

Bowen leaned forward, raising himself to a sitting position.

"Look!" he cried, his voice squeaking into a cough. A touch of his tapered finger nail had caused the pendant to fall into two halves. There before Roberts lay a tiny roll of tinted silk upon which vertical rows of black ideographs were revealed.

Roberts removed the silk carefully, spreading it across his knee.

"The key to one of the treasure caches of Kublai Khan!" shrilled Bowen. "It's mine. I found it. By using it, I managed to keep clean of body. It is the only hope for your friends—and you, if you venture in!"

Silently, and with a growing intensity of interest, Roberts deciphered the characters. The colophon furnished simple, straightforward directions, yet the tale it told was unbelievable.

"A—a *cure?*" he stammered shakily.

"Yes—or at least a preventive. *I* can answer for that."

"And is there plenty?"

Bowen cackled, raucous froth appearing on his lips.

"Forty jars!" he retorted. "Each jar with eight panels, and holding about a peck. Treasure, indeed! On those panels is carved the history of the reign of Kublai Khan!"

Roberts was on his feet.

"Let's start!" he commanded, his voice shaking with anticipation of high, terrible adventure. "There is the rim of the sun! Take one last drink of the whisky, Bowen...."

∽

ALL OF THE Chinese save two were left behind. This pair, stolid, fat, over-muscled giants who had been with Roberts for years, made a chair of their hands, and carried Bowen back across the rim of desert toward the Great Wall. All four of the men bristled with weapons, and had their pockets crammed with loaded clips.

To Roberts' surprise, Bowen directed the course of the journey back to the east, in the direction of Dadchin.

"Three corridors run the length of the wall in this section," he explained. "One corridor is not known to the *Yengi*...It is how I got among them first...."

Over tumbled ruins of wall climbed the four. At a black aperture, scarcely wide enough to permit the passing of a heavy man, Bowen signaled.

"Hang and drop," he commanded, speaking in a whisper. "The corridor floor is eight feet down. I know a better way to climb, but, going in, it is simpler to drop..."

From the black slit an odor rose which made Roberts stiffen. He had caught a faint suggestion of it from Bowen's clothes, but now it came to him, fetid and strong—a scent of rank, damp decay.

He snatched one last breath of desert air, knelt, swung himself down into space, and let go. As Bowen had said, the drop was short, but Roberts, in the dark, fell sidewise to the slimy bricks of the passage.

In a second he was up, shrinking involuntarily from the contact. When Bowen was lowered from the slit of light, Roberts caught him and set him down carefully. The Chinese did not follow.

"I told them to wait there," Bowen whispered. "They'd be useless down here. There's no sense in spoiling two brave boys."

"But can you make it?"

"Yes, if I don't have to cough. When we get in the third passage it won't matter. No one is there. Come on. Hold to this rag..." He placed a shred of his tattered blouse in Roberts' palm, plunging immediately into the blackness.

Roberts, stumbling blindly after—recoiling from each touch of the horrid, oozing walls—ran on tip-toe in order to match the silence of his barefooted guide.

They passed spots of light. These showed openings to right or left —openings to chambers lighted with flickering flames of green or yellow. Once Robert looked, his flesh acrawl with morbid curiosity. He saw within the place three sprawling things of rags and decay, things which did not—perhaps *could* not—move. Thereafter he kept his eyes averted, and clenched one fist about the solid butt of his revolver.

After perhaps ten minutes of travel, Bowen, wheezing audibly now, bent forward in a silent convulsion which brought blood to his lips. Only at the last did he make a noise. Then a gasping inhalation was not to be controlled.

A second later he crowded back against Roberts, crouching at the side of the passage. A leap...a dulled groan...Bowen had brought down the butt of one of his borrowed revolvers upon the skull of a newcomer whom Roberts had neither seen nor heard!

A moment later they squeezed through another narrow opening, descended a flight of block stairs, and were in another corridor—one much more populous than the upper, to judge from the sounds.

Roberts heard the subdued chattering of many voices. Here faint light showed.

Bowen led on hurriedly. At a point indistinguishable from the rest of the wall, so far as Roberts was concerned, he pushed inward a block of stone, which went to the horizontal, immediately swinging back when they had passed.

"Now we're all right for a minute...." began Bowen. His long-repressed coughing attacked him then and he surrendered to it for the time. "Lungs...filling up...won't last long..." he gasped then. "This corridor...no way out...get back in the other, if I am not...with...you..."

"We'll manage *that*; don't you worry!" answered Roberts. "Lead me first to those two men. After that, the Buddha...I feel unclean already!"

Bowen incomprehensibly laughed at that—a shrill giggle, half-hysterical. But he led on, of a sudden turning, squeezing through to the second corridor again, and then, without warning bringing up two automatics. Two streams of fire...four shots...

"Got 'em all!" he shrilled, laughing. "Come quick now!"

∽

Roberts found himself dragged forward at a half-run.

Again Bowen's two guns spoke. This time, in the light of flashes, Roberts saw two crouching things succumb. Through a black doorway they plunged. Then a faint light from a single insufficient wick lighted a chamber perhaps twenty by ten feet in size. Chained, backs outward, Porterfield and Christensen were spread-eagled against the fetid, oozing wall!

They were stripped to the waist. Across their white backs, greenish now in the light of the floating wick, were the red criss-crosses of flagellations.

"Thank God you've come!" cried the usually silent Christensen, as Roberts shot away the rusted chains binding his arms and ankles to the wall. "This place...do you know what it is?"

"All about it!" answered Roberts, succinctly. "Here, take these!" He handed a brace of revolvers and a handful of clips to his Norwegian comrade.

Then he turned to Porterfield. Four explosions, and a series of wrenches set free the boy, who did not wait to have the dangling shackles shot off his wrists and ankles.

Bowen, stationed at the entrance, was shooting now. A gathering handful of *Yengi* crowded in the passage. These threw lances, or cut at the defending figure with knives that were long, keen and curved.

Bowen was unharmed, however, except for scratches. His revolvers had kept him out of serious danger. He seemed to take inhuman delight in snapping away at every figure of a Chinaman that showed itself. When all had fallen between him and the turn of corridor, he still fired away. Before the four left, he had to reload all four of his revolvers.

Bowen and Roberts left in the van, Christensen and Porterfield were given the job of protecting the rear. The four hurried down the corridor, occasionally stopping for a second to pump out a shot or two at some unsuspecting hurrying figure.

Throughout the underground corridors weird shouts resounded. Cries in a tongue that even Roberts could not translate called for reinforcements from the chambers. Somewhere an eerie gong clanged its resonance.

The four pushed on, led forward by Bowen, who seemed to have reached an exhilaration which thought nothing of wounds. His bent figure now was wracked by continual coughing, but he paid no attention, grasping in sufficient breath somehow. Each five or six yards Christensen and Porterfield paused, to throw backward a fusillade at the gathering throng of maniacs.

They reached a triple fork in the passage. Without hesitation, Bowen chose the center one, which led on a gradual slant downward. Fifty paces further a brocaded curtain shut the passage. Here the light was bright from many swimming wicks set in the side wall.

"Straight in" cried Bowen, and flung himself upon the curtain. As his fingers clutched the cloth to pull it aside, a long keen blade reached out, puncturing his side in a swift flash.

"Ah-h!" he cried. "The priests! Kill them!"

He stumbled, and in falling, brought down the heavy weight of the curtain across his body. Through the aperture eight wizened specimens, flourishing drawn swords, charged the invaders.

∾

Roberts backed away, firing.

From the floor, however, came the streams of fire which dropped three of the priests.

"They're the ones who fixed *me!*" shrilled Bowen, firing as fast as his fingers could pull triggers.

The last toppled. The doorway was clear.

"You'll—you'll have to drag me...I'm done..." Bowen continued, his voice suddenly weakening. "I'll show you..."

Robert stooped, picking up the slight figure as he might have lifted a tumbled chair, and darted inside the last chamber.

Here he stopped a split second in open-mouthed amazement. He had expected a statue of Buddha. The colophon was explicit. Yet what a statue! From the wide base to the top of the broad forehead was at least fifty feet! The altar, surrounded by fire at the base, though itself the height of a man, seemed a puny thing.

"Hold the doorway!" cried Roberts to his two rescued companions. "Now, Bowen..."

But there was no need to ask the derelict. Reeling forward out of Roberts' arms, he pointed to a knob seven feet from the floor. "Turn... turn that...and press here...and here!" he gasped, choking.

Roberts obeyed. A second later he was scrambling up to force further open a slab which swung creakingly. Perched there on the slab to hold it open—it was weighted, and after the initial swing of opening, began to close—he glanced inward. There, stacked before him, were tiers and tiers of the eight-paneled jars that Bowen had mentioned. One, as if it had been opened, stood on the floor of the storage chamber. He seized it, finding it heavy in his hands, and leaped down.

Bowen clawed off the cover, reached in, and came forth with three greenish, soft masses clutched in his skinny fingers.

"The eggs!" he cried. "Seven hundred years old! Make...make each of them eat on right away! We'll have a hard time..." He choked, flinging a thin, trembling arm in the direction of Christensen and Porterfield, who were having their hands full at the doorway.

Roberts seized his own weapons, ran up, and in terse sentences explained the situation.

"A...a *cure?*" cried Porterfield, incredulously.

"Bowen says so. Try them, anyway. Eat one apiece. I'll hold the door. *Hm!*"

The last was an exclamation of pain. A thrown knife had sliced a six-inch cut just above his knee. He fired, conserving bullets now, for down the corridor as far as he could see the *Yengi* had banked themselves. Already a breastwork of Chinese bodies was growing in front of the chamber entrance.

Behind him, Porterfield sputtered over swallowing his portion.

"Awful taste!" he cried, grimacing.

"They're treated with something," answered Christensen, wiping his lips and leaping to Roberts' side with one of the ancient eggs.

Roberts stuffed half of the greenish mass into his mouth, swallowing it whole. The taste was not altogether unpleasant, yet acrid. As he fired on and on, emptying one after another of the revolvers, he caught himself wondering how long it had taken for the shells of those eggs to become resorbed...He ate the rest.

The fight was hopeless from the first. Though few bullets missed a human target—the narrow corridor was jammed with yammering, horrid humanity—and little damage could be accomplished by any of the *Yengi* at first, the inexorable pressure began to tell. Christensen, cursing in Scandinavian, plucked a lance from his shoulder. Later he dropped like a stone. The thin hilt of a knife quivered in the socket of his right eye.

Bowen, dragging himself to the entrance, diagnosed the reason.

'We're desecrating their shrine!" he yelled. "In a way, I don't blame them...They're...They're..." Coughs ended his sentence.

And then, catching up the eight-paneled jar, and begging from Roberts the silk colophon, he threw his mangled body out before the breastwork of dead Chinese. High and shrill rose his voice, a fast, excited jabber which Roberts could not decipher. It continued...

"Stop shooting!" Bowen flung back over his shoulder. The white men were glad to obey. Their ammunition was almost spent. Strangely enough, the *Yengi* of the front rank lowered their weapons. They turned, jabbering excitedly to others. Bowen flung out to them the square of ideographed silk.

"It—it's your only hope, my brothers!" gasped Bowen. "Take one jar—if you will..."

At this he pitched forward, clawing with his hands at the body of one of the *Yengi*. Roberts saw that the dead Chinese had leather pads in place of hands at the end of his wrists...

∼

WITH THE MELTING away of the horde of *Yengi*, Roberts—bearing Bowen, who was unconscious part of the time—and Porterfield found a way out. At the surface they saw full two hundred of the lepers, yet none of the latter moved to attack. The instant the white men left the opening, the *Yengi* fought in swarms to return.

"I told them...cure...Maybe it is...maybe not..." gasped Bowen. He shuddered and lay still. Roberts held a dead man in his arms.

Nevertheless he stalked on to the place where the two Chinese had been left. Then he relinquished his burden. Porterfield gave over to him the eight-paneled jar which represented the whole of their achievement.

"On the way back each of us will eat a dozen of these eggs." Stated Roberts. "Bowen may be wrong, but I believe what he said. Those old emperors knew..."

At the camp Porterfield collapsed, sobbing. The full horror of what he had experienced had begun to seep down to his consciousness. Roberts cared for him.

"Then I take it you won't be with me—when I go back?"

Porterfield roused himself. "Go back?" he cried. "I would not go back for all the wealth of the Indies! You don't mean to say...?"

"I do," answered Roberts grimly. "Within six months. Men may live or die, but the history must be written. The *Yengi* may not have smashed *all* of those forty jars...."

THE WISH, BY MYRTLE LEVY GAYLORD
AN ODD FRAGMENT OF FICTION

Burned and scarred by the hot breath of passion and the deep wounds of life, the mother took the newborn girl-child. Leonore, to her breast for the first time. She trembled with joy and pain at the touch of the greedy little lips.

Presently the woman and the child at her breast slept. The mother dreamed that out of a black sky a silver fairy appeared in a cloud of light.

"One wish, one wish only, for the newborn," the fairy offered.

The mother, clutching the child closer to her, trembled and choked, and it seemed that she would not be able to answer. Finally words came, as if involuntarily:

"That she may not feel, that she may not suffer, that passion love that scorches and does not warm, may never touch her!"

The fairy smiled a faint, far smile and inscribed a circle with her star-tipped wand.

'It is well," said she.

The cloud of light faded into a black sky. The child stirred, and the mother awoke, her heart aching, she knew not why.

∽

LEONORE, the woman, was tall, pale and exceptionally beautiful. She gazed out of clear, gray eyes that had lost the wonder of childhood without ever gaining the warmth of womanhood.

She passed through life as one in a dream. She saw much, she understood much, but when, in those intense moments that sometimes come, the quick tears of sympathy and love sprang to the eyes of those about her, her heart would seem a thing of stone. She knew that she *should* weep, but she could not. Then she would whisper to herself:

"Tears are not real. No one really feels. They just pretend."

Donald, the young poet, loved her suddenly, burningly, gloriously. He looked into her cool gray eyes and swore to himself that in their depths slumbered the answer to all life.

He wooed her passionately, beseechingly, and in vain. He laid bare to her all that aching beauty that was his soul. She smiled vaguely, detached as a pine tree outlined against the evening sky...

They dragged him from the little pond behind the house. He lay among the flowers, still and beautiful, with the fire that had burned so painfully forever extinguished.

There were tears in the eyes of those who had gathered around him in the great, gray room, tears in the eyes of all save Leonore. Leonore looked at the waxen face and thought only that it was beautiful. She did not weep.

"How cruel," she heard them whisper. "It was for love of Leonore, and she is a stone. She does not feel."

For many days she struggled with this thought. She did not feel. How could she feel? She began to look for misery that she might weep. She went to the funeral of a child who had died at its mother's breast. But neither the child in the little white casket, nor the mother, with her streaming hair and wild eyes, could bring tears to Leonore.

One night she sat before the fireplace in her bedroom, staring at the flames. The flickering light fascinated her. For a long time she sat motionless, watching it.

Then, out of the glowing heart of the fire, Donald spoke to her:

"Leonore, you *can* feel, but you will not."

She shook her head sadly. "I can not—I can *not*."

"The fire—feel!" he cried. "Surely you can feel the fire. Try!"

Obediently, she placed her slim, white hand into the flames.

"You feel? Now you *do* feel?" he begged her.

"No," she whispered. "No!"

"You are not a woman," he gasped. "Ice water, not blood, flows in your veins. See," he pointed to a keen-edged paper knife that lay gleaming on the table. Obediently, she reached for the knife, and with steady fingers she cut the artery at her wrist. Donald faded back into the flames....

When they found her in the morning they knew that she had sought death, but they could not understand why she had burned her left hand so cruelly.

THE WHISPERING THING (PART 1), BY LAURIE MCCLINTOCK AND CULPEPER CHUNN

DEATH AND TERROR ARE SPREAD BROADCAST BY THE ICY BREATH OF THE WHISPERING THING.

Chapter 1: The Thing Strikes

Jules Peret, known to the underworld as The Terrible Frog, hated the foul air in crowded street cars and the "stuffiness" of a taxicab, and, whenever possible, he avoided both.

Hence, having nothing in view that demanded hast, after leaving police headquarters, he had, in spite of the lateness of the hour, elected to make the journey home on foot. He had not gone very far, however, before he began to wish that he had chosen some other mode of traveling, for he had scarcely ever seen such a gloomy night. It was January, and the atmosphere was of that uncertain temperature that is best described as raw. The darkness was Stygian. A fine mist was falling from the starless skies, and a thick grayish-yellow fog enwrapped the city like a wet blanket.

The chimes in a church steeple, two blocks farther on, had just struck the hour of ten, and except for Peret and one other wayfarer, who had paused in the sickly glare of the corner lamp to light a cigarette, the street was deserted.

"A fine night for a murder!" muttered Peret to himself, as, with head lowered, he plowed his way through the fog. "*Diable!* I must find a taxi."

With this thought in mind, he was about to quicken his pace when, instead, he jerked himself to an abrupt halt and stood in an attitude of listening, as the tomblike silence was suddenly broken by a hoarse scream, and, almost immediately afterward, a cry of agony and terror:

"Help! Help! I'm dying!"

The cry, though muffled, was loud enough to reach the alert ears of Peret. It appeared to come from a tall, gloomy-looking building on the right side of the street. By no means certain of this, however, Peret crouched behind a tree and strained his ears to catch the sound should it be repeated.

But no cry came. Instead, there was a terrific crash of breaking glass, and Peret twisted his head around just in time to see a man hurl himself through the leaded sash of one of the lower windows of the house and fall to the pavement with a thud and a groan.

A moment later Peret was by his side. Whipping out a small flashlight, he directed the little disc of light on the man's face.

"*Nom d'un nom!*" he cried. "It is M. Max Berjet. What is the matter, my friend? Are you drunk? Ill? *Sacre nom!* Speak quickly, while you can. What ails you?

The man rolled from side to side, convulsively, and tore at the air with clawlike hands. To Peret, he seemed to be grappling with an invisible antagonist that was slowly crushing his life out. His face was blue and horribly distorted: his breath was coming in short, jerky gasps.

Suddenly his tensed muscles relaxed and he lay still. Unable to speak, he could only life his eyes to Peret's in desperate appeal.

"*Dame!* You are a sick man, my friend," observed Peret, feeling the man's pulse. "I will run for a physician. But tell me quickly what happened to your, *Monsieur.*"

There was an almost imperceptible movement of the dying man's froth-rimmed lips, and Peret held his head nearer.

"Now, speak, my friend," he entreated. "I am Jules Peret. You know me, eh? Tell me what is the matter with you. Were you attacked?"

"As-sas-sins," gasped the stricken man faintly.

"What?" cried Peret, excitedly. "Assassins?"

The look in Berjet's eyes was eloquent.

"Who are they?" pleaded the detective. "Tell me their names, *Monsieur*, before it is too late. I will avenge you. I promise you. I swear it. Quickly, *Monsieur, their names—*"

Berjet murmured something in a voice almost too faint to be audible.

"*Diz?*" questioned Peret, straining to catch the man's words. "You mean ten, eh?"

With his glazing eyes fixed on the detective, Berjet made a desperate effort to reply, but the effort was in vain. The ghost of a sigh escaped from his lips, a slight tremor shook his frame, and, with a gurgling sound in his throat, he died.

"*Peste!* What did he mean by that?" muttered Peret, getting to his feet. (*Diz* is the French word for "ten".) "Did he mean he was attacked by ten assassins? The devil! It does not take an army to kill a single man."

"What's the matter, old chap?" it was the pedestrian whom Peret had observed lighting a cigarette near the corner lamp a few minutes previously. "The old boy looks as if he had had a shot of bootlegger's private stock."

"He has been murdered," returned Peret shortly, after giving the man a keen scrutiny. Then: "Be so kind as to run to the drug store across the street and ask the druggist to send for a physician. Also request him to notify police headquarters that a murder has been committed. Have the notification sent in the name of Jules Peret. Hurry, my friend!"

Without waiting to reply, the man spun on his heel and dashed across the street. Dropping to his knees again, Peret made a hasty but thorough search of the dead man's clothing, but beyond a few stray coins in the pockets of his trousers, found nothing. As he was finishing his examination, the stranger returned, accompanied by the druggist and a physician who had chanced to be in the drug store.

Peret rose to his feet and stepped back to make room for the doctor.

"What's the trouble?" asked Dr. Sprague, a large, swarthy-faced man with a gray Vandyke beard.

"Murder, I'm afraid," replied Peret, pointing at Berjet's motionless body.

Dr. Sprague bent over the inert form of the scientist and made a brief examination.

"Yes," he said gravely, "he is beyond human aid."

"He is dead?"

"Quite."

"Can you tell me what caused his death?"

"I cannot be positive," replied the physician, "but he bears all the outward symptoms of asphyxiation."

"Asphyxiation?" repeated Peret incredulously.

"Yes."

Peret's skepticism was written plainly on his face.

"But that is at variance with the dead man's last words. I was with M. Berjet when he died and there was certainly nothing in his actions to suggest asphyxiation. However—" He exhibited his card. "I am Jules Peret, a detective. The man that you have just pronounced dead is Max Berjet, the eminent French scientist. If he was murdered—and I have reason to believe that he was—the murderer has not yet had time to escape, as M. Berjet has been dead less than two minutes. It is possible, therefore, that I can apprehend the assassin if I act at once. Can you stay here with the body pending the arrival of the police?"

Dr. Sprague glanced at the detective's card and nodded, whereupon Peret, with a single bound, cleared the iron fence that enclosed the little yard in front of Berjet's house. As he landed, feet first, on the lawn, he heard Dr. Sprague give a piercing scream.

So startled was he by the unexpectedness of it that he lost his footing and fell forward on his face. Leaping to his feet, he whirled around and directed the beam from his flashlight on the physician.

Dr. Sprague, with his hands clawing the air in front of him, appeared to be grappling with an invisible *something* that was rapidly getting the best of him. His lips were drawn back in a snarl; his eyes seemed as if they were about to pop from his head, and bloody froth had begun to ooze between his clenched teeth and run from the corners of his mouth.

As Peret was preparing to leap back over the fence, he heard a terrible scream issue from the throat of the unknown pedestrian, and saw him throw up his arms as if to ward off a blow. Then the man reeled back against the fence and began to struggle desperately with something that Peret could not see.

Whipping out his automatic, the detective again vaulted the fence, but before he could reach either of them, both Dr. Sprague and the pedestrian crashed to the pavement, the first dead, the second still fighting for his life.

Chapter II: The Mystery Deepens

Although the moment was obviously one that demanded caution, Jules Peret was never the man to hesitate in the face of an unknown danger.

He realized that he was in the presence of some terrible invisible thing that might strike him down at any moment, but, as he had no idea what that thing was and could not hope to cope with it until it attacked him or in some manner made itself manifest, he dismissed it from his mind for the moment and turned his attention to the two men who had gone down before its onslaught.

Kneeling beside Dr. Sprague's prostrate form, he bent over and peered into the physician's face. One look at the horribly distorted features and the glassy eyes that stared into his own, told him that the man was dead.

Turning now from the dead to the living, Peret jumped to his feet and ran to help the pedestrian who, with the help of the terrified little druggist, was in the act of staggering to his feet. Although the druggist's teeth were chattering with fear, his first thought seemed to be for the sufferer, and he helped Peret support the man, too weak to stand unaided, when he reeled back against the fence.

Choking, gasping, spitting, the pedestrian fought manfully to regain his breath. His face was purple with congested blood, and his glazed eyes were bulging. Great beads of sweat poured from his forehead and mingling with the froth that oozed from between his lips, flecked his face as he twisted his head from side to side in agony.

"What is the matter with you?" shouted Peret. "Speak! I want to help you."

The stricken man made a violent effort to throw off the invisible horror that had him in its clutches. Then the muscles of his body relaxed, and he ceased to struggle. Drawing in a deep breath of air, he expelled it with a sharp whistling sound. Then, exhausted, he shook off Peret's hand, and sank down on the pavement in a sitting posture.

"*Sacrebleu!*" yelled Peret. "Speak to me, my friend, so I can avenge you! One little word is all I ask. *What attacked you?*"

"I—I don't know," the man gasped. "It—it was something I could not see! It was a monster—an invisible monster. It whispered in my ear, and then it began to choke me. Oh, God—."

His head fell forward; he began to sob weakly.

"An invisible monster," repeated Peret, staring at the man curiously. "What do you mean by that?"

Before the man could reply, the police patrol-wagon swung around the corner and, with a clang of the bell, drew up to the curb. Detective Sergeant Strange of the homicide squad and two subordinates leaped to the sidewalk and approached the Frenchman.

"Well?" demanded Strange, with characteristic brevity.

"Murder," returned Peret, with equal conciseness, and nodded at the two bodies on the pavement.

"How?" Strange shot out.

"I don't know," replied Peret. "As I was passing the house ten minutes ago, Max Berjet, the man on your left, hurled himself through the window, cried out that he had been attacked by ten assassins, and died immediately afterward. After summoning a physician, I started to enter the house to investigate, and heard the doctor scream. When I turned I saw Dr. Sprague and this man"—pointing to the pedestrian—"struggling in the grasp of something I could not see. Before I could reach them, the two men fell to the pavement. Dr. Sprague died almost instantly; this other man, as you see, is recovering. He has just informed me that he was attacked by an invisible monster."

Strange's bellicose feature twisted into a grin.

"An invisible monster, eh? Well, if had better stay invisible if it's still sticking around." He whirled about, and to the patrolman: "I want all available men her on the jump, Bill. Call the coroner at the same time. O'Shane"—to one of the plainclothes men who accompanied him—"watch the front of that house and keep an eye on these bodies until the coroner comes. Mike, take care of the back of the house, and," he added with a grim humor, "keep your eye peeled for an 'invisible monster'."

Strange turned once more to the Frenchman.

"You're sure these two men are dead, Peret?"

"They will never be any deader," replied Peret shortly.

"All right—Who is that man?"—pointing over his shoulder at the druggist.

'I am the proprietor of the drug store across the street," spoke up the druggist. "I ran over with Dr. Sprague, who happened to be in the store when this gentleman summoned assistance."

Strange nodded.

"I may have to hold you as a witness," was his curt reply. "Stick around until I can find time to question you. Now, Peret, before we enter the house, spill the details. What do you know about this 'invisible monster'?"

"Little more than I have already told you," answered Peret, and launched into a detailed recital of his harrowing experience.

Although Detective Strange was a man difficult to surprise, he made no effort to conceal his astonishment when Peret brought his story to an end.

"You say Dr. Sprague and this other man were seized by the Thing when your back was turned?" he questioned.

"*Oui*; as I was leaping over the fence," nodded Peret, "I heard Dr. Sprague scream just as I landed on the ground. When I turned to see what was the matter, both he and the other man appeared to be struggling with some invisible antagonist. Before I could reach them, both men fell to the ground. Sprague was apparently dead before he fell. The other man, after a struggle, threw off the Thing—what it was or is."

"Didn't you see anything at all?" demanded Strange.

"Absolutely nothing."

"Hear anything?"

"No. But that man"—jerking his thumb at the pedestrian—"said he heard the Thing whisper."

"I also heard the Thing whisper," interposed the druggist, a small, bald-headed individual with a cataract over one of his eyes. Still in a state of nervous apprehension, he had edged up close to the two detectives as if seeking their protection. "I was talking to Dr. Sprague when he was attacked," he continued, darting furtive glances over his shoulder from time to time. "An instant before he screamed I heard a —a whispering sound."

Peret's eyes shone with interest.

"It's strange that I did not hear this sound," he muttered, half to himself. "Just what, exactly do you mean by a whispering sound, *Monsieur*?"

"I scarcely know," replied the druggist, after a moment's thought. "It was a whisper—nothing that I could understand. Just an inarticulate *whisper*. I had hardly heard it when Sprague screamed and began to struggle."

"Whence did the whisper emanate, *Monsieur*?" queried Peret eagerly.

"I do not know."

"You *saw* nothing?"

"Nothing."

"'S damn funny," growled Strange, scratching his ear. "An 'invisible monster' that whispers is a new one on me." He looked at the Frenchman perplexedly. "Queer business, Peret."

"It is," agreed Peret; then whirled around to confront the pedestrian. "Ah, *Monsieur*, perhaps you can help us a little, eh? How are you feeling now?"

"Considerably better," returned the other in a hoarse voice, and then added, "But I don't believe I'll ever recover from the shock. What, in God's name was it, anyway?"

He was a tall, heavy-set man with glittering black eyes, a close-cropped mustache and, though his features were irregular, had rather a handsome countenance. Although deathly pale and still a little shaken, he seemed to have himself pretty well in hand.

Strange looked at him shrewdly.

"What's your name?" he asked, taking out his notebook.

"Albert Deweese." Replied the man. "I am an artist and have a studio in the next block. I was on my way home when I heard the crash of breaking glass as Mr. Berjet jumped through the window-sash. Naturally, I ran back to find out what the trouble was."

Strange made a note and nodded.

"What attacked you?" he suddenly shot out.

"I don't know," replied Deweese. "The Thing, whatever it was, was invisible. I *felt* it. God knows, but did not *see* it."

"But you must have some idea of what the Thing was," Strange insisted. "Was it a man, or an animal, or--?"

Deweese shook his head slowly.

"I have said that I do not know," was his emphatic reply, "and I do not. How *could* I, when I did not see it? It was large, powerful and ferocious, but whether it was an animal of some kind, or a demon out of hell, I do not know."

"Perhaps your ears served you better than your eyes?" said Strange. "Did you hear the Thing when it leaped upon you?"

"I did," replied Deweese, with a shudder. "At almost the very instant that it attacked me I heard it whisper."

"*Eh, bien, Monsieur,*" cried Peret, "and what did it say to you?"

"It did not say anything intelligible," was Deweese's disappointing reply. "It just whispered."

Strange and Peret looked at each other in silence. The Frenchman shrugged his shoulders, and exhaled a cloud of cigarette smoke. Strange took a hitch in his trousers, and his face became stern.

"All right," he said curtly to Deweese. "Stick around till the coroner comes. I want to question you and this other man further, a little later on."

He gave an order to O'Shane, who was standing a little distance away with his eyes glued on the front of Berjet's house, then turned to Peret.

"I'm going in," he growled, and drew his revolver.

The Frenchman threw his cigarette on the pavement, drew his own automatic, and, opening the front gate, ran across the little yard. Followed by Strange and Deweese, who asked and obtained permission to accompany them. Peret buttoned his coat around his frail body, got a firm grip on the window ledge and, with the agility of a monkey, climbed through the broken sash of the window through which Berjet had projected himself.

The room in which the detectives found themselves had evidently been the scientist's sitting room. It was simply but comfortable furnished and was quite masculine in character. The walls were lined with well-filled book shelves, and in the center of the room was a large table, littered with a miscellany of papers, pamphlets, pipes, burnt matches and tobacco ashes. On the carpeted floor near the table lay an open book, the leaves of which were rumpled and torn. Except for this, the room was in perfect order.

"No signs of gas anywhere," said Strange, audibly sniffing the air. "The asphyxiation theory of Dr. Sprague's is a dud, in my opinion."

Peret, who had begun to make an inspection of the room, did not reply. Strange continued his investigation, while Deweese stood near the window looking on.

The result of Peret's examination, which, while brief, was more or less thorough, annoyed and confounded him. The detective sergeant also appeared to be puzzled. The Frenchman was the first to give expression to his thoughts.

"Three doors and the four windows in this room, sergeant, are *locked on the inside*," he remarked, as Strange paused for a moment to look at him with questioning eyes. "The key to that door on the far side of the room, and which I am sure is the door of a closet, is missing, but the other keys are in the locks. The windows, moreover, are, as you have no doubt observed, fastened with a form of mechanism that could not possibly have been sprung from the outside. Yet Berjet said he was attacked by ten assassins!"

"The point that you are trying to make, I take it," Strange grunted, "is that the broken window is the only means of egress from the room."

"Your penetration is remarkable," snapped Peret, who always became irritated when baffled.

"It's the devil's own work," commented Deweese, who had been watching the movements of the two detectives with keen interest. "Certainly there was nothing human about the Thing that attacked me, and I imagine that Berjet's death can be laid at the door of the same agency."

Peret flung himself into a chair and lit a cigarette.

"Any way you look at the thing, it seems preposterous," he said reflectively. "The 'invisible monster' theory is too absurd for serious consideration, and the other theories that have been advanced do not stand up in the presence of the facts. However, let us consider. We will assume that Berjet was, as he said, attacked by ten men. *Eh! Bien!* How did they get out of the room? All of the exits are locked on the inside, as you see.

"There is a small transom over that door opening onto the hall, it is true, but it is not large enough for a child to crawl through, much less a man. Dr. Sprague seemed to think that Berjet was asphyxiated. Yet this room, as you yourself observed when we entered it, sergeant, contained not the slightest trace of any kind of gas. As a matter of fact, the room is lighted by electricity. What are we to conclude from these premises? That the poison fumes, assuming that poison fumes were the cause of Berjet's death, were administered by human hands? If so, oblige me, my friend, by telling me how the owner of those hands got out of the room?"

"Well, if the murderers were invisible, and they were, if the testimony of you and Deweese counts for anything," rejoined Strange, "they might have followed Berjet through the window without having been observed by you."

"*Invisible* murderers!" snorted Peret, with a contemptuous shrug of his shoulders. "You are growing feeble-minded, my friend. Didn't Berjet say he *saw* his murderers?"

"So you say," returned Strange rudely. 'But *you* didn't see Sprague's murderer, although you claim to have been looking at him when he was attacked. Maybe your eyesight is failing you," he added.

Peret glared at the detective sergeant, but said nothing.

"Perhaps Berjet was subject to a hallucination," ventured Strange, after a moment's thought. "He may just have imagined he saw the murderers."

"Perhaps he just imagined he was murdered, too," retorted the Frenchman, and returned to his examination of the room.

At this juncture someone rapped on the door opening into the hall. Strange crossed the room, turned the key in the lock and, opening the door, admitted Central Bureau Detectives Frank and O'Shane.

"Well?" demanded Strange.

"Major Dobson sent us four men from headquarters, and we've searched the house as you ordered," answered O'Shane. "We drew an absolute blank. The house is empty."

"Hasn't Berjet got a family?" inquired Strange.

"The people next door say that Berjet's wife and daughter are spending the winter at Palm Beach."

"Ain't they any servants?"

"All of the servants go home at night except Adolphe, the murdered man's valet."

"Did you find him?"

"No."

"Was the front door, and the rest of the doors and windows in the house, locked?"

"The front door was not only unlocked but slightly ajar. The rest of the house was secured."

"Do you not think it possible that the murderer might have slipped out of the front door while you were watching without being seen by you?"

"Absolutely not." Said O'Shane, emphatically. "I didn't take my eye off the front of the house after you entered it until the men the major sent arrived. Mike watched the back of the house with equal care. Nobody could a-got out without one of us knowin' it. If a murder's been committed the murderer's still in the house somewhere."

The burly sergeant nodded his satisfaction.

"Well, if he's here, we'll get him," he declared. As an afterthought: "Got the house surrounded?"

"I've thrown a cordon around the whole block," replied O'Shane. "A mouse couldn't get through it without getting its neck broke."

"Good." Strange drew his revolver, which he had returned to his pocket after entering the room, and tried the handle of the closet door. 'Now, men, before we go any farther, let's get this closet open. It may contain a secrete exit, for all we know. Take a chair and burst it in, one of you."

"Wait, my friend, I know an easier way," said Peret.

He drew a jimmy from his inside coat pocket, inserted the flattened end in the crack between door and the jamb, and bore down on the handle. Yielding to the powerful leverage, the door creaked, splintered around the lock and flew open.

"Ten thousand devils!" cried Peret, leaping back.

The body of a dead man rolled out on the floor!

Chapter III: Arlington Finds a Clue

Violent death means nothing to the average police official; he comes in almost daily contact with the most brutal horrible form of it.

Therefore, while the utter unexpectedness of the corpse's arrival in their midst had a very noticeable effect on the excitable French sleuth, and more especially on Deweese, with his wracked nerves, the others, though momentarily startled, seemed to consider it all in the day's work.

Strange flashed a brief glance at Peret, and then finding him glaring blankly at the cadaver, shifted his gaze to encompass the gruesome object of the Frenchman's regard.

The dead man, like Peret, it was easy to see, was—or, rather had been—a native of France. The cast of his features was unmistakable. He was of medium height and build, was slightly bald, and his upper lip was adorned with a small, black, tightly-waxed mustache. The dagger that was buried to the hilt in his breast gave silent though ample testimony to the manner in which he had met his death.

His clothing was badly torn, and there was other evidence to show that he had put up a desperate fight with his murderer before the fatal blow was struck. In his present state he made a ghastly spectacle, for his face was badly discolored and smeared over with dried blood, and his eyes, one of which was nearly torn from its socket, were wide open and fixed on the ceiling in a glassy stare.

"Who is he?" asked O'Shane, after a brief silence.

"Adolphe," replied Peret, bending over the body. "Berjet's valet."

"You knew him," Strange stated rather than questioned.

"Yes, yes," said Peret. "I have seen him. He was *le bon valet.* See, sergeant, his limbs are cold and stiff. He was assassinated at least two hours before his master was. *Mon dieu!* What does it all mean?"

He rose to his feet, ran his fingers through his hair in a distracted manner and stared at the corpse as if he hoped to find an answer to the baffling mystery in the glassy eyes.

"Well, for one thing, it means that we got to get busy," was Strange's energetic response.

Whereupon O'Shane began to explore the closet. Strange, however, seemed to be in no hurry to follow the example set by his subordinate. He made several entries in his notebook, leisurely scratched his ear and looked at Peret from the corner of his eye. Though he would have died rather than admit it, the detective sergeant was one of the little Frenchman's staunchest admirers.

He had been associated with Peret almost daily for several years, and had given up a good many hours to the study of the other's methods in the hope that some day he would be able to emulate his friend's success. He knew that, mentally at least, Peret was his superior, and he was ever ready to place himself under the other's guidance when he could veil his real intentions sufficiently to make it appear that he himself was the leader.

"This case, at first glance, is the cat's meow," he said, tentatively. "It's the most complicated murder mystery I ever had anything to do with. What do you make of it, Peret?"

As Peret was about to reply, the door opened and three men entered the room. The first of these, a tall, middle-aged man, with a gray mustache and a fine, upright carriage, was Major and Superintendent of Police Dobson. Immediately behind him came Coroner Rane, an elderly man with penetrating gray eyes, and Police Sergeant Arlington, small, stoop-shouldered and addicted to big-rimmed spectacles.

"What's all the trouble about, sergeant?" was Dobson's greeting. He nodded to Peret, and continued: "I happened to be in my office when your call came, so I hurried over."

"I'm nighty glad you came," said Strange. "I'm afraid this case is going to prove troublesome. Did you view the bodies on the pavement?"

"Yes," said the major. "I helped Rane examine them."

"Well, here's another one for you to examine," said the detective grimly, and, stepping aside, he exposed to the view of the newcomers the body of the dead valet.

"This is not murder, it's a massacre!" exclaimed the coroner.

He knelt beside the body, and scrutinize the valet's face.

"This man has been dead for several hours, major," he continued. "Death was probably instantaneous, as this dagger is buried to the hilt in his heart." He tapped the hilt of the weapon with one of his fingers, and looked up at Strange. "Is this man supposed to have been murdered by the 'invisible monster' also?" he asked sarcastically.

"So you've heard about the 'invisible monster'," returned Strange, non-committally.

"Detective Frank, who was guarding the bodies on the pavement, told us some wild talk about an invisible murderer," remarked Dobson, with a quizzical uplift of his brows. Then, failing to draw an explanation from the sergeant, he asked: "Have you made any arrests?"

"I have not," replied Strange, then gave a rapid account of the measures he had taken to prevent the murderer's escape.

Dobson nodded his approval.

"Now, tell me all you know about these mysterious deaths," he suggested, and Strange, nothing loath, gave a brief though vivid recital of all the known facts in the case.

"This third murder," he said in conclusion, "instead of complicating matters, seems to make the going a little easier. In the dagger, with which this man was killed, we have something tangible, anyway. But as for Max Berjet and Dr. Sprague--."

"Dr. Rane," interrupted Peret from the depths of a morris chair into which he had dropped, "will you venture an opinion as to how Berjet and Sprague met their deaths?"

"It is impossible to reply with any degree of certainty until after the autopsy," answered the coroner: "but offhand I should say that they were either asphyxiated or poisoned."

Peret scowled at the coroner and relapsed into silence.

Strange, however, seemed to find comfort in the coroner's words. With a determined look on his hard-bitten face, he wheeled.

"Deweese," he rasped, in a tone calculated to impress on the hearer the absolute certainty of his words, "the coroner declares that you were poisoned." He shook a finger at the artist, as if daring him to deny it. "The poison was probably administered several hours before you felt the effects of it. Now thing! Who gave it to you? Who had the opportunity to give it to you? Who had a motive?"

"I was *not* poisoned," rejoined Deweese, quietly but emphatically. "I was choked—choked by an unseen thing that whispered in my ear. Not only did I hear it whisper, but I felt it breathing in my face as well."

Peret half rose to his feet, opened his lips as if to speak, then grunted and sat down in his chair again. Nevertheless, this new bit of evidence, if such it might be called, seemed to impress him, and he continued to eye the artist eagerly.

"Who is this man," asked Dobson.

Strange, with a gesture of helplessness, explained.

"You see what we are up against, Chief," he said. "I know how to trace a flesh and blood murderer, but, if you'll pardon me for saying so, I'll be damned if I know how to run down a spook, with no more substantial clues than a breath and a whisper."

"Mr. Deweese, you are positive, are you, that you were not attacked by a human being?" questioned the major.

"I am as certain of it as I am that I am alive," answered the artist.

"Nor an animal?"

"Yes."

"Nor something *inside of you?*"

"If you mean poison, or something like that, yes."

"Do you not think you might have been overcome by poisonous fumes of some sort?"

"Absolutely not. It was not that sort of sensation that I experienced at all."

"Have you any idea what it was that attacked you?"

"Not the remotest idea."

"You did not see it?"

"I did not."

"Could you have seen it if it had had substantial form?"

"Yes, because it was between me and the street lamp."

"Have you ever had any similar experience in the past—any experience that resembles it in the slightest way?"

"Never!"

Dobson threw a puzzled look at the coroner.

"Well," he began, and was interrupted by a blinding flash of light that suddenly illuminated the room.

With a cry of terror, Deweese whirled and, darting across the room, was about to hurl himself through the window, when Strange caught him by the arm and dragged him back.

"S'nothing but a flash-light, he said reassuringly. "Sergeant Alington is photographing the finger-prints on the dagger. "S'no wonder it scared you. Made me jump myself."

Deweese shook off the sergeant's hand and glared at the little finger-print expert.

"For God's sake, let me know before you set that thing off again," he cried in a shaking voice. "I've come through an experience that has shot my nerves to pieces and I can't stand any more shocks tonight."

"Sorry," apologized Alington, and then, like the little human bloodhound he was, turned once more to the business of nosing out and developing the finger-prints on the dagger.

"Now," resumed the major, after ordering O'Shane to have the house and vicinity toothcombed, "let us take up these murders and this assault in logical order and see if we cannot get to the bottom of this mystery. Granted that the evidence may at first appear to point that way, to contend that they were committed by a supernatural agency is absurd. Even if the murderers had some way of making it impossible for their victims to see them, we know that they were either human or animal, or, at least, directed or controlled by human intelligence.

"First of all, we have the death of Max Berjet. This man, it appears, died in the presence of our friend Peret. He hurled himself through that window, had a convulsion, and died. Before he died, however, he told Peret that he had been attacked by ten men. By the way, Peret, what were Berjet's last words?"

Peret sat hunched in his chair in an abstracted manner, staring into vacancy with knitted brow. He was evidently not pleased by the interruption, and showed his displeasure by scowling at the major.

"Just before Berjet hurled himself through the window," he explained, ungraciously, "I heard him cry, 'Help! Help! I'm dying!' As he lay dying on the pavement he gasped, '*Assassins...dix!*' just like that. *Dix*, in the French language, means 'ten,' and Berjet was a Frenchman. Figure it out for yourself."

The major nodded, thoughtfully.

"The words scarcely need any figuring out," he observed drily.

"They seem to figure themselves out. However, in view of the fact that all of the exits were fastened on the inside, and also because there is no evidence to show that any considerable number of men have recently been in this room, I think that we may leave the number of the scientist's murderers open to the question.

"Turning now to the second death, Dr. Sprague appears to have been attacked in the sight of at least two men, our amiable friend Peret and the druggist. Mr. Deweese was attacked at or about the same time that Sprague was, and the attack was also witnessed by the two persons named. Sprague and Deweese struggled with their antagonists, who, from all testimony, appear to have been of immense strength and ferocity.

"Sprague was killed almost instantly, and our friend the artist, after a desperate struggle, was fortunate enough to overcome, or at least to throw off the Thing that had him in its grasp. Deweese, the druggist and Peret declare that they did not see the Thing—that, in short, it was invisible; but both of the former gentlemen testify to the fact that they heard it whisper, and Deweese informs us further that he felt it breathing in his face.

"It seems safe to assume, therefore, that the Thing had substantial form, for even if we have to admit in the face of the facts that the Thing was invisible, we know that it could not have been a supernatural being, since supernatural beings are not supposed to whisper and breathe."

He paused, looked at the coroner as if inviting speech, and then, when only silence answered, continued:

"Let us turn now to the murder of the valet. There is certainly no doubt as to the manner in which *he* died. He was stabbed to death, and Dr. Rane has expressed the opinion that he has been dead for several hours. Yet, in spite of this, and in spite of the fact that the form of his murder is entirely different from that of Berjet and Sprague, it seems clear that the three murders, as well as the attack on the artist, are closely related to each other.

"Whether or not they are correlated is a matter which only the future can determine: but that they all bear some connection with each other and were committed by the same agency, there seems to be no doubt. The circumstances that surround the several murders speak for themselves. Therefore, in view of the fact that Berjet's valet was the first of the three men to meet his death, it is my opinion that if you find *his* murderer you will have found the man or Thing responsible for the other two murders, and for the attack on our friend, Deweese."

Strange heaved a sigh of profound satisfaction. He was now on familiar ground. Unseen and unknown forces that struck men down, forces that were apparently of some other world, were beyond his depth; but human knife-wielders were his meat. Given something tangible, a clue, or a motive, or even a theory that was not beyond his comprehension, there was no man on the force who could obtain quicker or more satisfactory results than he.

Therefore, while in his own mind, he had already settled on the dagger as the one key to the mystery in sight, it flattered him, in spite of the obviousness of the clue, to have the major's opinion coincide with his own.

"I agree with you, major," he cried heartily. "The man that we want most is the man that murdered the valet; and," he added with a tightening of his jaws, "I'm gonna get him!"

"Wait," said Sergeant Alington, who had been an interested listener to the major's summing up of that case. "I have some information to reveal which I think will be of interest to you."

He cleared his throat, set his glasses more firmly on the bridge of his nose, and glanced at several slips of paper he held in his hand.

"Before the bodies of Sprague and Berjet were taken to the morgue, I secured the finger-prints of both of them. I have since photographed a number of prints found on various objects in this room. Among the latter are a set of well-defined prints on the handle of the dagger that killed the valet. The photographs of these prints will not be available for purposes of comparison, of course, until I develop them; but the impressions on the daggerhandle are so clean-cut that they stand out clearly under the developing powder, when a magnifying glass is applied to them. While I cannot speak positively, therefore, I think that I have succeeded in identifying them."

"Well?" growled Strange, straining forward.

"Well," replied Alington, "instead of clearing up the mystery surrounding the murders of Sprague and Berjet, the finger-prints on the dagger tend to complicate it—that is, if we are to assume that the prints were made by the valet's murderer, and this, I am sure, all of you will agree with me in doing."

"Well?" repeated Strange, who saw his last glimmer of hope growing dimmer and dimmer. "Who murdered the valet?"

"If the prints were made by the man I think they were," said Alington slowly, as if to prolong the taste of the words, "the valet was murdered by Max Berjet."

Chapter IV: The Terrible Frog Takes The Trail

Strange, at once perceiving the blank wall into which his inquiry had led him, sat down on the arm of a chair and sought to hide his discomfiture by biting a liberal sized chew from the plug of tarlike tobacco that he fished out of his trousers pocket.

He had, very naturally, believed that the solution of the mystery was to be found in the finger-prints on the dagger, and his sudden disillusionment annoyed and angered him. He felt himself baffled and, having a profound dislike for the little fingerprint expert anyway, it incensed him to have to admit even momentary defeat at the latter's hands, especially in the presence of his superior.

The major, however, accepted the exploding of his theory with equanimity.

"It is obviously impossible for the scientist to have had any direct hand in Sprague's murder," he observed, "if he himself was murdered at least ten or fifteen minutes before the doctor was. And even if we assume that he had an indirect hand in it, and the circumstances surrounding the several murders would seem to disprove this, there is his own death still to be accounted for." He turned to the artist. "Mr. Deweese, did you know Max Berjet?"

Deweese shook his head.

"Never heard of him until tonight," he declared.

The major sighed.

"I thought as much," he asserted. "It seems a waste of time to try to fasten Sprague's murder and the attack on you on Berjet." He thought for a moment; then: "Sergeant Alington, you are sure, are you, that you have not been over-hasty in the conclusions you have drawn from your cursory examination of the prints? If there is any doubt in your mind, I suggest that you return to headquarters and develop the plates at once."

"You can judge for yourself, major," returned Alington, a little nettled. Like most experts, so-called and otherwise, it annoyed him to have a carefully-formed opinion of his disputed or even questioned. He could countenance such a thing in court, under the baleful eye of His Honor; but it was quite another thing at the scene of a crime, where he felt himself to be upon his own ground.

Strange, sensing his annoyance, paused long enough in his exploration of the table drawer to look at him and grin. Catching the latter's eye he winked, which exasperated the expert to such an extent that he dropped his magnifying glass. Strange, feeling fully repaid for any fancied injury, grinned again and dumped the contents of the drawer on the table.

With an injured air, Alington retrieved his magnifying glass and offered it to the major. He then held out for Dobson's inspection a set of finger-prints on a regulation blank and the dagger that the coroner had withdrawn from the breast of the dead valet. The dagger was an ordinary white bone-handle hunting knife, with a six-inch, double-edged blade. Dobson held it gingerly by the blood-smeared blade, in order not to disturb the thin coating of black powder that had been sprinkled over the handle.

Like most efficient police officials, Dobson had some knowledge of dactyloscopy, and the detectives awaited his verdict with eagerness. Applying the magnifying glass to the handle of the knife, the major leisurely examined the series of whorls and ridges that showed through the black coating. He then compared them with the finger-prints of the dead scientist, and, when he had concluded his examination, slowly nodded his head.

"You are right, sergeant," he was forced to acknowledge. "The two sets of prints are undoubtedly identical." He handed he dagger and glass to the expert. "Your evidence can not be combated, sergeant," he added.

Alington inclined his head slightly and retired to his place beside the table.

"Well," grumbled Strange, disappointed by the expert's vindication, "that at least clears up the first murder. As for the murder of Berjet, as clues are wholly lacking, in my opinion the only way we will make any headway is to motivate the crime."

"Has the ownership of the dagger been established?" asked the coroner.

"It has," replied Strange, without enthusiasm.

He held up to view the sheath of the hunting-knife, which he had found in the table drawer. A large "M.B." had been cut on the front of the leather covering by an unskilled hand. The letters were crude and the edges worn, and they had evidently been cut in the leather a long while ago.

The coroner examined the letters closely and returned the sheath to Strange.

"There can scarcely be any doubt as to the ownership of the knife," he agreed.

"What progress are your men making with their search?" demanded the major.

"The men have gone over the house twice without success," declared Strange. "O'Brill and Muldoon are now on the roof and the other men are searching adjoining houses."

"And have they found no evidence of any person having been in this house?"

"No one except Berjet and the valet."

"Dr. Rane, what do you think of this affair?" questioned Dobson impatiently. "We are progressing too slowly to please me. Have you any suggestions to offer?"

"I think it might help us if Mr. Deweese would describe in the most minute detail exactly what happened to him," returned Rane. "There is much of this story that has yet to be cleared up."

"Mr. Deweese," said Dobson, turning to the artist, "suppose you recount the details of your attack in your own way, and then, if necessary, we will question you."

Deweese had entirely recovered from his shock by this time and seemed eager to be of aid.

"On my way home from the theater," he began, "I stopped near the corner lamp, less than half a block away, to light a cigarette. As I was striking a match I heard a terrific crash of breaking glass behind me, and at once ran back to see what had happened. I found this gentleman"—nodding at Peret—"bending over the body of a man on the pavement. The body has since been identified as that of Max Berjet. Mr. Peret declared that the scientist had been murdered, and, at his bidding, I went to the drug store on the other side of the street to summon aid.

"While a clerk was 'phoning for the police I returned to the scene of the tragedy accompanied by the druggist and Dr. Sprague, who happened to be in the store at the time. Dr. Sprague examined and pronounced Berjet dead. Mr. Peret then informed the doctor that he was a detective and requested him to remain with the body until the police arrived, so he could make a preliminary investigation in the house. This Dr. Sprague agreed to do, and Mr. Peret ran across the pavement and jumped the fence in front of Berjet's house.

"I was standing a few feet away, talking with the druggist, and saw everything that followed. At the very instant that Mr. Peret leaped over the fence, I heard Dr. Sprague scream and saw him throw out his hands as if to grapple with something. He was standing by Berjet's body at the time. He appeared to have been attacked by some powerful and ferocious Thing, which I could not see, and I sprang forward to go to his assistance. It was then that I heard the whispering sound and felt the Thing hurl itself upon me.

"I could see nothing, but I felt my throat caught in a viselike grip and my chest crushed between two opposing forces. I cried out at once, and then my breath was shut off. I threw out my hands to grapple with the unseen Thing, but there appeared to be nothing to grapple with. My hands came in contact with nothing but air.

"Yet all of this while I could feel the monster crushing my life out. The terrible grip on my throat kept pressing my head back, inch by inch, and the pressure around my body seemed on the point of caving my ribs in. everything went black before me, and I could feel myself losing consciousness. Calling to my aid every ounce of strength I possessed, I made a last desperate effort to free myself of the Thing, and just as I felt life slipping from my grasp, the pressure on my throat and chest relaxed and, too exhausted to stand, I fell to the pavement."

"Unconscious?" asked the coroner.

"No, never for a single instant did I lose consciousness. Every terrible second of that eternity is indelibly stamped on my mind."

The recollection of his frightful experience made the artist tremble. Drawing a handkerchief from his pocket, he mopped his face.

"Was Dr. Sprague still struggling with his—ah—antagonist when you were attacked?" questioned the major.

"I cannot say," replied Deweese. "After I was attacked I had little thought to give to anything but my own defense."

"The testimony of both Peret and the druggist show that Deweese and Sprague were attacked at practically the same time," observed Strange, shifting his quid from east to west. "Both men struggled for a few seconds—about half a minute, according to Peret—and fell to the pavement at the same instant."

"Then it appears that we have more than one thing to contend with," interposed the major a little grimly. "Mr. Deweese, you are positive, are you, that you did not *see* the Thing? Think before you reply."

"It is not necessary for me to think," retorted the artist, "God knows, if I had seen the Thing I should not have been able to forge it this quickly!"

"When did you hear the Thing whisper—before or after it attacked you?"

"Before. After it hurled itself upon me I heard nothing."

"But you felt it breathing in your face"

"Not after the attack: no. it was immediately after I heard the whispering sound that I felt the Thing's breath on my face. After that terrible grip became fastened on my throat, everything else became negligible."

"You mean that even if the Thing had been breathing in your face it is doubtful if you would have known it?"

"Yes."

"Did this breathing sound or feel like the breathing of a man?"

"No; the Thing's breath was quick and jerky and cold as ice."

"*Cold?*" cried Peret, leaping to his feet.

He had been sitting back in his chair in an attitude of dejection, staring at a blank space on the wall. He had, with one ear, however, been drinking in every word of the conversation, and now he rose from his chair with such suddenness that he all but upset the little finger-printing expert standing in front of him.

"Yes, *cold*," repeated Deweese, the perspiration dripping from his brow, "cold and clammy."

"*Dame!*" cried the Frenchman, breathing on his hand as if to test the temperature of his breath. "Think well, my friend, of what you are saying. The breath of living things is *warm*. Perhaps it was not the breathing of a monster that you heard. It may have been--." He hesitated, and then, at a loss, stopped.

"There was no mistaking the—the thing I felt on my face," rejoined the artist grimly. "Except for the fact that it was cold and spasmodic it was like the breathing of a man."

"Like the breathing of a man choking on a piece of ice?" suggested the coroner.

"Exactly."

"Exactly."

"*Eh, bien!*" called the Frenchman, and smote himself on the forehead with his clenched fist. "Why did you not tell us this before?"

The Frenchman was transformed. Heretofore, in appearance at least, he had been an insignificant little man with no special capacity for the intricacies of unsolved crime mysteries. But now that the germ of an elusive idea had taken root in his mine he seemed to grow in stature as well as in intellect. His eyes became animated, his nostrils distended, his foolish little mustache took on an air of dignity, and his narrow shoulders seemed to grow straighter and to broaden.

Twisting the starboard point of his mustache fiercely between his fingers, he began to pace rapidly up and down the room. Dobson, who was acquainted with these symptoms, threw a significant look at the coroner. The look, however, failed to register, for Rane was staring at the floor, with knitted brow. He appeared to be thinking deeply.

Strange scratched his ear reflectively and stole a glance at the Frenchman. He, also was familiar with the latter's eccentricities and, like the major, was always a little awed by an outburst of his friend's temperament. Experience had taught him that this was a moment for silence, and he was determined to maintain it at all costs.

But even while he was rolling this thought around in his mind, and glaring threateningly at O'Shane, who was moistening his lips as if about to speak, the Frenchman put an end to it in a manner peculiarly his own.

"*Triomphe!*" he cried, with such suddenness and vigor that the iron-nerved detective sergeant jumped. "I've got it! At last I see the light!"

In his excitement he danced up and down in front of the major, to the secret amusement of the coroner and the astonishment of Deweese. Strange, however, knowing what this overflow of energy denoted, leaned forward eagerly and strained his ears to catch what would follow.

"Well, what have you got?" asked the major calmly, though the coroner thought he could detect a note of vast relief in his voice.

"The answer to the riddle, major," yelled Peret too excited to contain himself. "I've got it! I've found it! The mystery is solved. *Nom de diable!* The Thing is—"

"Stop," said the major, truculently. "We must use some discretion here. Are you sure you know what you are talking about, Peret, or are you simply making a wild guess?"

"I know it," shouted Peret, making a heroic though futile effort to lower his voice. "Ah, it was too simple! Like taking the candy from the mouth of the little one! *Oui, m'sieu;* The mystery is solved! I stake my reputation on it. I will show you—Stay!"

To the horror of the central office men, he grasped the dignified major by the lapel of his coat and dragged him (not unwillingly) out of his chair and half across the room. When they were well out of earshot of the others, he drew the major's head down and poured a perfect torrent of whispers in his ear.

Dobson heard the Frenchman out without interruption, but, while evincing the deepest interest, he did not appear to be altogether convinced. However, Peret had once been under his command, and there was no one who had more respect for his ability. It was he himself who, a year or so previously, had characterized the Frenchman as "an accomplished linguist, a master of disguise and one of the most astute criminologists on this side of the Atlantic."

In his present extremity, moreover, he was like a drowning man clutching at a straw. He was not in a position to reject a possible solution of the mystery advanced by a man of Peret's ability, no matter how unsound it might appear to him.

"What you say seems plausible enough," he remarked, when Peret paused for want of breath; "but it is, after all, only a theory. There is not a shred of evidence to give weight to your words."

"Evidence is sometimes the biggest liar in the world," said Peret, a little dashed by Dobson's lack of enthusiasm. "In this case, however, there is, as you say, no evidence of any kind—yet. We must therefore look for it, before it sneaks up on us and bites us. Ah, my dear friend. Think! Consider! Reflect! Why, the thing is as clear as a piece of crystal."

"What suggestions have you to make?" asked the major, visibly impressed. "I suppose you have in mind some plan--."

"*Oui!*" cried Peret, with fierce enthusiasm. "Except for one little thing, I ask that you give me a free hand. I will either prove or disprove my theory within twenty-four hours. Your men in the meantime, can make an independent investigation."

He made several hieroglyphics on a page torn from his memorandum book and handed it to the major. Dobson studied the characters for a moment, and then nodded.

"All right," he said briskly. "I give you a free hand. Call headquarters when you want, and in the meantime let me know at the earliest possible moment, if you learn anything of importance. *Allez—vous-en.*"

"Remember—no arrests!" hissed Peret, and, clapping his hat on the back of his head, he fled from the house as if pursued by the devil himself.

Chapter V: The House of the Wolf

Jules Peret was a man of parts. Born in the slums of Paris, he had migrated to America at an early age and, following the vicissitudes of a dissipated youth, had, by the sheer power of will and ability, forced himself to the top of the ladder of success in his chosen profession.

Eccentric, high-strung and affected, he was nevertheless something of a genius in his particular line. As a plainclothes man under the command of Major Dobson, his success had been outstanding. This was largely due to his love of the dramatic, and his knack of making the most unpretentious case assume huge proportions in the eyes of the public.

His methods were simple, apparently infallible, always spectacular. For which reason the newspapers gave him much space on their front pages and delighted in referring to him as the Terrible Frog and the Devil's Sister—appellations, by the way, that had their origin in the dives of the underworld.

Three months ago Peret had severed his connections with police headquarters and established himself as a "consulting detective." And because of the enviable record he had made while serving his apprenticeship on the "force," he had at once found his services in great demand.

At this time Peret was about thirty-four years of age. A small effeminate man, with delicate features, small hands and feet, rosy cheeks and trick eye-brows, one would have taken him for almost anything in the world but a detective. In manner and dress, he was typical of the *boulevardiers* of Paris. He affected a slender black mustache about the same general size and shape of a pointed matchstick, and he had a weakness for pearl-striped trousers and lavender spats.

Exteriors, however, are sometimes deceiving, and this was true in the case of the little Frenchman. When aroused, Peret was like a tiger. It was not for nothing that he had earned his terrible *noms de guerre* in the world of crime.

Erratic in manner as in dress, his departure—or, rather, his flight —from the home of the murdered scientist, was as distinctive of the man as was his mustache. The mirth of the coroner and the astonishment of Deweese meant nothing to him. He was too wrapped up in his own thoughts for the moment to consider the effect of his behavior on the others. He had simply felt the impulse to action and had obeyed it with characteristic promptness, energy and enthusiasm.

On the sidewalk he paused for a moment.

The night was pitch-black. Not a star was visible. The fog still hung over the city in heavy folds and at a distance of fifteen or twenty feet almost obliterated the street lights. A little crowd of morbidly curious sensation-seekers had gathered in front of the house and, much to their dislike, were now being herded away from the immediate scene of the crime by two uniformed policemen.

Turning up the collar of his coat, Peret wriggled his way through the crowd and sped across the street to the drug store. Entering a telephone booth, he ordered a taxi. He then called up his office, and when the connection was made, poured a volley of instructions into the receiver in language that must have burnt the wires.

Replacing the receiver on the hook, he left the store and, when his taxi arrived a few minutes later, started out on a feverish round of inquiries.

His first call was at the Army and Navy Building. Evidently luck was against him, for after a moment's stay he emerged from the building, with a scowl on his face. Hopping into the taxi, he ordered the chauffeur to drive to the Treasury Department.

Owing to the lateness of the hour, he had, as expected, some difficulty in gaining admittance. A cabalistic message sent to some mysterious personage within however, had a magical effect on the watchman, who swung wide the doors for him.

Hi stay within was brief, and after the portals had again been opened to let him out, he sped down the flight of steps in front of the building and crossed the street on a dead run. From the corner drug store he fired a message over the wire to police headquarters, then, quitting the store, once more boarded the taxi and instructed the chauffeur to drive him to a certain street corner.

After a short run, the cab came to a stop at the corner of a dark street in one of the residential sections of the city. Instructing the chauffeur to wait for him, Peret left the car and, wrapping his coat around him, glided off in the darkness.

Half way down the block, at the intersection of an alley, the Frenchman paused. Through the fog had lifted somewhat, the mist had turned into a heavy sleet and, if such a thing were possible, it was even darker than it had been an hour previously. Except for the taxi waiting at the corner, the street, so far as Peret could see, was deserted.

Stepping behind a tree-box, Peret surveyed the row of houses on the opposite side of the street. A dim light burned in several of the vestibules; otherwise the houses were wrapped in darkness. Satisfied that he was not observed, Peret stepped from behind the tree-box and gave a peculiar, birdlike whistle.

In answer to the signal, the eye of a flash-light blinked near the front door of one of the houses in the middle of the block, and Peret, clinging to the shadows, crossed the street. Drawing his automatic, he traversed the lawn to the house.

"Bendlow?"

"H'luva night to be abroad, Chief," came a hoarse whisper. "What's the row, anyway?"

Although it was too dark to distinguish the speaker's features, or, as a matter of fact, even to see the outline of his form, there was no mistaking the foghorn voice of Harvey Bendlow, former Secret Service agent and, at the present time, night manager of Peret's Detective Agency. Restoring his automatic to his pocket, the Frenchman gripped the other's hand.

"Haven't time to explain now," he said in an undertone. "We've got a big job ahead of us. How long have you been here?"

"'Bout an hour," croaked Bendlow. "I came on the jump just as soon as your message was received at the office. I've been prowling around taking a look-see."

"Seen anything of the occupant of the house?"

"Nope. I guess the Wolf is in the hay," was Bendlow's enigmatic reply.

"What's that?" asked Peret sharply. "Who is this that you call the 'Wolf'?"

"Say, don't you know whose house you sent me to watch?" demanded Bendlow in surprise.

"No; I have a suspicion that the man living in this house is a foreign agent, but I'm not sure that I know who he is."

"Well, your suspicion does you credit. This house at the present time is occupied by Count Vincent di Dalfonzo, better known to the Secret Service as the Wolf."

"*Tiens!*" exclaimed Peret, with rising excitement. "Are you sure?"

"None surer! Known him for a long time."

"Tell me what you know about him, quickly, my friend."

"Take too long now. He's got a record. Had a coupla run-ins with him when I was attached to the Secret Service. He's a clever and dangerous guy. International agent. Famous spy during the war. Plays only for big stakes, and the harder the game the better he likes it. Renegade Italian nobleman. His mother was an American. Takes after her in looks, I reckon. Never know he was a wop to look at him. He's been a thorn in the side of the foreign Secret Service for years. Too clever for them. They know he's the milk in the cocoanut, but they can't crack his shell, so to speak. He's a bad medicine, and no mistake. He kills at the drop of a hat."

"Bud how do you know he is living in this house, he? Have you seen him?"

"Nope. You ordered me to watch the house, and, not knowing what your game is, I haven't made any effort to see him. He's here, though, and it's damn funny, too. Last time I heard of him, two months ago, he was in Petrograd."

"If you have not seen him, how do you know he is living in this house?" asked Peret impatiently.

In a subdued voice, Bendlow rapidly related all he knew about the man he called the Wolf, and gave his reasons for believing him to be the present occupant of the house. When he concluded, Peret could scarcely control his elation.

"*Voila,*" he exclaimed softly. "You have done your work better than you know, my friend. Everything fits together beautifully. Now, let's to work. I wonder if there is any one in the house now?"

"Can't say for sure, but I doubt it."

"Well, we're going in, regardless. It's dangerous business, but necessary. I must clear up the mystery of the whispering Thing."

"The Whispering Thing?" questioned Bendlow.

"*Oui,*" whispered Peret tersely. "I cannot tell you what it is, for I do not know. But it's a demon, my friend, be sure of that! Keep close to me and be prepared for any eventuality. Ready?"

"Yep," laconically. "Lead on."

Peret tried the door behind him and found it locked. After several unsuccessful attempts, he opened it with a master key and, followed by Bendlow, entered the cellar. Closing the door, Peret brought his flashlight into play, and then, like a phantom, he passed over the concrete floor and ascended a flight of steps in the rear.

Unlocking the door at the head of the steps, the two detectives stepped out into the carpeted hall and paused for a moment to listen.

No sound greeted their ears. The house was as dark and silent as a grave. Even the light in the vestibule had been extinguished.

"Where next?" whispered Bendlow.

"The first floor, then upstairs," breathed Peret in his ear.

Guided by frequent flashes from Peret's flashlight, the two detectives explored the parlor, dining-room and kitchen, and found them empty, cold and silent. When they returned to the hall, Peret leaned over and put his lips to his companion's ear.

"Wait at the bottom of the front stairs and watch," was his whispered order. "I'm going up. Warn me if any one enters the house, and if you hear me cry out, turn on the lights and come to my help as rapidly as you can. The Whispering Thing strikes quickly, and, having struck, moves on. *Comprendez-vous?*"

"Yep," croaked Bendlow, and took up his stand at the place designated.

Flashing his light around the hall once more, so as not to lose his sense of direction, Peret began his slow and cautious ascent to the second floor. Placing his feet carefully on that part of the steps nearest to the wall so they would not creak, he worked his way up to the top of the steps. There he paused to listen.

No one knew better than he how fatal it would prove to be caught prowling around the house of a man as desperate as the Wolf was reputed to be, in the dead of night. There was not only the man himself to be feared; there was the Whispering Thing, for it Dalfonzo was, as he suspected, implicated in the murders he was investigating, it was certain that the invisible assassin, be it man, beast or devil was in league with the renegade Italian.

Yet a search of the man's house during his absence, or at least without his knowledge, seemed necessary, since Peret not only had no evidence against the Count, but had as yet to learn the exact nature of the Thing; and it would be useless to make an arrest until he could fasten the crimes on their perpetrator.

Having assured himself that no one was stirring, therefore, Peret began to explore the second floor. The house was a small one, and it did not take him long to go through the four rooms that comprised the second floor, especially as two of them were unfurnished. The other two rooms, which contained only the necessary articles of bedroom furniture, bore signs of recent occupation, but Peret was unable to find in them anything of an incriminating or even of an enlightening character.

Rendered moody by his failure to find the evidence he sought, the Frenchman returned to the hall and was about the retrace his steps to the first floor when he felt a pressure on his arm and heard Bendlow's hoarse, low-pitched warning in his ear.

"Something's in the vestibule."

Peret's muscles grew tense.

"Somebody coming in?" he asked quickly.

"Nope," came the reply. "It's something in the vestibule between the two doors. It musta been there all the time we've been here, as the front door hasn't been opened since I've been on guard."

"How do you know something's there?" whispered Peret.

"Heard it moving around, and when I put my ear to the keyhole I heard it breathing," was Bendlow's startling reply.

Peret's jaws closed with a snap, and his grasp on his automatic tightened.

"*Eh, bien,*" he hissed. "Follow me down stairs. Keep hold of my coat so we won't get separated. If anything approaches you from the rear, shoot first and ask questions afterwards. It begins to look as if we had tracked the Whispering Thing to its lair. *En avant!*"

Cautiously and noiselessly, the two men made their way down the dark steps to the first floor. Followed closely by Bendlow, who had an automatic in his hand, Peret tip-toed across the hall and applied his ear to the keyhole in the front door. He heard a slight movement on the other side of the door, and his spine stiffened.

Peret waited, with his ear glued to the keyhole. He could plainly hear something moving around restlessly in the vestibule, but, for the moment, he could not determine what it was. Suddenly, however, he heard a *thump* on the door and a scratching sound on the floor. This was followed by a loud whining yawn.

Peret caught Bendlow by the arm and drew him away from the door.

"It's a dog," he whispered disgustedly. "Dalfonzo doubtless placed him there to guard the entrance during his absence. Lucky for us we entered by the way of the cellar, eh?"

"I thought it might be a dog when I first heard it," muttered Bendlow; "but after what you said about the Whispering Thing I thought I better not investigate alone. Maybe the dog'll convince you that the Wolf is a tough customer. He's a hard man to catch napping. Going back upstairs?"

"No. I am through. There is no one in the house, and I can find no trace of the Whispering Thing. *Sapristi!* What a blind trail it is that I follow. Are you sure, my friend, that you have not made a mistake in thinking that Dalfonzo—"

"Not a chance," was Bendlow's emphatic reply. "This house, however, may be a blind. The Wolf may be laying low and working through his confederate. He may not even be in the city. However, as I am working in the dark, I will not hazard any more guesses. But you can bet your bottom dollar that the Wolf—"

"*Hist!*"

But Peret's warning came too late. Engrossed as they were in their whispered conversation, neither of them had heard the outer front door open, or the whine with which the dog welcomed the man who entered the vestibule. Peret's alert ear had caught the sound made by a key being turned in the lock of the inner door, and he hissed his warning just as the door was opened to admit the man and the dog. At the same instant a match flared in the hand of the new-comer, and the two detectives, as if on pivots, whirled.

"The Wolf," croaked Bendlow hoarsely, and, with Peret following darted down the hall.

"Halt!" commanded the Wolf, and the dog, with an angry growl, shot between his legs and hurled itself after the detectives.

Reaching the door at the head of the cellar steps, Bendlow grasped the knob and wrenched it open. A streak of flame stabbed the darkness and a bullet *zummed* by in Peret's ear and buried itself in the wall.

"Get him, Sultan," cried the Wolf, and fired another shot.

Sultan tore down the dark hall, his lower jaw hung low in readiness, but when he reached the end of the hall he found the two prowlers had disappeared and the cellar door was closed.

Chapter VI: The Whispering Thing

If Sultan was doomed to disappointment, so, too, were Peret and his husky companion, for they were not to make their escape as easily as they had at first believed then would. As they climbed from the basement window a dark form loomed up in front of them and a harsh voice commanded:

"Hands up!"

At the same instant the cold muzzle of a revolver came in violent contact with the Frenchman's nose.

"*Diable!*" swore Peret softly, and, realizing that he was at the other's mercy, elevated his hands with alacrity and, with a backward swing of his foot, kicked Bendlow on the shin.

Bendlow, however, needed no such urging. At the first spoken word, he had raised his automatic and taken deadly aim at the dark form in front of Peret. Something in the speaker's voice, however, made him hesitate to shoot.

"Climb out of there, you!" ordered the voice harshly. "No funny business if you're fond of life. C'mon out."

"Dick Cromwell!" spoke up Bendlow suddenly. "Drop your gat. It's Bendlow and Peret."

"Well, for the luva Mike!" exclaimed the central bureau detective, and lowered his revolver. Then, to someone behind him, "It's the Terrible Frog, Sarge."

With a sigh of relief that was not unlike a snort, Peret scrambled out of the basement, and, without loss of time, tersely explained the situation to the three city detectives who crowded around him and his companion. His explanation, however, did not altogether satisfy Sergeant O'Brien, who was in charge of the party. Although he and the other two detectives had been set to watch the house at the Frenchman's suggestion, he had not been informed of this and had no knowledge of Peret's connection with the cause, and further, while the two private detectives were both well and favorable known to him, he had been ordered to arrest any one who attempted to leave the house, and orders were orders.

The only thing he could do, therefore, was to hold the two men until he could telephone for instructions. Having explained this to Peret, he went to the patrol box in the next block to get in communication with headquarters, while the others retired to a safe distance from the house to await his return. When he rejoined them, a few minutes later, the two prisoners, after being subjected to much good-natured badinage, were released.

At the corner, where he found the taxi still waiting for him, Peret gave Bendlow his orders for the night, then climbed in the cab and left his lieutenant to shift for himself. His only desire now was to get home and crawl into bed. The past hour's work had disgusted and depressed him. The only thing he had accomplished had been to put Dalfonzo on his guard, and that was the last thing in the world he desired to do. Nevertheless, he felt that he had the case pretty well in hand and that within the next twenty-four hours he would be able to act decisively. And in this he found consolation.

Reaching his apartment house, he descended to the sidewalk, paid and dismissed the chauffeur without doing him bodily harm—which, considering the size of the far, was little less than remarkable —and even wished the bandit good-night.

Peret entered the apartment house with a sprightly step. Had he been attending his own funeral he would have done no less. His vast supply of nervous energy had to have some outlet, and even in moments of depression he walked as if he had springs in his heels.

It was long after midnight, and the front hall was deserted. Rather than awaken the elevator boy, who was dozing in his cage, Peret mounted the stairs to the second floor. At the front end of the dimly-lighted hall, he came to a stop and tied the door of his sitting-room. As he expected, he found it locked.

Inserting the key in the lock, he opened the door and entered the dark room. As he replaced the key in his pocked with one hand, he pushed the door shut with the other.

He heard the spring of the nightlatch close with a loud *click*. He was about to reach out his hand to find the push-button that operated the electric lights, when, suddenly, his head flew back with a snap and his body became tense.

The silence in the room was suddenly broken by a loud though inarticulate *whisper*—a loud, jerky, sibilant sound, that departed as abruptly as it had come.

The blood in the Frenchman's veins congealed. He could see nothing. The darkness was so intense that he could almost feel it press against his eye-balls.

Moistening his lips, he waited, with every sense alert, half believing that his ears had deceived him. But no. almost immediately the silence was once more broken by a blood-curdling *hiss*, and, at the same instant *Peret felt an ice-cold breath on his cheek.*

He shuddered, too paralyzed with fear to move. The hiss, or whisper, seemed to come from in front of him, and in his mind's eye he could see the invisible Thing gathering itself for attack. He shuddered again as *It* moved around in back of him and, after chilling his fevered cheek with its icy breath, whispered in his ear.

There was nothing human about the whisper: it had an unnatural and ominous sound, and the breath of the unseen Thing, which now fanned his face, was as cold and clammy as the respirations of an animated corpse.

Peret was undoubtedly a brave man. He had the heart of a lion and the strength of many men twice his size. But for once in his life he knew fear—real fear—a terrible, overpowering apprehension of impending danger.

The tragic happenings in the vicinity of Berjet's house were still so fresh in his mind that even his lively imagination could scarcely have lent color to the deadly peril in which he knew he stood. In a flash he recalled everything that Deweese had said about the whispers and the breathing that had preceded the attack of the monstrous Thing, and he remembered the death struggles of the scientist and Dr. Sprague, and their horribly distorted features as they lay stretched out on the pavement at his feet.

Again he heard the agonized scream of the physician and saw his bulging eyes as he battled for his life with the invisible monster.

He wanted to move, to scream, to strike out, to do anything but remain inactive, but, for the moment, he was helpless, for his soul was gripped by the icy fingers of terror. The hair of his head bristled and beads of cold perspiration burst from his brow.

That he stood in the presence of the Whispering Thing—the whispering and respiring supernatural horror that had, but a few short hours before, crushed the life out of the two men whose death he had sworn to avenge—he could not, and did not, for a moment doubt.

This story will be concluded in the next issue of Weird Tales. Tell your news dealer to reserve a copy for you.

THE THING OF A THOUSAND SHAPES (PART 2), BY OTIS ADELBERT KLINE

THE LAST THRILLING CHAPTERS OF THIS WEIRD NOVEL.

H ERE'S WHAT HAPPENED IN THE EARLY CHAPTERS:
William Ansley, who tells the story, receives word that his Uncle Jim is dead in Peoria and goes at once to his uncle's home. Later, while gazing upon the body in the gray casket, he hears himself say, as if against his own reason, "*He is not dead-only sleeping.*" Subsequent events indicate that this is true. William, watching beside the body in the lonely house at night, is visited by a number of terrifying apparitions. At midnight he fears that the worst is yet to come.

THE STORY CONTINUES FROM THIS POINT

∼

THE STORM SLOWLY ABATED, and finally died down altogether, succeeded by a dead calm.

An hour passed without incident, to my inestimable relief. I believed that the phenomena had passed with the storm. The thought soothed me. I became drowsy, and was soon asleep.

Fitful dreams disturbed my slumber. It seemed that I was walking in a great primeval forest. The trees and vegetation about me were new and strange. Huge ferns, some of them fifty feet in height, grew all about in rank profusion. Under foot was a soft carpet of moss. Giant fungi, colossal toadstools, and mushrooms of varying shades and forms were everywhere.

In my hand I carried a huge knotted club, and my sole article of clothing seemed to be a tiger skin, girded about my waist and falling half way to my knees.

A queer-looking creature, half rhinoceros, half horse, ran across my pathway. Following closely behind it, in hot pursuit was a huge reptilian monster, in outline something like a kangaroo, in size larger than the largest elephant. Its monstrous serpentlike head towered more than twenty-five feet in the air as it suddenly stopped and stood erect on its hind feet and tail, apparently giving up the chase.

Then it spied me. Quick as a flash, I turned and ran, dodging hither and thither, floundering in the soft moss, stumbling over tangled vines and occasionally overturning a mammoth toadstool. I could hear the horrible beast crashing through the fern brakes, only a short distance behind me.

At last I came to a rocky hillside, and saw an opening about two feet in diameter. Into this I plunged headlong, barely in time to escape the frightful jaws which closed behind me with a terrifying *snap*. I lay on the ground, panting for breath, in the far corner of the cave and just out of reach of the ferocious monster. It appeared to be trying to widen the opening with its huge front feet...

Someone had laid a hand on my arm and was gently trying to awaken me. The cave and the horrible reptile disappeared, and I was again in my uncle's living-room. I turned, expecting to see Mrs. Rhodes, but saw no one.

There was, however, a hand on my arm. It ended at the wrist in a sort of indescribable, filmy mass. I was now fully awake, and somewhat startled, as may be imagined. The hand withdrew and seemed to float through the air to the other side of the room.

I now observed in the room a sort of white vapor, from which other hands were forming. Soon there were hands of all descriptions and sizes. They were constantly in motion, some of them flexing the fingers as if to try the newly-formed muscles, others beckoning, and still others clasped in pairs, as if in greeting.

There were large, horny masculine hands, daintily-formed womanly hands, and active, chubby little hands like those of children. Some of them were perfectly modeled. Others, apparently in the process of formation, looked like floating bits of chiffon, while still others had the appearance of flat, empty gloves.

Two well-developed hands now emerged from the mass and moved a few feet toward me. They waved as if attempting to attract my attention, and then I could see they were forming letters of the deaf and dumb alphabet. They spelled my name:

"B-I-L-L-Y."

Then:

"S-A-V-E M-E B-I-L-L-Y."

I managed to ask, "Who are you?"

The hands spelled:

"I A-M-"

Then they were withdrawn, with a jerk, into the group.

I could now see a new transformation taking place. The hands were drawn together, dissolving into a white, irregular fluted column, surmounted by a dark, hairy looking mass. A bearded face seemed to be forming at the top of the column, which was now widening out considerably, taking on the semblance of a human form. In a moment a white-robed figure stood there, the eyes turned upward and inward as if in fear and supplication, the arms extended toward me.

The apparition began slowly to advance in my direction. It seemed to glide along as if suspended in the air. There was no movement of walking, just a slow, floating motion.

The phantom, when at the other end of the room, had seemed frightful enough, but to see it coming toward me was unnerving-terrifying. The nearer it approached, the more horrible it seemed, and the more firmly I appeared rooted to the spot.

Soon it was towering above me. The eyes rolled downward and seemed to look through mine into my very brain. The arms were extended to encircle me, when the instinct of self-preservation came to my rescue.

I acted quickly, and apparently without volition. Overturning my chair and rushing from the room, I ran out the front door and down the pathway. I did not dare look back, but rushed blindly forth into the night.

Suddenly there was a brilliant glare of light. Something stuck me with considerable force, and I lost consciousness.

When I regained my senses I was lying in a bedroom, the room I had occupied in my uncle's house.

A beautiful girl was bending over me, bathing my fevered forehead from time to time with cold water. Sunlight was streaming in at the window. Outside, a robin was singing his morning song, his farewell to the Northland, no doubt, as the stinging snow-laden winds of winter must soon drive him southward.

I attempted to sit up, but sank back with a groan, as a sharp pain shot through my right side.

My fair attendant laid a soft hand on my brow.

"You mustn't do that again," she said. "The telephone wires are down, so father has driven to town for the doctor."

Memories of the night returned. The apparition-my rush down the pathway-the blinding light-the sudden shock-and then oblivion.

"Do you mind telling me," I asked, "what it was that knocked me out, and how you came so suddenly to my rescue?"

"It was our car that knocked you out," she replied, "and it was no more than right that I should do what I could to make you comfortable until the doctor arrives."

"Please tell me your name-won't you?-and how it all happened."

"My name is Ruth Randall. My father is Albert Randall, dean of the local college. We had motored to Indianapolis, intending to spend the week-end with friends, when we were notified of your uncle's death. He and my father were bosom friends, and together conducted many experiments in psychical research. Naturally we hurried home at once, in order to attend the funeral.

"We expected to make Peoria by midnight, but the storm came, and the roads soon were almost impassable. It was only by putting on chains and running at low speed most of the time that we were able to make any progress. Just as we were passing this house, you rushed in front of the car.

"Father says it is fortunate that we were compelled to run at low speed, otherwise you would have been instantly killed. We brought you to the door and aroused the housekeeper, who helped us get you to your room. Father tried to phone for a doctor, but it was no use, as the lines were torn down by the storm, so he drove to town for one. I think that is he coming now. I hear a motor in the driveway."

A few moments later two men entered-Professor Randall, tall, thin, slightly stooped, and pale of face, and Doctor Rush of medium height and rather portly. The doctor wore glasses with very thick lenses, through which he seemed almost to glare at me. He lost no time in taking my pulse and temperature, pushing the pocket thermometer into my mouth with one hand, and seizing my wrist with the other.

He removed the thermometer from my mouth, then, holding it up to the light and squinting for a moment said "*Humph,*" and proceeded to paw me over in search of broken bones. When he started manhadling my right side I winced considerably. He presently located a couple of fractured ribs.

After a painful half-hour, during which the injured ribs were set, he left me with instructions to keep as still as possible, and let nature do the rest.

The professor lingered for a moment and I asked him to have Doctor Rush examine my uncle's body for signs of decomposition, as it was now more than three days since his death.

Miss Randall, who had left the room during the examination, came in just as her father was leaving, and said nice, sweet, sympathetic things, and fluffed up my pillow for me and smoothed back my hair; and if the doctor had taken my pulse at that moment he would have sworn my auricles and ventricles were racing each other the world's championship.

"After all," I thought, "having one's ribs broken is not such an unpleasant experience."

Then her father, entered-and my thoughts were turned into new channels.

"Doctor Rush has made a thorough examination," he said, "and can find absolutely no sign of decomposition on your uncle's body. He frankly admits that he is puzzled by this condition, and that it is a case entirely outside his previous experience. He states that, from the condition of the corpse, he would have been led to believe that death took place only a few hours ago."

"If you can spare the time," I said, "and if it is not asking too much, I should like to have you spend the day with me. I have much to tell you, and many strange things have happened on which I sorely need your advice and assistance. Joe Severs can take the doctor home."

The professor kindly consented to stay, and his daughter went downstairs to locate Joe and his flivver.

"The things of which I am about to tell you," I began, "may seem like the visions of an opium eater, or the hallucinations of a deranged mind. In fact, they have even made me doubt by own sanity. However, I must tell someone, and as you are an old and valued friend of my uncle's, I feel that whether or not you accept my story as a verity you will be a sympathetic listener, and can offer some explanation-if, indeed, it be possible to explain such singular happenings."

I then related in detail everything that had happened since my arrival at the farm up to the moment when I rushed head long in front of his automobile.

He listened attentively, but whether he believed my narrative or not I could not tell. When I had finished, he asked many questions about the various phenomena I had witnessed, and seemed particularly interested when I told him about the disappearance of the bat. He asked me where the book, which had been used to dispatch the creature, might be found, and immediately went downstairs, bringing it up a moment later.

A dry, white smudge was still faintly discernible on the cover. This he examined carefully with a pocket microscope, then said:

"I will have to put this substance under a compound microscope, and also test it chemically in my laboratory. It may be the means of explaining all of the phenomena you have witnessed. I will drive home this afternoon and make a thorough examination of this sample."

"I should be very glad indeed," I replied," to have even some slight explanation of these mysteries."

"You are undoubtedly aware," he said" that there are no vampires or similar bats indigenous to this part of the world. The only true vampire bat is found in South America, although there is a type of frugivorous bat slightly resembling it, which inhabits the southeast coast of Asia and Maylayan Archipelago, and is sometimes erroneously called a vampire or spectre bat. You have described in detail a creature greatly resembling the true vampire bat, but it is probable that what you saw was no bat at all. What it really was, I hesitate to say until I have examined the substance on this book cover."

"Well, whatever it was, I am positive it was no real vampire, as Glitch says," I replied.

"I don't like this vampire story that is being circulated by Glitch," said the professor. "It may lead to trouble. It is most surprising to find such crude superstition prevailing in these modern times."

At this juncture there was a rap at my door. I called, "come in," and Joe Severs entered.

"Well, Joe, did you get the doctor home without shaking any of his teeth loose?" I asked.

"Yes, sir, I got him home all right, but that ain't what I come to tell you about," he replied. There's a heap of trouble brewin' around these parts an' I thought I better let you know. Somebody's sick in nearly every family in the neighborhood, an' they're sayin' Mr. Braddock is the cause of it. They're holdin' an indignation meetin' up to the school house now."

"This is indeed serious," said the professor. "Do you know what they propose to do about it?"

"Can't say as to that, but they're sure some riled up about it," replied Joe.

Mrs. Rhodes came in with my luncheon, and announced to the professor that Miss Ruth awaited him in the dining-room below, whereupon he begged to be excused. Joe went out murmuring something about having to feed the horses, and I was left alone to enjoy a very tasty meal.

CHAPTER IV

A half hour later the housekeeper came in to remove the dishes, and Miss Randall brought me a huge bouquet of autumn daisies.

"Father has driven to town to analyze a sample of something or other that he has found," she said," and in the meantime I will do my best to make the hours pass pleasantly for you. What do you want me to do? Shall I read to you?"

"By all means," I replied. "read or talk, or do anything you like. I assure you I am not hard to amuse."

"I think I shall read, " she decided. "What do you prefer? fiction, history, mythology, philosophy? Or perhaps," she added, "you prefer poetry."

"I will leave the selection entirely to you," I said. "Read what interests you, and I will be interested."

"Don't be too sure of that," she answered, and went down to my uncle's library.

She returned a few moments later with several volumes. From a book of Scott's poems, she chose "Rokeby" and soon we were conveyed, as if by a magic carpet, to medieval Yorkshire with its moated castles, dense forests, sparkling streams, jutting crags and enchanted dells.

She had finished the poem, and we were chatting gaily, when Mrs. Rhodes entered.

"A small boy brought this note for you, sir," she said, handing me a sealed envelope.

I tore it open carelessly, then read:

"*Mr. William Ansley.*

Dear Sir:

"Owing to the fact that at least one member of nearly every family in this community has been smitten with peculiar malady, in some instances fatal, since the death of James Braddock, and in view of the undeniable evidence that the corpse of the aforesaid had become a vampire, proven by certain things which you, in company with two respected and veracious neighbors witnessed, an indignation meeting was held today, attended by more than one hundred residents, for the purpose of discussing ways and means of combating this terrible menace to the community.

"Tradition tells us that there are two effective ways for disposing of a vampire. One is by burning the corpse of the offender, the other is by burial with a stake driven through the heart. We have decided on the latter as the more simple and easily carried out.

"You are therefore directed to convey the corpse to the pine grove which is situated a half mile back from the road on your uncle's farm, where you will find a grave ready dug, and six men who will see that the body is properly interred. You have until eight o'clock his evening to carry out these instructions.

"To refuse to do as directed will avail you nothing. if you do not bring the body we will come and get it. *If you offer resistance, you do so at your peril, as we are armed, and we mean business.*

"THE COMMITTEE.

P.S. No use to try to telephone or send a messenger for help. Your wires are out of commission and the house is surrounded by armed sentinels."

As the professor had predicted, this was indeed a most serious turn of events. I turned to Mrs. Rhodes.

"Where is the bearer of this letter?' I asked. "Did he wait for a reply?"

"It was given to me by a small boy. " she answered. "He said that if you wished to reply, to put your letter in the mail-box, and it would be given to the right party. There was a closed automobile waiting for him in front of the house, and he ran back to it and was driven away at high speed."

"I must dress and go downstairs at once," I said.

"You must do no such thing," replied Miss. Randall. "The doctor's orders are that you must keep perfectly quiet until your ribs heal."

I heard a swift footfall on the stairs, and a moment later the professor entered the room, very much excited.

"Two farmers," he said, "poked shotguns in my face and searched me on the public highway. That's what just happened to me!"

"What do you suppose they were after?" I asked.

"They did not make themselves clear on that point, and they didn't take anything, so I am at a loss to explain their conduct. They merely stopped me, felt through my pockets and searched the car: then told me to drive on."

"Perhaps this will throw some light on their motive," I said, handing him the letter.

As he read it a look of surprise came over his face.

"Ah! It is quite plain, now. These were the armed guards mentioned in the postscript. It seems incredible that such superstition should prevail in this enlightened age; however, the evidence is quite too plain to be questioned. What is to be done?"

"Frankly, I don't know," I replied. "We are evidently so well watched that it would be impossible for anyone to go for help. Of course, they cannot harm my deceased uncle by driving a stake through the corpse, but to permit these barbarians to carry out their purpose would be to desecrate the memory of the best friend I ever had." "What are they going to do?" asked Miss Randall in alarm. I handed her the letter. She read it hastily, then ran downstairs to see if the telephone was working.

"What would you say if I were to tell you there is a strong possibility that your uncle's body is *not* a corpse; or, in other words, that he is not *really dead?*" asked the professor.

"I would say that if there is the slightest possibility of that, they will make a corpse of me before they stage this vampire funeral," I replied, starting to dress.

"I am with you in that," said he, extending his hand, "and now let us examine the evidence."

"By all means," I answered.

"According to the belief of most modern psychologists," he began, "every human being is endowed with two minds. Ones is usually termed the objective, or conscious mind, the other the subjective, or subconscious mind. Some call it the subliminal consciousness. The former controls our waking hours, the latter is dominant when we are asleep.

"You are, no doubt, familiar with the functions and powers of the objective mind, so we will not discuss them. The powers of the subjective mind, which are not generally known or recognized, are what chiefly concern us in this instance.

"My belief that your uncle is not really dead started when I first heard your story. It was later substantiated by two significant facts. I will take up the various points in their logical order, and you may judge for yourself as to whether or not my hypothesis is fully justified.

"First, upon seeing him lying in the casket, you involuntarily exclaimed, 'He is not dead-only sleeping.' This apparently absurd statement, unsubstantiated by objective evidence, was undoubtedly prompted by your subjective mind. One of the best know powers of the subjective mind is that of telepathy, the communication of thoughts or ideas form mind to mind, without the employment of physical means. This message was apparently impressed so strongly on your subjective mind that you spoke it aloud, automatically, almost without the subjective knowledge that you were talking. Assuming that it was a telepathic message, it must necessarily have been projected by *some other mind.* May we not, therefore, reasonably supposed that the message came from the subjective mind of you uncle?

"Then the second message. Was it not plainly from someone who knew you intimately, someone in dire need? You will recall that, just before you fell asleep, you seemed to hear the words, '*Billy! Save me, Billy.*'

"And now, as to the phenomena: I must confess that I was somewhat in doubt, at first, regarding these. Not that I questioned your veracity in the least, for no man rushed blindly in front of a moving automobile without sufficient cause, but the sights which you witnessed were so striking and unusual that I felt sure they must have been hallucinations. On second thought, however, I decided that it would be quite out of the ordinary for you and two other men to have the same hallucinations. It was therefore, apparent that you had witnessed genuine materialization phenomena.

"The key to the whole situation, however, lay in the seemingly insignificant smudge on the book cover. Two years ago your uncle advanced a theory that materialization phenomena were produced by a substance which he termed 'psychoplasm.' After listening to his argument, I was convinced that he was right. Since then, we have attended numerous materialization seances, with the object of securing a sample of this elusive material for examination. It always disappears instantly when bright light is flashed upon it, or when the medium is startled or alarmed, and our efforts in this direction have always been fruitless.

"Needless to say, when you described the deposit left on the book by the phantasmic bat, I was intensely interested. Microscopic examination and analysis show that this substance is something quite different from anything I have ever encountered. While it is undoubtedly organic, it is nevertheless remarkably different, in structure and composition, from anything heretofore classified, either by biologists or chemists. In short, I am convinced it is that substance which has eluded us for so long, namely, psychoplasm.

"No doubt you will wonder what bearing this has on the question under discussion-that is, whether or not your uncle still lives. As far as we are able to learn, psychoplasm is produced only by, or through, *living* persons, and in nearly every instance it occurs only when the person acting as medium is in a state of catalepsy, or suspended animation. As most of the manifestations took place in the room where your uncle's body lay, and as he is the only one in the house likely to be in that state, I assume that your uncle's soul still inhabits his body.

"The final point, and by no means the least important is that in spite of the time which has elapsed since his alleged death-in spite of that fact that it lay in a warm room without refrigeration or embalming fluid-your uncle's body shows absolutely no sign of decomposition."

"But how is it possible," I asked, "for a person in a cataleptic stated to simulate death so completely as to deceive the most competent physicians?"

"How such a thing is possible, I cannot explain any more than I can tell you how psychopalsm is generated. The wonderful powers of the subjective entity are truly amazing. We can only deal with the facts as we find them. Statistics show that no less that one case a week of suspended animation is discovered in the United States. There are, no doubt, hundreds of other cases which are never brought to light. As a usual thing, nowadays, the doctor no sooner pronounces the patient dead than the undertaker is summoned. Needless to say, when the arteries have been drained and the embalming fluid injected, there is absolutely no chance of the patient coming to life."

Together, we walked downstairs and entered the room where Uncle Jim lay. We looked carefully, minutely, for some sign of life, but none was apparent.

"It is useless," said the professor, "to employ physical means at this time. However, I have an experiment to propose, which, if successful, may prove my theory. As I stated previously, you are, no doubt, subjectively in mental *enrapport* with your uncle. Your subjective mind constantly communicates with his, but you lack the power to elevate the messages to your objective consciousness. My daughter has cultivated to some extent the power of automatic writing. You can, no doubt, establish rapport with her by touch. I will put the questions."

Miss Randall was called, and upon our explaining to her that we wished to conduct an experiment in automatic writing, she readily consented. Her father seated her at the library table, with pencil and paper near her right hand. He then held a small hand mirror before her, slight above the level of her eyes, on which she fixed her gaze.

When she had looked steadily at the mirror for a short time he made a few hypnotic passes with his hands, whereupon she closed her eyes and apparently fell into a light sleep. Then, placing the pencil in her right hand, he told me to be seated beside her, and place my right hand over her left. We sat thus for perhaps ten minutes, when she began to write, very slowly at first, then gradually increasing in speed until the pencil fairly flew over the paper. When the bottom of the sheet had been reached a new one was supplied, and this was half covered with writing before she stopped.

The professor and I examined the resulting manuscript. Something about it seemed strangely familiar to me. I remember seeing those words in a book I had picked up in that same room. On making a comparison, we found that she had written, word for word, the introduction to my uncle's book, "The Reality of Materialization Phenomena."

"We will now ask some questions," said the professor.

He took a pencil and paper and made a record of his questions the answers to which were written by his daughter. I have copied them verbatim, and present them below.

Q: "Who are you that writes?"

A: "Ruth."

Q: "By whose direction do you write?"

A: "Billy."

Q: "Who directs Billy to direct you to write as you do?"

A: "Uncle Jim."

Q: "How are we to know that it is Uncle Jim?"

A: "Uncle Jim will give proof."

Q: "If Uncle Jim will tell us something which he knows and we do not know, but which we can find out, he will have furnished sufficient proof. What can Uncle Jim tell us?"

A: "Remove third book from left top shelf of book case. Shake book and pressed maple leaf will fall out."

(The professor removed and shook it as directed, and a pressed maple leaf fell to the floor.)

Q: "What further proof can Uncle Jim give?"

A: "Get key from small urn on mantle. Open desk in corner and take out small ledger. Turn to page sixty and find account of Peoria

Grain Company. Account balanced October first by check for one thousand two hundred forty-eight dollars and sixty-three cents."

(Again the professor did as directed, and again the written statement was corroborated.)

Q: "The proof is ample and convincing. Will Uncle Jim tell us where he is at the present time?"

A: "Here in the room."

Q: "What means shall we use to awaken him?"

A: "Uncle Jim is recuperating. Does not wish to be awakened."

Q: "But we want Uncle Jim to waken some time. What shall we do?"

A: "Let Uncle Jim alone, and he will waken naturally when the time comes."

The professor propounded several more queries, to which there were no answers, so we discontinued the sitting. Miss Randall was awakened by suggestion.

"We now have conclusive proof that your uncle is alive, and in a cataleptic state," said the professor.

"Is there no way to arouse him?" I asked.

"The best thing to do is to let him waken himself, as he directed us to do in the telepathic message. He is, as he says, recuperating from his illness and should not be disturbed. You are, perhaps, unaware that catalepsy, although believed by many people to be a disease, is really no disease at all. While it is known as a symptom of certain nervous disorders, it may accompany any form of sickness, or may even be caused by a mental or physical shock of some sort.

"It can also be induced in hypnotization by suggestion. Do not think of it as a form of sickness, but, rather, as a very deep sleep, which permits the patient much needed rest for an overburdened body and mind; for it is a well-known fact that when catalepsy intervenes in any form of sickness, death is usually cheated."

"Would it be dangerous to my uncle's health if we were to remove him to his bedroom?" I asked. "It seems to me that a coffin is rather a gruesome thing for him to convalesce in"

"Agreed," said the professor, "and I can see no particular harm in moving him, provided he is handled very gently. Ruth, will you please have Mrs. Rhodes make the room ready? Mr. Ansley and I will then carry his uncle upstairs."

While Miss Randall was doing her father's bidding we tried to contrive a way to outwit the superstitious farmers, who would arrive in a few minutes if they made good their threat.

My eye fell upon two large oak logs, which young Severs had brought for the fireplace, and I said,

"Why not weight the casket with these logs and screw the lid down? No doubt they will carry it out without opening it, and when they are well on their way we can place my uncle in your car and be out of reach before they discover the substitution."

"A capital idea," said the professor. "We will wrap the logs well so they will not rattle, and, as the casket is an especially heavy one, they will be non the wiser until it is opened at the grave."

I ran upstairs and tore two heavy comforters from my bed, and with these we soon had the logs well padded. Miss Randall called that the room was ready. The professor and I carefully lifted my uncle from the casket and were about to take him from the room, when a gruff voice commanded:

"Schtop!"

A dozen masked men, armed indiscriminately with shotguns, rifles and revolvers, were standing in the hall. We could hear the stamping of many more on the porch. I recognized the voice and figure of the leader of those of Glitch.

"Back in der coffin," he said, pointing a double-barreled shotgun at me. "Poot him back, or I blow your tam head off."

Then several other men came in and menaced us with their weapons.

CHAPTER V

I dropped my uncle's feet and rushed furiously at Glitch, but was quickly seized and overpowered by two stalwart farmers.

The professor, however, was more calm. He laid my uncle gently on the floor and faced the men.

"Gentlemen," he said, "may I ask the reason for this sudden and unwarranted intrusion in a peaceful home?"

"Ve are going to bury dot vampire corpse wit a stake t'rough its heart. Dot's vot," replied Glitch.

"What would you do if I were to tell you that this man is not dead, but alive?" asked the professor.

"Alive or dead, he's gonna be buried tonight," said a burly ruffian, stepping up to my uncle. "One o' you guys help me get this in the coffin."

A tall, lean farmer stepped up and leaned his gun against the casket. The the two of them roughly lifted my uncle into it and screwed down the lid.

In the meantime, another had discovered the wrapped logs, to which he call the attention of his companions.

"Well, I'll be blowed!" he said. "Thought yuh was pretty slick, didn't yuh? Thought yuh could fool us with a coupla logs? Just for that we'll take yuh along to the part so yuh don't try no more fancy capers." "Gentlemen," said the professor, "do you realize that you will be committing a murder if you bury this man's body?"

"Murder, Hell!" exclaimed one. "He killed my boy."

"He sucked my daughter's blood," cried another.

"An' my brother is lyin' in his death bed on account of him," shouted a third.

"Come one, let's go," said the burly ruffian. "Some o' you boys grab hold o' them handles, an' we'll change shifts goin' out."

"Yah. Ve vill proceed," said Glitch. "Vorwarts!"

"If you will permit me, I will go and reassure my daughter before accompanying you," said the professor. "She is very nervous and may be prostrated with fear if I do not calm her."

"Go ahead and be quick about it," said the ruffian. "Don't try no funny stunts, though, or we'll use the stake on you, too"

The professor hurried upstairs and, on his return a moment later, the funeral cortege proceeded.

It was pitch dark outside, and therefore necessary for some of the men to carry lanterns. One of these led the way. Immediately after him walked six men bearing the casket, behind which the professor and I walked with an armed guard on either side of us.

Following, we were the remainder of the men, some twenty-five all told. There was no talking, except at intervals when the pallbearers were relieved by others. This occurred a number of times, as the burden was heavy and the way none too smooth.

I walked as one in a trance. It seemed that my feet moved automatically, as if directed by a power outside myself. Sometimes I thought it all a horrible nightmare from which I should presently awaken. Then the realization of the terrible truth would come to me, engendering a grief that seemed unbearable.

I mentally reviewed the many kindnesses of my uncle. I thought of his generous self-sacrifice, that I might be educated to cope with the world; and now that the time had come when I should be of service to him-when his very life was to be taken-I was failing him, failing miserably.

I cudgeled my numb brain for some way of outwitting the superstitious farmers. Once I thought of wrestling the gun from my guard and fighting the mob alone, but I knew this would be useless. I would merely delay, not defeat, the grisly plans of these men, and would be almost sure to lose my own life in the attempt. I was faint and weak, and my broken ribs pained incessantly.

All too soon, we arrived at the pine grove, and moved toward a point from which the rays of a lantern glimmered faintly through the trees. A few moments more, and we were beside a shallow grave at which the six grim sextons, masked like their companions, waited.

The casket was placed in the grave and the lid removed. Then a long, stout stake, sharply pointed with iron, was brought forward, and two men with heavy sledges moved, one to each side of the grave.

Here a discussion arose as to whether it would be better to drive the stake through the body and then replace the lid, or to put the lid on first and then drive the stake through the entire coffin. The latter plan was finally decided upon, and the lid replaced, when we were all startled by a terrible screaming coming from a thicket, perhaps a hundred yards distant. It was the voice of a woman in mortal terror.

"*Help!* Save me-save me!" she cried. "Oh, my God, will nobody save me?"

In a moment, all was confusion. Stake and mauls were dropped, and everyone rushed toward the thicket. The cries redoubled as we approached. Presently we saw a woman running through the underbrush, and after a chase of several minutes over took her. My heart leaped to my throat as I recognized Ruth Randall.

She was crouching low, as if in deadly fear of something which she seemed to be trying to push away from her-something invisible, imperceptible, to us. Her beautiful hair hung below her waist, and her clothing was bedraggled and torn.

I was first to reach her side.

"Ruth! What is the matter?"

"Oh, that huge bat-that terrible bat with the fiery eyes! Drive him away from me! Don't let him get me! Please! *Please!*"

I tried to soothe her in my arms. She looked up, her eyes distended with terror.

"There he is-right behind you! Oh, don't let him get me! Please don't let him get me!"

I looked back, but could see nothing resembling a bat. The armed men stood around us in a circle.

"There is no bat behind me." I said. "You are overwrought. Don't be frightened."

"But there *is* a bat. I can *see* him. He is flying around us in a circle now. Don't you see him flying there?" and she described an arc with her hand. "You men have guns. Shoot him. Drive him away."

Glitch spoke, "It's der vampire again. Ve'll put a schtop to dis business right now. Come one, men."

We started back to the grove. I was nonplussed-mystified. Perhaps there was such a thing as a vampire, after all. But no, that could not be. She was only the victim of overwrought nerves.

Once more we stood beside the grave. Two men were screwing down the coffin lid. The three with the stake and sledges stood ready.

I saw that Miss Randall was trembling with the cold, for she had come out without a wrap, and, removing, my coat, I placed it around her.

The professor stood at the foot of the grave, looking down calmly at the men. He appeared almost unconcerned.

The stake was placed on the spot, calculated to be directly above the left breast of my uncle, and the man nearest me raised his sledge to strike.

I leaped toward him.

"Don't strike! For God's sake, don't strike!" I cried, seizing his arm.

Someone hit me on the back of the head, and strong arms dragged me back. My senses reeled, as I saw first one heavy sledge descend, then another. The stake crashed through the coffin and deep into the ground beneath, driven by the relentless blows.

Suddenly, apparently from the bottom of the grave, came a muffled wailing cry, increasing to a horrible, blood-curdling shriek.

The mob stood for a moment as if paralyzed, then, to a man, fled precipitately, stopping for neither weapons nor tools. I found temporary relief in unconsciousness....

My senses returned to me gradually. I was walking, or, rather, reeling, as one intoxicated, between Miss Randall and her father, who were helping me toward the house. The professor was carrying a lantern which one of the men had dropped and fantastic, swaying, bobbing shadows stretched wherever its rays penetrated.

After what seemed an age of painful travel we reached the house, Miss Randall helped me into the front room, the professor following. Sam and Joe Severs were there, and someone reclined in the large morris chair facing the fire. Mrs. Rhodes came bustling in with a steaming tea wagon.

I moved toward the fire, for I was chilled through. As I did so, I glanced toward the occupant of the morris chair, then gave a startled cry. *The man in the chair was Uncle Jim!*

"Hello, Billy," he said. "How are you, my boy?"

For a moment I was speechless. "Uncle Jim!" I managed to stammer. "Is it really you, or am I dreaming again?"

Ruth squeezed my arm reassuringly. "Don't be afraid. It is really your uncle."

I knelt by the chair and felt Uncle Jim's arm about my shoulders. "Yes, it is really I, Billy. A bit weak and shaken, perhaps, but I'll soon be as sound as a new dollar."

"But how-when-how did you get out of that horrible grave?"

"First I will ask Miss Ruth if she will be so kind as to preside over the tea wagon. Then I believe my friend Randall can recount the events of the evening much more clearly and satisfactorily than I."

"Being, perhaps, more familiar with the evening's deep-laid plot than some of those present, I accept the nomination," replied the professor, smiling, "although, in doing so, I do not want to detract one iota from the honor due to my fellow plotters for their most efficient assistance, without which my plan would have been a complete failure."

Tea was served, cigars were lighted, and the professor began.

"In the first place, I am sure you will all be interested in knowing the cause of the epidemic on account of which some of our neighbors have reverted to the superstition of the dark ages. It is explained by an article in *The Peoria Times*, which I brought with me this afternoon, but did not have time to read until a moment ago, which states that the countryside is being swept by a new and strange malady known as 'sleeping sickness,' and that physicians have not, as yet, found any efficient means of combating the disease.

"Now for this evening's little drama. You will, no doubt, recall, Mr Ansley, that before we joined the funeral procession, I requested a moment's conversation with my daughter. The events which followed were the result of that conversation.

"In order that the plan might be carried out, it was necessary for her first to gain the help of Joe and Sam here, and then make a quick detour around the procession. I know that there are few men who will not rush to the rescue of a woman in distress and I asked her to call for help in order to divert the mob from the grave. She thought of the bat idea herself, and I must say it worked most excellently.

"While everyone was gone, Joe and Sam, who had stationed

themselves nearby, came and helped me remove your uncle from the casket. As we did so, I noticed signs of returning consciousness, brought about in some measure, no doubt, by the rude jolting of the casket. Then the boys carried him to the house, while I replaced the lid. you are all familiar with what followed."

"But that unearthly shriek from the grave," I said. "It sounded like the cry of a dying man."

"Ventriloquism," said the professor, "nothing more. A simple little trick I learned in my high school days. It was I who shrieked."

∼

UNCLE JIM and I convalesced together.

When my ribs were knitted and his strength was restored, it was decided that he should go to Florida for the winter, and that I should have charge of the farm. He said that my education and training should make me a far more capable manager than he, and that the position should be mine as long as I desired it.

He delayed his trip, however, until a certain girl, who had made me a certain promise, exchanged the name of Randall for that of Ansley. Then he left us to our happiness.

THE END.

THE CONQUERING WILL, BY TED OLSON
CAN THE DEAD RETURN TO LIFE?

Gordon Paige is dead now, and surely there can be no harm in giving to the world this mad story, contained in the manuscript he left behind. Many will think that the man WAS mad; many will believe that he was attempting to perpetrate an immense and grotesque hoax. I do not know. I do know that Gordon always impressed me as the sanest of men, and surely he never seemed a man to father so strange and horrible a practical joke. But it is not for me to tell you what I believe, or attempt to force upon you my own opinion. Rather I shall offer the story as he left it, and let you interpret it as a joke or a madman's dream, or a remarkable document from that mysterious border realm of which we know so little.

What is Soul? Who can define it? What is that intangible quality that makes me what I am, that brands me as a creature distinct, individual, with an entity that is my own and none other's?

Who can answer? I do not know. I can only tell you my story—the story of Malcolm Rae—and ask that you give it what credence you can.

It was two years ago that I bade Jane Cavanaugh good-by at the railway station in our little home town of Radford. She was weeping, and clumsily I tried to comfort her.

"I sha'n't be gone long, dearest," I said. "A year isn't long. I'll be back in June, when my work is done. Then—we'll be married, and we'll never be separated again."

"I know," she answered. "I'm foolish" She smiled up at me bravely, an April smile, with the tears still glistening in her brown eyes. "But —I've been frightened, somehow. It seems so far, up in that cold wilderness, and I've had you such a short time. I won't be foolish again."

The northbound train began to move, and for the last time I caught her in my arms and pressed my lips to hers.

"In June, dear. I'll be back. I promise. Don't worry," I said again, as I swung upon the step of the Pullman.

She was smiling—that brave, April smile—and I watched her until the train carried me beyond sight of her.

&

Northward we went, Dan Murdock and I. Somewhere in those barren mountains in the untrammeled Northwest of Canada, a grizzled old prospector had unearthed a store of that precious stuff, tungsten. Murdock and I had been sent by our government to investigate it, determine its value, its quantity, and report.

It was a long task that awaited us. August was already upon us. The road inland was long and hard. It would be winter when we reached the prospect, spring before we could hope to complete our data and return.

Four days took us to the end of the railroad—a station tumbled in the midst of scarce-broken prairie and timberland. There we met the prospector, a shriveled, wiry, hairy old man, marked indelibly with the brand that men bear who have lived much in solitude.

From there our trail led northwest. Up waterways we pressed, across silent, silver lakes, hemmed in to the very brim with an untouched growth of pine and spruce; across portages, where streams thundered down precipitous canyons while we laboriously transported canoe and duffel through the timber, following faint paths that told plainly how rarely they had known human foot prints.

August passed—a series of long days filled only with the toil of paddle and portage. September was on us, and the days grew shorter, and sharp at either end. We were in a veritable untrodden land now. The mountains were close upon us. The portages grew more frequent, the way more rough and toilsome. Norton, the leathery-skinned old prospector, informed us curtly one morning "Four more days, and we're there."

That day we abandoned the canoe, cacheing it safely in shrubbery ad underbush. For two days we pressed upward, packing across a ridge that tested our strength to the utmost.

The morning of the third day found us once more on water. We had reached a deep, swift river, a stream that flowed to the north. We had crossed the divide and were on a tributary of the Mackenzie. From a cunning cache Norton drew forth another canoe, and we sped at ease down the stream.

And then—came the tragedy. It was noon of the fourth day. From round the bend in the river we heard the unmistakable roar of rapids.

"Portage?" queried Dan of our guide.

Norton shook his head. "Shoot 'er," he answered curtly.

A moment later we swung around the bend. Before us the banks drew suddenly closer together, and the river narrowed and shot down between granite walls. The channel was checkered with boulders, around them the tortured waters spat and hissed, flung themselves high in unavailing anger, yelled their rage in deafening uproar.

Dan and I glanced questioningly. One narrow channel we could see—perilously narrow, perilously swift. But it was too late to reconsider. Already the waters quickened beneath us, bore us on with an insidious smoothness that was belied by the speed with which the canyon walls shot by. Norton sat poised at the bow, alert, ready. Murdock and I gripped our paddles. In a moment we were in it.

With sickening speed we shot into the turmoil. The roar rang in our ears terrifyingly. Spray shot over and drenched us. We battled furiously, plunging our paddles deep as Norton signaled us. The light craft seemed to leap and bound, like a runner at the hurdles, gathering impetus at each new thrust.

Then—a rock seemed to leap up in our very path. Dan, kneeling amidships, gave a cry of terror, and plunged wildly with his paddle. The delicately-balanced boat swayed, lost for a moment its poise, slued sideways.

A splintering crash, and I found myself in the seething water.

How I lived I do not know. I was a strong swimmer, but in that blind turmoil, skill availed littler. I was borne headlong. I was conscious of boulders bludgeoning me cruelly. But suddenly the waters grew quieter. I was swept into an eddy at the foot of the canyon. Somehow, I struck out weakly, and, blind, breathless, and beaten, drew myself on a gravelly bar.

How long I lay there I can only guess. Bit by bit my strength returned. I sat up. I was on the edge of a mountain meadow, through which the stream swept, still foaming and boisterous. The thunder of the canyon came to me noisily.

The sound of it called me suddenly to a realization of my position. I strove to rise. A sickening, terrible pain shot through me, and as I dropped back to the sane I knew that my left leg was shattered.

It was not long before I knew the worst. Murdock and Norton were dead. I could not doubt the truth. Dan, as I knew, could not swim; and even had he been an expert swimmer it would be but through blind good fortune that any man could live in that seething torrent.

By such blind luck I had been saved. For what crippled, alone, with neither food nor shelter, in a wilderness hundreds of miles from human aid, with winter hanging imminent, what chance did I have? Saved? Yes—for death by slow torture!

For a moment, as the realization sent a sick despair through me, I was tempted to plunge once more into the river, and let the waters finish their work. But I dismissed the cowardly impulse. I would not despair. I *would not die!*

I took a more careful review of my surroundings. For the first time

I saw, on the bank not a hundred yards away, a cabin—a mere pen of mud-plastered logs, but still a cabin. On the hillside above it was a scar in the earth. It was Norton's cabin, Norton's mine. But Norton was dead.

The sight gave me new courage. There was yet hope. I dragged myself to a kneeling position, gritting my teeth until the pain cleared a bit, and then began to creep toward the cabin.

∼

IT WAS TORTURE, every inch of the way. Twice I fainted with the sheer agony. But I kept on. It had been noon when we neared the canyon. The sun was setting when I drew my body across the cabin door and fell in a stupor on the floor. There I lay until morning.

The pale dawn found me tossing in a high fever. I must have been delirious for days. But after a time I woke, very weak, but rational. I began to take stock of my surroundings.

I had hoped to find the cabin well stocked with provisions. A hasty survey proved that my hopes were vain. The tiny room was almost barren. A hand made cupboard stood in one corner, but it was all by empty. A driblet of flour, a strip of moldy bacon, a few shreds of jerked venison. Again despair shook me nauseatingly, again I banished it was grim resolve.

With the scant supply of wood I built a fire, dragging myself somehow around the room to get what I needed. There was water in a pail by the fireplace. I brewed the jerked meat for an hour. The resultant mixture was a weak, tasteless broth. Yet it was food—the first I had tasted for days. I drank some of it, and felt stronger.

My shattered leg had begun to knit. I had set it as best I could before the fever took me. Now it pained greatly, but with the aid of an old broom that I found I made shift to move around. And again hope flared warm in my heart. I built the fire high, and crawled under the robes in Norton's bunk.

In the night I woke uneasily. First I was conscious of the throbbing in my leg; then I realized that what had aroused me was the sound of the wind roaring and shrieking past the walls, yelling like a horde of demons without.

Above my head was a window, made of caribou skin scraped parchment-thin, and against this I could hear the spit and rattle of snow. The fire had died to embers, and a bitter chill crept through the cabin. Winter had come.

At dawn it was still storming. For three days the blizzard kept up. I huddled in my robes, fed the fire from the diminishing pile of wood, ate sparingly of the scanty food. And again the fear began to play upon my heart with chill fingers; again I strove to banish it was grim resolve.

On the fourth day the snow ceased, but the wind remained unabated. It grew terribly cold. And on that day my woodpile dwindled to nothing, my last scrap of food vanished.

It grew colder, I kept the fire burning charily, feeding it, bit by bit, the scanty furniture that Norton had made with axe and hammer. I husbanded every bit, crouching over the merest spark of a flame, wrapping my thin body in robe and fur to conserve the precious warmth.

And still the storm raved around the cabin. Still the screaming wind drove the snowflakes against the windows, through badly-chinked crevices—a malicious, devilish wind that seemed to my disordered brain, to be an embodied spirit of evil bent on my destruction. And still the cold penetrated, mocking my efforts to stave it off.

Hunger and cold and pain combined to sap my strength. I grew delirious. For hours I forgot where I was, lived again the hours I had spent with Jane, saw her as I remembered her, a slim, exquisite thing, dark of hair, luminous of face, a spirit thing, too fine for man's possession. And again I pressed her in my arms, and swore that I would return.

Waking from such visions, the will to live burned very strong in me. I *would* live; I *would* return. I swore it. Death could not conquer me; could not conquer love. Yet all the time I grew weaker; the flame of life flickered lower in my emaciated body.

The body was dying. I knew it. It scarce had strength now to cast more wood on the dying fire. Within it the pulse of existence flickered feebly. But never was the real *me* more alive. I burned fiercely with the desire to live. I swore I should not die.

Then one morning I awoke. The fire was out. Yet I was not cold. I attempted to rise; my body did not answer. I attempted to speak; no words came. Then I knew.

In the night the body had died. It lay there now, stiff, still. It had ceased to live.

But *I* was not dead. I could see my body lying there, a cast-off thing. But *I* was here.

The entity that was I had not perished with the flesh. The will to lie was still mine. And I was alive! I was infinitely alive.

My perceptions were a hundred times clearer. I saw, I heard, I felt, as I never had before. And it seemed as if my whole being were concentrated in the one desire—to see Jane, to tell her I still lived.

And then there shot through my brain a terrible, sickening thought. To all the world's knowledge I was dead. I was no longer flesh, but spirit. I could see Jane, no doubt, but I could never make myself known to her. I had lost her.

∼

THE MOST EXQUISITE torture of soul racked me as the realization came. I was not dead. There was no death; my will had conquered it. But I was hopelessly and forever exiled from the world I had known. That warm familiar word that held love and so many other things, was forever taken away from me.

Hopelessly exiled! Again my will revolted at the thought. Why was I forever condemned to such exile? There lay the body. It had ceased to live, in truth. I had shed it as one does a garment. But why could I not don it again?

The body had stopped because of external, physical reasons. The soul had fled because living soul could not inhabit dead flesh. But if the physical conditions that had ended life were removed, could not the soul again restore it to life. If aid, food, warmth were to come, could I not live again in the body?

And so I waited. Soul kept vigil over body in that room—the two that had been linked so inextricably for thirty-one years, now divorced so irrevocably. You call it bizarre? That is because I tell it to you thus. How do you know but that it has happened times without number? You have watched by dead bodies, perhaps. How do you know that strange, invisible guest may not have shared the vigil with you?

And so I waited. Night came. The wind had died a little outside, and through the cold I heard the distant howl of wolves.

Again the howls came, and closer this time. It was a pack in full cry, spurred on by hunger, questing through the frozen solitudes for food. And now I could hear them in the clearing and suddenly I realized what they sought.

Forgetting my impotence, I strove with desperate hands to bar the door more tightly. I seized my rifle—or tried to seize it. It was vain. Spirit has no fear from dangers of this world; equally it has no means of defense.

Round the cabin the wolves circled cautiously. I could hear them sniffling at the door.

Then one brute dashed himself against the panels. The stout frame quivered, but held. A long-drawn howl came; it thrilled me with terror. Then another clawed at the caribou-skin of the window.

A gleaming claw shot through, a pair of slavering jaws followed. In a minute they were in.

Can you dream of a thing so horrible as to watch your own body being torn apart by wild beasts?

They snarled, they fought. Their fangs clipped and tore. I grew sick with despair. The night was hideous with their snarls and yowling.

Unable to endure it, I fled. And horror tore at my heart. For now I knew I was indeed exile. The fleshly cloak that I had forsaken, that I had hoped to resume, was torn, destroyed.

I had only one wish now. To see Jane again, even though I could not speak to her, could not hold her in my arms. To see her at least, bitter as it would be, were still consolation.

There are no bounds of time or space to the unfettered soul. And so I found myself, without knowing how, in that long, homelike room where we had sat so often, with the fire flaming cheerily on the great hearth, the friendly books and pictures, everything that was so good a setting for the girl I loved. In the quiet peace of it I forgot that desolate solitude, that cabin with its howling, fighting inmates.

Jane was seated reading by the window, but as I watched she laid aside the book, and sat looking out of the window across the silent, moonlit fields. And I saw two tears glide from her eyelashes, and glisten on her cheeks. She spoke my name.

That evidence of her love was more than I could hear. I knelt beside her, strove to take her in my arms, whispered a thousand broken endearments. And she sat pensive, unresponsive, utterly unconscious of me. The tragedy smote me again. I was spirit; she spirit in flesh. I was exiled.

And, with the ecstasy of despair, there flamed once more in me that dogged, unreasoning will to live—to live again, I must say.

And, with it, I fled the room, guided somehow, blindly, by new hope.

I found myself in another house—in a bedroom that was very quiet, with an unnatural silence. In the bed lay a man. I knew him. It was my old friend, Gordon Paige.

There were others, too. Gordon's mother sat with her face in her hands. His sister, her eyes dry and bright, knelt beside her and pressed her in comforting arms. Then I saw the white-haired doctor turn mutely away. And I knew why I had come.

The body of Gordon Paige lay there, inert, lifeless. With all the power I knew I willed myself toward it.

The body of Gordon Paige stirred. He spoke. The light of sanity came back into his dead eyes. The doctor turned to him in amazement. A minute later he turned again.

"He lives! God knows how, but he lives. The crisis is past. He will recover."

And he *did* recover. The body of Gordon Paige won back to life and health.

But the soul within his body was the soul of Malcolm Rae!

∽

WHAT IS SOUL? What is self? I speak to you with the voice of Gordon Paige. I write, and the handwriting is that of Gordon Paige.

But I—the entity that dwells in the body of Paige—*I am Malcom Rae.*

In the spring they brought the news of Malcolm Rae's death to Jane Cavanaugh. She loved him—she was heart-broken. But she found comfort in the presence of her old friend Gordon Paige.

We were married last week, Jane and I. It was June, just a year after the June in which Rae had promised to return. When I told Jane I loved her, she said:

"I do love you, Gordon. But sometimes it seems wrong—after poor Malcolm dying. But—you're like him, Gordon. You're so like Malcolm that I can't blame myself for caring.

I wish I could tell her—that I am Malcolm.

But the word is too incredulous. I do not dare.

SIX FEET OF WILLOW, BY CARROLL F. MICHENER

THE STRANGE TALE OF A YELLOW MAN AND HIS BELOVED REPTILE

It was for no love of the Chinese that Allister risked his life in the shark-plagued waters off Samoa.

The motive was largely a rigid sense of fair play, which had led him into more than one hazard. Also, he hated the second mate, who was so ridiculously afraid of Ssu Yin's serpent.

Therefore the Chinese need have nourished no great feeling of obligation. Scales for weighing honor and indebtedness, however, are not the same in the East as in the West, where motives are perhaps more closely scanned; and it would have been difficult to persuade Ssu Yin that he did not owe more than life to Allister. He felt that he owed *two* lives; that of his own leather-yellowed body and that of the woman whose soul, so he believed, now sojourned on its vast pilgrimage along the Nirvana-road of incarnations, within his snake's scaly longitude.

To the Chinese, an obligation clearly understood is a collectible asset. Death or the devil—or dishonor that is worse than either—claims him who escapes payment of a just debt. Therefore it need not be surprising that the magnitude of his fancied obligation to Allister discomfited Ssu Yin, and left him more than melancholy for the remainder of the voyage.

On the other hand, his devotion to the serpent, a poisonous six feet of willow-green relieved by the satin-white ribbon of its belly, was greater than before, and the venom of his regard for the second mate, who had dared toss the reptile's basket overboard ,was disquieting to observe.

The thing had happened in a flash that gave Allister no more than a moment for reflection before the action than had bound him with inseverable fetters to the destinies of Ssu Yin. The second mate, who was Irish, with a soul fed upon belief in banshees and leprechauns and the traditions of St. Patrick, had chafed bitterly at the captain's indifference toward the Chinaman's obnoxious galley-pet.

His irritation had grown steadily since the third day out from Panama, when the reptile's presence on board had been discovered. The captain was one of those rare humans in whom a snake breeds no particular revulsion; he merely winked at Ssu Yin's vagary, stipulating, as an afterthought, that the serpent should be tied by the neck and at all times safely confined to its bamboo cage.

The mate's displeasure grew into agitation, and then into a saturnine fear. Ssu Yin's notion that the serpent was animated by the spirit of his dead wife, a creature of frail morals whose fate it had been to be slain in an act of infidelity, reduced the mate to paroxysms of superstitious rage. A suggestion of insanity blazed from his eyes, and he vented his irritation upon the crew in a variety of diabolical mistreatment. Stealthily he plotted the serpent's destruction.

He had long to wait, for Ssu Yin was rarely beyond sight of his somnolent pet. But one day, growing reckless from the excess of his somewhat alcoholic fear, the mate seized the bamboo cage, well beyond reach of its occupant's fangs, lifted it brusquely through the window of the cook's galley—from under the very eyes of Ssu Yin—and gave it a triumphant heave overboard.

With a yell that seemed to supply added impulse to his flying heels and to stiffen his queue into a rigid horizontal, Ssu Yin darted from the galley and flung himself after his ophidian treasure.

Allister turned automatically toward a life boat, but the mate thrust him back. A fanatical cruelty colored the leer in the man's face as he watched Ssu Yin bobbing helplessly some yards from the bamboo cage, quite evidently unable to swim.

"Aren't you going to launch that lifeboat?" Allister bawled at him.

The mate spat over the rail, with a sullen negation.

"The hell you won't," snarled Allister, poising swiftly to plunge after the Chinaman. "Let's see if you'll do it for a white man, then."

∼

THE MATE LOWERED THE BOAT, not so much because Allister was white as because he was a brother of the captain. There was a calm sea, and no difficulty in the rescue. The crew fished up the three of them, Allister supporting the exhausted Ssu Yin, who in turn held aloft, out of the wash of the sea, his most unhappy dry-land reptile.

The mate shut himself up in his cabin and drank Jamaica run with such proficiency that it became necessary to lodge him in the brig. He wallowed there for the remainder of the voyage into Penang, where Ssu Yin, with the serpent clasped to his meager bosom, scuttled ashore and vanished from the mate's bleary ken.

Allister, for whom the world was in its opening chapters, lost himself in bizarre and dizzy pages of Oriental life. At the end of three years he was "on the beach," tossed up with other human jetsam from the slime of the Orient's undertow.

He had brawled with sailors from many seas in the dives of Hongkong, tasted the wickedness of native inland cities, and squandered himself in a thousand negligible pursuits between Bangkok and Peking. He was the eternal parable of West meeting East, a conjunction perpetually fatal to the insecure soul. For it is only the strong who can sip safely at the pleasant vices of a mellower civilization.

On a day squally with the pestilent dust of an obscure Chinese outport, Allister sat gazing at a wooden door in a wall. He was oblivious to outward discomfort, although his clothes were remnants through which the wind drove chill misery. He felt only one need, and his mind had room for but one thought, and that was the gratification of an unholy lust. It was three days since opium had caressed his shrieking nerves.

Beggars, exhibiting their unspeakable sores, the ghastly souvenirs of real or simulated disease, jostled him in their crawling search for charity; it was the plaza of a temple where he had taken up his watch.

Curses, and the muttered insults that are flung to foreigners, came to him from the crowd, but he appeared not to hear; his senses were subject only to one diversion, and that was the wall before him, with its wooden door, and the peephole that for an hour of eternities had remained blind. If he could not gain the attention of Ssu Yin, he would be doomed to another night of drugless terror.

To knock on the door would be useless; he had tried that. Only a certain alarum would gain admittance, and no amount of cunning had been capable of revealing this to him. To shout was equally futile, for Ssu Yin had become almost wholly deaf, the result of his barber's unskillful wax-scraping—an accident with an equally unfortunate sequel, the barber having been bitten to death shortly afterward by Ssu Yin's serpent.

It was necessary, Allister well knew, to wait for the soya-brown eye that glistened intently through the peephole at a certain hour of the day—the eye of Ssu Yin, focused expectantly upon some indeterminate object within the temple grounds.

The impatient accents of a woman, half-concealed behind the discolored marble flank of a stone lion with the head of a dog, roused Allister. He had been long enough in the Orient to absorb an understanding of many dialects.

"The serpent-eared grandfather of a skillet is late," complained the voice, and there was an answering murmur from another woman at her side.

Allister stole a glance at them, and saw that they, like himself, were interested in the wooden door. One was young, and probably, though not definitely, a courtesan; she may have been merely an adventurous and discontented second-wife. Her companion was an older woman, evidently a servant.

His eyes returned to the hole in the door, but his ears continued to listen for the words of the women. The servant was speaking:

"How long, Tai-tai, must my Crimson Lotus submit to the vile attentions of this opium hawker? Surely it should not be difficult—"

"It is more difficult than thou thinkest, mother of no sons."

"Will he not take my Peach Blossom—my Lotus—into his stinking hovel? Will he look upon your beauty in no place other than the teahouse?"

"He fears the serpent."

"The serpent?"

"Have I not told thee, daughter of an addled egg? He cherishes a creeping creature that he swears was once his wife in a former life. He fears the fangs of her jealousy."

"A serpent may be crushed by the heel—"

"That shall be thy task, then. Nay, find the way, and it shall be my heel, and mine the silver *sycee* that lies under the bricks of his *kang*."

"Find the way?"

"The secret of the knocks that gain admittance, O Half Moon of Wisdom—buy it from one of the slaves of the pipe that come here each day."

Allister heard no more, for there was of a sudden a deeper shadow, a more animate void, within the aperture of the door. He shook himself together, and arose, for he was conscious of the eye of Ssu Yin.

After a moment the door opened, and the opium seller stood forth. He was imperceptibly startled when Allister touched his sleeve, for his attention had been directed to the vanishing glint of embroidery that beckoned him toward the tea pavilion of a Thousand and Three Beatitudes.

There was no greeting from either, and there was no need of word or gesture. Allister's drug-lust uttered its own argument, and Ssu Yin bowed with the air of both acquiescence and of acknowledge obligation. He shouted backward into the passage behind the open door, and shuffling feet responded.

The door closed behind Allister's starved figure, and Ssu Yin, conscious of the street-crowd admiration that followed the unwonted gayety of his attire, crossed a miasmatic lotus pool and entered the teahouse.

∽

ALLISTER WAS able to think more clearly when the stupor wore away, though mind and body were torn by a devastating revulsion. He lifted himself abruptly from the filthy bunk in which he lay, and the feeble, awkward movement upset a stand upon which was his chandoo pipe, still nauseous with burnt opium. The effort left him suddenly faint, and with alarm he shuddered back into the bunk, closing fiery-lidded eyes.

"Can't be far from the end," he murmured to himself. "If I could only get away—if I could only get back to the States!"

This was the usual burst of remorse; it was like all the rest, a feeble protest against ill-directed destiny. He knew that, of his own effort, he never would get back to the States, away from the insidious East. He had tried that; he had worked until the money was in his hands, only to dive more steeply for a time toward the poppy fields of oblivion.

The consul-general had shipped him out on a transport, but he had gone only as far as Manila. The call of the drug had been too insistent. If the vessel only had been going straight East, without a stop, to the California coast, he might have made it.

He *would* make it! He would get the money once more—earn it, perhaps, but somehow he would get it, and go Home.

After a second effort, he succeeded in struggling to his feet, then in staggering out of the room into a larger one where there was the light of a horn lantern, and the comforting aroma of tea.

Ssu Yin sat gurgling contemplatively at his water-pipe, his eyes fixed upon two brilliant points of light in the half-shadows over the *kang*. He did not stir at Allister's approach, though he muttered an acknowledgement of the other's presence. Slowly Allister's bleared sight, following the direction of Ssu Yin's comprehended the significance of those cold-blue darts of phosphorescence. They were set in a rigid, cylindrical, limblike standard, projecting motionless from a pyramid of symmetrical coils. Often as he had beheld the serpent of Ssu Yin, on the poppy excursions that brought him so frequently to the sea cook's illicit den, he had never conquered a subtle fear, a rage for crushing, stamping out, obliterating. He had tried to explain this as an expression of man's traditional enmity toward the creeping creatures of the earth. Curiously, to witness the same fear in another was his sole antidote. In the presence of one who was more afraid than himself he could laugh down his own feeling, as had happened in the case of the second mate.

He sat down beside the brazier and helped himself to a gulp of tea. Ssu yin, removing his eyes from their fixed stare, with a gesture that suggested the snapping of an invisible thread binding them to the eyes of the serpent, regarded Allister with an attentive but unfathomable look. Though his countenance expressed nothing, he was, Allister observed, in an unwonted mood. It was as if there had been a misunderstanding between himself and his reptilian familiar.

"Was there sweetness in the Elder Brother's honorable pipe of August Beginnings?" inquired Ssu Yin, bringing forth the foreign ear-trumpet that looked incongruous against its oriental setting.

A grimace of pain was Allister's only answer.

"And was the sleep of this poor worm's wise and illustrious benefactor filled with the jasmine-incense of celestial happiness?"

"May your flesh be jellied and your bones splintered," was Allister's discourteous shot into the trumpet. "May your ancestors—"

"Harmless is the bluster of the paper tiger," interrupted Ssu Yin, with a playful malice. He went on in a more kindly vein: "A gem cannot be polished without friction, or a man perfected without adversity. The friction has been thine, Elder Brother, even as it is written; also the adversity; but a wise man also has said that the gods cannot help him who loses opportunities."

"Oh, drop the classic, Ssu Yin, and tell me what you're driving at!"

"The Elder Brother must set his feet unto new paths, or he will learn to walk soon in the Eternal Shades."

"I'm through, Ssu Yin. No more chandoo for me. Tomorrow—"

"The man who overestimates himself is like a rat falling into a scale and weighing himself."

Allister was stung by the contempt of his host's words, but he feared to retort. His sense of need came more fully upon him. His head swam, leadenly, and his tongue was thick.

"The pipe, Ssu Yin—only once more. And tomorrow—"

"Spawn of frog begets but frog; the wise man does not give his cloak to the stealer of his coat; and to cure a habit by indulging it is to push a stone with an egg."

"No, Ssu Yin, I mean I this time—"

"Dragging the lake for the moon in the water, adding fuel to put out a fire," ran the relentless river of Ssu Yin's scornful proverbs.

Nevertheless, Ssu Yin arose and led the way to the sleeping-room. He set forth within Allister's reach a bamboo pipe with black tassels and a mouthpiece of jade, lighted the lamp, and from a receptacle within his capacious sleeve jealously produced three miniature cylinders of amber-hued opium.

Cynically, Ssu Yin observed the trembling hands of the white man as he held one of the precious morsels over the flame, watched it sizzle, dissolve, evaporate. He waited until the operation thrice had been performed, each puff sending Allister nearer to the paradise of drugs, and stood gazing at the young man's emaciated features long after the squalid room had been translated, for Allister, into a pearly grotto through which he stepped forth on the winged feet of inexhaustible youth into a world of unimaginable color, transcendent beauty and unspeakable delight.

"A just debt—a just debt is mine," muttered Ssu Yin, solemnly, "and it is thus that I have paid. For this I have merited no less than the reproach of the gods."

∼

WHEN ALLISTER RETURNED AGAIN from the lotus fields of Elysium, his eyes were more fevered, his yellowed skin closer drawn over cadaverous cheeks, and his weakness even greater than before.

This was the tomorrow of which he had spoken to Ssu Yin.

But what had any Oriental tomorrow to do with him? Here there were promises only of more lethal hours that did not relieve so much as they accented the deepening miseries leading toward an indubitable end.

Tomorrow—

He sprang up suddenly, the effort startling his heart into wild uncertainties. The recurrence of a feeling of resentment, long nourished, supported him.

"Ssu Yin, the superstitious dog—rich—preaching to me in nasty proverbs and feeding me this spawn of hell when he might be sending me home!"

The thought took possession of him, made him stealthy and steel-nerved. He would take the money—Ssu Yin owed it to him, the heathen ingrate; this time he would have a share in that hoard of *sycee* beneath the bricks of the *kang*.

He crept into the other room, fearing to find Ssu Yin there, a delay to his plot. But Ssu Yin was not in the room; the house seemed empty even of servants. The seller of opium probably was at his daily tryst, Allister thought, in the teahouse of the Beatitudes.

For the moment Allister had forgotten the serpent, and it was only in the act of turning his darting steps toward the *kang* that he remembered. In that instant a ray of sunlight revealed the still creature, eternally somnolent, as immobile as the stones against which its gelid coils were ranged.

The old fear seized him, and with it the rage to kill; but his weakness returned, and he was incapable of that. He remained as motionless as the snake, thinking of its reputed iniquities. The opium den of Ssu Yin was not without a reputation for crime. It had had its murders, strange deaths that baffled the native doctors of both "inside" and "outside" anatomy.

The serpent, he knew, was master of man in a duel of eyes, and Allister felt relief at a sound of interruption. Someone had entered the house. The shock loosened his limbs, and he crept back to his foul bunk, waiting for the philosophical gibes of Ssu Yin, sick with revulsion at thought of his intended theft.

His ears told him in a moment, however, that the wary step and the listening caution of the one who had entered, were not Ssu Yin's. Presently there were hurried movements, unwonted sounds, a breathless intenseness that took audible form, in the outer room. Stealthily, Allister moved nearer to see.

The figure of a woman was beneath the ray of sunlight now, cutting off its warning of the coiled spectre of dissolution. She stooped over the *kang*, lifting the bricks, laying them aside with a careless impatience. A cavity grew, and from it presently, with a sigh of gratification, she plucked a silver ingot—followed it with others, until a mound of them, too heavy for her own strength, lay at her feet.

Allister watched her in amazement. Was she unaware of the snake? Or was she, like Ssu Yin, its master, immune to the ophidian fear?

She stood up, turned toward Allister, as if at some psychic warning of his presence, and he recognized her as the woman of the temple yard—the Crimson Lotus, Ssu Yin's teahouse siren.

Doubtless her apprehensions heightened her error, but in the half-light it must have been easy to mistake Allister's immobile figure for the darkly vengeful one of Ssu Yin.

She cried out, took an involuntary step backward, tripped upon a *sycee* ingot, and a bared arm, thrust outward to break her fall, met the serpent's fangs.

∽

IN THE NINE-TONED sing-song of a Cantonese who is at peace with himself, Ssu Yin entered his hovel incanting a bar of that old song of Cathay, "The Millet's in Flower."

He paused at the door of his inner room, in the middle of a note, and allowed the details of the tableau to etch themselves upon his brain.

Across the *kang* lay his woman—his Crimson Lotus—inert, lifeless. Upon her still breast, its viridescence blending strangely with the soft tints of her silk tunic, was piled the deadly pyramid of the coiled serpent—flat, arrowy head drawn back awaiting the impulse to strike, glistening red tongue stirring with forked vibrations, and phosphorescent eyes blazing with a sinister fury.

Within reach of its fangs was crouched Allister, one hand touching, with a suggestion of pity, the face of the woman, the other, clasping a silver ingot, poised cataleptically in the midst of an intended blow. His was the arrested animation of craved marble, the impotent fascination of a bird obeying the hypnosis of the serpent's eye.

Slow rage filled Ssu Yin—a calm cruelty. Here lay his broken Lotus Bud; a thief, an accomplice, a wanton, or a viperous traitor to his heart's homage—what did it matter? And here was his "Elder Brother" his benefactor, the white man—dog despoiler—who would have robbed him of all.

Well, a simple solution—the fangs of his serpent, slavering for their prey....

But the poise of a hundred philosophical generations began to quiet his thick pulses—the restraints of a race that has schooled itself to play the game of life by meticulous rule. A debt was his—he must pay it.

Ssu Yin realized, suddenly, that an abrupt movement, the slightest translation of Allister's rigid pose into activity, would bring to him the darting caress of oblivion.

Cautiously, Ssu Yin approached, uttering a curious sound that always, until now, had brought an answering acquiescence into the eyes of the serpent. He came closer, at last laying his parchment-skinned hand upon the vibrant coil, seeking a grip that would keep him safe from a scratch of fangs.

But something was amiss with Ssu Yin's mastery over the snake. He recognized this in a thrill of terror at the moment when he knew it was forever too late. He would have explained, had there been time for such inquiry, that it was jealousy in the soul of the transmigrated woman who had been his wife—jealousy of the Crimson Lotus. This it was, he would have said, that animated the serpent's yellow needles of death.

The poison gripped him, but a sense of unfinished justice gave him strength while he battered the cringing reptile into an amorphous, hideous mass.

With Allister, dazed, half understanding, he still had the business of words. A courteous smile crackled the parchment of his face as he took from his sleeve an envelope and held it out to Allister.

"Three lives for two," he murmured, "and the debt is more than paid. May the August Elder Brother's voyage into the friendly bosom of the West be as pleasant as the repose of Buddha."

Allister's wondering fingers disclosed within the envelope a steamer ticket to Seattle. He put out a protesting hand, began self-accusing phrases, but the seller of opium was beyond argument. Ssu Yin was on his knees murmuring before the shelf of the gods:

"Unabashed, Great Ancestors—into the Val of Longevity Ssu Yin walks without shame."

THE HALL OF THE DEAD, BY FRANCIS D. GRIERSON

THE OCCULTISM OF ANCIENT EGYPT PERMEATES

"You have good nerves?" asked Professor Julius March, with a somewhat cynical smile.

Annette Grey shrugged her shoulders.

"People who work for their living," she replied "cannot afford nerves."

The Professor nodded.

"There is something in that" he answered thoughtfully. "At the same time, I must make the position clear to you. As you are aware, I am an Egyptologist, and in my house here I have many queer things. Some people dislike the idea of working among mummies and—"

Annette interrupted him with a deprecating gesture.

"Believe me," she said, "that sort of thing does not affect me in the least. As your secretary, I am prepared to work where and when you like."

"My former secretary—" the professor began, and paused.

"Your former secretary disappeared,' said the girl. "Of course I know that; you will remember that I applied for the vacancy after reading about her in the paper. I do not propose to disappear; the terms you offer are too good."

She smiled faintly, and the Egyptologist shrewdly eyed her.

"Well," he said at last, "your qualifications and education appear to recommend you for the work I should want you to do. It is secretarial work in the broadest sense of the term—from typing my notes (when you have learned to decipher my abominably bad handwriting) to looking up references in the British Museum, or—should occasion arise—accompanying me on a flying visit to Egypt. I give you fair warning that I shall work you hard, but, apart from the salary and board, which I have already named, you will not find me ungenerous if you prove yourself valuable."

"Then may I consider myself engaged?"

March bowed.

"Certainly," he replied. "You will probably learn presently," he added, in his cynical way, "that I am regarded as an eccentric person, and somewhat of a hard taskmaster—"

"I prefer to form my own opinion," said Annette quietly.

Again he smiled. It was not a pleasant smile.

So Annette Grey took up her residence in the rambling old house on the outskirts of London in which Professor Julius March had gradually accumulated relics of ancient Egypt that were regarded with respect by the curators of some of the greatest museums in the world.

There were those who hinted that the Professor had not always been scrupulous in the methods he adopted to secure his rarer curios; but March laughed at such stories when anyone had the hardihood to repeat them to him, openly attributing them to the jealousy of less fortunate rivals. Wealthy and profoundly learned, he had become known as one of the greatest Egyptologists of his day.

Annette studied her new employer with the patience characteristic of her nature, and she found the study an interesting as well as a useful one. March, for the most part, was reserved and silent, but he was capable of bursts of extraordinary excitement. He devoted himself, with an almost religious fervor, to the pursuit which he had made his life study, and the few friends he possessed—for he was not a popular man—were almost all brother archeologists.

Tall and thin, with black eyes peering through large tortoise-shell-rimmed spectacles, his gray hair tumbled in a shaggy mass over his broad forehead, he had a habit of thrusting his square chin aggressively forward when he spoke. His long, graceful fingers moved in nervous sympathy with what he was saying, and he would spring from his chair and walk rapidly up and down with catlike steps that reminded Annette of a panther ceaselessly pacing to and fro behind the bars of its cage.

Possessed of great endurance, he would site for hours at a stretch poring over an ancient papyrus, disdaining food and sleep. Then, plunging into a cold bath, he would emerge glowing, eat an enormous meal and set off for a long walk, indifferent as to whether it happened to be day or the middle of the night.

When March first asked her whether or not she had good nerves, Annette had supposed him to be referring to the disappearance of Beatrice Vane, his former assistant. Beatrice, a beautiful girl just budding into the maturity of womanhood, had vanished utterly, leaving her clothes and other possessions behind her, but no clue as to where she had gone. March, with his lawyer, Henry Sturges, had sought the assistance of the police, and every effort had been made to trace the missing girl, but without success.

Attorney Sturges, who had recommended Beatrice Vane to Professor March, had been the girl's guardian. An orphan, she had been left a small annual income, the capital of which was under Sturges' control as trustee. She had received a good education, and the lawyer had procured her employment with Julius March in order that she might occupy her time and at the same time supplement the scanty income which declining financial conditions had left her.

March spoke highly of her work, and was more affected by her disappearance than many, who saw only the cynicism of the man, would have believed. He feared, Annette supposed, that his new secretary would think it unlucky to step into the shoes of the girl who had vanished so mysteriously, and she hastened to disabuse his mind of any such idea.

But Annette soon found that there existed an additional reason for his question. The old house, she found, was divided into two parts. In one, the smaller of the two, lived March and his staff. A bachelor, he was looked after by an elderly housekeeper, one or two maids, a chauffeur and a confidential valet, who had been with him for years. These people attended to what he called the "domesticities" of the place.

The larger part of the house was consecrated to his hobby, and had been, indeed, altered and partially reconstructed to suit his unusual requirements. Into this Egypt in miniature the servants were sternly forbidden to penetrate. There March would bury himself amid his mummies and papyri, and sometimes, in his morose moods, even his secretary was forbidden access.

Annette had a comfortably-furnished sitting-room of her own, and a little room furnished as an office, but a great part of her work, she found, was to be done in the room which March grimly called the "Hall of the Dead."

It was, indeed, an apartment in which only a girl of strong nerves could have worked without glancing fearfully over her shoulder. Floored with black-and-white marble, alternated in a curious pattern, it was dimly lit by a lamp swung from the roof by bronze chains. To afford the stronger light necessary for the study of ancient inscriptions, a smaller lamp stood on each of two small tables, the incongruous effect of their electric wiring being mitigated by their antique shape. These lamps, however, illuminated only their immediate neighborhood, leaving the greater part of the huge room in semi-obscurity.

Round the room were placed at regular intervals mummies and mummy-cases, whose grave immobility seemed by a mask which they could tear off at will, descending to move about the hall with measured steps and to converse on topics that had been of living importance to a long-dead civilization.

In the center of the hall stood a great stone table, curiously grooved and hollowed, and between the mummies were placed objects of metal and earthenware, the uses of which Annette could only guess.

In this strange room March would pass hour after hour. Annette soon learned to understand and accommodate herself to his methods. The sharp sound of an electric bell in her room would bring her to the Hall of the Dead, notebook and pencil in hand. The heavy door, controlled by an automatic mechanism, would roll back as she approached, closing silently behind her as she entered and took her seat, without a word, at one of the smaller tables.

Acknowledging her presence only by a gesture, March would stride up and down the room with his quick tread, pausing now and again to examine a document or to apply a magnifying glass to the inscription on a mummy-case, muttering to himself as he resumed his rapid pacing. Suddenly, without warning, he would commence to dictate, in sharp, staccato sentences, admirably lucid and without a superfluous word.

He would cease as suddenly as he had begun, and for perhaps half an hour, or longer, he would remain buried in thought, resuming his dictation as unexpectedly as he had ceased, but without ever losing the sequence of his ideas.

Sometimes this would go on for hours. On such occasions he would recollect himself suddenly, glance at the ancient water-clock on its carved pedestal, and dismiss Annette with a word of apology for his forgetfulness.

Once an incident occurred which revealed yet another side of this man's complex character.

Annette had received a lengthy piece of dictation, and had been at work in her office for nearly an hour, transcribing her notes. She was a competent writer of shorthand, but some of the technical expressions which March used were quite unfamiliar, and she did not care to interrupt him, preferring to wait until he had finished before asking him any questions. On this occasion it had seemed fairly plain sailing, but toward the end of her notes she came across a sign the significance of which completely baffled her.

Finding that the context was of no assistance, and not wishing to delay the work, which she knew the Professor required as quickly as possible, she resolved to consult him.

It was the first time she had visited the Hall of the Dead unbidden, and she was uncertain how to attract his attention from the outside, for there was no knocker or bell on the great door. The mechanism which controlled it, however, either did not depend on the person inside, or could be so set as to work independently, for as she reached the threshold some concealed spring was put into operation and the door opened before her as usual. Still standing on the threshold, she was about to enter, when she stopped as though turned into stone.

Inside the hall she saw Julius March kneeling before one of the mummy-cases—the mummy-case of a woman. His head rested against the knees of the image, and his body was shaken by great sobs.

Amazed, moved by the strange sight, Annette turned and fled to her own room. Behind her the door of the Hall of the Dead swung noiselessly into its frame.

∼

A WEEK LATER, Annette entered the little-used drawing room of Professor March's house shortly before seven o'clock in the evening, and sat down near the bright fire ready to receive his guests. For March was giving one of his rare dinner-parties.

A few moments later the door opened, and the servant ushered in Attorney Sturges and a friend of his, a pleasant, rather simple-looking man named Sims.

"I fear we are a little early, Miss Grey," said Sturges, when he had presented his friend.

"Not at all," Annette replied easily. 'Professor March asked me to make his excuses to you; he was detained at the British Museum and only arrived a few minutes ago. He is dressing, and will be down in a few minutes. Meanwhile, I must play hostess."

"And most adequately," murmured Sturges, with old-fashioned courtesy.

Then, as the door closed behind the servant, he spoke rapidly:

"We came a little early on purpose," he explained. "You are prepared, Miss Vane?"

"Quite," said the girl calmly.

"Good. Inspector Sims agrees with me that if we are ever to discover the mystery of your sister's disappearance, it will be tonight. Sims has been practicing his part, and does it admirably."

The Scotland Yard man smiled.

"I think I can play it," he said. "And I congratulate you, Miss Vane, on the way you have handled the matter. This idea is an excellent one, and I admit I should never have thought of it myself. I hope, too," he went on, without the slightest alteration in his tone, as a step sounded outside and the door opened, "that Professor March will not deny me a peep at the wonderful treasure he keeps here."

"Why, of course not," cried March heartily, as he entered the room. "I caught your last words, Mr. Sims," he went on, "—for I am sure you are Sturges' psychic friend—and I shall be delighted to show you round my little museum. Well, Sturges, I must apologize to you both for keeping you waiting like this; but you have been in good hands."

He bowed courteously to Annette.

"It is very good of you, Mr. Sims," he went on, "to come and visit a recluse like this. Sturges has told me of your powers of necromancy, and I confess I am hoping to see something very wonderful."

The words were polite and were uttered with perfect civility, but the old lawyer laughed gently.

"It's no good, March," he said; "you cannot quite get the true ring. You scientific fellows always scoff at the unseen, and decline to believe anything that cannot be set down in writing, like an algebraic equation."

"Not at all," replied the Professor, with sudden gravity. "On the contrary, my researches have convince me that there are mysteries to which, if we only had the clue—but we'll talk of that later," he added, with a sudden change of tone. "My first duty, as your host, is to feed you; come and help me perform the sacred rite of hospitality."

Laughing, he opened the door and bowed Annette to the head of the little procession to the dining-room, where they were presently seated round a candle-lit table of richly-polished mahogany.

It was a strange dinner-party, at which two, at least, of the diners found it difficult to appreciate the sallies of the host. Mr. Sims, however, expanded under the influence of the Professor's geniality. March was in unusually high spirits, for he had just succeeded in translating a hieroglyphic inscription which had defeated the Museum authorities, and he devoted himself to the sport of drawing out his psychic guest with a delicate irony which, to do him justice, never passed the bounds of good taste.

The innocent Mr. Sims responded to this subtle flattery with a readiness which delighted the Professor, and even Annette and the lawyer could not refrain from smiling at the naiveté with which Sims played his part.

At last the dinner drew to a close, and March rose.

"I am not going to let you off, Mr. Sims," he said. "I am eager to learn something of the methods of the modern spiritualists, for I admit I am more familiar with those of the past. But I think we ought to have a more suitable atmosphere for the *séance*," he added, chuckling. "Miss Grey, I hope you will not leave us? I think my Egyptian room would form an admirable background for Mr. Sims' experiments."

Annette smiled, with something of an effort, and led the way to the Hall of the Dead.

Despite himself, Sims could not repress an exclamation of awe at the sight of the great, gloomy room, with its solemn figures and mysterious shadows.

The Professor rubbed his hands, well pleased at the effect he had produced.

"Now, Mr. Sims," he said, "here is a carved chair on which a Pharaoh once sat. Enthrone yourself there. We will sit, metaphorically, at your feet, and listen to what you are pleased to tell us."

Sims bowed, but did not return the Professor's smile. Gravely he seated himself in the heavy wooden chair, rested his elbow on one of the quaintly-carved arms, and let his head sink onto his hand. The others grouped themselves near and waited, in a heavy silence.

Sensitive to impressions, the Professor's gay mood faded gradually into a tense expectancy that made his long fingers work nervously. He startled as Sims' voice broke the silence sharply.

"I am aware, Professor March," said Sims in a hard, level tone that startled his hearers, "that you are a skeptic."

The Professor murmured something, but Sims went on, without heeding him.

"I feel tonight that I am going to prove to you that I can see things that are hidden...."

He paused, and again the silence was broken only by the sound of heavy breathing. As suddenly as before, Sims spoke again:

"Listen!" he said. "I see a great room, half lit by a lamp in the roof. There is a brighter light near a table in the center of the room. It is a stone table, such as was used in ancient Egypt by the embalmers."

The Professor drew in his breath with a sharp gasp, but the voice went steadily on:

"Beside the table I see a man. He is bending over something—something white. It is the body of a woman—"

"*Stop*, damn you!" screamed the Professor; and Sims, springing from his chair, took something from the pocket of his dinner-jacket.

The Professor laughed discordantly—the laugh of a madman.

"Put up your pistol," he cried. "You will not need it. I don't know who you are, and, damn you, I don't care! Do you hear that? *I don't care!* Listen, all of you; listen, I say! Today I have completed my task; I have learned the secret which I have sought so patiently. I am going to join my Princess, my Hora."

He ceased, and threw his arms out in a great gesture to the mummy-case in front of which he had been standing. Huge drops of sweat stood out on his forehead, and he tore open his linen collar with a madman's strength. But it was in a controlled, almost tender voice that he went on:

"Listen to me, and I will tell you a wonderful thing. Countless years ago I—I who speak to you here tonight—was a priest in Egypt. I was vowed to the service of Isis. But one day there came to the temple, where I ministered, a woman. A woman? Nay, a goddess! A being of such beauty that my heart leaped within me at the sight of her loveliness.

"She was the Princess Hora. We loved. Ten thousand words could say no more. But an evil fate tore her from me; the Pharaoh had seen her, and coveted her. Sooner than lie in his foul embrace she plunged a dagger into her white bosom...."

He paused, and for a few moments covered his face with his hands, his shoulders quivering. Then he tore his hands away and stretched them once more toward the painted image that looked so calmly down at him.

"Hora, my Hora!" he cried passionately. "I have sought thee for centuries, through age after age. And now, at last thou hast come to me—and gone again. But only for a little while, a few brief moments, for I follow thee tonight."

Again he paused, and again he resumed, mastering his emotion:

"She came to me here, here in this house, where I have labored so long, striving to regain my knowledge of that past which is sometimes so clear, and sometimes, O Isis, so terribly dark! She came to me, my beautiful Hora; came clad in the garb of today, bearing the name of Beatrice."

A low sob broke from Annette, but he went on, unheeding:

"I told you, Hora, I *tried* to tell you—but your eyes were filmed by the gods. You could not understand....You spurned me. Then it was that I understood that for us there could be only one way. One touch of this little knife, steeped in a poison so deadly that your soul had flown ere your body had fallen into my arms.

"Tenderly I bathed you and poured into your veins the secret essences that keep the flesh firm and fair as in life, and bore you to the tomb where you sit, waiting for me. But in another word, Hora, you wait for me, a thousand times more beautiful, and knowing that I, your lover, have sought you and found you at last. Hora, *I come!*"

With a wild cry, he raised the little dagger which he had drawn from his pocket. Sims sprang forward, but before he could reach him Professor Julius March had buried it in his heart. Hardly had the blade touched his flesh than he swayed, stumbled and crashed down at the feet of the mummy-case.

For a moment the others gazed at the prostrate form. Then Inspector Sims sprang forward and fumbled with trembling fingers at the fastenings of the mummy-case. Suddenly the front fell forward, and Annette uttered a terrible cry.

In the case, thus revealed, sat the girl who had been Beatrice Vane. She was nude, the chaste beauty of her lovely form standing out against the dark interior of the case. So wonderfully had the madman done his work that no scar marred the grace of the firm bosom, the long, rounded limbs, the head set proudly on the ivory neck. She sat as might have sat the Princess Hora, had she so wished, beside the Pharaoh himself on his Egyptian throne.

Sims drew back and bowed his head reverently as Annette, stumbling forward, laid her head on her dead sister's knees in a grief too terrible for tears.

THE PARLOR CEMETERY, BY C. E. HOWARD

A GRISLY SATIRE

"Good morning! I'm getting the information for the new city directory. May I step in and rest a moment while I'm asking you a few questions?"

"Well, ye—es, I reckon yuh kin come in and set," conceded the old lady who had answered my knock, "but I won't give yuh no order, Mister. I haint much of a booker."

"Oh, I don't sell the books," I hastened to assure her, as I laid y sample volume on the floor by my chair and placed my hat on it. "I just go around from house to house gathering the names for it. The company publishes and sells the book. I don't have anything to do with that part of it."

"Oh, you jes' do th' authorin'? It must take yuh consid'ble time to write as big a book as that! Do yuh do it all 'one?"

"No; we have fifty-four men working on it now, and it will take about two months to get it all. Now may I ask--?"

"How much does it cost?"

"This year they will sell them for fifteen dollars—"

"*Apiece!*" she shrilled. "My land o' livin'! Whoever buys th' things?"

"All the big stores keep them, especially the drug stores, for the benefit of the public, you know. Now your name is--?"

"Well, what's it all 'bout, anyhow?" she insisted. "An' what's it fur? Is it a tillyphone dickshanary?"

"Something like that. It contains the names and addresses of everybody living in this city, and all the big establishments keep one so that if anybody wishes to find out where anyone else lives they just go in some store and look in this directory and there it is. Now, will you give me your name for the new book, please?"

"*My* name? W'y, my name is—Now, is this a-goin' to cost me anything? Yuh know I said I wouldn't take none afore I let yuh in."

"It will not cost you a cent," I told her earnestly, "and it may do you some good. See"—running through the leaves of the book in which I entered the statistics—"how many people I have interviewed this morning, and all of them gave me he information I asked for. Now you will see all there is to it; right down here on this top line I write your name—what did you say it was?"

"I never said yit; but it was Cook."

"Ah!" We were off at last! "Cook"—I paused at the "k" and asked, "Do you spell it the short way or with an 'e'?"

"Which?"

"How do you spell it? 'C-double-o-k,' or 'C-double-o-k-e'?"

"No; not with no 'e' on to it! That would be cooky! It was jes' plain Cook—C-o-o-k."

I was willing to let it go at that and wrote it down. "And your first name now?"

"My fust name? I don't tell my fust name to no strangers—'specially *men!*"

"I beg your pardon, but I am not asking that from impertinence, Mrs. Cook," I explained carefully. "We do not mean to pry into people's personal affairs—such things are of no concern to us—but you see there are probably a hundred or more Cooks in this city and if we didn't have their first names there would be no telling them apart. All the ladies so far have told me their first names," I declared, holding my book toward her with the evidence.

After peering at it intently for some time she relaxed in her chair, reassured. "Well, 'tain't no name to be 'shamed of, if 'tis old-fashioned. It's Ann."

"Ann—'A-n-n'." I spelled aloud, to give her the chance to correct me if necessary. Thinking of the famous query connected with that name and thankful I didn't have to ask that, too, I continued:

"You have a husband?"

"No, not now. I've had 'em, though."

"Ah, a widow, then—that is, I presume your husband is not alive, Mrs. Cook?" I essayed gently, avoiding, as always, the direct interrogation as to grass-widowship.

"No; they're all on 'em dead now; but, Mister, my name ain't Cook —it's Hay!"

"What!" I exclaimed. "Why, I understood you to say it was Cook?"

"Well, yuh understood right. It *was* Cook—that what's yuh asked me, what it *was*—but it's Hay now. 'Bout two years after Cook went up in smoke I married a feller named Hay, see?"

∼

"Oh yes," I smiled cheerfully, and, reversing my pencil I endeavored to rub off the former husband's name.

Of course the flimsy paper tore. I yanked out the sheet and began again.

"'H-a-y,' Hay," I put down, writing lightly with an eye to more erasures or corrections. "Just the plain, short Hay, I presume?"

"Yes, jus' th' plain Hay—not timothy ner alfalfy ner none l' them fancy hoss brekfus foods. My lan'!" she broke out in astonishment, "I sh'uld think the' comp'ny'd git men to do this work that c'uld spell!"

"That is one of the things we are told to be most careful about, Mrs.—ah—Hay. We must always ask everybody's name and just how they spell it, even if we think we know. Often people having the same sounding name spell it differently, and if it goes in the directory wrong they generally blame us. And now, may I ask," I said sympathetically, recalling the peculiar way in which she had spoken of the late Mr. Cook's decease, "if your former husband lost his life in a fire?"

"Who, Cook? Oh, yuh mean what'd I mean when I spoke o' 'im goin' up in smoke? No, he was plumb dead—I was sattyfied o' that, afore he was burned. That's th' way I've had 'em all done; kin' of a habit I got into, I reckon, but seems to me 'twas a pretty good habit. That's Cook, second from th' right-hand end," she said calmly, pointing to an object on the humble mantel as though she were indicating a specimen in a museum.

"*How! What?*" I gasped, as every separate hair on my head arose and tried to spring from its root-cell.

"W'y, I had all my husban's' bodies consoomed by fire—what d'yuh call it, cremated?—w'en they up an lef' me, an' that's the' ashes of all on 'em in the dishes there! Seems t' me that's th' bes' way t' do with dead folks—have your own cem'terry right in your house where it's handy. It's 'specially nice when one moves 'round a good deal like I've done. I never c'uld a-forded t' gone visitin' here an' there t that many graves scattered 'bout in dif'rent states. Besides, it saves tumstones an' th' 'spense o' takin' care o' the lots."

Gradually, I grasped the woman's meaning as she continued to rock back and forth and utter her placid Mrs. Jarley explanation. The men who had been so unfeelingly abrupt as to "up an' leave" this poor creature had evidently, each in his turn, been cremated, and now their ashes, side by side, served to adorn the mantel and comfort the heart of the faithful widow. 'Imperial Caesar, dead and turned to clay....' I gazed at the row of assorted receptacles with awe and back at the woman with feelings still more curious.

"Some folks thinks them's odd kin' o' coffins," she continued, "but I d'know what c'uld be more 'propriate. Yuh see, I've tried t' have each one sort o' repasent either th' man himself or his trade. Now, for instance, this one here," she explained, rising and placing her hand on a small stone jar at the left end of the line—there were five of these unique memorials altogether—"this was my fust husban', John Marmyduke. Th' label on th' crock, yuh'll notice, is 'Marmylade', an' that's purt' near his name, an' then it almose d'scribes his dispazishun, too. Th' grocer tol' me that marmylade was a kin' o' English jam, an' John was sort o' sweet-tempered, fer a man, so I thought one l' them stun things 'ud do fine to keep him in.

"This is William Thompson here," she continued, tapping a small tea caddy with her thimble. "He was a teacher, an' I always called 'im Mr. T. So w'en he departed I thinks to myself, thinks I, 'One o' them little chests that Chinymens packs tea in is jes' th' ticket fer *yuh*'—tea standin' for both his name an' his callin', do you see?"

I expressed my admiration for this delightful idea, and she proceeded with her cataloguing:

"This third cuhlection, in th' fruit jar, is Mason. That was his name an' his trade, an' he belonged to that lodge an' that's the make o' th' jar, so, considerin' all them facks, I d'know what c'uld be a fitter tum fer '*im*. Mason fell off a roof one day an' broke his back, an' though he lived six months, somehow, he was never much 'count arter that. He was a big man—weighed 225 afore breakfus—an' he made such a pile l' ashes, spite l' their keepin' him in then over double time, that it took a gallon jar to hol' his leavin's. I had some quart jars on hand already an' 'suspected to put 'im in one of 'em, but I never begrudged buyin' a bigger one fer he was always, or purt near always gen'rous with me, an' then I knew I was savin' an undertaker's bill, anyhow.

"Now, I wa'n't altogether sattyfied with th' coffin I fin'ly chose fer Cook," she said, looking at me doubtfully, as she motioned toward the small japanned tin bread-box that was the next mortuary souvenir on the shelf. "I worried over th' matter th' hull time he was sick, but I never got a mite o' help from '*im*. Ev'ry time I tried to get that man to suggest what he thought he'd rest comft-ble in he'd go on frightful. Doctor said his temper prob'bly shortened his life.

"Well, at last I *dee*-cided on the bread box as comin' as near to repasentin' him as anything I c'uld think on—his name bein' Cook an' him havin' occupated as a baker as long's he was 'live. What's your 'pinion 'bout it, Mister?"

I declared that if Mr. Cook did not now rest in peace and content he was certainly a hard man to please.

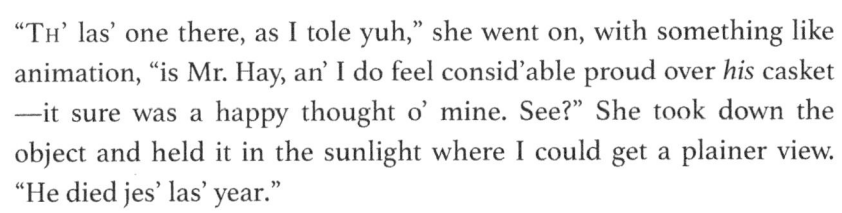

"Th' las' one there, as I tole yuh," she went on, with something like animation, "is Mr. Hay, an' I do feel consid'able proud over *his* casket—it sure was a happy thought o' mine. See?" She took down the object and held it in the sunlight where I could get a plainer view. "He died jes' las' year."

Mr. Hay's ashes reposed in one of the large square glass perfume bottles such as most druggists carry, and the ornate label thereon had become the painfully true epitaph, "New Mown Hay"!

When I could trust my voice, I inquired, "was he ill long?"

"No; he wa'n't ill a-tall. He left me kinda on'spectedly. However, he always *was* a great man fer doin' things on th' impuse o' th' moment. We was livin' out on a farm then, an' one day Mr. Hay was cutting' grass in th' orchard an' I 'spose he must 'a' struck a nest o' bees. Anyhow, somethin' started th' team an' they run 'way an' throwed him off in front o' th' knives, an' th' horses stepped on him a few times an' th' machine finished it up. He cert'inly was most completely dead when we reached him. Hired man tole me he had to gether him up with a rake an' wheelbarrer. Only forty-six years ol', too, he was—mowed down in his prime!

"Well, this is a funny world, ain't it? Some women kin take one man an' keep him 'live an' whole fer fifty or sixty years, but I sure had bad luck with my batch o' husban's. It's a comfort to me, though, that I kin have 'em with me in death, at least. I take down their monnyments ev'ry mornin' an' dust 'em off, an' w'enever I go on th' keers vis'tin' anywhere I pack one in my valeese an' carry it along. When I get it out an' put it up in my room, w'erever I be, I feel right to hum."

I succeeded in getting answers to the rest of my questions in another half hour, and I went on my way, dazed. And though, when my day's work was over, I had no rarebit for supper, yet a vision came to me something between the dark and the daylight. I thought I saw myself fall ill and die, and my body was prepared for cremation.

I struggled to escape, to call out, but in vain. They slid me into a kiln and the inexorable heat dissolved flesh, blood, and bone. Then some brutal, careless wretch came and swept me up on a dustpan, and put me in a sack and delivered me over to an eager old woman, whose face seemed strangely familiar.

The ghoulish woman bore me away to her home and went to work trying to pack me down in a catsup bottle. It was too small. It seemed to press on my throat. I was choking. I struggled. I shrieked.

And I awoke—to find, thank Heaven, that a large crayon portrait above my bed had fallen down and was now around my neck, and the man in the next room was hammering on the wall with his shoe and shouting and swearing at me.

GOLDEN GLOW, BY HARRY IRVING SHUMWAY

A "HAUNTED HOUSE" STORY WITH A TOUCH OF HUMOR

When you're rolling along through the country at forty miles an hour, and have been so doing for several hours, any excuse to stop and stretch is a welcome excuse. It gives you an opportunity to light a longed-for pipe and takes the kinks out of your back. I lighted mine.

My friend, Doctor Wilbur Hunneker, whom I have never called anything but Hunky, vaulted from the driver's seat without the formality of opening the door.

"Judas Iscariot!" he grunted, slapping the dust from his shoulders and digging at his eyes. "Some dust and some breeze!"

"What you stop here for?" I asked him, propping my feet up on the windshield. "Nat that I don't welcome any hesitation in the fierce procedure which you call touring. But why here?"

He grinned and pointed toward a tumbled-down, decrepit-looking cottage, almost entirely covered with woodbine. In front of it grew the most magnificent clusters of Golden Glow I have ever seen. There were hundreds of these beautiful yellow heads swaying in the sunlight, and they were in strange contrast to the drab and weather-beaten background of the house.

"Going to pick you a nosegay," he said. "You haven't energy enough to gather wild flowers for yourself, so I'll do it for you."

"Go to it," I said, relieved, and sank back on the deep cushions in a cloud of my own smoke. "But look out for the pooch. Also day-time ghosts. That old shack may have both."

"I'm not afraid of either," he replied, and moved through the high grass toward the house.

Lazily, I watched him selecting the choicest blooms. Then my gaze wandered over the old squatty-looking house.

It was indeed a derelict, a perfect example of the abandoned home. I couldn't imagine anyone having been near it or in it for a score of years. The small window-panes were covered with cobwebs and the marks of falling leaves and pelting rains of many years. The door in the center was innocent of paint, and great seams ran down and across its sections, witnesses of the battles it had put up against the roaring storms.

The stone slabs, slanted and sunken, which served as steps to the door were moss-covered and almost hidden from sight by the luxuriantly growing grass. Not a sound came from the place, or indeed from anywhere else.

Hunky returned to the car, grinning at me with a huge bunch of the golden flowers. He presented them with a sweeping gesture. Not to be outdone in courtesy, I rose and made him a mocking bow.

"Accept these tokens of my esteem, I prithee."

"I do, Sir Knight, and go to hell," I replied. "If you're through with this horticultural business what d'you say we get to the flashing? That's what we started out for—trout, not yellow bellies."

He held up his hand in protest.

"There is no element of romance in your sordid make-up. You're as flat in the head as the fish you catch. Take a look at that old house. What stories it might tell! What ghosts may have prowled about in its somber interior! I see a broken pane in the quaint side window of the door. Adventure calls. Watch me."

The nut! He noiselessly moved toward the door. Then he gingerly thrust his hand through the jagged opening in the side window and felt for the key. I saw by the smile on his face that he had found it. He removed his hand, turned the outside knob—and the door opened. He peered around, and then went inside.

It wasn't premonition or an unknown feeling of anything that prompted me to leap over the side of that car and beat if for the inside of that house. It was a glimpse of one corking fine mantle that I caught through the open door. Old mantels, newel-posts and corner china-closets exert an influence over my artistic soul that brooks no laziness. I'll walk ten miles through a bog any day to get a peep at something rare and fine in old woodwork. This one called to me, and I went.

I had on rubber-soled shoes, as did my companion, and hence made little noise. Hunky was nowhere in sight, but there was a side door beyond the fire-place and I knew he must be prowling about on the other side of it.

"Say, Hunky, did you see this old mantle?" I called, moving toward the door.

I went through it—and found myself looking at two most unexpected things—Hunky, with his hands raised above his head, and a nice, blue-black automatic held in the unwavering hand of an old woman who was sitting in a chair.

~

"You, too!" she snapped at me, "Up with 'em! Now what the hell are you two crooks breaking into an old woman's home for?"

"Good heavens, ma'am," stammered Hunky. "We—that is—I thought it was a deserted farm house. No intention of annoying anybody. We are simply touring—just a lark to break in here."

"'Lark', hey?" said the old woman, a most unpleasant glare in her eyes. "D'you call it a lark to bust into my home and maybe rob me? How do I know you mightn't have murdered me?"

"I assure you, madame," I interrupted, "my friend here had no intention of doing the slightest harm. It was, as he says, a lark—just to show off to me. I followed him because I was interested in the old woodwork—and not your modern hardware" I added.

She lowered the gun slowly.

"Hum. Well, you don't look like desperate characters now I take a good look at you. I was frightened, I guess."

"Sorry," said Hunky. "No intention of frightening anybody and it was sill of me to break in. I apologize."

"Well, I guess that's all right. I'll let you go. But don't come round here scarin' me again," replied the evil-looking old woman. "Now you get!"

We got. Hunky stepped on the gas and we traveled. I hope I am not a saffron member of the coward league, but just the same I own there are many views I prefer infinitely more than the muzzle of a dog that both barks and bites. Hunky was not much upset. He's familiar with guns. I prefer fishing rods.

"A quaint old party," he mused, as we got under way. "Old house, everything all dust-covered, old woman—and an up-to-date automatic in her fist. How many old farm ladies pack new guns?"

Now I was awake. "Yes, and how many old ladies up in this section of the hinterland speak with an unbucolic accent. I know the local dialect, and she doesn't belong.'

"We'll stop here for gas," said Hunky, guiding the car around another which was filling from a tank by a country store.

A thick-set young man was turning the gasoline pump-handle and another man, athletic in build and in his early thirties, was watching the flow into the tank of his car.

Nobody up in that section of the world ever hurries, and the conversation between the two was easy and unruffled.

"Sure you won't disappoint us?" asked the store-keeper.

"No fear," answered the other. "Cases all taken care of and I can get away with no trouble. Better give me two quarts of oil, Ed, medium."

The one called Ed went inside, and Hunky and I followed him in search of tobacco. He obliged me with a package and also some conversation which he seemed anxious to spill.

"That feller out there is our district attorney," he said. "Wouldn't think it, would you? Young and all that. Fact, he's the youngest district attorney in our state. He plays short field on our baseball team—the Hunterville Tigers."

"So he's district attorney?" inquired Hunky.

"Sure it, and smart as they make 'em."

Hunky wandered out to the cars in front. I followed. He approached the young official, who was putting up the hood of his car in readiness for the oil.

"Sir," said Hunky to him. "Are you District Attorney for this county?"

"Yes, sir," answered the man, straightening up and gazing back at Hunky with a pair of very frank and fearless gray eyes.

"In that case I want to tell you something," said Hunky. "I just broke into an old house about three miles down the road. It looked to be a deserted house, all covered with woodbine and a lot of golden glow in the front of it."

"That's the Old Collishaw House. It *is* deserted. No one has lived there for fifteen years."

"I thought so, too—consequently when I ventured through a door and looked smack into the barrel of an unprepossessing revolver you can realize I was surprised some."

The young District Attorney pushed his hat up from his forehead. There seemed nothing at all that could be hidden from his eyes, and now he bent their gaze on Hunky.

"Hum," he said finally. "If that had happened at night I'd say that you were seeing things."

Hunky laughed.

"My friend had the same pleasure and also assisted me in reaching for the sky. It was an old lady who was on the other end of that gun."

"Old lady?"

"Yes. She searched us mentally and told us to get out. We did. That wasn't more than fifteen minutes ago. Here's the strange thing about it to my mind. Old house, old lady, everything moss-covered and dusty—and a brand new up-to-date automatic in the old dame's hand."

The other man mused over this without comment. Finally he shot a question at us.

"Where are you two going?"

"Fishing in Cold Stream Pond. Come up here every year. My name is Doctor Wilbur Hunneker and my friend's is Edward Triteham."

"You wait here for me," said the District Attorney, quickly making a decision. "I'm going to run down there. If some one is hanging around that house I want to know who it is and what they want. Will you wait here until I return?"

"Certainly," Hunky replied. "Or I'll go with you if you like."

"No," the other quickly answered, getting into his roadster. "I'll go it alone. See you later."

∽

He shot off down the road in a cloud of powdery dust.

Hunky and I went into the cool interior of the country store and regaled ourselves with root beer and the store-keeper's conversation, which for the moment was wholly of the young District Attorney. He was a most remarkable county official, we were told.

It seemed but a moment when the subject of the talk was back in another swirl of dust. He jumped out of his car. We went out to meet him.

"Gone," he said laconically to our inquiring look. "But somebody was there all right. What the devil they wanted is more than I can fathom. Nothing disturbed—isn't much to disturb. But it bothers me. You're sure about that gun?" His eyes bored us.

Hunky faced him.

"Quite," he said quietly. "I know guns. Also, I know the look in the eyes behind them. I'm a physician and I have to know people. This old woman had some good reason for wanting to scare us away."

'I know that," replied the young man, with his mouth set in a line. "Guns and deserted houses don't make a very reassuring picture."

"Did you look all around the house?" inquired my friend.

"Sure. Probably those old eyes were on me while I was doing it. She couldn't have gone far; possibly she was in the woods nearby. I made only a cursory examination so as not to excited suspicion if she or anybody else had been watching. Now let's see, what's back of that house. The old wood lot—a pasture—"

"That's all," spoke up the store-keeper. "Then the railroad cuts through beyond that."

"Railroad!" said the District Attorney sharply. "Why, that's about the point where that wreck was yesterday afternoon."

"Yes," replied the store-keeper. "The pasture lot runs right down to the bend, and it was on that bend that the cars left he track."

"By George! You're right" exclaimed the District Attorney.

He seemed to ponder the situation for a few moments. Then he made a movement as if to be off.

"I won't detain you gentlemen,' he said quickly. "If you want to fish you'd better be on your way. Just about time to make it before sundown."

Hunky smiled.

"I'm not so keen on fishing as my friend Triteham here," he said quietly. "I'd much rather go along with you to see that wreck."

The District Attorney eyed him carefully. Then:

"All right. I'd be glad of your company if you feel that way about it."

"Something tells me I had better leave the fish to their watery beds today," said I.

"All right," answered our new acquaintance.

And the three of us started on a brisk walk in what seemed a circuitous direction. The District Attorney knew the lay of the land, and after about twenty minutes we came upon the railroad tracks. Here we turned back in the direction of the deserted house.

In about three-quarters of an hour we came upon a distant view of the wreck around a bend. A railroad gang was at work, straightening the tangled mess caused by three freight cars which had left the rails.

The District Attorney approached the foreman of the gang and made himself known.

"Anybody hurt?" he asked.

"Nope. Not going very fast. We hope to get the tracks cleared by tomorrow."

"Do you mind if I look around—over the cars?' asked the District Attorney.

"Go ahead," replied the foreman.

The three of us began inspecting the whole train from engine to caboose. The District Attorney scrutinized everything.

After the examination, which seemed to offer up nothing of special interest, our new friend suggested we retrace our steps. We straggled along the ties, each to himself, nobody having much to say.

"Something tells me," finally spoke the District Attorney, "that your old woman with the gun and this wreck are connected in some way. Certainly there is nothing either mysterious or valuable about that old house. Why should someone become suddenly interested in it enough to go around armed to warn away intruders. The only thing significant is that wreck. If it is that—then developments will take place quickly and in darkness."

"It is getting dark now," I suggested.

"Yes. I'm going to stick around here and see what I shall see. You boys can find your way back to the store. Just follow the tracks and turn into the path at the bridge."

Hunky smiled. "If it's all the same to you, we'd like to stick."

The District Attorney hesitated a moment, then said: "All right. If will be a lonely vigil, and maybe you can help if anything does happen."

We stopped about half a mile from the wreck, and sat down to wait for darkness. In the woods twilight is short, and we hadn't long to wait. Back we turned and worked cautiously toward the wreck.

The gang was still at work, and in the distance we could see their grotesque shapes by the light of their lanterns. The operations were up ahead and we kept just in the rear and about a hundred feet to one side of the caboose. This vantage point enabled us to command a view of the wreck and the approach to it from the pasture and woods. Our own position was well concealed.

Four hours went by, slowly because of the damp and cold of the night. The illuminated hands of my wrist watch told me it was between eleven and midnight. Banks of fleecy fog clung here and there to the low trees and the ground. The night sounds of the woods mingled eerily with the sharp noises made by the wrecking crew. It was cold and damp.

Suddenly the sharp eyes and ears of the District Attorney must have told him something, for his hand went out in warning. Whatever the warning was, it proved correct because we became aware, almost at once, of five dark figures stealing up the slight incline toward that part of the train which remained on the rails. Then we noticed two more figures edging their way toward the front end of the wreck where the operations were being conducted.

～

"Let 'em start whatever they intend doing," whispered the District Attorney. "We are outnumbered, two to one, unless the crew backs us up. You're both set?"

"We're both armed and we're both good shots," answered Hunky.

The five figures showed no hesitation in their movements, but made for the fourth car from the caboose. We could see two of them hold a third man upon their shoulders while he worked at the door.

Beyond, the other two had surprised the work gang and we could see their hands go up in the flickering light.

"Let's get nearer," whispered the District Attorney.

Slowly, we began to move forward. We were about one hundred and fifty feet from the larger group when an unexpected shot rang out. The men working on the door became alert in a second.

We could see the five men dragging boxes from the car, the door of which they had slid back. They weren't any too quiet about it, so our footsteps were not heard.

The District Attorney ran quickly forward in a crouching position. We followed and spread out so as not to be in his line. When he was within twenty feet one of the robbers turned—and he never turned again in this world. The District Attorney dropped him with one shot.

Both our guns barked at the same time. So sudden and unexpected had been our onslaught that we had a bully jump on them. The resistance, while spirited and desperate for a few seconds, was quickly overcome. Three of them were laid out, either wounded badly or dead. One tried to get into the car, and Hunky dropped him right in the doorway. He came down with a thud on the ground. The one remaining man surrendered, and we disarmed him.

Shots were coming from the head of the train, and, leaving the scene of our first encounter, we rushed down there. The two on guard had turned for a minute, and the boss of the wrecking crew had drawn his gun and opened upon them. They were caught between two fires and couldn't get away.

In a matter of minutes we had them all trussed up. The others we carried into the caboose for the time being.

The District Attorney wasted little time on them. He turned his attention to the car which had been opened by the robbers. When Hunky and I came up he was a puzzled man.

"Turnips!" he exploded. "A whole carload of 'em! Must be something else in here."

The three of us tugged and hauled for a quarter of an hour, while a brakeman held a lantern for us to see by. Our efforts were finally rewarded by something which we were not surprised to find by that time.

Yes, indeed. Case after case of whisky! That was the cargo those birds were after.

It was plain enough now. The gang was part of an organized whisky-ring engaged in smuggling whisky from Canada into the United States. They had, through the connivance of confederates, secreted the liquor at the point of embarkation beneath a larger load of turnips. The car would have reached its destination and been secretly unloaded by members of the gang waiting for it, possibly in the big train yards at night.

Then had come the wreck. Perhaps someone in the employ of the road had wired the gang. Anyway, they had learned of it and hustled to the scene desperate on getting the liquor.

The connection must have been between the old deserted house, which we had stumbled on by mistake, and the wreck. Evidently they had planned to carry the stuff in cases to the deserted house and thence over the road by automobiles. Undoubtedly, we would find several big high-powered cars when we got to the house.

The District Attorney, Hunky and I went into the caboose after checking up the loot which proved to be over one hundred cases. Some of the crooks were stretched out and some sitting up. Two of them would never do any more robbing in this sprightly existence.

One was sitting hunched upon a stool and a mighty evil-looking bird he was. His black eyes scowled all kinds of malevolence at us. He looked vaguely familiar and when I caught his eye I recognized him.

"Hum. Changed your sex, I see," I snapped at him.

He didn't favor me with a reply—just glared at me.

"Recognize our old pal, Hunky?" I said to my friend. "This is the old lady who gave us the scare in the farm house."

"By George, you're right," said Hunky. "What was the idea of the masquerade?"

But the fellow wouldn't tell. And he never did say, as far as we ever could learn, why he had chosen to play the part of an old woman. Perhaps he had figured that in that role he would be better able to avert suspicion if he had been seen around the deserted farm house. Perhaps it would have worked, too, had he not made the mistake of holding us up with that suspiciously new and modern gun.

THE EYRIE

Here we are with the second issue of WEIRD TALES—and we're going strong! Or at least—judging by the number of congratulatory letters that the postman drops on our desk every morning—we're making lots of friends.

But, says the boss, are we also making money? A fair question! As we remarked before, WEIRD TALES is an experiment. There has never been another magazine quite like this, hence nobody knows whether or not such a magazine will pay. And, of course, if a magazine doesn't pay it promptly ceases to exist.

We do believe, though, that WEIRD TALES has entered upon a long and flourishing journey. We know there are multitudes of readers who like this kind of magazine and are willing to buy it. Are these readers numerous enough to support WEIRD TALES? The answer is up to you.

But we'll never get anywhere unless we all work together. It's our job to publish the right sort of magazine. It's yours to buy it. If we both do these things as we should—why, then, of course, WEIRD TALES is sure to succeed. Nothing can stop it.

And if anybody thinks that ours is the easiest task he should sit at our desk for a day or so and wade through the rivers of manuscripts that are flooding us like the waters of spring. From this great welter of material we must select such stories as we think you'd like to read. And since it is manifestly impossible to know the likes and dislikes of some ten of thousands of readers, we are often uncertain what to put in and what to leave out. Generally, we try to solve this perplexing problem by choosing only those stories in which we ourselves can become genuinely interested, assuming that anything that interests us will likewise interest others. Maybe we're wrong about this; but—what would YOU do if you were editor of WEIRD TALES?

Although most of the manuscripts we receive are obviously hopeless, all must be read. Of the thousands of manuscripts sent to our office not one has been returned, or ever will be returned, unread. We cannot afford to take a chance on missing something really good.

Too many authors place too much stress upon atmospheric conditions when they take their trusty typewriters in hand to turn out a goose-flesh thriller. Seven in ten, when opening their stories, employ a variant of the well-worn dictum: "'Twas a dark and stormy night." Why is this? Must the heavens weep and the thunder growl to make a weird tale? We think not. Weird indeed, is "The Forty Jars," published in this issue, and yet the story takes place on a red-hot desert beneath a blazing sun.

But let's look through some of these letters on our desk. Here's something short and snappy from H.W. of Sterling, Illinois:

> "My dear Mr. Baird: I have just notified my attorney to start suit against you and your new magazine for personal injury. My eyes are rather poor, and the first number was so interesting that I sat up nearly all night reading it—and as a result I've been wearing smoked glasses ever since. WEIRD TALES seems to me to fill a long felt want in magazine circles. I have always delighted in stories of the 'Dracula' type and that Sax Rohmer stuff, and I never could understand why the editors didn't wake up. You, as a pioneer in the field, are giving them something to think about.

Meanwhile, if you make the next number as interesting as the first, I'll likely go blind."

Despite the danger to H.W.'s eyesight, we tried to make this number even more interesting than the first. And we're going to make the next number more interesting than this.

We have here a letter from C.L. Austin, 328 Locust Avenue, Amsterdam, N.Y., that simply must be printed if for no other reason than as an answer to the last ten words of it:

> Gentlemen: Having read the first issue of your magazine, WEIRD TALES, I must admit that I like the stories very much. They are entirely out of the ordinary. There is no question but what this magazine will be a big success, providing the editor is not hedged in by a multitude of 'don'ts's' from the managing department. It is a well-known fact that many times an editor would like to accept material that in many ways would conflict with the policy of the magazine, and there is a loss of what no doubt would be valuable material. In fact, I have known for some time that adverse criticism of half a dozen people in different sections of the country have power to change the entire editorial policy of a magazine.
>
> "And unless the editor is the kind of man who is brave enough to stick for his ideals, regardless of his job, there must be much vacillation, with a consequent loss of valuable material and a depreciation in the reading value of the magazine. I notice that you say you will publish all letters received, providing there is no objection by the writers. Well, really now, old chap, I've no possible objection, but I doubt that you have the nerve to do it."

With no desire to engage in a controversy with Mr. Austin, we must say to him emphatically that the editorial policy of WEIRD TALES is not dictated by the business office. We will stand or fall on our platform of "something new in magazine fiction." If you support us, we shall be able to give you what you want. If you turn thumbs down, we'll blow out the gas and go home in the dark. In any event, there will be no compromise. WEIRD TALES, as long as it lives, will always be "The Unique Magazine."

Here's another:

"Dear sir: I have just read your new magazine, WEIRD TALES, also The Eyrie by yourself. SOME magazine, I'll say! There is a real kick to these stories—something that is pitifully lacking in the stories of most magazines. Why editors shy at 'weird' and 'horror' stories has always been a mystery to me. I like meat in my literature the same as I do in my menu. This willy-nilly stuff of would-be cowboys (when there aren't any such animals nowadays) is sickening. So is sugar when eaten to excess. Keep this magazine going. There is a demand for such literature. We all love mystery and stories that give us cold spine (we of the public), whether the editors think so or not. This magazine of yours will prove it, I'm sure. Believe me, I'm for it! For the same reason I have always read Poe. And to prove this, I am enclosing a check for a year's subscription. Money talks. We are always willing to pay for what we like."

That letter came from Dr. Vance J. Hoyt, suite S18, Baker Detwiler Building, Los Angeles, California, and that's the sort of letter we particularly like to read. As the doctor says, money talks—and it speaks with an eloquent tongue!

So, also do letters of frank criticism such as the following:

"I'm glad to say that I think the first issue of WEIRD TALES very good. I read 'Ooze,' 'The Ghoul and the Corpse,' 'Fear,' 'The place of Madness,' 'The Unknown Beast,' 'The Sequel,' 'The Young Man Who Wanted to Die.' Of these I was mightily taken with 'The Ghoul and the Corpse', which, to my mind, ran a close race with 'Ooze'—in fact, as to handling, I think the best written, by far, of any that I read. Taylor's story was good—my wife read it, and like it—and so did I, as to theme. The handling left something to be desired in the way of smoothness, but, as a story, it was the cat's whiskers. 'The Unknown Beast' was about the poorest, pressed for honor by Story's 'Sequel.' But, all in all, I am heartily in accord with your editorial dictum that people DO like and want grim stories. I know that I'm one who does. And I read 'The Grim Thirteen,' with some amazement that none of these stories had sold previously.

"I think some of our editors are so hide-bound, so cribbed, cabined and confined within the narrow limits of an increasingly myopic purview that, for the life of them, they can see nothing but stereotypes. Or else they're not really editors, but just hired men who have to pass the stuff up to a 'business' boss who doesn't know a single thing about fiction, or life, either, for that matter. All in all, I congratulate you on something really god—AND new. —H.C., Summit, N.J."

We have received a considerable number of letters like the following from S.O.B. of Beulah, New Mexico:

"Your enterprise hits me in the right spot. I am a lover of Poe's stuff, and have often felt that the general editorial prejudice against weird stories today isn't, after all, a true reflection of the people's taste. I hope my opinion is correct and that WEIRD TALES may receive a hearty welcome."

And also like this:

"Congratulations on your new magazine, WEIRD TALES! The first edition was a veritable ghastly, ghostly knockout! Most every one enjoys an occasional ghost story, and a thrilling novelette like 'Ooze' is a better tonic than Tanlac.—D.L.C. Denver, Colorado.

Victor Wilson of Hazen, Pa., writes us:

"I have just finished reading the first installment of 'The Thing of a Thousand Shapes.' It is fine, and one who has a good imagination should not 'start it late at night.' I wish to congratulate you on your fine fiction magazine. I am a reader of several other magazines of up-to-date fiction, but yours is the first of its kind. I have not read all of the stories, but I like 'The Place of Madness,' 'The Grave,' and 'Hark! The Rattle!'"

And here's a line I' type or to from our star contrib, Anthony M. Rud:

"WEIRD TALES seems to have hit your mark excellently well. It possesses glamor for me in every yarn but two—which I won't attempt to criticize as both well may suit other readers exactly."

We wish Rud had told us the names of those two yarns. Strange as it may seem, we're always more interested in adverse criticism than in praise.

Still, we can't deny that we like to get letters like this one from C.P.O of Gainesville, Texas:

"Dear Mr. Baird: Allow me to number myself among the first subscribers to the new venture. Check enclosed. The sub-title, 'unique,' really describes the magazine, even in these days of specialization in the magazine field....WEIRD TALES appears at a time when the public is interested in this type of story, I believe, as I notice in the monthly bulletins of Brentano's, McClurg's and Baker & Taylor that quite a collection of ghost, psychic and weird tales are appearing in book form. Most famous authors wrote one or more weird tales; to mention a few: Dickens, Thackeray, Poe, Bierce, O'Brien, F. Marion Crawford and DeMaupassant. I fear you will find greater trouble in securing good material for WEIRD TALES than for DETECTIVE TALES, for, after all, the detective story is a matter of craftsmanship while the really first-class ghost or weird tale is a matter of art.."

It is hard to get good material for WEIRD TALES; but we're glad to work hard for it—to go almost to any length for it—if, by so doing, we can offer something distinctive and worthwhile and UNIQUE in magazines.

Here's another letter from Texas:

"Dear sir: I just bought a copy of WEIRD TALES, and I have read most of the stories and consider them very good. I believe that a magazine of this type will be very popular. In fact, I am sure it will be, and I trust nothing will happen to change your policy in regard to the type of material you are now using and expect to use in the future.—J.H.C., Houston, Texas."

William S. Saudby of Washington, D.C., wrote to us, "You have struck the right key with WEIRD TALES, and congratulations are in order for Vol. 1, No. 1," while E.E.L of Chicago wrote to us, in part, as follows:

"Gentlemen:...You will probably be deluged with a lot of stuff, for everybody who writes is sometimes compelled to commit to paper some seductive phantasm of his brain for the sheer pleasure of doing it...Poe took more than 5,000 words to develop his supreme story of horror, and those who have an ambition to imitate the Master will often require a larger canvas. Your story lengths—1,000 to 20,000 words—will give everybody a chance to show what he can do. May I not express the hope that your magazine will prove a success, and that you will publish therein stories that otherwise would molder in filing-cases, and which will be lifted from your pages to become a permanent part of our literature?...If the contributions can maintain a sufficiently high level you can count on me as one of your permanent subscribers, for I dearly love to read stories of this character."

With regard to WEIRD TALES for May: We meant to say a good deal about it in this month's Eyrie, but we've consumed so much space with our correspondence that we've precious little room left. All we can tell you now is that if you are seeking the "usual type" of fiction you will not find it in the May issue of WEIRD TALES. But if you are looking for "something different"—something that you've never expected to see in any magazine---then the place to find it is in the May WEIRD TALES. Need we say more?—THE EDITOR.

MORE PULP FICTION

We'd love for you to join our community! For more Pulp fiction and classic texts, visit some of the links below!

The Website
www.mythbank.com

Facebook
www.facebook.com/mythbank

Made in the USA
Monee, IL
15 February 2021